Praise for

MARK ANDREW OLSEN and *The Assignment*

"A writer who can take your breath away with a single sentence. A welcome, fresh voice that must be read!"

—Ted Dekker

"Olsen's multifaceted plot of good and evil is a page-turner. [*The Assignment*] will also appeal to readers of Ted Dekker and Frank Peretti. Highly recommended."

—*Library Journal*

". . . a nonstop thriller . . . a smoothly plausible story. [Olsen] includes a religious perspective without being preachy. The concepts he presents are fascinating and well plotted. His characters are involved in a good vs. evil struggle from the start and the journey to the ending will keep you on the edge of your seat and awake until it's finished."

—*Heartland Reviews*

"In his first single major inspirational thriller, *The Assignment*, Mark Andrew Olsen weaves a riveting and unforgettable tale . . . His characters walk straight off the pages and will give the reader not only an edge-of-the-seat, thrilling read, but a life-changing experience."

—*MyShelf.com*

"Surprisingly, this is not a preachy or apostatizing story but reads more like an urban fantasy in which the powers of good and evil fight for supremacy. Mark Andrew Olsen is a talent comparable to Frank Peretti and Jerry Jenkins."

—*ReviewCentre*

"Mark Andrew Olsen blasts action into his story and keeps us up until the wee hours of the morning wanting to finish, yet not wanting the story to end . . . His pen writes with spiritual ink that captures and captivates."

—*The Road to Romance*

"His non-preachy yet grounded style is both refreshing and thought-provoking . . . I found myself moved—both by the outcome and by the sense of this author's living faith in God."

—*FaithfulReader.com*

"*The Assignment* is the perfect blend of Christian fiction and suspense, with something for fans of both to enjoy."

—*BookLoons.com*

"[Olsen's] power of description is beautiful. The concept of the story is fascinating. The main characters are instantly captivating and likeable. Glimpses of Ireland, Jerusalem, and France through the eyes of the characters are so vivid you feel you've been there. The conclusion of the story, at least for the main male character, is satisfying enough to induce tears."

—*Focus on Fiction.net*

"A good book that relies on its story and characters rather than on sermonettes and churchy cliché."

—*Infuze Magazine*

"Olsen weaves the present and the past together to show a man tormented by immortality . . . [and] combines well-developed characters, a fast-paced plot, and an intriguing problem into a fascinating suspense novel."

—*Christian Book Previews*

". . . a well-told story, a unique combination of characters, with scenes and plot development that should please mystery readers . . . Spiritual messages come across as part of the essence of the story, not broken twigs or branches sticking out unnaturally to interrupt the flow . . . I'm keeping it for a second read."

—*Rambles Magazine*

"Wow! I've read hundreds of thriller, international-intrigue whodunits. But few of them have grabbed my imagination like this. *The Assignment* is rife with exciting action, rich characters, complex plot movements, and especially fulfilling in its historic panorama. A great read!"

—*ChristianBook.com*

THE
WATCHERS

Books by Mark Andrew Olsen

Hadassah: One Night With the King[1]

The Hadassah Covenant: A Queen's Legacy[1]

Rescued[2]

The Assignment

The Watchers

[1]with Tommy Tenney   [2]with John Bevere

MARK ANDREW OLSEN

THE WATCHERS

BETHANYHOUSE
MINNEAPOLIS, MINNESOTA

Published by Bethany House Publishers
11400 Hampshire Avenue South
Bloomington, Minnesota 55438

Bethany House Publishers is a division of
Baker Publishing Group, Grand Rapids, Michigan.

Printed in the United States of America

ISBN-13: 978-0-7642-2818-6
ISBN-10: 0-7642-2818-8

Library of Congress Cataloging-in-Publication Data

Olsen, Mark Andrew.
    The watchers / Mark Andrew Olsen.
        p. cm.
    ISBN-13: 978-0-7642-2818-6 (hardcover : alk. paper)
    ISBN-10: 0-7642-2818-8 (hardcover: alk. paper)
    1. Young women—Fiction. 2. Assassins—Fiction. 3. Secret societies—Fiction.
I. Title.

    PS3615.L73W37   2007
    813'.6—dc22   2006038325

To my own precious

Abigail,

more beautiful and delightful

than any character in a book,

and forever our

Miracle Child

THE WATCHERS

CHAPTER

_1

PACIFIC PALISADES, CALIFORNIA—MIDNIGHT

The blue flickers of her television danced across the housekeeper's unmoving pupils. She neither budged a muscle, nor leveled the odd tilt of her head, nor wiped the crimson trickles crisscrossing her neck, nor rose from the stain darkening the sofa cushions beneath her. Nor did she notice that, twenty feet away, a man gripping the weapon of her murder had now reached the bedroom door of her *pequeña angel-ica*. Her angelic one.

Her employer's beautiful, sleeping, twenty-year-old daughter, Abigail.

No, deep in the final tremors of her death, the housekeeper did not hear her assailant turn the bedroom's door handle or see him enter the room. Nor did she scream when he took two padded strides into shadow.

Paused just inside the threshold, the killer breathed in deeply and tried in vain to calm his pulse by drinking in the darkness, savoring the smell of clean sheets and dissipating perfume. He badly needed the pause. The ecstasy of the previous slaying still fired through every synapse of his nervous system. In fact, the bliss so enthralled his faculties that he could only stand motionless while it subsided, peer down at young Abigail's bed, and focus all his energy on recovering his poise.

That, and resist the urge to harvest the new prey now sleeping before him.

Breathing as silently as he could, he tried to relax by forcing his thoughts back to the instant his first kill of the evening had awakened from her TV-induced stupor and realized what was happening to her. His soul was fed by the montage of terror that had blazed across those sleep-swollen eyes: disbelief, shock, rage, numbness, and finally heavy-lidded resignation as the laws of biology asserted themselves.

Oh, how the woman's death had electrified his every sense! Each layer of fear delighted him like nothing else. His Order had never overstated how delicious it was to savor those last moments of someone's life like a mouthful of caviar. He never tired of it. He doubted he ever would.

And best of all, as the Order of the Scythe would faithfully insist, was his assurance that in the process he had fulfilled one of earth's most necessary and neglected functions. The recycling of an inferior being.

Culling the herd.

Now he scowled and focused on this second girl, on his actual purpose for being in this place. *She* was a different matter. No thrill-harvest here. He could not shake from his mind the fact that taking her life without authorization—or deviating one inch from his orders—could prove his last mistake.

Beyond the surface value of sparing the world one more parasite, the woman out there on the sofa had been little more than a contingency. But now the sleeping girl embodied the assignment of a lifetime, one whose failure he might not survive.

Even *that* danger gave him a rush.

He stared harder at the beauty before him, the insolent serenity of the woman's slumber, of her blond hair tossed casually across the pillow.

Sleeping soundly like any other untroubled youth, probably dreaming of pimple-faced boys and MTV. She'd have no idea. . . .

He gazed at the placid face, the contours of her cheeks, and the long, thick eyelashes that lay atop sculptured cheekbones. Full lips parted gently around an escaping breath. *Beautiful girl,* he acknowledged. He followed the outline of legs under quilted blanket and realized that in another context the sight might have pierced him with a different desire altogether.

But tonight there was serious business at hand.

Inwardly he compared her sleeping expression to the photos he had studied. A lean, tanned face, a winsome, carefree smile, and hair bleached sandy blond by the sun. In her photos she'd worn no makeup, sporting an ordinary, unglamorous hairstyle. She might have been even more stunning if only she paid attention to such things.

She's the one, he reassured himself.

Next to his shoulder, on the dresser, sat an open laptop. He merely had to touch the space bar to wake it up.

He peered closer and started reading, shaking his head and smiling. These kids. They all think they're so bold and trailblazing, and yet they're so predictable.

It was her personal home page. Not a keystroke required; it was right there waiting for him. Her MyCorner site. The latest cyber-fad, a computer page festooned with photos of the girl, her friends, covers of her favorite albums. Her own personal corner of cyberspace.

It all began with a welcoming block of text, a sort of electronic handshake beckoning visitors into her own private world.

> Congratulations. You just reached my own little corner of cyberspace.
> Who am I?
> Abby Sherman, that's who. Just your basic, young, messed-up California beach girl.
> Who are you? And why are you checking me out?
> Drop me a few pixels and let's find out!
> Oh yeah, vital statistics: I'm twenty. I'm Caucasian. Californian. Upper . . . Know what? I don't like the way all these labels

make me sound. I know you're supposed to spit out all your demographic info for this MyCorner welcome block, but these facts don't tell the truth about me. They make me sound like some spoiled, privileged person I really want to believe I'm not.

Those handful of sloppy social labels don't tell you that I've taken four mission trips to orphanages in Romania, the Cité Soleil slum in Haiti, the Payatas landfill in Manila, and Mexico City's red-light district. That I volunteer ten hours a week at a local rape shelter. Or that I've taken ten semester credit hours of college courses.

How about the fact that my best friend isn't some debutante named Ashton like my "vital statistics" might indicate, but a very cool and wise 50-year-old expatriate from El Salvador named Narbeli. Who happens to be our ecstatic-to-have-the-job house-keeper (she's legal!) and has been since my mom took off when I was three. Who loves me so much that, even though she has her own apartment, she sleeps every night on the couch outside my door to make sure I'm okay.

I'm not telling this to be a goody two-shoes or puff myself up in any way. I'm no saint. But neither am I some girl who sits around the pool polishing her nails all day and snapping at "the help." Please don't slap easy labels on me without knowing what's under the surface.

Okay—so on that surface, some people might feel compelled to label me a rich, tanned, well-educated American beach chick. I suppose if you want to classify me, I am in the upper—see, I even hate that. I'll say, quite freely, that I'm one of the most privileged people on earth. How's that? I may not apologize for it, but I'm definitely grateful. So let's move on.

Like I started to say, I live in California. Near the beach. I love the ocean almost as much as I love the God who made it.

I've been taking college classes since high school, but I'm totally unmotivated because I have no idea what I want to do with my life. My dad's so frustrated with me. He just wants me to pick something and forge ahead, but I'm one of those people who says, if I have no idea what I'm supposed to do, then what's the point? Why waste time and effort on a major that's not for me? So I'm currently pounding on God to give me a clue just how He wants me to serve.

And yeah, my dad's one of those Type A wheeler-dealers you've never heard about unless you memorize the faces on the cover of *Inc.* and *Forbes* magazine. In which case, I feel sorry for you. In fact, if you've heard of my dad, then you're probably not gonna relate to this site. His name's Robert Sherman, or Bob, I suppose. We live in Pacific Palisades with his wife Teresa. And my half sister, Caryn, who's four.

My mom? Forget it. I'm not talking about that. Not yet. We don't know each other near well enough.

If you're a friend, stay awhile. Check out my other friends, my fave tunes, my blog.

Oh yeah. I'm about to post some pretty bizarre stuff on my blog. Some far-out things have been happening to me—at least in my dreams. Maybe if you're a true mystic, you can IM me, tell me what in the world's going on.

Meanwhile, welcome to MyCorner. . . .

Definitely *her*, the killer told himself, shaking his head at people's willingness to display intimate knowledge of themselves in the most unsecured places. He breathed in deeply. She was the one. A typical young, attractive, well-advantaged American woman, except of course that . . .

. . . if all the heat around this op was true, this woman lay dead center in the crosshairs of history itself.

CHAPTER
_2

"Sister? You have a visitor . . ."

The monk frowned and lowered his voice to a whisper, which a gust of hot desert wind seized and blew away, over the tan rooftops, past the shining church cupolas and into the stifling haze of a Judean midday. He bent over the reclining figure and hesitated, unsure what to try next. He ventured a finger toward her thin, black-clad shoulder and prodded once, gingerly.

She was so still, so weak.

Her eyes fluttered softly and parted. Beneath this five-inch strip of shade—all the monks could spare her today—she winced and her eyelids fluttered again. Her first motion in nearly three hours.

Behind the monk, the voice of the visitor floated out on the softest of whispers. "It is I. Sister Sarha, from Eilat."

A faint smile slowly took hold of the death-mask mouth and tugged it upward at the corners.

"Greetings, my dear. You have traveled far." The mouth closed again, appearing to gather strength for the very next word. "Have you felt it too?"

In response, Sarha bent over suddenly, her eyes ablaze.

"Yes! Oh, Sister, please tell us what it means. We have never sensed anything like this—ever, it seems. Many of us feel something, yet we are all so puzzled. Is this a person, a warning about you? A threat?"

"Yes, it is a danger," the reclining one said. "A terrible peril. Beyond that, I cannot explain. You are right; it is odd beyond anything I have ever witnessed."

Her voice mimicked the word it was conveying, trailing off into nothing.

"Is this the one we've been praying for?"

"I cannot tell."

"What can we do?" the visitor asked.

The other shook her head ever so slightly. "Pray like our fate depends on it. Pray desperately that the threat will pass. And then maybe, if we survive, we can learn more."

PACIFIC PALISADES—THAT SAME MOMENT

The killer forced his senses to re-acquire. Straining to hear the faint inhale and exhale of young lungs, he grimaced, for despite the gravity of the mission he could not keep himself from picturing the homicidal delights this kill might have offered.

Had he been allowed to take her in the usual manner, that is.

Thick eyelashes opening just so wide, narrowing to identify him in the gloom. Then a curious and alluring squint contorting with terror as she realized what he was doing. . . .

Perhaps in a moment, when these preliminaries were over, his hidden earpiece would crackle with a muttered "Go ahead" to indulge this fantasy, to take the girl after all. But not until then. He could hardly risk the thought of it. And even then, he had been ordered to take her with unusual means. A potent and untraceable poison. All the fun removed for the sake of caution.

So be it. He bit into his lower lip so deeply that a crimson trickle ran down his chin. He licked it as far as his tongue would reach, then bent to his appointed task.

It only took five seconds more to find what he was looking for. Her blog entry for the day. Raw and just entered, not yet uploaded onto her site.

He read the title and blanched.

"The most mind-blowing dream I've had yet."

He clenched his jaw. *There it was. The entry that had brought him here . . .*

Without turning away, he reached down to his thigh pocket and pulled out a strip of Velcro elastic holding a dozen short cords. He pulled off one, inserted its end into the laptop's USB port, the other into the recesses of the backpack strapped across his shoulders.

The pack beamed the book's contents to a laptop concealed in the backseat of his van tucked into an alley half a mile away. From there, a wireless Internet server sent an encrypted, electronic message to three e-mail accounts scattered hundreds and even thousands of miles away, at diverse points of the planet.

BEVERLY HILLS, CALIFORNIA—THAT MOMENT

On a marble-floored veranda high above the Los Angeles basin, an impeccably manicured hand reached over to the output drawer of a chrome-plated printer. The first page had hardly even begun to emerge and yet the fingers trembled and reached hungrily for the shuddering vellum edge.

NEW YORK CITY—THAT MOMENT

In a walnut-veneered library in Manhattan, gnarled and wrinkled fingers did not even pretend to wait, but snatched the first page of the very same transmission from the maw of a clattering dot-matrix. The sheet, still connected by a thin perforation to the one that followed, gave way and seemed swallowed up by a palsied grip that shakily raised it high, into the beam of a single recessed light.

ST. PETERSBURG, FORMERLY LENINGRAD—THAT SAME MOMENT

In a nondescript warehouse loft in St. Petersburg, Russia, a head of gray tousled hair bent closer to an old console television jury-rigged as a computer monitor. Here, there was no printer, for the occupant did not trust paper records of any sort. In fact, he considered it fool-hardy enough to let the old *Gorizont*'s pixels hold even a moment's grasp of the image, this all-important picture.

In all three places, curses filled the air as the words unfolded. . . .

CHAPTER

_3

Abby Sherman's Dream Blog

I slammed this out one morning after the dream itself. Please read it and pass it along, and watch for my plea at the end.
—Abby

Dear World,

What in the world just happened to me?

I still don't know if this was just the wildest dream in the history of dreams, or something real. It sure *felt* real. So here goes . . .

It started with being jerked out of my sleep and thrown to one side of the bed and thinking the wind might have slammed a shutter against the house or lightning struck close by. Or maybe I'd overslept again and my stepmom Teresa was acting like my maternal unit that morning (even though she isn't, and never will be), shaking me and yelling that I have to wake up now or miss my ride to class.

Only this light hammered against the outside of my eyelids, like when I lay out on the beach on a really hot day. And I thought, this is weird—did I sleepwalk and wake up out in the backyard or something?

So I opened my eyes. And I was definitely outside—only outside on the hottest, brightest day of the year. I had to raise my hand up over my face, the sun was so intense, and I could actually feel it burn my forehead and cheeks. But how did I get here?

My nose instantly filled with a bunch of weird smells, like old dust and meat barbecuing and woodsmoke and even a whiff of animal poop that I can still smell right now. And I was wearing this thick robe thing that grated against my skin. Reminded me of when I played the shepherd in the manger scene last Christmas, and Mrs. Carter had cut my costume out of these old canvas bags that chapped me so bad that later that night I had to rub chamomile over my arms and legs.

Sorry to take so long getting to the story, but I just really want you to know that I'm not making this up when I say it was a totally *real* experience. Everything I just described sank in so fast, it was like, less than a split second. Before my eyes could even take in what was actually in front of me. Like layers of stuff filling my senses one at a time.

Then I looked out and saw that I was sitting on a pile of old blankets on a really hard floor in the middle of this desert kind of city. I thought, no wonder I'm smelling all these things, because everything is totally dusty and made out of stone and the air is dry and really, really hot. I was actually *in* this place, in some way more real than watching any TV. Actually way more than that. More like the coolest sensurround, high-def, 3-D, IMAX, smell-a-vision—all of them put together—show in the world.

Oh yeah. And I was someone else.

Back to that later, 'cause I'm not through telling you what I saw. Right in front of me this stone wall almost blocked out the sun, it was so high. And other walls just as high stood way behind it, all around me. But I finally realized I was inside a courtyard at the edge of some huge kind of campus or ancient mall, or something.

And thousands of people were walking on every side of my spot, this thick crowd just separating around me at the last second like those shows about animal stampedes where the camera's down on the ground and all these legs slam around it and you're wondering how it doesn't get stomped on. I know you're thinking, how can something that intense take me so long to get around to—but remember, there was so much sensory overload rushing at me in that second, I was just barely keeping up.

All these people were dressed the way I remember from some of the movies and pictures of Bible times. I saw men in robes with blue and purple and yellow turbans over their heads. And a lot of them were pulling donkeys behind them all loaded with packages and blankets and huge bottles. And women walking behind them, only most of them had their heads down, looking at their feet. And men in white church-type robes with these blue fringes coming down their shoulders, who were clasping their hands over their tummies and checking me out real sneaky-like from the corners of their eyes.

And the funny thing is, everyone was quiet, this huge crowd was just walking around all hushed, just the sound of their feet— which made this big clapping sound since they were all wearing sandals. Like some huge crowd touring a museum, or walking through some really strict library.

Every now and then one of them would look over at me and smile or nod at me, all solemn the way people do when they pass by my pastor on Sunday but they don't really want to stop and tell him what they thought of the sermon.

Then things got even freakier. I realized that I was sitting up, only I didn't remember moving anything more than my eyelids. Worse, my body felt way different than just that. Like I said before, it felt like it belonged to somebody else.

Yeah. Stay with me, cause it gets even weirder.

See, I was feeling all these emotions, but not through my own mind. Another one. I can't really explain how I knew that, but I did.

I was an old woman, I realized. It was an instinct, like all these sensations just added themselves together and totaled up: "old woman." And these old woman's thoughts and memories weren't right in front of my mind, but kind of hanging back in the corners, just out of sight. Even though I wasn't experiencing them straight on, in a sideways kind of knowing I knew that these were memories of a really hard life.

I saw—I know you're not supposed to "see" feelings, but I could—her worrying over whether she'd eat that day, her stress over where she would live. I saw this young man yell at her and call her crazy, that she couldn't just waste her life waiting around all day, every day. I saw her memory of a man lying in a dark room gasping for breath and clutching his hands at the air above him, and I was totally sad because I knew he was dying. And I knew that she loved him. I saw day after day of loneliness and depression. All of these really sad days, like picture screens strung together in a row until I couldn't see them all. Just stretching on and on, clear over the horizon.

And I saw the city square where I was, at a bunch of different times of the year. People walking under a low sun with breath fogging out of their mouths. Then everything all green and flowery with spring. Then walkers almost bowing their heads to keep out of the summer heat. I saw the place lit by every hour of the day—purple shadows that looked like dawn, noon glare, hazy afternoons, sunset throwing this golden shadow over everything. I saw it both empty and crammed with people. Time. Lots and lots of time passing by.

And I knew that the man who had died was my husband, and that I was a widow. An old widow who sat in this same spot day after day and waited, waited, waited. And people didn't know what to think of me—whether to treat me like a lunatic, or a saint, or a prophet.

And at the same time, another part of me was Abby Sherman going, "Whoa girl, did you eat too much late-night salsa?" And wanting to shake my head and clear this hallucination out of my senses and get back to reality. *Real* dreams, like showing up for finals in my underwear.

Only the head wasn't mine, and I just knew the moment wasn't mine either. It belonged to *her*. Whoever this woman was.

Then her heart started beating so hard, I thought it might just run out of strength at any moment, and her thoughts got all jacked-up and alert. And I realized something else. Somehow, I knew this without knowing how it came to me.

What this old woman had waited for all these years was happening. It was coming her way that very second.

ST. PETERSBURG, RUSSIA

The old fingers clawed at the television's glowing glass, as though some grip or sharp fingernail could wrest the young American's offending words out of their curved enclosure. The voice which now rang through the cavernous room behind it hardly sounded human anymore. In fact, it did not even bear any resemblance to a terrestrial utterance of any kind—man *or* beast. The only sound competing with it was the incessant pounding of an index finger upon a single, abused key, the *down arrow*, to continue the reading at all cost. . . .

CHAPTER
_4

BEVERLY HILLS, CALIFORNIA

A deep retching sound echoed across the broad, barrel-ceilinged sitting room, propelling thirty dollars' worth of half-digested sashimi from the *Matsuhisa*—the most exclusive sushi house in Beverly Hills—out across a terrazzo of exquisitely checkered Carrara marble.

The butler appeared at the French door windows, peering in worriedly despite his express orders to stay away.

Elegant fingers waved him off, then plucked up a linen napkin and hurriedly dabbed clean their owner's mouth. The nauseated man did not move again, but reached instead for the next page of text from the printer as if no stench or disarray was worth an interruption. . . .

ABBY SHERMAN'S MYCORNER DREAM BLOG, PAGE 7

I—or this old woman, it's hard to make a difference now, because I was her, she was me—felt blown away by an emotion that was strange and new even for her. It was a mixture of like, amazement and gratitude and off-the-chart happiness and fear and awe and humility and wanting to cry a little, all at once. It reminded me of when I saw Caryn being born, when I felt these tears cross my face, and like a freak I didn't even realize I was crying until my emotions caught up with my mind.

But now, last night standing there, I had no idea what was causing all this. I only knew that the feeling was growing stronger. It was coming closer, the cause of all this. Toward me.

I remember seeing a couple of soldiers pass by. I didn't need this old woman's mind to tell me they were Roman because I recognized the fringe on their helmets and the style of their armor from Bible stories and movies and even that trip to Caesar's Palace last year.

And just then, I saw them coming through the crowd.

They were a little family. A short bearded man with really buff forearms and a bone-tired look in his eyes. And a very young woman—a girl, I'd call her, actually. She couldn't have been more than a high school junior back in my reality. Only she was holding a baby, all awkward and tender-like the way Teresa held Caryn coming home from the hospital. This new mom was beautiful. Her skin was all pale and perfect and she had these deep, intense eyes like her husband. I remember she turned and stared right through all the passersby and locked onto me. Her mouth widened into this almost-smile that seemed to light up her whole face.

And I too felt all lit up inside. It sounds stupid to just say ''there was something about these two,'' because it was way more than just *something*. But it seemed like this aura, some intense force field, was following them, and it definitely wasn't coming from the sun. I felt my sight go all fuzzy and then bear down into this soft doughnut haze like the ring around the moon. Like all of a sudden they were the only people in the world. Made me think of that scene in *Jaws*, Dad's favorite movie, when the sheriff sees the shark fin for the very first time, and his face goes all slack with shock while the whole world zooms away behind him.

Then, without even deciding to, I started to stand, and man, was *that* a scary trip. I felt all wobbly, my muscles thin and stringy and weak. My legs didn't really take orders very well. But I was going to stand if it was the last thing I did. I reached up to grab something when these big hands took hold of my forearms, and I realized that a couple of men had stopped to help me.

The men pulled me up and my legs straightened under me. But when I let go and tried to settle my weight down, my knees weren't sure they wanted to hold me. Gradually things got steadier, and the men nodded and mumbled something like "shalom" and hurried back on their way.

And then my legs stepped forward, all on their own, and my mouth moved and my throat made this sound that was half sob and half cry. My arms pulled outward, hands open, as if I'd been asking that young mom to hold her child. Only she wasn't near me anymore. She was walking away.

I cried out. The second the old woman's voice left my mouth, I knew it was a foreign language. But in the very next moment I realized that I could understand it—don't ask me how.

"The Messiah! The Redeemer of Jerusalem!"

AMSTERDAM—THAT MOMENT

A guttural bark, almost a growl, ripped apart the darkness. In the light of the glowing monitor, with the words *Redeemer of Jerusalem!* still blinking in a glowing blue upon it, a hand quickly formed a fist. It struck the screen's glass surface and knocked the machine from its tabletop perch, crashing onto the floor.

More curses now rose, laced with the slightest howl of pain, as the words continued. . . .

ABBY SHERMAN'S MYCORNER DREAM BLOG, PAGE 11

I felt tears run down my cheeks. And felt my chest pump up and down, just fighting to keep up. And this thrill ran like a shower of warm honey down from my head and across my limbs. And this feeling of love and adoration blew up in my chest so big that I wasn't sure I could stand it a second longer.

And my mind flooded with these thoughts: "Thank you. Thank you, dear God. You have vindicated my wait. My whole life. You have brought salvation to Jerusalem."

These weren't Abby Sherman thoughts, I'm sure you can tell. I don't think like that. At that moment the old woman's thoughts just kind of stepped up and were running all over mine, which was cool with me.

A second later, after my cry stopped echoing, the crowd around me slowed down like someone had just turned down the speed button on the whole scene. But that young couple, they stopped dead in their tracks. The young mom turned back to me again, and this time the look on her face had to be as intense as mine. Her brown eyes opened wide and her lower lip went all shaky and trembly. She looked like she was about to cry and shout out for joy and maybe run for her life, all at the same time.

Except the girl stepped toward me, still holding that child in front of her, and she took a step. The distance between us felt all of a sudden like that last three feet of pool water after you dive into the deep end with your breath running out.

And then a whole new set of feelings just exploded. I felt space open up and whisk me along as if some kind of resistance had been sucked away, like someone had opened one of those space-movie air locks and its vacuum was pulling me ahead. I wasn't this barely walking old woman anymore. I was on a moving sidewalk that wouldn't stop for anything in the world.

And I thought I heard music just fill my ears. These millions of soft voices in my ear reminding me of Enya singing, not really words but just a note, a syllable, with all these minor-chord strings swelling behind her. I'm still not sure I imagined it, or if I truly heard it somehow. Either way it made me feel that although I was already super old I could have lived a thousand more lifetimes and this would have still been my ultimate moment.

My legs kept pulling me toward the mother and child. I stopped three feet from her and she stopped too, and then it got really obvious that as beautiful as she was, it wasn't the girl who was setting off all these emotions.

It was the baby.

I looked down at the tiny face framed in blankets. He was chubby and perfect and a beautiful baby, for sure, only there wasn't anything so special about his features themselves. It was how looking at him made me feel. It was the emotional fireworks show going off as I got closer to him—so strong now that I wasn't sure I could keep standing.

I stood and held out my arms. My fingers shook a little

because part of me couldn't believe my own audacity at thinking I could actually hold this child in my very own hands.

There was a pause until the mom moved again, and it seemed to stretch out into a whole year. I heard the tiniest sounds all around me. I heard my heart thump out of control. I heard the child make this tiny little whimper. I heard feet hit the dirt somewhere behind us.

Then I saw the little body come closer to me, being held out. My hands reached him. My fingertips touched his blanket, felt his weight, and I pulled him to my breast. I remember for a split second how tiny and light he seemed. I can't really describe what happened next. But since this is my blog, I'll try.

I felt like I was holding the center of the universe—like someone had sucked the core of one of those supernovas and laid it in my arms. My whole body tingled and throbbed, starting from my chest outward. And it seemed that light was pouring from his little face, like he was the brightest shopping-mall spotlight you've ever seen, aimed right at me, yet I was the only one who could see it.

And that was just the outside of me. Somewhere deep down in my heart, or maybe my soul, was just . . . the only way to describe it is like when an opera singer belts out some high note that just lasts forever and ever. Only this note was all about pure joy. The sound itself wasn't actually sound but this incredible happiness just pouring out from the deepest part of me.

And the next thing I knew, it got to be almost too much. The worst thing in the world was happening—with this precious one still in my arms I was starting to sway, the whole world just moving sideways. It was more than I could stand—literally. But thank God, people had jumped to my side and were holding me up.

My voice was making those words again, only I was so weak that I could only whisper them.

"Messiah. He has come at last."

And the part of me that was Abby Sherman started to cry, because I knew somehow that the baby *was* Jesus, and I was totally there in Jerusalem, two thousand years ago, and I was actually holding Him in my arms. Don't ask me how I know—but if you put a gun to my head and swore to shoot me if I was wrong, I'd still tell you I've been there.

And how can I say it?—every nerve in my body screamed out

that He was divine, that He really was the Son of God. Both the old woman part of me and the Abby Sherman part of me knew the same thing, in a way beyond doubt or question.

Five minutes later I was awake in my usual bed at midnight, back in California, my body still shaking and my mind just spinning like a top. And my fingers still tingled from knowing I had held Him. I don't know why, or how, or what it all meant, but I had held the most important person in the history of the world. That moment had really happened, exactly the way I had lived it.

Then I closed my eyes and started to cry real quiet, not wanting to wake anyone up. I don't know if I was just punch-drunk from the whole trip, or truly feeling nostalgic, but I swear I couldn't stop crying for wanting to go back there, to be back in that time and place and in that old woman's body all over again. The thought of having to stay in this dull, dead world just broke my heart.

So, visitor, you tell me. If you've ever had a dream remotely like this, would you e-mail me and let me know? Because I'm convinced it isn't some random occurrence. It was too intense not to have meaning beyond some product of a spicy dinner or a lumpy pillow. I'm serious—I'm waiting to hear from you.

Abby Sherman

_5

PACIFIC PALISADES—TEN MINUTES PAST MIDNIGHT

The first kill order came only six minutes later.

The assassin had barely tolerated the wait. He stood rigidly with his heart throbbing inside his chest. He had only managed to calm his thoughts by reminding himself that his superiors were duty-bound to pore over every word.

The first order's arrival caused his display backlighting to switch on its eerie blue glow. *Take her. Elder one.*

He breathed out through pursed lips. "All right . . ."

Malibu blinked in. *I concur. Two.*

Amsterdam came, as usual, last and most verbose. *Target is definitely awakening. She is indeed the one we have feared. Harvest at once. Three.*

Seeing again the word *harvest* triggered an inward smile, for it reminded him of the privilege headed his way. Indeed, the assignment before him not only reflected great risk but the opportunity of a lifetime. True, the pleasure of harvesting someone this coveted might prove the sensation of a lifetime, but far more important, this go-ahead reflected enormous trust in his skill and ruthlessness. When he succeeded at the kill, he would single-handedly leapfrog whole ranks of his fellow Scythians and forgo years of ordinary, unremarkable slaughter. Surely that would vault him high into the Scythe's upper echelons, obscure and secret as they might be.

Reassured, he breathed in again and forced his sluggish thoughts to plod through the steps ahead. Despite the honor of the moment, he could hardly afford to get a single thing wrong. The triumvirate had spoken. The order had been issued. Completion now had to be a mere formality.

Sedate with three pumps of the mist bottle. Then remove the needle, expose forearm, and inject. . . .

ST. LOUIS, MISSOURI—THAT MOMENT

In near-total darkness, long fingers lowered and tightened around the faded photograph of a smiling, luminous little girl. With the economy of a long-familiar motion, they slowly, meticulously traced the creases in its paper and folded their sides together.

Finally the picture was restored to a tightly folded square. The fingers clasped the paper to a bony, thinly clad breast. A woman's torso began to rock forward, ever so gradually, then backward again. And again.

A faint mumble broke the silence of the tiny room, echoed through the gloom, across the antiseptic tiles, the bare white walls, the thick locked door.

"Dear Jesus, I beg you to protect my precious one. . . ."

Patient 64 launched into her familiar ritual. The one she performed several hundred times a day and every night before succumbing to sleep, for over thirty-five hundred evenings to date.

This night, her prayers did not end until dawn.

PACIFIC PALISADES—THAT MOMENT

The assassin's hand moved toward the syringe in his breast pocket, but in the millisecond that followed, something in the air before him slowed his motion. It was a force he could hardly distinguish from a tangible, physical resistance. Nothing large and unmovable, like furniture, but more like a body, a strong one, unseen yet pushing resolutely against his hands and face.

He gritted his teeth and flexed through the motion. His eyebrows furrowed. Was fear clogging up his brain? Nervous tension short-circuiting his muscles?

He fought for control and began to sense an almost palpable opposition against every twitch of his body. He scowled. He hadn't been warned of this. He served the ultimate power in the universe—surely at such a time as this it would come to his aid. What was happening?

Panic screamed through his thoughts. He had never encountered anything like this. Several times before he had felt twinges of something odd, but never outright force. He could almost sense a personality in the space just ahead of him, invisibly grappling with him.

His left arm was now trapped in the vise of an invisible hand. His right wrist felt paralyzed; the syringe quivered in his fingers as though an iron grip was trying to wrest it from him. A thousand panicked thoughts hammered his mind. He pushed them away to concentrate on the struggle. He was now being pushed physically back by a force so powerful he wondered if he could stay afoot.

He grunted audibly, for now even his will was beginning to falter. Usually unwavering, his resolve began to flicker like a tungsten filament losing contact with its current. A voice inside him cried, *Quit! Run now while you still can. This one's off-limits. Keep trying to harm her and you will pay!*

His mind quailed at the renewed warning that he could pay for failure with his life. Desperation seared his senses. He strained forward with every ounce of his strength, straining to push the needle closer to her arm. Forget the sedation at this point. . . .

Then he remembered his briefing data. If the poison even touched one of her membranes, it might do the job. Her mouth lay open, her eyelids fluttering at the nearby commotion. Perhaps if he could send a stream of the liquid in the right place . . .

He pressed his thumb on the plunger. Again the resistance came. He only managed a feeble spray, which arched through the air and landed on her wrist. Toxic stuff, to be sure.

But was it enough?

Suddenly his mind shattered like a branch snapped over an upraised knee, and his determination fell apart—simply fled into a void so deep that his unmoored soul could not follow. He broke from the task, turned away and began to run. He ran from the room, past the housekeeper's body that now lay pitched forward on the living room carpet, out the door and into a cold rain lofted by a midnight sea breeze. He felt his feet labor like pistons beneath him, hardly making contact with the ground. He sensed the house and that hateful presence retreating while the night engulfed his long, furious strides.

They had told him he served the greatest power in existence. Yet they had never warned him of this. He could not factor this, could not contemplate a power greater than the bloodlust of Mother Earth. And now having encountered it, he no longer wanted to go on, for its implications were too horrific to think about.

He reached his van in just over a minute, panting now like a marathoner. In a flurry of motion he would soon forget completely, he climbed inside and sped away.

The summons blinked over his pager before he had reached the end of the block. *Congratulations, young Brother. Your honor awaits you.*

He read it once, then twice, and furrowed his eyebrows. Surely they had no idea. How could they possibly know already what had taken place? Not without his telling . . .

THE HOUSE—FIFTEEN MINUTES LATER

Abigail awoke to a flurry of sensations: her father's arms, chilly with the scent of car exhaust and the outdoors, clamped tight around her neck, his face pressed against hers, his voice broken and weeping. Only once before had she heard his voice that high-pitched, seen him that unhinged. Now commotion reigned all about her. Blue and red lights sweeping across her still-darkened ceiling. The screeching of police radios. A woman wailing in the next room.

They all swept her up at once, and all she could think of were words from her childhood.

"Oh, Daddy! Make it go away!"

"Darling, darling. Oh, baby. I'm so sorry I left. I wish I could—"

"What happened, Daddy?" She heard her voice, soft and plaintive like that of a six-year-old, but tonight it did not bother her. At that moment, being adult and independent didn't matter in the least.

Then the memory started to return. A presence in her sleep. A dark and menacing terror just beyond her slumber. Danger as real and palpable as the air in her lungs.

"There was a man," she panted. "In here. He wanted to kill me— I know it wasn't a dream. It wasn't, was it? I sensed it."

Her father drew back and nodded at her, his face streaked with tears.

"It was so horrible, Daddy. I didn't wake up. Not quite. But I knew. It was like a darkness. A personality. It was like . . . craving my death. I know that sounds bizarre, but I felt it. It was . . . I don't know, all specific, like an actual person. It was that real. That close. And there was a struggle. I don't understand, maybe someone else was here, maybe a lot of someones, but there was a fight. And he left. He *did* leave, didn't he?"

Her father nodded again, and the quiver in his lip told her that something worse was true, that an even darker thing had happened.

"Narbeli? What about Narbeli?"

Her father's features disintegrated then, dissolved into an incoherent mask of twitching facial muscles, flowing tears, and uncontrolled sobs.

Then she heard screaming, as wild as that of an animal, and realized it came from her own throat.

MALIBU, CALIFORNIA, THE COLONY—ONE HOUR LATER

The ornate glass door uttered a faint mechanical click and swayed open nearly a foot, seeming to anticipate his approach. The killer froze. He took a silent, shallow breath and cemented his decision to face whatever lay ahead.

After all, he asked himself for the fifth time, what was the point of evasion? The Elder knew he had arrived. If they wanted to kill him, he was already as good as dead. As a frequent purveyor of their carnage, he knew that fact as well as anyone. Someone like him, an invisible and unstoppable assassin, would come and harvest him.

Either way, defying them was out of the question. No, he told himself while trying to ignore a chill like ice water cascading through his veins, he would ride this night to its fated conclusion. And one way or the other, he would end the evening with some explanation of the bizarre force which had opposed him.

He strained to keep his body from shifting into its customary tactical mode. Forcing it to stand still before the door and see what the moment held in store, he willed himself to stop breathing. To not move even an inch. He would bear it like a man.

Ten seconds later he had felt nothing. No bullets piercing his body. No wisps of gas rising to his nostrils. No blackout. His reflection still stood askew in the open door, staring back at him.

And why should they kill me now? he reassured himself. They had no way of knowing he'd failed. Or did they? True, their ability to know impossible things had never ceased to amaze him, but yet . . .

He pushed the slab open with a nudge of an outstretched hand, glancing down at his palm-held computer to verify the address. Yes, he'd gotten it right. Besides, he told himself, front doors did not simply open of their own accord to strangers. Not in beachfront Malibu.

Please walk straight through and meet me on the veranda was the text message's final words. Without moving his head, he trailed his gaze across the surrounding walls. Although the house was unlit, he could still make out the high vaulted ceiling, the open contemporary architecture. There was lots of blown glass as well as squares of dark color to his left and right—framed patches of modern art. He smirked. *Probably overpriced and totally incoherent.*

White seemed to be the room's dominant palette, though it now stood dimmed in the gray of early morning. He noted that most of the scant light glowed from a large two-story window. Through it his eyes made out a band of deep blue floating over one of even deeper cobalt, both halves swimming in the luminescence of a full moon.

The Pacific. The only neighbor to be trusted with an easy view.

He finally allowed himself to breathe out and in again. Tried to pound into his brain the notion he had succeeded, that this was a happy occasion. Surely he would look back, ten minutes from now, and kick himself for having stolen his joy of anticipation—

A dull noise.

His heart stopped; his trained reflexes threw him to the floor. The blow of cold marble against his body shocked him, and he stiffened and shook his head. Suddenly his mind was awash in dread, his mouth sour with the taste of gunmetal. A thin, screaming sound stabbed his ears. He forced his awareness outward to inventory his body for injuries, for he knew that in this current state of adrenaline overload, he could be mortally wounded and hardly even know it.

But no, his senses reported: his body was intact.

He glanced in the direction of the sound and saw, just beyond the window, a dark shape lounging in an Adirondack chair. The round back of a silver-haired head turned as if anticipating his approach. He stood, walked to the door, opened it and forced himself to ignore the soothing kiss of cool, salt-scented air. The person, now to his left, remained still, his gaze seemingly fixed somewhere out on the dim ocean horizon.

"Welcome, my Brother," came a low and confident voice. The purr of an older man quite at ease. "I hope I didn't give you a scare."

The assassin stood dumb for a moment, unable to formulate a coherent reply.

"No—thank you, my Elder," he finally answered. He tried not to stare directly at the man's face, yet his peripheral vision brought him a rough outline of craggy features topped by well-coiffed gray hair. Legs crossed casually in elegantly draped white slacks. It was nobody he recognized—probably one of those highest-echelon Elders he had only heard whispered about.

"Please. Have a seat." The phrasing was smooth and cultured. "I apologize, by the way, for not greeting you at the door. But I am mesmerized by the sea tonight. Is she not captivating?"

"Ah, she is. Certainly." Elaboration seemed beyond his capacity just then.

"Besides, I wanted you to see for yourself that I bear you no ill intentions. You are truly here to reap the reward of a most pivotal mission."

With those words the killer sat down in a deep-cushioned patio chair. He was quickly surrounded by the sour taste of thick cigar smoke. Breathing it in, he allowed himself to laugh nervously at his host's reassurance.

"That is most thoughtful of you, my Elder."

"Think nothing of it." There was a pause while the two men stared out at the sea. The older man chuckled as the crying of seafowl drifted to their ears and a flight of birds churned upward in a damp gust of wind. "Actually, it's not really the ocean that has me so entranced. It's the *gulls*. They fascinate me tonight. Think of it: almost three o'clock in the morning and there they are just as frantic, still straining the air and sky for food. Their appetite is insatiable. Don't you find their drive relentless?"

"Yes," the killer replied. He thought for a moment, then added, "I admire determination."

"Yes, we all do. May I pour you a glass of my favorite single malt? It's world-class."

"Sounds good."

While his host rose and turned to an unseen bar in the corner, he relaxed into his seat and watched the lights of a freighter plow toward the glow of L.A. Harbor. A brief moment later a finely etched crystal tumbler lowered into his field of view, grasped in manicured fingers. He drank deeply. It was indeed a complex scotch, rich with undertones of peat, barley, and malt.

"I wonder if you gained a sense," the older man continued, sitting back with a glass of his own, "as you went about your work, of how many great and powerful minds were frantic for news of your progress. I daresay that nothing you do again may be as closely watched in so many high places."

"No, I was too intent on my work to feel much beyond my immediate duty. But I did have a sense that the mission had a very high profile."

A low snicker drifted over to him. "High profile indeed."

He decided to strike. "Yes, my Elder. And that is why I wonder why no one chose to warn me of the opposition I would face."

He had expected the older man to react strongly, but the tanned face only lowered toward the glass and chuckled audibly. As though the outburst had been completely anticipated. "Opposition?" the man finally said. "Please elaborate."

"I have a feeling you know exactly what I'm referring to."

The voice grew an edge testier. "Nevertheless, I would like you to describe it for me."

"Well, it wasn't a physical barrier. More like an invisible guardian, it would seem, posted there to thwart me. The problem is, as you know I don't believe in such things."

"And how strong was this opponent?"

"Very strong."

"Stronger than *you*?"

Burning eyes bored into his own, so searing that they seemed to be devouring him. He felt his brain lock down. Could he answer now? Or lie successfully?

"I'll ask again. Stronger than *you*?"

He shook his head slowly.

"Just speak, my boy. I assure you, deception right now would prove far more trouble than it's worth. Just start talking, and the answer will come out on its own."

It was easier just to relent, he told himself. Just open your mouth and speak. . . .

"Yes. It was stronger than me. I failed to inject the full dose." Saying it, he felt a tinge of nausea sweep over him.

The wrinkled face drew closer, its expression completely slack. The killer now sat staring at his host's patrician mask and into green heavy-lidded eyes. No longer friendly yet not entirely hostile, either. More like the impassive gaze of a lion watching a gazelle.

"I managed to apply a partial dose on her wrist," he said, his voice rising. "It should do the job eventually. But it may take some additional time."

"Did you see your enemy?" The two men were close enough now for the older one to bite his nose.

"No. But I felt him. I . . . I suppose it was a *him*. His strength was overwhelming."

"You're certain you did administer some of the poison."

"Yes. I saw it. I even smelled it reacting with her skin."

"And this document you discovered—did she actually post it to her website?"

"I never had time to find out," the killer answered. "I found it in a MyCorner text field, and it looked like it hadn't been posted, but I was never able to find out for certain."

The older man sighed loudly and pulled away, settled back into his chair. "Our masters told me as much," he said in a low voice, almost to himself. "That must be why they chose you for the honor."

The killer pursed his eyebrows and wondered what the "honor" was. But no explanation was offered. His host must have meant the meeting at hand. He leaned back and the two fell silent for several minutes.

The gulls grew closer, their cries louder now, angry and accusing. The old man turned to his guest, his expression now bemused like that of one who had just birthed a great, surprising thought.

"My younger Brother, our true masters have asked to bestow on you an honor which not even I have been offered."

"I am flattered, my Elder, but I have no idea what you're referring to. What is this honor?"

"They have asked you to join them."

"Who are *they?*"

"Are you ready to hear this? The oldest, most powerful, deepest secret human history has ever hidden?"

"I'm more than ready."

"I'm sure you are." The older man took a deep drink, swallowed with a loud sniff and exhaled. "Well, all the dark portents are real.

The mystics and the soothsayers were right. Although the full truth and power of what actually exists would quite literally blow them away."

"*What* actually exists?" he asked for the second time, now hardly bothering to conceal his impatience.

"The force you encountered tonight. And those who oppose it. Like the entity which defeated you, they are invisible. They are what, for lack of better terminology, we'd call disembodied spirits. Does that surprise you, my Brother?"

"Nothing surprises me this night. But please. Tell me more."

"Well, I don't need to elaborate much. You will soon know more than I could ever dream of telling. But I will tell you the basics. You see, everything you've been told about the Scythian Directive is pure nonsense." The speaker's voice was now tinged with contempt. "Well, not untrue, necessarily, but the thinnest veneer of truth. All the stuff about ridding the planet of inferior beings. Bah. As though we were carrying out some crude form of population control. There's no deny-ing that most humans are worth less than the ground they walk on, but you're a bright young man—did our grand Directive never strike you as a bit out of kilter? A rancid bit of rationalization, perhaps?"

The assassin inhaled slowly, though only as a pretext for giving himself an extra second. He struggled to form an answer as the shock of what he was hearing sent his thoughts in a thousand different directions. His breath returned to the night, unspent.

"Oh, admit it," the older man continued. "You're a killer. Every bit of your soul has been caught up in the lust for death. Why deny it? I certainly don't. I slaughtered three people before dinner tonight. A man, a wife, and a homeless bum. I'm still basking in it as we speak."

"I think I understand." It was the best reply he could manage.

"No, you don't! You don't understand any of it!" The sudden venom in the man's voice drifted away at the outburst's end and the previous voice returned, conciliatory as before. "Well, perhaps I exag-gerate. You only understand the slightest edge of the tiniest bit of the truth. That's because deep down you realize that you're not just serving some disembodied planet, some gauzy spirit of Gaia. Our Order and its killing serve a far higher and historic purpose."

His voice grew loud and pompous again. "You were opposed by an invisible being many fools in this world would call an *angel*. The very word makes my stomach churn. You see, as you might have surmised, nothing is as it seems. Up is down. Black is white. Good is cruel. Behind the drivel of organized religion lies a bitter parody of truth. There *is* an invisible realm. Call it the spirit, heaven, the veil, the other side—whatever you will. Angels, spirits and all that. Of course the religious fools have gotten it all backward. What they call angels are actually the instruments of oppression, of despair and betrayal. What they call God is actually the entity dripping with injustice and cruelty. And what they call evil is in fact the side to be pitied, to be shown sympathy and aid. *These* are the real purpose for our Directive."

The man stabbed his cigar into his goblet's remaining ice. His facade of patrician charm was now spent. The flush on his cheeks and the quiver of his jowls showed he was clearly enraged.

"It's quite a saga, especially given that it's older than history itself. The beings whom we serve have been condemned to roam this planet invisible, without purpose, companionship, or hope of redemption. They do not even possess the ability to inhabit a human body, which is a spirit's deepest craving. And the cruelest part? Their only nourishment is something quite rare and elusive: the byproduct of human damnation. The spiritual essence of death itself. It's something they cannot set in motion without our help. They literally feed off of the dying of souls. If you think of death as also a process of rebirth, then they consume the afterbirth of that ethereal delivery. Which means that even finding sustenance is a process over which they have no control. We Brothers provide them that, when we kill. *You've* provided them that dozens of times. Our Order is their lifeline, and has been for thousands of years. Of course, the minions of the so-called loving God have formed their own army to fight us, to deny them their only sustenance. Since the dawn of history there's raged a war between our Brotherhood and their idiotic foot soldiers."

He turned to the younger man. His smile had now returned. "Around the world we are close to exterminating the fools' army once and for all. Final victory is within sight. I tell you this because the young girl you visited tonight is a key battleground in this war. If we do not kill her, all could be in vain. You will learn why in due time."

"She will soon be dead. I'm sure of it."

"I am sure too, my boy. Do not concern yourself with that. As I said already, I have invited you here for a great honor. In fact, tonight you have catapulted to the very highest privilege our Brotherhood can offer. A status far higher than my own. As I told you before, our masters have asked you to join them."

"How do I do this? Join them, I mean. If they're disembodied . . ."

"A most practical, commonsense question. I respect that. One whose answer I suspect you already are beginning to guess."

"And the answer is?"

He was beginning to tire of all the evasions.

"I'll have to take your life, of course."

The younger man felt his fingers quiver. A dead weight plummeted from his grasp and the sound of shattering glass reached him from a strange distance—a hollow sound from a faraway room.

"Yes. Again, remember: It is the highest honor imaginable. I do not know if it is a result of your abject failure, or some inadvertent triumph. At this point, as I've said before, it matters little. All I know is that my personal master, who stands here with us on this veranda right now, has asked to consume you and bring you into himself."

The host reached out and caressed the younger man's forearm. He spoke in a lascivious whisper. "It is forward and rather off-putting for a man to touch another in this manner, is it not? But can you brush away my hand? I rather doubt it. That's because the paralyzing agent in your whiskey is taking effect right on schedule. Death is the medium of our commerce, you understand that. In your case, an exquisite agony which will produce the very sweetest and highest communion imaginable. And the more prolonged it is, the more exalted it will be."

The Elder knelt now in the front of the immobilized man.

"I will give you a choice. I am about to flay you alive over the course of many hours. You will feel every twinge, for while the agent has paralyzed your limbs, it is expressly designed not to impair sensation. You wouldn't believe the chemical balancing act required to bring *that* off. Then I can either dissolve you, quite slowly, in hydrochloric acid, or, since you enjoyed tonight's aerial display as much as I did, I can feed you one morsel at a time to these remarkable seabirds. So— blink once for the acid, twice for the birds. Your eyelids will be functional for another minute or so."

The killer closed his eyes and kept them shut. He clamped them as tightly as his body's last flutters of electrical energy would allow.

"Fine. I'll take that as *two*. Here's the scalpel."

The old man knelt and plucked a generous shred from his shoulder. He held it up and allowed a fine spray of crimson droplets to fly into a sudden gust of wind.

"Birdies! Come here, sweethearts . . ."

LATER

The furious flock remained, hovering, over the beach house veranda for most of the day. Passersby along the sands of America's most famous beach shook their heads and concluded that the home's eccentric owner had taken his odd passion for the birds to a new height of generosity.

_6

The door was opening; Abby's eyes flew open. Then, seeing the expression on her doctor's face, she felt her heart sink. The man's eyes were almost half shut with the heaviness of someone facing a dreaded task. Her father and Teresa followed with their gazes averted. Her father seemed to be breathing strangely. She thought Teresa's eyes looked red and puffy.

They slunk in and sat in twin chairs at the far corner while the doctor settled on the end of her bed and gave her a smile not matching the cast of his eyes.

"Abby."

He said it flatly, like a statement.

"Are you gonna level with me now?" she asked.

He shut his eyes against the frustration in her voice. "Now, there's no need to talk like that. We've told you everything we could at every step."

She'd been hoarding this frustration since shortly after her admittance twenty-one days ago, and it was sweet release now to let it flow.

"I don't believe that. You've been managing me all three weeks I've been here. My nurses won't even tell me my temperature without asking your permission."

"We're unsure, that's all. We've been trying to figure things out."

"But now you know, I can tell. What is it?"

He breathed in deeply, ponderously, then out again. "We're not sure—"

"Oh, stop it," she interrupted, until he held out his hand to stop her.

"Abby, a very aggressive and destructive infection is moving through your body. We've never seen anything like it before. We've tried to analyze it against every known treatment known to medical science. And frankly, the results so far are inconclusive. But the effects on your body aren't."

He sighed again, and from the corner of her eye she saw her father look down and wipe his eyes.

"As you already know, your left arm is fully engaged. The infection is traveling along your neural pathways, your nerves, and simply shutting them off. I don't know how long it will take, but without an effective cure—which we don't seem to have—it will reach your heart at some point in the near future, your brain soon after that."

"Say it to me." Her voice was a mixture of dread and defiance. "Say the words."

Finally, he looked straight into her eyes, his gaze clouded with sadness. "You're going to die, Abby. Very soon. I could give you false hope, and I can truthfully say that we'll keep trying. But there's very little hope."

She felt her breathing skip somewhere beyond her control, her lungs fight for breath. The room began to sway. Her thoughts suddenly slowed as if unwilling to process the knowledge pounding at the gates of her conscious mind.

Finally she felt her throat force out a few words.

"So you've done all you can for me."

"No. We can give you our very best care. Manage your pain. Increase your comfort immeasurably. I'm so sorry, Abby . . ."

"Does this have something to do with Narbeli's murder?"

He shook his head. "Not directly. But it seems your infection started around the same time. I don't know how you could have acquired this thing. Only that it's on the move, and I have no idea how to stop it."

She closed her eyes and wished the act could erase the sight of all of them—doctor and family together.

"Pretty ironic, isn't it, Dad?" He looked at her blankly, uncomprehending. "I mean, here you and I have been arguing the last six months over what I should do with my life. How badly I need to figure out what I want to *do with my life*. And now, it doesn't even matter. It's over. Do you think maybe now you and I can start getting along better?"

He shot her a brokenhearted smile. Blackness replaced the white light and stark expressions, then overtook her.

THE NEXT DAY

Abigail awoke to the sight of her father gazing down at her through eyes full of tears. His index finger lay poised atop her hand, grazing it like one afraid to apply too much pressure on a delicate object. Immediately the truth behind his expression burst upon her with an inner sensation like that of being drenched in ice water.

He was already saying good-bye.

No doubt about it—her father was weeping with a shocked distance she had only seen him adopt once before: a week and a half prior, after returning from Narbeli's gravesite. At the time, she had barely possessed the strength to look about and register anyone else's reactions, for the murder had knocked her into a pall of depression from which she had yet to catch her breath. But her father's expression had been so altered that day, such a departure from his usually cool and competent demeanor, that even then she had taken note.

And now he was looking at her with that very same unhinged expression.

For a second she had the macabre sensation of already being in the grave, peering up at the mourners of her own funeral.

"Daddy?" she heard herself say in alarm.

Then the cause of his devastated expression came rushing back to her.

Third week in this bed. No answers. No encouraging signs. Not even a diagnosis to speak of. Only the knowledge that she was dying. Yes, dying. Inexplicably, inexorably, painfully.

At the age of twenty.

Maybe his premature reaction to the sight of her wasn't so un-justified.

"I'm still here," she said in a weak voice. "Daddy. Please. Don't look at me that way."

Startled from his grief, he stirred himself and allowed a paternal smile to warm his features once more.

"I'm sorry. I didn't mean it."

Instead of returning the smile, she scowled and peered at him. A fierce shudder cascaded down her spine.

She had just seen . . . felt . . . *something.* A breeze, a wisp, a flutter. A chill through her heart. A dark wing across the empty air just in front of her.

"Dad, did you just feel something?"

"Something what?"

"I don't know. Something passing, a shudder, a presence even?"

He stared at her. "No, sweetie . . ."

She sighed and shut her eyes. Yes, she had seen it—*or had she?* Had she glimpsed an eerie haze drift in front of his shoulders?

She saw something again, and almost screamed—for it was now clear.

And terrifying.

A gauzy face, revolting and horrific at once. A mouth, leering and ravenous. A palpable shroud of something that made her want to crawl out of her skin.

"Are you okay, sweetie?" came his voice through what sounded like a thick cloud.

She shook her head. "I'm sure it's part of the sickness. I don't know—this morning my vision started to get blurred with these opti-cal illusions. These little vapors, wisps of something. And every hour they get more . . . distinct. And horrible. Sometimes it even seems I can see faces on them. Just now it became totally clear. It was the scariest thing I've ever seen. I can't explain it, 'cause they're very . . . I know it's childish, but they really give me the creeps."

"They're just hallucinations, honey," said the nurse at the foot of her bed. "I'm sure we can get you some drugs to make them—"

"No, please," Abby interrupted. "No drugs. I don't want to spend my last . . ." She realized what she was starting to say and paused. "I don't want this time to be a haze."

"I'm so sorry, sweetie," her dad said. He sighed with a heaviness that made the nurse, even his wife, Teresa, who stood to one side, glance at him sharply. "But please, don't tell me. Don't bring up these things. Please. Just don't."

"But, Dad, if I can't talk to you about it, who can I talk to?"

His head began an almost involuntary shake. "I don't know. One of your friends? A counselor? I'll pay."

"Please. Don't make it about money."

"I'm not, Abby. I'll even bring in a chaplain, if that'll help."

Abigail stretched her face into an exaggerated look of surprise. Anybody who knew her father knew about his feelings toward organized religion. Ever since her mother had led Abigail in a sinner's prayer at the age of eight—during one of her calmer periods just before her disappearance—the subject had been a wedge between her and her father. After her mother had vanished, Abigail had clung to her new beliefs, and then her church, as a source of solace. Then, as she matured, it had turned into far more. It had blossomed into a truly voluntary, vibrant core of her character. At the same time, her father had angrily rejected Christianity, managing to remain grudgingly tolerant of his daughter's faith. The most he would offer was a continual complaint that on Sunday mornings, one of his most available times in a hectic professional schedule, it would have been nice to spend *quality time* together. Instead, she had to rush off to *that place.* . . .

That was why this offer was indeed a concession.

"No, Dad. I want you to tell me why. Come on—I'm the one who's, who's . . ."

"Don't say it."

"But I am. And that's why you owe me an explanation. This is too important; I can see it in your eyes."

He sat down quickly, with the suddenness of someone whose knees had abruptly lost all their strength. Not a man who racked up a dozen treadmill hours a week.

"I always thought I'd go to my grave without ever telling you about these things. But now . . ." He raised his eyebrows as if to finish by saying, *Now with you about to go before me, it's all changed.*

"Tell me, Daddy. You're scaring me."

"It's about your mother."

Abigail felt a hard wall of inevitability rise within her. *Of course,* she told herself. What other topic would push him so close to the edge?

"Go ahead."

He sighed and blew out loudly. "Right before the end, right before she disappeared, your mother started complaining of all sorts of strange sights. It started with these strangely real dreams. They seemed to involve folks who lived in ancient times. Biblical characters. She seemed to think these were more than your average dreams, but actually some kind of invasion, a *possession* almost. Except not like the normal possession. In these dreams, she was the one possessing the body of these historical people."

Abigail inhaled slowly, self-consciously. It felt like her life depended on gathering that next breath. She felt an actual swimming sensation in her head and knew that she was in danger of fainting. She could hardly believe the words buzzing about her tympanic membrane.

"Anyway, that's not the most important part," he continued. "But see, right around that time, she started talking about seeing things. About all of a sudden experiencing some kind of, what she called 'spiritual vision.' She started really freaking out, talking about seeing things swimming around in front of her. Just like what you said. I'm sorry. But it was so pronounced . . . the similarity. The words you chose—they could have come out of her mouth. Some of the last words she ever spoke to me."

"So, is that what you think drove her to abandon us?"

He paused and turned to Teresa, whose eyes seemed to have recently gone cold. As abruptly as the flicking of a switch.

"Honey, I have something to confess to you."

Teresa exhaled angrily and stormed off toward the door. Her father watched her go, then turned back to Abigail with a weary expression.

"Your mother didn't exactly abandon us the way I've always told you," he said in a low voice, as though someone was eavesdropping on the conversation.

"What?"

"Your mother didn't just leave. She disappeared under suspicious circumstances. If you were to track down her case with the FBI, you'd find that her file states her as presumed dead. *Murdered*, to put a finer point on it."

"So you thought it would be better," Abigail said, her voice rising, "to let me grow up thinking that my mom was a tramp who never loved me and thought it would be more fun to run off with a cult of dope-smoking hippies than stay and raise me?"

"Yes," he answered, his lips stretched tight. "I thought that would be easier to live with than knowing your mother had transformed into a schizophrenic and ran off in sheer insanity, rejecting all my attempts to help her, and who, if she isn't a homeless junkie, is probably lying in a potter's field cemetery."

Abigail dropped her head back on her neck in resignation. She let out a groan. Her father's explanation had been a convincing one. Neither scenario of her mother's fate seemed appropriate for contemplation by a young girl's tender heart and soul.

"I'm sorry," he said softly. "I shouldn't have been so blunt."

"Thanks," she said, "but I did sort of provoke you. And so you're saying you have no idea what's actually happened to Mom?"

A look of regret flashed briefly across his face. "Before I answer that, let me tell you something. I spent much of your childhood years doing everything imaginable to find your mother. I was on a first-name basis with the missing person's coordinator of every state in the union. I hired so many investigators that I bet there's not a shelter west of the Mississippi that hasn't been visited by somebody on my payroll. I've personally driven every mile of the L.A. Basin's freeways and homeless areas. No man alive could have tried harder than I did."

"I'm not calling you a failure, Dad. I'm just asking what you know."

"Well, I did find her, and she came home. For a while."

"Of course. When I was eight. I remember."

"But I know something else still."

She grimaced this time. "Dad, I'm not sure I can survive any more surprises today."

"Then brace yourself, because this may be my last chance to tell you this. I'm pretty sure she was kidnapped and murdered."

This time Abigail did not utter a word in response. She did not even move a muscle to entice him into going further. She was incapable of either. Finally, however, it became obvious that he did not have the will to elaborate unless she provoked him.

"Dad? Are you going to explain?"

He snapped back from some strange reverie and met her eyes. "It had something to do with these visions of hers. Many years later, after talking to several forensic psychologists, I became convinced that it wasn't a mental illness at all."

Abby used the last of her strength to prop herself upright in bed and face him directly. "What do you think it was?"

"I don't know for certain. Some kind of strange gifting, I suppose. A variant of what psychics experience. The real ones, that is—if there is such a distinction."

"But how did that lead to her being kidnapped?"

He sat on the side of her bed and sandwiched her right hand between both of his.

"Because a lot of things don't add up about the night she disappeared. I can't go into all of it, but there seemed to be a forced entry. At first the detectives thought it was her breaking her way out of the house, but when my private investigators looked it over later, it was obvious someone had broken in. Someone very skillful, very adept at hiding his tracks. There was a scuff mark on a wall. Really—I don't want to give you all the reasons. But suffice it to say, they add up in the dozens. And they haven't faded over time. I think these strange sightings of your mother's got her abducted and probably killed."

"Oh."

"Are you satisfied now? Do you feel any better?"

"Not really."

"I didn't think you would. That's why I never told you. And why I didn't want to tell you today."

She squeezed his hand tightly, because she had heard a rare quaver of emotion in his last few syllables. What would she do without him?

He rose, gave her a weak smile, and walked out.

Abigail sank back into the mattress and let the tears flow. She wasn't sure why she'd held them back—maybe because she'd always prided herself on being Daddy's strong girl, the flinty one who had bounced back from her mother's disappearance with such obvious wholeness that everyone in her world marveled at her resiliency. Perhaps she simply didn't think she had the strength to burden her father with a disclosure of her strange dreams.

But there, just below the surface, lay something far more troubling yet. In the span of a single conversation her personal mystery had just tripled its depth.

Mommy . . . For her whole life, the subject had been a fairly straightforward, although deeply painful, tale of mental illness and abandonment. A good mother who had lost her mind and tragically left her family forever. In the Southern California of decades past— haven to free spirits, psychedelic drugs, and profound eccentrics—it hadn't proven such an unusual story.

Yet for Abby, it had always been tinged with a hint of doubt she had never wanted to fully wrestle with.

For such an unstable person, Abby's mother had done one thing her daughter had never forgotten.

She had only to close her eyes for the images to rush back. . . .

She was eight years old. It was late evening, and the ranch house in Reseda—two homes removed from the mansion in which she now

lived—lay wreathed in shadow. Her bedroom was lit only by her faithful Cinderella table lamp. Her mother's face hovered close, her sandy
brown ponytail accented by the single light source. She spoke in the
low husky voice she only used at bedtime. But tonight her speech
sounded even more laden with emotion than ever before.

"Are you sure, sweetheart? You really know what this prayer
means?"

"Yes, Mommy. I want Jesus to come into my heart. I want to live
for Him."

It was something mother and daughter had talked about for
weeks, ever since a clear though childlike understanding of spiritual
things had clicked into place within her young mind. Years of Bible
reading and quiet nighttime talks about God had taken hold and
yielded a realization, however rudimentary, that she was prone to sin
and needed Him in her life.

Abby remembered every bit of the conversation, especially the
sight of one lingering detail—the crystal-like tears that had wandered
down the contours of her mother's face while she watched her pray.
Puzzled at the display of emotion, Abby had asked her mother why
she was crying. At first, her question had only seemed to multiply the
tears. Then her mother had cradled her cheek with one hand and
spoken in a wavering voice.

"Honey, I'm just so happy to be able to pray this prayer with you,
that's all."

"Well, who else would do it?"

"I don't know, Abby. No one. But I've been away so much the last
few years. I'm just overjoyed to be the one sitting here with you."

"Daddy wouldn't do it. He doesn't even believe in God."

"Abby . . ."

"Isn't that why he doesn't go to church with us?"

"Sweetie, your father loves you very much. He's a good daddy."

"Yeah, but he never prays at dinner, and when we do he keeps his
eyes open. I've seen him."

"Really?" she said with a relieved smile. "Well, you must have had
your eyes open to see it, didn't you?" And she brushed off the subject

with an affectionate squeeze of Abby's forearm.

The weeks that followed became a bewildering time for the little girl. In the aftermath of her prayer, her mother's behavior seemed to split into dual and utterly contradictory paths. When speaking to Abby directly, she had continued to be nurturing and loving. Their bedtime conversations now stretched into the better part of an hour as her mother patiently answered countless questions about God and this newfound faith of hers. Abby had been a precocious little girl, and her ponderings had led her into an unusually deep understanding of what it meant to live out her faith.

Yet whenever her gaze was directed away from the little girl, Abby's mother had transformed into a frightened, jittery woman. Abby retained a vivid memory of her mother's voice, sharp and panicky, ringing out through the house. There were the sounds of doors slamming at odd hours. Her parents' voices rose in anger, the echoes muffled only by closed doors and sheltering walls.

The night of her mother's disappearance had come only a month or two later. Abby had little memory of that fateful night—at least until the worst was over. She awakened to being shaken by her father, his face white and his voice brittle with an edge she had never heard before. He must have told her then, but her sleep-fogged mind had not absorbed the words. It had taken several days, and several repeatings, for the fact to penetrate her mind.

Mommy is gone. They're looking for her, but we don't know if she'll ever come back. Ever . . .

It had taken years for the gloomy tentacles of that grief to dissipate from her life. And still they had a persistent way of returning sometimes, wrought by the most random of provocations, late at night or abroad in her daytime pursuits, sparked by a television commercial or an overheard remark or the sight of a young girl hand in hand with her mommy.

And now, all these years later, to discover that her distant grief, her mother's disappearance, might also be tied to this present business. The thought stole her breath away and set her thoughts tumbling with a fury she felt powerless to stop.

She had an idea of how to calm herself. *Her laptop.* She leaned over to the hospital side table and pulled the computer closer. Ever since her injury she hadn't had the heart to glance at the document she'd been typing right before falling asleep on that fateful night. Her retelling of the strange dream she had lived through.

Her account of exactly what her father had described. A dream where she'd possessed the body of an ancient old woman. A blog entry she'd never found the courage to upload to her MyCorner site. A document whose final paragraph included the words . . . *visitor, you tell me. If you've ever had a dream remotely like this, would you e-mail me and let me know?*

Making up her mind, she moved the cursor over a small rectangular box outlining the word *Upload.*

Up to now, she hadn't been sure if it was worth the trouble of posting this latest blog to her site, let alone an announcement of what had happened since: Narbeli's murder and her own mysterious illness. But now, after her father's explosive revelation, everything had changed. Suddenly that final question throbbed with more urgency and meaning than any question she could ever have imagined. She needed to know. She *had* to know. She couldn't leave this world without some closure on this curse that had claimed her mother and now seemed poised to claim her as well.

She clicked to begin the upload of her dream.

Abruptly, she was overwhelmed by a feeling that she'd just set off an atom bomb.

Reply to: Abby Sherman, BeachDreamer@MyCorner.com
Message received at Server, marked UNREAD

Girl, I'm gonna try my best and get around to what I've e-mailed you about. But give me a second. Right now, all I can do is try and catch my breath. I can hardly keep enough air in my lungs to stay conscious—forget trying to type.

This is crazy. It's not possible.

I'm sure I don't know you. I live in Detroit. No one I know has ever met you. No one I've ever talked to. But even that doesn't matter, 'cause I haven't talked to anyone about this.

YOU DESCRIBED, WORD FOR WORD, A DREAM I HAD
LAST WEEK!
Rochelle at MyCorner

P.S. Yeah, I'm as freaked out by it as you are. But no, I don't
know anything more about what it means than you seem to. If you
find out any more, would you e-mail me back? Please?

[MyCorner.com Admin: MESSAGE not read. Recipient's mail-
box at 367% capacity]

HOSPITAL

On day twenty-three, Abigail's nurse came to collect the remains
of lunch accompanied by another African-American nurse in her late
forties. The moment the newcomer walked through the door, Abigail
stiffened up in her bed and threw a forearm over her eyes as if trying
to shelter her vision from an oppressively bright light source.

"What's the matter?" the new nurse asked, looking around her.

"Don't you see them?" Abby said in a high-pitched voice. "They
came in with you."

The woman turned to Abby's nurse. She lowered her head and
raised her eyebrows. An expression which read, *I'm glad I came.*

But Abby's nurse seemed to stiffen with the opposite impression.
"Maybe it wasn't such a good idea, you coming with me," she told the
newcomer in a low voice.

"No, no, please—I think it's more important than ever," the older
nurse said, her eyes fixed on Abby.

"Are you okay?" her nurse asked Abby.

"There's nothing wrong with me," Abby answered. "It's just these
bright, white men standing beside her."

"This isn't going to work," her nurse said to the other through the
side of her mouth. "I need to get a consult."

"No you don't," the new nurse said. "I know what this is. Now,
Kathy, you've known me for ten years. You know that I know my job.
If I only ask you one time to just trust me, this is it."

"I trust you, Gladys. But that trust isn't worth losing my job over."

"It won't come to that. I promise."

The older woman walked forward to Abby's bedside and sat down on a visitor's chair. "Please, Sister. Tell me what these men look like."

Abby paused for several reasons—not the least of which was the unfamiliar sensation of being called "sister" by an African-American woman.

"Please, won't you tell me?"

Abigail narrowed her eyes and scrutinized the nurse. The woman's tone was neither pleading nor insistent. Just very, very passionate.

"You mean you can't see them?" Abby asked.

The woman turned around, stood, and remained utterly still for a long moment. Then she turned back to Abby.

"I don't have it as strong as I used to, see. These days I can see their glow, mostly. And if I stand real still, I can almost see the edges of their wings against a darker background. It's like any other gift, you know. Comes and goes. It fades a little with age, and neglect. So go ahead—it sounds like you're just awakening to it. It must be powerful with you."

Abby suddenly felt a strange boldness come over her. She felt compelled to stare right at the apparitions and call them out like one of those last-minute witnesses at a murder trial.

"The one on your right is tallest, and his skin is dark—as black as coal. I say 'his skin' because every other part of him, his eyes, his smile, his whole countenance, his whole body even, glows so bright I find it hard to look at him straight on."

"Does he have wings?" the nurse asked, her voice trembling with joy.

"Okay, that's it," her first nurse interrupted. "Gladys, you need to leave. Or I call security."

Oblivious to the interruption, Abby squinted and leaned forward. "Why, he *does* have wings," she said in a breathy, amazed voice. "Although I hadn't even noticed them before! They're huge, and dramatic . . . so beautiful."

"One, two . . ." the first nurse counted at Gladys in a darkening tone.

Nurse Gladys turned to the woman and looked downward, gathering her determination in one long, loud breath. "Kathy. Please. Two minutes."

"You've got *one*."

Gladys now seemed to search the ceiling tiles for inspiration. "Kathy, I know what you're afraid of. I promise you that I'm going to help this poor girl, not hurt her."

"But you two are talking nonsense. You sound like a couple of girls fantasizing about fairies and pixie dust. Thirty seconds . . ."

Gladys reached out and touched Kathy's forearm, briefly, tentatively, then retreated like someone struck by an electric shock. "How many times have you and I sat in the lounge and whispered stories to each other about the mysteries of life and death we've seen in this place? Do you remember the elderly woman just last week, who popped up in Trauma Three after having been declared dead an hour before? Do you remember the things she said?"

"Yes, but . . ."

"And what about the blind girl who flatlined on the operating table and came back telling you the color of your hair and the number of dust bunnies on the top of the OR supply cabinet and a whole host of things she had no way of seeing?"

"That's different."

"No, it's not, Kathy. This is one of those things. It's something I'll be glad to tell you about someday, when we're truly in a safe place. But you've got to trust me. This is something I know about very personally. It's part of my past. Part of my family."

Kathy glanced about her with an exasperated look. "Okay," she said at last. "You have five minutes. After that, I can't protect you. Everyone knows you don't work this floor. The other girls will be by—"

"I know," Gladys interrupted. "I'll hurry."

She turned back to Abby, reached out and grazed her forearm tenderly.

"Does this mean I'm dying?" Abby asked. "Right now, I mean? Is that why I'm seeing them? Have they come for me?"

"Oh no, Sister," Gladys said. "You may be in bad shape, but this right here ain't about dying at all. I got it when I was eighteen, and my momma when she was twenty-two. Momma's still alive, and Lord willing, I should be around a long time, if my children don't put me in the grave themselves."

She leaned forward almost into Abby's face now, and her voice refashioned into a fierce whisper.

"You've been seeing the other kind too, haven't you? The evil ones?"

Abby nodded, unable to speak a reply.

"How long has this been happening?"

The young girl swallowed hard and blinked her tears away. "Just a few weeks. It started right before all this."

"And did it all start with a dream?"

"Yes!" said Abby. "A dream about an—"

"An old woman at the Temple."

"That's right. How in the world. . . ?"

The nurse's grip on Abby's forearm tightened. "My Suzette was right. She read your blog—along with half the sisters in town, apparently. She recognized your dream from the stories I used to tell her as a young girl. She doesn't have the gift herself, but she remembered. And she was right on the money—you got the Sight."

"The what?"

"The Sight is just a gifting from the Lord, honey. It manifests in young women every generation or so. I heard of it stretching back all the way to plantation days, in my family and two of the others in my church. It isn't spoken of much. More of a myth these days, one of those shivers-down-your-back kind of stories that women tell each other when the men are out of earshot. Tell me something. Do you love the Lord?"

"Well, yeah . . ."

"No, I don't mean some namby-pamby twice-a-year pew-warmer. I mean, are you on fire for Jesus?"

Abby smiled at the old woman's vivacity.

"How do I prove that to you?"

The older woman's eyes fell to the bed where Abby's hands lay still. She smiled. There, still clutched in Abby's fingers, was her gnarled old study Bible.

"You have to know that He's all that's getting me through," Abby said in a breathy voice, on the thin edge of tears.

The nurse reached forward and with an index finger lifted a tear from Abby's cheek. "You don't have to prove nothin'." Kathy glanced over with an impatient expression, and Gladys rose to leave. "One thing. This is a strange question to ask, so you can tell me to mind my own business. But do you have any color in your family tree?"

"What?"

The older woman smiled indulgently. "Any African forebears?"

Abby lifted up a blond lock of her hair. "No, not a bit. Not that I know of anyway."

The nurse shook her head. "It didn't seem like it—you're blonder than vanilla pudding. That's the strange part, though. I've never heard of it coming to a white person before."

She blew a kiss and walked out. Then her face reappeared in the doorway.

"One last thing, I promise. Suzette would kill me if I didn't tell you. But you've gotta check your e-mail. You done stirred up something big. And word is, you don't even know it."

Abby felt a surge of curiosity and longing well up inside her, and called out weakly, "Come back?" But the old woman was gone.

Reply to: Abby Sherman, BeachDreamer@MyCorner.com
Message received at Server, marked UNREAD

Whoa. Up until I read your blog, I was sure that it only happened to members of my family or my church. See, I had that same exact dream, down to the smell of animal dung and the difficulty standing up, and especially the feeling of holding that Child. *Especially that part . . .* Only it was three years ago.

I started to tell my family the next morning, and my momma looked over at me from the stove with a look that told me I'd get whupped within an inch of my life if I said another word. So I made up some other ending, like some Elm Street nightmare. And an hour later, she took me aside and told me something.

Now, I'm gonna go ahead and tell it to you. Not because what she told me wasn't a major secret, but because you sound like someone who needs to hear this secret as badly as I did. See, she told me these dreams were like the beginning of what she called a "wondrous" thing that was going to start coming to life inside me. It almost sounded like when she had "The Talk" with me, you know, the one about getting your first period and becoming a woman and sex and all that, only that happened six years ago.

She didn't tell me what the next part would be, because she didn't want to bum me out in case it didn't happen. But she said there would be more "giftings," as she called them. And we'd wait for them. Then she told me that if I got them, it would be proof that I had something she called, in this really deep whisper, "The Sight."

It was something only a few women in my family had been blessed with. My great-aunt Lavinia had it, she told me, along with a couple of old-timey great-grandsomethings I only heard about growing up. And that wasn't any surprise, because me and Laveen, as I used to call her, were as tight as thieves all through my childhood, until she passed from a stroke one week after my ninth birthday. We had a bond, they always said. Laveen would always squeeze me to her bosom and say "Ooooh, this is a special child," even if no one was listening. It was she who first prayed the prayer of salvation with me, and who told me about making God the delight of my heart.

And I always knew that folks listened to Lavinia. There was just something different about the way people cocked their heads and turned their eyes when she said something important. She had *respect*. Don't mean to sound like an Aretha Franklin wannabe, but I'll bet you know what I mean when I say that.

So now it seems like I'm still in the process of getting the Sight. And I'm not going to tell you everything that comes next.

Except I will ask you a question, Abigail Sherman. Are you starting to see things? Spirits? Has the veil lifted yet?

You IM me, Sister. And we'll talk.

Jackie at MyCorner

THE FOUR SEASONS, NEW YORK CITY—MORNING

His satellite phone rang with that spectral ring tone that never failed to send an unintended shiver down his spine.

Five long, droning chimes.

Hell calling.

His back and neck stiffened and his eyelids fluttered the way they do when someone braces for impending impact. Like a child running full speed toward some sensitive part of his body. A door swinging into his face.

Yet despite all his training, his ferocity of will and his commitment-to-the-death, that particular ring tone never failed to make some long-buried part of him recoil. He knew it was childish and beneath a hardened warrior of the Brotherhood, yet the sound drenched his spirit with a distinct and otherworldly chill.

Creepy.

And still—the sound's gloominess paled next to the ghastliness of the caller waiting to speak with him. He knew that without a doubt.

The world knew him as a highly successful if somewhat unapproachable investment banker. But in the only world that truly mattered to him, he was known as Elder of the Order of the Scythe, or in simplistic American parlance, Elder. He hated the simplified term. First of all, it made him sound like some *éminence grise*, a grizzled old septuagenarian—when in fact he was by far the youngest of all his peers among the other Elders.

But the titles were about so much more than nicknames and semantics. They meant entrée to the world's most hidden and secretive halls of ultimate power. A pivotal role in the innermost collusion of nations and multinational corporations. Most of all, terrifying glimpses into the true nature of good and evil, of spiritual powers ordinary people would never believe. He couldn't remember how he had endured his existence before being shown the other side, beyond the gate. He now walked through life with his secret like a throbbing place deep inside him, a warm glow of superior knowledge. He would rather die now than go back to a barren existence most people lived— mere work, financial advancement, family travails.

Abandoning his usual grace, he jerked his hand into the Armani pocket and yanked out the phone. As he held it up and flipped it about expertly in his grip, his gaze instinctively lingered on its heft, its thickly utilitarian design. The oversized display that read, *caller ID out of area.*

Yeah, he thought with a bitter chuckle. *It's out of area, all right.*

He glanced around him at the other café diners and noticed, against a dozen well-scrubbed ears, cell-phone snobbery in full bloom. Handhelds trimmed in silver and gold and even platinum, each seemingly thinner than the next. He wondered if anyone would notice his phone's thicker bulk and be sophisticated enough to ascribe it to the device's global range, and not a lack of elegance.

Stop it, he told himself. *Enough petty elitism. You're about to talk with . . .*

He couldn't even bring himself to think it. He rarely did. Instead, he winced and flipped the phone open.

"I've just received a disturbing report," the voice said. There was no greeting, no introduction. Just that growl halfway between that of a wolf and of a Harley throbbing out of first gear. Few but he could even understand it.

"What is it, master?"

"The girl did indeed post, or upload, the account of her dream onto her website shortly after surviving our attempt."

"I believe we were anticipating that."

"Yes, but we weren't anticipating *this.* Apparently, her narrative ended with a challenge, an open request for anyone who has ever experienced that dream to contact her."

"Great. It will have to be sabotaged."

"It's too late for that. Listen to this: in less than twelve hours her challenge has set off an avalanche of responses over the Internet. At last report, just before I dialed you, sixty thousand individual responses had been sent to her account. Fifty-thousand-plus of these young women have signed up as Abigail's MyCorner *friends.* Already, media is beginning to look into this brand-new Internet celebrity with the mystical story."

"I had no idea . . ."

"Of course you didn't. None of us knew how powerful these personal websites have become. But it cannot continue. This could spiral out of control and become a worse threat than anything we've ever imagined. In fact, it may already be too late."

"I understand."

"Do you? Then instruct our contact and kill her. Assemble the team. Now."

He sighed. His master never minced words, never one for euphemisms or fancy talk. Another reason for the bulky handheld, embedded with the very latest encryption technology and supposedly impervious to NSA snooping. Every month, it seemed, another box arrived by overnight carrier from some obscure Asian port, bearing the very latest secure communications unit.

He decided to push his luck an inch further. "But she is dying, master. She has less than three months left. Isn't that enough?"

"You miserable idiot! It'll make things worse. At her rate, she'll have half the world on their knees fondling crosses by the time she passes. She's more dangerous than ever!"

He paused. He had pictured this day coming, so many times. But not like this. Not now, or here.

"I understand. I'll assemble the team."

"Can you do this? Am I going to have a problem with you?"

"No problem, master. My allegiance is absolute, as ever."

"It better be. Because if she starts to awaken even more, and it finds its way onto that website, it's all over. You give the order immediately. A clean hit, disguised, untraceable. I'll give you one week. And then if she's still alive, you die before she does."

And then a click and a merciful dial tone.

CHAPTER

_7

"I want a massage."

"Right now?"

"Yeah. My wife told me last night that you degenerates offer your prisoners massages. And I have a sore back from that pathetic flight and that van drive over here."

A smile formed—a slight, deliberate turning of the lips and nothing more. The lean face and dead eyes remained unaltered.

"So, I want a massage."

The Dutch prison warden scowled at the man—his newest inmate, the infamous Serbian general and accused mass murderer, Radovan Mladov.

The warden felt the spotlight of international media attention surrounding Mladov's arrival like a physical sensation, an invisible heat lamp trained upon his body. It seemed to radiate from the dozen or so satellite trucks parked outside the walls, from his telephone ringing incessantly with calls from every news organization on earth, and from the glare of camera lights nearly blinding him and his men when the prisoner's van had finally glided through their gates.

Mladov's arrest had made headlines across the planet, as had the assertion of jurisdiction by the World Court and the general's eventual extradition here. The world was watching, clearly. And now, for just a moment, he could sense the focus of that scrutiny fixed squarely on him.

Indeed, it was a pivotal moment for the warden, and he would not fail. He would uphold both the honor of the United Nations and the memory of those victims this man was accused of—and most assuredly *guilty* of—having murdered.

But the warden was a professional. No matter how strongly he shuddered in the mere presence of this creature, he inwardly vowed to maintain his high principles.

"Mr. Mladov," he replied, "we at the United Nations pride ourselves on treating our inmates as persons. As a result, you have heard correctly—we do provide certain humane amenities to those we house. They are intended to foster an atmosphere of respect and concern for basic human rights."

The six-foot-four general now smirked at the handcuffs still binding his wrists, and over at the nearly adolescent guard four yards away in the corner. He glanced up and down at the boy's blue UN uniform. He took note of the Heckler & Koch MP5 submachine gun held tightly in soft, unblemished hands.

Three seconds with that gun and I could be out of here, the general told himself. *I'd wager the boy doesn't even know how to flip off the safety.*

Then he began to shake his head almost mournfully as though he could not believe the nonsense he was hearing.

"And yes," the warden continued, "under certain circumstances, that includes medical massages for inmates who suffer from the tensions and ills of incarceration. Therefore, I will grant your request, but just this once. Are we clear on the matter?"

Mladov smiled coldly at the rising undercurrent of indignation in the bureaucrat's voice. He nodded just barely enough for the man to notice, but no more.

"Fine," the warden said. He turned to the hallway behind him and frowned at a man standing in a flawless pinstriped suit. "As soon as the inmate is processed into his cell, grant him a medical massage. Rudi is out sick, so you'll have to call in the reserve man. Sixty minutes, and not a second more."

Without meeting Mladov's eyes another time, the warden turned on his heels and strode away.

Less than one hour later, Radovan Mladov was not sitting sullenly on a prison bench, as thousands of Croats and Muslims back in Yugoslavia had wistfully imagined. He was stomach down on a padded massage table deep within the Scheveningen prison complex, bare to the waist with his eyes closed in bliss.

An impassive and impressively fit man in white clothes had awaited his entrance, standing against the wall with his arms crossed behind his back. The armed guard had retreated, locked the door, and taken up station behind a large, thickly glassed window. Then the man had finally moved. He stepped forward and began the session as emotionlessly as a robot programmed for the task.

Within a few minutes the general had turned his face toward the therapist. Ignoring the young man's unusually thick shoulders and narrow build, he forced one eye to take in the masseur's young, inscrutable face. "So, do I get a cigarette after this?" he asked.

The man had not even rolled his eyes at the comment. Without looking up from his vigorous kneading of the prisoner's back, he merely said, "You may smoke anytime you like, Herr General."

Mladov furrowed his eyebrows at those last two words, not caring for the parting use of German and its obvious implication. The man had even pronounced *General* with a hard *g*, just like the Nazi lackeys in those old war movies. Despite his having no German accent whatsoever.

The Serb decided to overlook the comment and preserve the mood. He moaned softly and soaked in both the bliss of the procedure and the absurdity of this moment. *Who would have believed prison life could be so coddled. . . ?*

Then he felt pain spread like a puddle of fire across his back.

"Hey!" he said sharply, rising to face the man. "You trying to hurt me? What is happening here?"

The stranger lowered himself, faced him squarely in the eye, and shook his head without a change in expression. Mladov noted that the man's eyes radiated a glacial calm. A poise he glimpsed in few men. Back in Zagreb and under different circumstances he might have recruited such a man for one of his shock troops. He now looked like a man who could mow down an entire family without flinching. Sadly, he'd often told himself, soldiers like that had grown scarce in this world of weak wills and soft allegiances.

The man's voice spoke close in his ear—very close. And now there was expression, a smile in the words.

"Mladov, by the time I finish this sentence you will be incapable of crying out for help, or for that matter, of any speech at all. You are experiencing the onset of total paralysis from a lethal dose of parathion I've just rubbed into your back. You will be immobilized for approximately a half hour, during which you will endure the most intense pain the human nervous system can inflict. Doctors could stop the poison with a high dose of atropine or even soothe your pain with a nerve block. But they will think you are merely suffering a stroke, and will not suspect the truth because you will be unable to tell them. Before the hour is up you will choke to death on your own bile—fully conscious. Then I pray there truly is a hell, for you will certainly go there."

Even as he spoke, the man continued to knead the general's now twitching back as though nothing had happened. The guard behind the window had not moved; he could not hear but only see what took place in the chamber.

"I am not accustomed to telling my packages what is happening to them," the man continued, "but in your case I saw footage of what you did to those civilians back in Mitrovica. And *they* knew what was going to happen. Even the children. Now *you* know too. I wish I could make your death more painful, but that is not neurologically possible. Rest in hell, Herr General."

This time he not only used the hard *g* but rolled the *r*'s in *Herr*.

It was the last bit of speech Mladov's brain would clearly process.

At once, just as the general's eyes rolled back in their sockets and a tremor began to seize his arms and hands, the massage operator whirled back toward the mirror and shouted with the appropriate level of alarm in his voice and face.

"Alert! Alert! This man is suffering some kind of seizure!"

Doors flew open and the guard rushed in with a handheld radio at his mouth while muttering furiously in Flemish. Twenty seconds later, three more men ran in, clad in white just like the massage therapist.

The assassin had flattened himself against the wall, watching closely but letting the emergency team do their work. He waited until the ambulance gurney arrived and met the inmate's pleading eyes as he was carted away.

Yet by the time the prison warden arrived to debrief the staff, he had vanished.

_8

Five minutes later, Dylan Hatfield, originally of Billings, Montana—a.k.a. Jonathan Peruggia, Marcus Bryce, and Joseph Stevens of various North American passports and mailing addresses—was clad in street clothes and walking amiably down a tree-shaded sidewalk of Scheveningen, a pleasant suburb barely two miles from The Hague.

Hatfield hummed "La Marseillaise" under his breath and smiled at his feet with the blurry grin of a departing lover. He had reason to be pleased. The uniform was discarded in a hospital dumpster. The job was over—executed flawlessly, as near as he could tell. A fatal stroke would emerge as official cause of death. Who could deny that entering prison was a stressful event?

A gust of October wind blew into him, misty with suspended rain and the threat of winter. The cold wetness across his face and hair made him briefly picture himself as a fleeting, shadowy angel of death—an inexorable dispenser of righteous vengeance. He smiled even wider at the thought. With beasts like Mladov roaming the earth, he didn't mind the analogy one bit.

He was particularly pleased with himself over the poison he had employed. Acquiring the right concentration of parathion, the world's most lethal and agonizing neurotoxin, had required a trip to Caracas, to South America's vilest back-alley *Mercado de veneno* or poison market. The blackest heart of one of those third-world bazaars that most tourists require a laminated street map to find their way out of.

On its outer peripheries lay a labyrinth where every sort of exotic or conventional animal could be purchased in any state of life or death. The kind of rancid slum uninitiated Westerners would only breach with surgical masks pulled tightly over their mouths, or a ready barf bag swiped from the flight over. And then, only with a trusted guide.

But farther within, there lay a hardened sector the tourists would never approach. A criminal sector which attracted a steady stream of the world's slimiest and most cruel assassins.

It had taken nearly five thousand dollars in bribes, two tense body searches, and a nauseating blindfolded journey through several dozen hard spins and jogs along dirt paths. It all culminated with a brutal blow—from the stock end of an AK–47, he would later learn—on the back of his head, which knocked him to the ground. He had expected it. Although with his old Delta Force training he could have killed them all in seconds, he also conceded that abuse was part of the bargain. A ritual greeting, an initiation of sorts.

He had regained his senses in a pool of shadow, lying on the hard floor of a small, dimly lit hut. He jerked upright and froze at the sight of an old Indian man aiming an antique Colt pistol at his gut with a gnarled right hand.

"*Veneno?*" came the feathery old voice.

Actually, Dylan had come in search of a *curare* derivative he had heard about years before in Israel. Although the Caracas *mercado* had evolved into a source of every poison known to man, it had first gained notoriety as the world's definitive source for the Amazon's most lethal and exotic compounds. And curare, favorite of Indian arrow tips, was definitely a product of the Amazon.

But the old man was fresh out, a young female translator said from a corner. Worse yet, it was the rainy season, she explained as he interpreted with a dismissive wave of the old man's hand. Travel up the Orinoco was disrupted.

Instead he smiled, exposing a mouthful of large, greenish teeth, and waved a vial filled with amber liquid. The young woman had whispered that he had just taken the substance in trade from a Russian hit man. *Veneno muy potente.* Very potent stuff.

She read the details from a wrinkled sheet of paper. "Parathion. Chemical first cousin of Sarin, the nerve gas of Tokyo subway fame. Diethyl nitrophenyl thiophosphate. A powerful insecticide one hundred percent fatal upon skin contact at present concentrations. Pre-death symptoms including initial paralysis, headache, spasms, abdominal pain, muscle weakness, involuntary twitching, diarrhea, convulsions, nosebleeds, nausea, loss of sphincter control, heart block, respiratory distress, and pulmonary edema."

Death within thirty minutes of respiratory failure—a slow asphyxiation consistent with neurological damage from a stroke.

He had paid a bargain price and considered himself lucky. Curare would have been quick and difficult to detect, not to mention natural, but this poison would give the man what he deserved. And it would be simple to administer. A simple drop or two rubbed into the skin, assuming the proper precautions against accidental inhalation.

Perfect for use by the UN wing's newest backup massage therapist.

And just right for the ill-timed demise of one of Europe's most hated men—Dylan's latest assignment, commissioned by a one-time UN commander in Serbia who was wrongfully blamed for failing to stop one of the Balkans' worst massacres. The disgraced functionary had promptly resigned and "gone native"—which in this case meant vanishing whole into the former Yugoslavia's substantial population of displaced refugees. And which also meant that, known only to the holders of the world's deepest intelligence secrets, he had become the head of a Croatian terrorist cell. A dispenser of justice to the Serbian killers of women and children who had ruined his life.

Dylan couldn't wait to make the call. He would ask the go-between to patch him through in person for a firsthand report. It was risky and irregular, he knew, yet he wanted to personally tell his client the truth about those vague reports just beginning to surface from the world's satellite news networks, hinting at a sudden death in Belgium.

The man would laugh, he imagined, maybe sing a triumphant ditty in his native Portuguese, and gleefully hang up. Then within the hour, seven sweet digits would blink into the digital vaults of a bank deep in Switzerland, whisked effortlessly into his balance register from the distant end of some electronic corridor off in Asia or the Caribbean.

On days like today, he loved his job.

CHAPTER

_9

The killer of Radovan Mladov took a cleansing breath, glanced up at the darkening sky, and thought again of his gradual and unlikely descent into a career as a shadow-world assassin.

His earliest childhood victims had been mule deer on his grandmother's farm, followed by firing-range target silhouettes at age eighteen after enlisting in the army. His skill had quickly channeled him into sniper training, then Special Forces, and eventually five years in Delta Force "wet work." Solo sanctions.

He trailed his memory across some of those early missions with a wistful shake of the head. He could still taste the thrill of jumping solo from the roaring entrails of a C–130 over the night-darkened terrains of Afghanistan, Columbia, and Somalia. He had worn little more than a standard-issue ghillie suit—a poncho fastened with camouflage-painted ribbons to break up his outline against the ground. The suit had concealed a bristling array of high-tech survival, killing, and communications gear stashed about his body.

More than all that, though, he had loved the solitude, the intoxicating self-reliance. Melting into the landscape completely alone and concealed. A passing shadow. A human trigger already pulled. A bullet of flesh and blood, homing in on its doomed target.

Yet he'd always taken a special satisfaction in knowing that his targets had been bad guys. African warlords. Balkan drug traffickers. Terrorists of every stripe. His mode of national service might have been more disturbing, although he had considered it no less honorable than the work of a mortar operator or artillery gunner.

Even when the Cold War had ended and his identity dissipated into the realm of joint CIA/NSA black ops, he had always taken pride in the necessary nature of his work. The righteous choice of targets. It might not have made polite conversation, but the fact remained that the world had people in it who needed killing. And he was often on a short list of the best men alive to answer his nation's call for the job.

The homicidal chill of centering a man's head in the crosshairs, of ending someone's life with a twitch of his trigger finger—that was simply the operational downside. The burden of his mission, just as claustrophobia was to a submariner, or boredom to an officer in a missile silo.

And now that he had disappeared even further from the mantle of government service—barely knowing even the identity of his employers, but instead trusting in decades-old relationships, code words, and drop-boxes—he still clung to the fraying mantle of his perennial rationale. Today's bad guys might have been lesser threats to national security, yet they were still major-league scumbags.

No, he wasn't some mere hit man, he reminded himself. No conscience-for-hire. He was one of the best in the world at a job that might seem alluring to some yet was agonizingly difficult, incredibly dangerous, and despite its justifications, he realized—potentially corrosive to the soul. If those hazards did not make his occupation exactly respectable, well, they nevertheless enabled him to hold his head up high.

Most of the time he wasn't even a killer. He was an unspecified artistic type—painter, actor, writer, musician—living alone in Manhattan's Tribeca district, a bohemian existence that none of his girlfriends or acquaintances questioned or took special notice in. Men of such hazy pursuits were a dime a dozen in his neighborhood. For some reason, no product of a life's work was ever expected—only the means to continue paying the rent on shabby-chic lofts and the tabs on never-ending supplies of morning espresso and trendy overpriced cuisine.

He traveled a great deal, and most of his casual acquaintances thought this was due to his sideline of occasional modeling. According to Gretchen—the latest raven-haired jet-setter with an undetermined European accent to grace his bed—he was here on some German magazine shoot of unspecified duration.

A faint vibration at his thigh told him the pager was going off. He had several impulsive clients. Some refused to wait even one second before either granting him an assignment or shifting it to someone else. Sometimes one of them would even call in the final seconds of a sanction to cancel the order. Naturally he resented the vacillation, but it was better than killing someone unnecessarily. The clients still paid, of course. But they always appreciated the ready access.

Without breaking stride he reached down into a low-slung pocket of his cargo pants and retrieved the pager. A well-dressed elderly couple was approaching him on the sidewalk. He could feel their gazes on him, their eyes probing him for some polite nod or affirmation. He glanced down with a vague smile to avoid eye contact.

The display's green letters read, *555–310–2998*. His eyes widened at the sight.

Two minutes later he stepped onto a quiet cobblestone street overshadowed by residential buildings. There a dark blue Mercedes sedan with Dutch plates awaited him. He climbed inside; instantly the engine roared and he sped away in European fashion.

Before he'd gone a hundred yards, he was on the cell phone to America.

"This is Rover," he said.

"Shadow Leader here. Remember when I told you the day would come when we needed some extreme backbone from you?"

"Yeah, I remember. I told you I had no shortage of that, if you cared to take another glance at my record."

"Yes, but I did not explain myself. And that day has now come, my friend. It couldn't be a nobler cause or a higher risk to the world if you fail. But it won't be easy."

"Yeah?"

"The target is a young girl. A beautiful young girl who's dying of a rare infection."

"What possible threat could this girl pose?"

"It's not necessarily her fault. But she's about to provoke a very dangerous international incident. She could trigger a world war. You're gonna have to trust me on this, because I can't elaborate."

Dylan paused and thought for a minute. He had never been obliged to trust a client before on the suitability of a target. And he certainly didn't like the sound of this.

"I don't know," he replied. "I've never sanctioned anyone over unintended consequences. They've always had to be an intentional bad guy. And a young girl—that's taking it really far."

"I hear you, but there's no other way, Rover. You'll have to trust me when I tell you that millions could die if she stays alive."

"Look, this is a whole new ball game for me. I kill bad guys, period. You know that. All this crystal-ball stuff about possibilities and consequences—I'm not sure that's for me."

There was a pause. Then the voice returned, now with a harder edge.

"I could tell you that I'd just take the assignment elsewhere, but the fact is I need *you*. This needs to be handled with the lightest touch imaginable. Completely covered up. The other guys are bunglers compared to you. Now, remember all the assignments I swung your way during the lean years?"

"You know I do."

"Well, you've refined your operational tradecraft to the extreme. You're the best in the world. But now it's time to hone a new skill. Moral toughness. There's pressure on this one, my friend. And, oh yeah . . ."

His voice trailed off, and Dylan thought he had lost the connection.

Shadow Leader returned with a trace of mirth in his words. "Five mill down, ten upon completion. Not to buy your conscience, mind you. Just in recognition of the degree of difficulty. It's what this kind of job commands."

Dylan whistled softly. He was no mercenary, yet he couldn't deny that fifteen million was the fee of a lifetime. Retirement money— enough to let him fade away and start a new life. He returned the phone to his ear.

"I'm still listening. . . ."

CHAPTER
_10

Abby waited until each of her chief mourners had left her room in turn—the nurse, her best friend, Bonnie, half sister, Caryn, and even her father, who had lingered until his usual 10:00 p.m. "kick out time"—before she allowed herself to lean down beside the bed and pull her laptop from its case.

She noticed a tremor as she typed in the address for her My-Corner site, then glanced down at her hand. She hadn't felt such trepidation at the computer since learning to use her first Macintosh in junior high school, nearly a decade before.

There it was—*MyCorner.com*. She typed in her username and password, then pressed Enter.

She read, frowned, and cocked her head. Instead of the usual animated graphic depicting an aerial approach through a thatched roof into a warmly lit cottage, leading down into a hearth, a brightly blazing fire, and a weathered leather armchair—in other words, a graphic of a *corner*—she saw a stark and uninspired warning.

ADMINISTRATOR WARNING TO USER ABIGAIL SHERMAN!

MyCorner.com user Abigail Sherman: your corner's data size has exceeded purchased bandwidth capacity by 1006%. This surplus consists of 21,597 unread and waiting messages, and 19,372 Corner Friends registered since your last log-in. Access to your site has been blocked until you either contact Technical Support for a paid upgrade of your storage size or dispose of 97% of unread messages and accept or reject your unprocessed Friends during your very next log-in.

Ms. Sherman, please contact us to resolve this matter immediately.

Without even pausing to consider the consequences, she logged in and opened the very first message in her queue.

Abby,

My best friend Tonya e-mailed me the text of your dream with the subject line, 'Wasn't this Lady Marietta's story?' I read it, and my friend was absolutely right.

Let me explain.

When we were little girls back in Alabama in the mid-sixties, this fascinating old lady showed up at a church social one day. No one even saw her walk up; she just seemed to gather out of the old pine floor. I say that because we were a tight-knit church body of about 45, it was the height of the Civil Rights movement, and newcomers were most definitely noticed. Not that we were unfriendly, but conversation would just pause and no one failed to know when a stranger had entered our midst. And yet this lady somehow seemed to be known by someone, as if she was some member's old friend or long-lost aunt. But I never learned whose.

So Tonya and I turned our attentions back to the potluck until we noticed that all the ladies had formed this tight circle around the visitor. She was talking so low that no one but them could hear her words. Naturally, Sonya and I were overcome with curiosity, so we crawled down on our hands and knees and scuttled through my mama Nettie's skirts, which, believe me, were plenty wide enough for the two of us. And as soon as we broke through to the middle of this ring, that old lady looked down at us, then kind of peered around our faces, and broke into tears! She pulled us up and told us that we both had the most beautiful and strapping guardian angels you'd ever want to see. Then she just looked back up again and continued her story, as though it had been nothing unusual.

What she spoke was *your* story.

The one you told in your Corner, that is. Of course I learned later that it was the story of the prophetess Anna, who the Bible describes as an old woman who had waited most of her life at the Temple for the Messiah to come, and who saw Him as a tiny baby being brought in by His parents. It wasn't the story itself that was so memorable and so similar to yours. It was more the way the old woman seemed to experience it. How she saw the prophetess' thoughts and emotions and memories, even while her own thoughts still hovered there, suspended.

It was exactly the way you described it.

Abby, I don't know if this is good news for you or not. For you see, this old woman, who everyone began to call Lady Marietta — no one was quite sure whether it was because she was born in that Georgia town, or it was truly her name — stirred up quite a hornet's nest in our church. She told the women that she'd been driven out of her congregation in a neighboring county for the things she'd been seeing. See, the dream seemed to have awakened some kind of spiritual sight within her. She'd started walking up to people and describing the beings, good and evil, that followed them around. It turned out there were far more dark spirits abroad than anyone would have liked. And her church people had become so frightened that even her own family had told her to leave. She had nowhere to go.

Marietta started sleeping on a pile of blankets on the back pew of our tiny choir loft and doing odd jobs in our members' houses. But soon our own pastor questioned her. And he didn't like what he heard. Pastor became convinced that she was either possessed of a demon or actually some kind of sorceress, and he threw her out without so much as a good-bye.

Well, you can imagine that this created quite a row among the women, who, as in so many country churches, were the congregation's true leaders and hard workers. One after another of them took in the old woman to sleep on their sofas. Yet our pastor would not relent. He traveled to each of her benefactors' homes and threatened the whole families with excommunication if they did not heed the warning of the Lord. The conflict reached such a boiling point that one of the husbands took a swing at the pastor, and a neighbor wound up calling the police. Before the patrol car

arrived, though—we were in Freemantown, the black neighborhood, and so police cars always took their time—Marietta stepped
up to the pastor and described, in horrible detail, the appearance
of the giant warrior demon that had its claws embedded deep into
the pastor's back.

Acting like someone roused from a very deep stupor, the old
woman straightened up and began to shout at the entity in a commanding and totally abnormal tone of voice. According to the witnesses, it wasn't an exorcism so much as one whale of a harangue.
But one thing every spectator knew for certain: that old woman
was not the least bit afraid of what she was speaking to.

And so instead of the old woman fleeing, it was our pastor who
turned tail and ran screaming into the head-high briar and kudzu
vine that draped down from Freemantown's old railroad trestle.

He was never seen in our town again.

But then, neither was Marietta. Police found a decomposed
body outside of town late that fall, and with their usual lack of dil-
igence, never even bothered to identify her after finding out it was
that of a black woman. Somehow the rumor that this was Marietta's body swept through church like a revival swoon.

So my message to you? Yeah, you may have something special.
But watch out. It's not only a blessing in disguise, it's also a curse.
I wish I could tell you more than that, give you some direction or
contact point. But this is just an old, weird story from my childhood.

So you take care, Sister. Watch who you speak to about such
things, and make sure you stay square with the Author of all True
Fairy Tales.

Abby shook her head in amazement, then read further down. The
next letter, and the letter after that, and the letter after that . . .

. . . *all bore the same message.*

She was not alone. Others had dreamed her same dream. Walked
through similar aftermaths.

There were hundreds. Thousands.

She found herself weeping, swept away on a wave of awe and gratitude. Even as the tears flowed she continued to read. And as she did,

she began to slowly realize one common denominator in her responses.

Each respondent was as clueless, as pleading, as lost as she was. No one had any answers. There were shadowy tentacles of the phenomenon reaching back into the history of the last hundred years, but they largely consisted of rumors and oral folktales. No one could give her any more clues or direction other than a simple confirmation that, no, her experience was not unique.

Beyond that, her sisters were all of them, each one, alone.

In the early hours of the morning, after fatigue had conspired with the sheer number of responses to numb her capacity for reason, Abby reached both hands to the keyboard and began to type out a response.

CHAPTER
_11

Dear Sisters,

Thank you all for your responses to my ignorant and aimless plea. I am humbled and awed by the passion, kinship, and love in each of your letters. I just finished my first attempt to read through all of your posts, so I am still reeling, to be honest. I had no idea, when I sent my blind question out into the cyber-void, that there were so many of you out there.

And now, since so many have honored me with your stories, I have some news for you. I'm writing from a hospital bed. A few hours after I finished typing my dream-blog on my laptop, someone very twisted and unspeakably evil broke into my house and not only murdered my beloved friend and housekeeper, Narbeli, in monstrous fashion, but then tried to kill me. He did not succeed. At least not immediately. But my doctors tell me that he infected me with some sort of poisonous substance that they are not able to identify, but whose effect is unstoppable.

So, if you pick up and read the electronic clipboard hanging from the end of my bed, it seems I am dying. No one can tell me whether it will be next week or next month. Nor can they treat with any great success the pain that wracks my body while the poison does its work. My mind is fine. For that fact, even my body is remarkably functional, except for the pain itself. I can move around still. It just hurts like crazy. I'd be up and walking, although more slowly than usual, if I wasn't in this place for round after round of never-ending tests.

Even as I type these words, it occurs to me that there must be meaning to all this. There just has to be. I'm not here to tiptoe up to the edge of this mystery and simply pass away, leaving it all unsolved. You didn't write me so the unanswered questions in each of your stories could only deepen, sit there and rot.

There must be an answer. I sense it in my deepest spirit. Don't you? I think I can feel it "between the lines" in each of your replies. There's a reason for all this. We've all been stranded on the very edge of something really big, and up until now apparently unseen.

Pray for me, Sisters, and gather round, if there's an Internet version of such a thing. We've got a mystery to solve. A bridge to find, and to cross.

(One thing about being told you're going to die very soon and way too young. It sharpens your sense of purpose like no kick in the head you'll ever get on any soccer field or karate dojo. It clears the mind and everything else about you. Leaves you keen and sharp as a knife's edge. That's what I'm feeling right now.)

Forget this. I'm not going to sit here and wait to die. I'm going to get up from this bed and figure out what's up.

Are you with me?

Abby Sherman

She woke up the next morning with a sense of determination, if anything, beating stronger and more urgently within her. Her father entered the room shortly after seven o'clock and, instead of finding her still dozing as he had every morning before, saw his daughter finishing up an early power breakfast.

"Abby, what's up?" he asked.

"Dad, I have something to tell you."

He stared hard and long at her, for he had not heard such steel in her voice for quite a long while. "I have something to tell you too," he said. "But why don't you go first."

"Dad, I'm getting out of here. I can't explain it, but I just know that God doesn't mean for me to sit here and wait for the end. You know how many arguments you and I have had about what I should do with my life. You know I've always thought He had a special purpose for my life, and as weird as this sounds, I know that now more than ever. I just have far less time to waste. And now I have a direction I never had before."

He took a seat in the visitor's chair, crossed his leg and pretended to wave some invisible dust bunny from his knee. "Have you really thought this through? You know that the doctors want you here. If you check yourself out against their orders, you may be shutting yourself off from pain management, from the kind of treatment you're going to need as this thing progresses. Worse still, you could be cutting off their research just as they're about to discover what's wrong with you."

"Dad, they've taken enough of my blood to fill a swimming pool. They've got their samples. They don't need me to stick around. I'm not just going to lie here and waste my last days being a guinea pig. Look up at these lights. Would you want this to be the last sky you ever gazed up on? Would you want this to be your last bed? The last sight your eyes ever saw?"

He gave the sigh he always let out when her logic had gotten the best of him.

"So where are you proposing to go?"

"I have no idea, Dad. I just know I've stumbled into something big, and I'm supposed to do something about it. But all I know is the first step, and that's to get out of this bed. After that, it's all on faith."

"Well, now it's my turn," he said after a pause. "And I may just know what your second step may be."

"What do you mean?"

"Take a look outside."

She slowly swung her legs down and walked gingerly over to the window, waved aside the flimsy curtain and peered out. Three floors down, the sidewalk lay jumbled with a mass of television trucks, glowing reflector screens, and camera lights.

"What's going on?" she asked, turning to face her dad. "Some kind of celebrity in here with me?"

His gaze bore into hers. "It's you, sweetheart."

"Me? What are you talking about?"

"I think you know. It seems that Internet blog you posted has made a huge splash. You're the flavor of the day. The web celebrity of the hour, honey. In less than twelve hours you've registered more friends than anyone in MyCorner history."

She sat back down, her head swimming.

"What in the world did you write about?" he continued. "Was this something about Narbeli's death? Your sickness? What could have provoked a response like this?"

"Both of those, I guess. But it's more than that, Dad. It was actually a dream I had."

An incredulous look crossed his handsome features. "A dream. That's it?"

She picked up the laptop and handed it to him. "It's too involved to explain right now. Here, read it for yourself. I have to go."

"*Where?*" His voice had become tinged with exasperation. "Where are you going? Don't think I'm just going to let my little girl take off and leave her to the wolves."

"Who're the wolves, Dad? Those people outside?"

"Some of them. You know the media. They don't care about your privacy or your peace of mind."

"I'm not after peace of mind. I'm after answers."

He sighed deeply. "Well, Abby, maybe I can help. Just before I walked in here, I got a call from a producer working for Mara Mc-Queen. Mara wants to interview you."

Abby began to shake her head slowly, as though answering a question only she could hear.

"Wow. Mara. I'll talk to her. Tomorrow morning."

"I'll arrange the interview, sweetheart, on one condition. Just stay in the hospital one more day. Let her interview you here, and in the meantime give your doctors one more chance to help you. Will you do that for me?"

She nodded and glanced glumly around the room. "For you, Dad. Only for you."

CHAPTER
_12

Dylan's Sidekick hummed to life on the airplane tray before him, vibrating with the special ring tone that announced a warning from the one contact in the world he could least afford to ignore.

His apartment.

First, he tensed his body out of the half-dozing state in which he'd allowed himself to lapse. He furtively glanced around him to gauge the prudence of checking in right away. The first-class cabin lay dark and deep in that nocturnal midflight interlude when all its privileged occupants were either sleeping or spellbound by some form of seat-back entertainment. Apart from the plane's droning engine noise and a light snore from the businessman beside him, no sound of life emanated from anywhere around the space.

Dylan picked up the Sidekick, flipped down its keyboard, and pressed on the touch screen to respond. A password dialog box appeared. He glanced around him again and typed in five digits to reach his most urgent contact.

It was Camera One calling. As usual. The one he'd had hidden inside the crown molding of his loft's vestibule to catch any visitors, welcome or unwelcome. It was the most-used camera in his inventory. Naturally, as the one that recorded people's initial approach, it was nearly always the one that responded first.

He winced. The video, even while it stuttered with the imperfections of its airborne bandwidth, clearly revealed the person approaching. Actually, two persons. One of them was Gretchen, his current prime candidate for what one might loosely label a *girlfriend*. Her companion, stumbling drunkenly and giggling, was her favorite fashion photographer, Claude. Gretchen had introduced him to Dylan at various parties, always failing to conceal her infatuation with the man.

Dylan allowed himself a small groan. He'd always known that Gretchen wasn't the epitome of faithfulness. For one thing, their relationship could hardly be thought of as monogamous, a fact for which he was as much to blame as she. But the blue-eyed Swede was so exotic that he'd willingly overlooked the drawbacks.

Still, bringing a man to *his* apartment . . .

The Sidekick broadcast the rattle of his industrial garage-sized door being yanked upward. Camera Two switched on, its motion detector installed to catch activity just inside the loft.

He heard laughter, then Gretchen's voice giggling in that alluring Scandinavian accent of hers. "He's in Europe, scaredy cat. Come on in. It's beautiful."

And it was. Since he was a bit vain about the place, the remark caused him to feel a twinge of goodwill for Gretchen. His apartment was indeed the quintessential Tribeca loft: shabby-chic industrial, sprawling, devoid of walls, open on three sides to high windows, bright with views of the neighborhood's distinctive Romanesque Revival architecture.

The scene switched over to Camera Three, Dylan's kitchen. The cheaters had ducked in for a quick perusing glance. Then Camera Five kicked in as they hurried into the bedroom, a vague area bounded by only a bookcase and a large ficus tree.

Dylan sighed and for the first time began to question how long he could endure this. It certainly gave him no voyeuristic thrill. His index finger quivered with an autonomous urge to click Shutdown. Just as he was poised to switch off the whole transmission, Camera Three abruptly switched back on.

What burst upon his screen nearly made him forget to breathe. A male figure dressed in tightly fitting black clothes hid behind a column, a long revolver gripped in one fist. For the first time in several years, Dylan lost external control and audibly gasped. The security system, prompted by activity in dual locations, abruptly switched to a split screen. On the left, the gunman tiptoed forward with the slowness and exaggerated mannerisms of a trained professional. On the right, Gretchen and her lover stood beside his bed, kissing ardently and beginning to peel off each other's shirts.

Dylan's fingers now flew into a flurry of action. *Was there time?* He'd armed his apartment with four layers of cutting-edge security systems. The fourth, which the gunman surely would not have disabled, might save . . .

There came an angry sound of bone striking flesh, then the sight of furious movement flooded the underlit image. Claude's head flew back and violently struck the headboard, his body flung along with the force of the intruder's brutal kick. Gretchen screamed so loudly that Dylan was forced to punch down the Sidekick's volume.

Too late.

The security module had loaded, but not in time. In the top right-hand corner of the screen, discreetly positioned to avoid obscuring his view, sat three dialog boxes he only had to press in order to release one of a trio of gases.

The first, labeled K for Knockout, contained a relatively harmless cocktail that would swiftly put an intruder to sleep. The second, N for Noxious, was a variant of tear gas, intended to incapacitate the intruder and drive him, coughing, away. The third, framed in bright red, warned F for Fatal. It would kill within two seconds, also triggering a sophisticated exhaust system that would render his apartment uninhabitable for several days to anyone not wearing a special gas mask.

"It's not him!" Gretchen screamed at the man, even as she clawed frantically from a pathetic kneeling position. The gunman paced, striding away from Claude's unconscious body, which he had kicked over for a better look. At her side, he brandished the weapon in her face and growled at her to be quiet.

Dylan grimaced again. Obviously the gunman was surprised to find that he had knocked out someone other than him. Claude did resemble Dylan, true, but in a twinge of professional objectivity he observed that the intruder should have been one hundred percent certain. At least he'd been prudent enough to choose a hard kick over a wild first shot.

Now the man was in a bind. Surely whoever had hired him to kill someone like Dylan would not be the sort to tolerate near-misses, extra bodies, or complications like unnecessary parties to the plot. Collateral involvements added to the event's visibility and invariably multiplied the odds of getting caught. This man was probably now in serious, if not mortal, trouble. The intruder sank into a crouch, then jumped up. The abruptness of it told Dylan that awareness of peril had finally begun to sink into a brain seething with equal parts adrenaline and testosterone.

Gretchen's own agitation was surging louder, more out of control. Dylan peered closer for a better look at the gunman's body language, and *yes*, just as Dylan had feared—the man's gestures were growing more impulsive, staccato and sudden. His instincts flung a chilling and certain verdict into Dylan's conscious mind.

He was seriously thinking about hurting Gretchen too.

Perhaps the woman deserved the same fate as her lover. Somewhere deep under the competing strata of reactions fluttering across Dylan's mind, he could have located rage and resentment. But *no*, he realized—whatever he felt toward her wasn't justification for letting her be brutalized. Certainly not sitting here and watching it happen from some godlike perch high in the sky.

He pressed Knockout.

No mist appeared on his screen, for the system had been designed for invisibility. Yet automatically a stopwatch appeared inside the dialog box and began counting. The desired effect was touted to take effect within eight seconds. The gunman, however, was breathing so heavily that at second six his body slumped over—ironically, on the bed right next to a fast-blinking Gretchen. Two seconds later, both lay completely unconscious.

Amazing what I can do with a jacked-up cell phone, he chuckled to himself, despite the gravity of the situation. He had saved a life, narrowly missed stopping a vicious assault, and incapacitated a killer. All without leaving his seat. And all from over a thousand miles away.

He slipped the unit shut, looking around to see if anyone was watching him, and replaced the phone on his tray as though terminating a routine text message.

NEW YORK CITY, JOHN F. KENNEDY AIRPORT

When the plane landed at JFK two hours later, Dylan did not afford himself the luxury of a return-as-usual. He knew that the killer may have lain incapacitated on his bedroom floor, knocked out for a possible duration of at least eight hours, according to his chemist. For now, the killer wasn't the problem. The problem was that the man had been sent by *someone*.

And that someone would be growing antsy by now.

As an expert on the protocols of high-tech murder, Dylan knew that some form of check-in would normally be expected soon after a successful hit. After failing to receive any acknowledgment, the group behind the contract would soon grow agitated. If they possessed any other assets in the area, then those too might be already deployed—at least in surveillance and perhaps even active attempts at reentry. If not, then he had the luxury of three, four hours tops before the response would escalate.

The focus of attention, of course, would be his apartment. A place he'd worked very hard to render attention-free.

At JFK's first-class lounge, he pulled out his laptop to gain a fuller picture of the security system and how the gunman had managed to defeat it. Or, at least, part of it.

While he sat in a leather chaise and waited for the bulky system to boot up, he thought back over the arduous evolution of his private, custom-designed intruder repellent.

Dylan had considered it part of basic survival to install the most rigorous and advanced security imaginable. As someone who made it his living to defeat such systems, he'd had it built to be substantially more intricate and powerful than anything a killer like him would expect. Normally, the best installed security network had at least two, and up to four, independent systems. That did not include built-in redundancies, complex power protection, and increasingly devilish concealment features.

So Dylan had designed the first three layers with as much complexity as sophistication required, but little more. They were throwaways, intended to convince an expert that the basics had been observed.

First came a biometric thumbprint reader at the door. Highly effective in keeping out petty burglars, the odd meth freak and homeless squatter. But no great shakes to a true pro. Second was the array of concealed, motion-activated video cameras featuring hidden, but otherwise conventionally wired, power sources. That network might take a skilled intruder around an hour to find its hidden and dedicated electric wires. Yet, once located, one snip of the needle-nosed pliers and the scanners were down.

Dylan's third layer was more than adequate to challenge the most exacting and paranoid techie. He called it his Rapid Gas system, and it was this system that had brought down the recent intruder. Only the use of a decoy or fatal guinea pig would be guaranteed to detect that contingency. However, another killer who knew what Dylan did for a living would expect defenses beyond the pale, and therefore, if he spent the time and effort to find it, would likely be satisfied that he had extinguished all the options.

But Dylan had a fourth layer, his *coup de grâce*.

Obtaining the necessary technology had obliged Dylan to launch a small front company to penetrate all the layers of secrecy as well as the legal safeguards. The application of that technology was his own idea, derived from an obscure yet exotic innovation. Dylan had read about the raw advances in a small, innocuous newspaper article three years before. *"Smart concrete: the Chinese are high on the stuff!"* Turns out a Chinese-American scientist had developed a way to imbed threads of tiny sensors inside otherwise ordinary blocks of concrete. Those sensors, when installed in a construction setting, could gather and transmit a number of measurements back to a central computer for a range of vital, and until now unobtainable, calculations. Those included structural fatigue, ambient stress, sturdiness, and—of most interest to Dylan—the presence and weight of anyone walking across the blocks.

Slumped over his monitor in the British Airways lounge, Dylan suddenly stopped his typing and leaned back in pleasant surprise.

Layer four had worked.

The intruder had successfully disabled power to systems one, two, and three before setting foot in his apartment. But then he had wrongly considered his efforts sufficient and stepped inside. With that first footfall, he had activated layer four's smart-concrete sensors, including its crowning feature—an infrared reactivation of all the other systems, regardless of whether their conventional power sources had been disabled. Tiny, undetectable emergency batteries containing three hours of power, imbedded inside each system, had instantly blinked to life. Each was activated by an infrared beam triggered by the unauthorized weight of a human foot on the concrete floor.

Still, Dylan hesitated. If layer four had reactivated the other three systems, then why had the gunman not been the very first sight broadcast through the video system? Why had Gretchen and Claude come on-screen before him?

Then he remembered—it took approximately four seconds for the infrared beam to finish reactivating all the systems and all three to come back fully online. The gunman could have entered, then found his place of concealment and frozen still within that interval.

Preoccupied with its reactivation tasks, the system's motion detectors would have effectively forgotten about the man whose step had triggered it. Upon its restart, it would have focused on the amorous pair in the bedroom.

Reassured that his system had worked as desired, Dylan hopped a cab for the Tribeca district. On his way through midtown he instructed the driver to pause at Grand Central Station while he darted out, stashed his luggage in a travel locker, and returned. He needed to make his return light-handed.

Two blocks from his building, he exited to trace his circuitous tactical return.

NEW YORK CITY, TRIBECA DISTRICT

Even though it was only late afternoon, Dylan noted with frustration that Church Street was already crowded with young couples and clots of partiers ambling through the district's artsy storefronts and outdoor cafés.

Worst possible time to shake off a tail.

He spent ten minutes wandering in circles, detected no obvious pursuit and so decided, for the first time, to forgo his usual counter-surveillance regimen and head straight home. Normally he would have bar-hopped through a sequence of progressively emptier clubs and bistros before returning well after quitting time. This routine was a great way to spot any followers, recurring faces or silhouettes. Of course it wasn't a bad excuse for partying in some of America's best watering holes, but Dylan rarely admitted that to himself.

Tonight he had no time to lose. The intruder would be waking up soon. If there was danger, it now awaited him at home. From within, not without.

In the last half block he pulled out what appeared to be an MP3 player and threaded its stylishly thin earphones around his head. Rather than a music device, however, the card-deck sized unit was a small PDA whose wireless receiver displayed, rather than song titles and album covers, the latest footage from layer two's half dozen external video cameras trained on the surrounding perimeter. He manipulated the small screen with his thumb, scanning each of the miniscreens to verify that no ambush awaited him in any of his apartment's cunningly designed sight lines.

He walked past his building's front door, swerved abruptly through the side entry of a neighboring French restaurant, and disappeared.

CHAPTER
_14

Claude's attacker stirred and inched open an eyelid. The only sight greeting his hazy vision was a bewildering chaos of shadows and gloom. He groaned—whether from the challenge of clearing his eyes or the pain of something jabbing him in the ribs, he could not say.

Finally, in a cool, bracing rush, his discipline and warrior's training roared back to his senses. Ignoring all else, he willed his legs to straighten and stand.

A hammer blow to the face threw him onto his back again.

Awash in fury, he rolled away and jumped to his feet, assuming his best fighter's stance before he could even see his assailant.

Another kick swept his ankles from beneath him and drove him to the floor. Faster than his still-addled senses could respond, a fist yanked into his hairline, brutally jerking his head back.

"Who are you?" a snarling voice said, close in his ear.

"A messenger," the man said, after a pause. "And you?"

The fist threw him forward onto his face. "I live here. I don't have to answer questions."

The man lowered his gaze into the gleaming bore of a chrome handgun, held perfectly still mere inches from his nose.

"Let's cut the nonsense," Dylan said in a more normal voice. "I know what you do for a living. I've got it on tape. And I'll bet you know what I do. You know I have sanction, maybe even a professional duty, to blow your brains out. And you know I have the means to make you talk before I do it. So why don't we chat?"

"Fine. Let's chat," the killer said, as the resignation of the utterly defeated settled into his eyes. He glanced over at the bed where Gretchen and her would-be lover still lay unconscious, still immobilized.

The two men sat facing each other. Dylan's eyes traveled up and down this so-called killer, sizing him up. "Fairly new at this, aren't you? I mean, in the civilian realm."

"Delta Force, who cares," the other said with a defensive wag of his chin. "I was set up. They gave me a rough description of your wiring grid, and I believed that was enough."

"Maybe they did too. Maybe I outsmarted you and your clients. So who are they? You gonna tell me?"

The man stared into the bank of windows and winced against a beam of dying sunlight. "Yeah. I can either take my chances with you, or die for sure with those guys."

"Oh, I don't know about that," Dylan countered. "After all, those guys chose you. You were obviously the best they had. You might still evade them."

The man shook his head and chuckled bitterly. "No. Actually, I was just a test. I overheard one of them. I'm just here to rile you, to test your readiness. I wasn't supposed to kill you, just knock you out. Although I was authorized to shoot back in self-defense."

"You're kidding! This client wouldn't have been Shadow Leader, would it?"

"Yeah, that's one of his names," the man said, shaking his head. "And you must be that hotshot they've been whispering about all these years. The one who's so precious, they haven't even bothered to bring you in."

"Bring me in to *what*?"

"To the Brotherhood, man. The Brotherhood of the Scythe." It was the intruder's turn now to drip with condescension. "Man, you don't know nothing. You have no idea what you're dealing with."

"I've known Shadow Leader for twenty years. He was my CO in Grenada and Desert Storm."

The man glanced up at Dylan and laughed, revealing a top row of blood-smeared teeth. "Like I said, you're greener than grass. That Shadow Leader was harvested over a decade ago. Even I'm too young to have met that guy, although I've heard stories about him."

"Harvested?" Dylan asked, wincing at the coldness of it.

"Yeah. You want me to draw you a picture?"

"No pictures necessary." Dylan blew out heavily as the knowledge settled into his mind. "So tell me—what's this Brotherhood?"

The man blinked, then fixed a suspicious stare on Dylan. "You don't want to know."

"Yes, I do."

"Look, it doesn't matter. I screwed up this assignment royally. These guys don't tolerate screwing up. So just kill me now. Make it quick, okay?"

"I may not know much about this Brotherhood, but you don't know a thing about me. I only kill bad guys."

"Hey, I just gave this pansy over here a nasty concussion, a broken nose, maybe even a shattered spine. Doesn't that qualify me?"

"I mean *real bad* guys—not just wet boys like you who mess up training ops. I mean dope dealers, dictators, and arms brokers. The kind out there ruining the world, killing innocents by the tens of thousands. That's who I've always gone after. It's one of the reasons your bosses kept me pure. At least until now."

"Well, then you're about to cross the line, dude. 'Cause, member or not, they're intent on motivating you to take this heavy assignment you've been waffling about. And if you want to live, I wouldn't think about telling them no."

"What is so stinking important about some twenty-year-old chick?" Dylan said with irritation crackling in his voice. "How can she be worth all this trouble? I'm not in the business of sanctioning girls. I mean, *girls*. Think about it."

"I wouldn't tell you if I knew," the man said, his voice rising. "But I do know that these are men who wouldn't bat an eyelash at killing a child. In fact, they kill children by the hundreds, every day."

"What are you talking about?"

"Man, you have no idea—"

A pistol shot shattered the air, punching a neat black hole dead center in the man's forehead. He fell backward, his eyes wide in shock.

Dylan's instincts flooded back into place. He snatched up a second revolver from his waist and whirled around.

The gunman was less than ten feet away. He wore a crisp, green military-type uniform. His weapon was not visible.

He smiled the smile of a reptile. "Dylan, I am Shadow Leader."

Dylan moved forward and shoved his revolver into the man's face. Shadow Leader did not flinch. "I don't know you," Dylan said. "You *sound* like the man I once knew as Shadow Leader, but no more than that. Why did you do that to my old friend?"

"I gave him a life beyond anything you could ever imagine," the man said. Dylan almost retched. *There went that smile again. . . .*

"Yeah?" Dylan pointed to the intruder's bleeding body. "Like you just gave *him*?"

"No, this idiot traded his soul far too cheaply. I'm talking about something far more glorious. Listen, don't worry about him. The only thing he told you right is that he was merely a warm-up for you. And, if necessary, a warning."

"About turning down your assignment? I never turned it down. I just said I needed to think about it."

"Well, the time for thinking about it has ended. The girl has just agreed to go on the Mara McQueen show. Which, without briefing you *ad nauseam*, happens to be the worst possible news. Are you in or out?"

Dylan rubbed the bruised side of his face, then turned back to the man. "How did you get in here undetected, anyway?"

"Oh, you mean the floor sensors you installed? Nice touch, Dylan. But you will never be able to defend yourself against me or the people I represent. Remember that."

Dylan breathed in deeply. This latest assignment had gone from being a gold mine attached to a dubious target to a desperate bid to save his own life. He wondered—could he use the seven-figure fee to escape this man forever?

"Tell me about this girl," he said. "Why is she the target?"

"I don't have time for a full explanation. But just think of it this way. What if you had a hundred-yard bead on a darling little four-year-old girl, who happened to be sitting there playing with the trigger to an atomic bomb? In fact, she's two seconds away from detonating the biggest, baddest nuclear device ever conjured up by the black heart of man. Do you sit there and moralize about the right or wrong of taking out a little girl, and let millions of people get incinerated in the process? Or do you take the shot? See, even though she's innocent, and sweet, and completely well-meaning, what this young woman threatens to unravel is incredibly dangerous. Dangerous to the whole world, in ways I could take days to explain to you. She cannot be allowed to continue, and she won't. The question is, will we have Dylan Hatfield with us to perform the hit safely, in a sanitary fashion? Or will Dylan Hatfield miss out on fifteen million bucks and wind up in a dumpster somewhere?"

"I hear you. But you know what I hate?" Dylan said, anger stealing back into his voice. "You—or whoever was you, back then—used to value the fact that I had a moral backbone. That I went after real evil as someone with a righteous cause. Now you're treating my principles like they were an afterthought."

The man smiled patronizingly. "That's not true, Dylan. I always warned you that the day would come when we'd have to consider a paradigm shift. When moral backbone would become much less simple, less cut-and-dry. Well, that day has come, and the clock's ticking." He held up a Glock 9 pistol. "So what's it gonna be?"

"Don't insult me," Dylan growled. "Put down the gun and let's go."

CHAPTER

_15

MyCorner blog: Abby Sherman
I Just Returned From Heaven!

Dear Friends,

I had another dream. Actually, much more than that. Another experience, another journey to someplace else. I wasn't looking for another one—you know, some sort of sequel. That first dream has revolutionized my life enough that I was quite comfortable marking it down as a once-in-a-lifetime event. In fact, even the strange "spiritual sight" which developed after that first dream seems to have subsided. I'm told it may come back at any time, but for now I'm grateful for a reprieve from the horrible things I was seeing all around me, even if they were balanced by the appearance of angels and plenty of beauty.

But as they say, God has a sense of humor all His own. See, if I wasn't looking for a sequel, I definitely wasn't expecting anything to top the first one. For one thing, I wouldn't have thought it was possible. Not until now.

But friends, I've gotta be honest. This one rocked. It blew the first one out of the water. I guess I gave it all away in the blog title, but I couldn't help myself.

And I realize I'm running the risk of falling into the oldest cliché of the chick-journal—the dandelion-doodled, hearts-over-the-I's, estrogen-drenched tale of some buff savior whisking me off to Beulah Land.

But check this out, friends, because this dream wasn't like that. If you think I'm deluding myself, I trust y'all to tell me. There's enough bandwidth now for you guys to let me know.

My guess is, if I tell this right, you won't. Here goes . . .

I was right here in the hospital bed, so exhausted from a day of tests that I hardly knew where I was. In fact, now that I think of it, I'm not exactly sure it was a dream at all. That's the only ready word I can think of, but it doesn't do it justice. True, it started while I was in bed, and when I was exhausted beyond belief. Yet I wasn't actually asleep. I was lying here when suddenly I felt this presence.

If you've lived awhile, you've probably had that weird sensation when someone walks up behind you, no matter how silently they approach. I know I have.

This was the same sensation, only jacked up a million times. This may not make sense, but at first it was like this "intensity" coming toward me, this concentrated pocket of importance. More of a force field or a power source than anything else. I remember whipping around in my bed, because the sensation was so powerful and so frightening.

And then I paused, and I took stock for a second.

Because now I recognized it.

This is going to sound weird, but it was the same personality I sensed pouring out of the baby in my last dream.

Then something inside me jumped for joy, because I realized who it was.

It was Him!

THE HOSPITAL—NEXT MORNING

Abby heard the familiar intro music swell and the familiar credits flash across the large monitor wedged in the corner. It was surreal—the woman featured in its quick-cutting, choppily edited montage stood only three feet away.

It struck Abby that, despite the strange context where she now stood, the woman beside her bed was probably the most familiar human figure in the modern world. Globally adored, self-made billionaire, spiritual seeker and shepherd to a large swath of the human population, star of the most lucrative daily television franchise in media history . . . the superlatives went on and on.

And now all those abstractions were distilled into one human face, one plump female body standing an arm's reach away. She could hear her African-style bracelets jangle softly. Smell her exotic perfume. Feel the press of her unusually long fingers upon her own, lingering from their handshake just moments before.

Mara McQueen. The last name wasn't necessary, of course. Both the show, her magazine, her television network, even her supermarket line of household goods bore the single first name. *Mara*. The two syllables seemed to quiver with the promise of wholeness and harmony.

Suddenly the music ended. A leather-clad man wedged in the room's doorway turned from the monitor to the woman herself and pointed. Abby felt the camera lights turn on and the attention spark to life in a flash of heat.

"Friends, you can see I'm not in the studio today," Mara began in her trademark friendly cadence. "No audience. No stage. I'm here in the presence of one of the most remarkable and unlikely media stories in recent history. Chances are, if you know anyone with a MyCorner site—and who doesn't? I have one myself—then you've heard of Abby Sherman and the amazing dream she shared over the web. Friends, there have been Internet celebrities before. Private individuals thrust into an odd, Andy Warhol–like few minutes of notoriety by some media fluke. But most of them were seeking something. Something gainful, I mean. A career. Attention. Vindication. Even revenge. But all Abby Sherman wanted when she threw a desperate plea out into cyberspace was a wee bit of closure. A little knowledge in order to finally put something behind her."

Finally, Mara turned toward her. It was hard to tell what felt more jarring—the gape of the camera's large glass eyeball, or the glare of

Mara's own charisma directed at her.

"Abby didn't really imagine anyone would answer her plea. But to date, over thirty-eight thousand young women have. And yes, all women. In fact—and here's part of the mystery—all African-American women. They've all written in to reveal a remarkable kinship with someone, who on the surface has little in common with most of them. A self-admitted, rich California girl who likes surfing and church, in that order."

Abby had never heard the paradoxes of her situation described that pithily before, and the sound of it made her chuckle. Instantly the camera panned over, seeming to take note of her reaction.

"And this morning, even as we met Abby for the first time, while preparing to bring you this broadcast from the hospital room where she lies dying of an unknown disease, this remarkable woman had another surprise in store for us. In case you haven't watched the late-breaking news, or personally checked the most followed blog on the Internet, let me just read the title of Abby's newest upload. Do you want to read it, Abby, or do you want me to?"

"You go ahead, Mara. It sounds better coming from you."

Now the chuckle came from Mara. "All right, Abby. The title is 'I just returned from heaven.' Abby, is that a true statement, or just a fanciful description meant to attract more attention?"

"It's the truth, Mara. As you know, I'm here because of a terminal diagnosis. So attention is the furthest thing from my mind."

Mara flashed her trademark reassuring grin. "I know it is, honey. I just wanted to acknowledge that it's a pretty incredible claim."

"It is. But still, I can't escape the fact that it's completely true. I was . . . taken on a journey, a preview of sorts. To the real heaven."

"By no less than Jesus Christ."

Abby cocked her head in a rueful assessment of how to reply. Clearly it was a tall order. "Mara, I don't expect anyone to believe what I'm saying. I just know what I experienced. Inside myself, I know it beyond the shadow of a doubt. But that's personal. It's based on a lot of perceptions that are completely real to me, including the first dream I wrote about."

"Well, clearly, Abby, an awful lot of people have chosen to place their faith in what you've been experiencing. Do you think it's because, as a person with a terminal illness, they find you easier to believe?"

"Maybe so," Abby replied with the surprised look of someone who had not considered that angle. "I know that I'm not interested in wasting anybody's time with idle fantasies, that's for sure."

"So, Abby, for the benefit of those last few people on earth who haven't logged in as your friend and perused your blog, why don't you tell us the story in your own words?"

CHAPTER
_16

MANHATTAN

The drawing room's three windows, which rose to its ceiling height of twenty-one feet, usually looked out onto the green expanse of Central Park. Right now, however, their full-length mahogany blinds were drawn shut and the vast space darkened. In the near corner, a sixty-inch plasma screen glowed with the pale images of a hospital room. In it floated two faces. One was brown and exceedingly famous. The other was young, white and, until today, unknown to most people except the man standing in a silk track suit before the scene, clenching and unclenching one fist at his side, and in the other holding a silver-plated cell phone to his ear.

"I don't care if it creates a firestorm! I want her silenced now, do you understand?"

He paused and turned away from the screen while the other party replied, seemingly unable to bear any more of the television program.

"I know it's delicate, but isn't that what we're paying him for? Isn't that why you've been hyping this guy to me all this time? His ability to pull off long-distance or high-difficulty harvests without being caught?"

The Elder turned back to the monitor, unable to contain his curiosity. It bore a close-up of Abby Sherman, luminous and, in the morning light, beautiful despite her prolonged hospital stay. She was speaking intensely.

"Hold on. I have to hear what this little snot is saying. It may be too late. . . ."

ABBY'S HOSPITAL ROOM—THAT MOMENT

"It was the same person, the same spirit living inside that little baby. That's the only way I can say it. What I felt coming from that infant was so powerful that there's no way I could mistake it. As He carried me out of this room, He was communicating to me somehow. I'd call it speech because it was very specific—He was comforting me, calming me, telling me how much He loved me—only I couldn't say for sure whether the words were spoken or I even heard words at all. I just felt them register in my own spirit, and I knew exactly what He was saying and who was speaking.

"I know it all sounds airy-fairy, vague and New Agey, but the experience of it was very intense and real. He was telling me, 'Do not be afraid, Abby. Let me show you what lies ahead, and you will not fear it any longer.'

"Because I wasn't in my body anymore. We'd left it behind. I actually looked down on myself, lying trembling and wide-eyed on the bed. The rest of the hospital floated past under us. I saw panels and wires and darkness, followed by more floors, beds, and nurses walking, then more beds until finally we were shooting past the rooftop into the night air over Los Angeles.

"And you know what else is strange? As incredible as it might sound to float up high like that, it meant almost nothing to me. That is, nothing compared to the wonder of who was carrying me. I didn't care about the sights near as much as the feeling pouring into my soul from the One guiding me.

"Man, I had no idea I could feel so much love. Of any kind. I remember my mother's love from a long time ago, magnified the way we all distort old memories, and it was strong. Everything a mother's love should be—except maybe for having been interrupted so soon.

"But while this love was in some ways similar, it was also a million times stronger. I felt like I was bathed in it, like I could swim around in this warm bath of pure love from this . . . yes, I'd call Him a parent. And if anyone on earth ever invented some lotion that soaked into your skin and healed every bruise, every cut, every abrasion you'd ever suffered, then in the spiritual sense this love was like that. I felt it soak into every pain, every inner wound I've ever endured. I could almost feel every tear I've ever shed dry up like it never happened— or the pain that had provoked it. Like time was moving in reverse and my life's sorrows were being rolled up and tossed away.

"At the same time, I felt so close to Him. I remembered for a second the almost smothering feeling of kinship I'd felt with my best friend when I was six years old. Beth Vega. She came over for a sleepover, and we stayed up long into the night telling each other all our stories, all our secrets, and when the sun finally started peeking through the shutters, I felt like she and I had become a single person.

"That old memory was just the tiniest shadow of this new experience. The sense of being so close to Him made me feel like I'd been somewhat of a recluse all my life, a hermit who'd never even been in the company of another being. And unlike being forced unpleasantly close to others like the way you feel on elevators, this was an extreme closeness that I craved. In fact, I desired it beyond any longing I've ever felt.

"You have to understand: His person was radiating—all at the same time—unthinkable power, vast wisdom and knowledge, a solemn and kingly sensation I can only call *majesty*, along with this incredible love I've been talking about. If I could have crawled up inside this personality somehow, I would have. I wanted it as close to me as I could get.

"It's taking me this long to describe it, but I have to say again that the actual experience didn't take any time at all. This was all one very rich and complex sensation. Because in like no time at all, we'd left the earth behind and were flying over the shores of something new. Something beyond the experience of any living human."

NEARBY ROOFTOP

The tiny receiver in Dylan's ear buzzed with the vibration of an incoming voice. He winced, feeling his grip on the rifle barrel waver slightly. The crosshairs poised on the young woman's chest barely trembled—but at this distance, it was easily enough of a deviation to throw his shot far off course, his trajectory magnified by 324 yards of rising air, a fitful morning breeze, and the impact of shattering vinyl glass on a descending bullet.

"Can you make it?"

"Eighty percent chance. But you gotta know—the camera's aimed straight in my direction. If I take it, I'm blown."

"Aren't you in good cover?"

"Excellent. But it's not that. There'll still be a whale of a muzzle flash. As soon as I take the shot, I'll have to egress within seconds. Expose myself. Everything about me—my weapon, uniform, my body, my direction of escape. I'll be identified by NSA within an hour."

"Can you take out the camera first?"

He breathed out and hesitated, thinking. "Much harder. The angles, the margins, they're all much tighter. I'd have to hit straight on."

"Can you disrupt in some other way? Cut the building's power maybe? My brothers are climbing all over me to shut her up."

"Their video camera will be battery driven. I suppose a warning shot through the window would make them stop and seek cover. But I doubt that it would be a complete guarantee. Look, I'm using the scope mostly for recon. I wasn't really considering a shot. My verdict is, if you want the interruption to look benign, you'll have to wait. My only options will be high profile, high impact. Impossible to conceal."

A vicious oath buzzed through the earpiece.

"Then wait. She's already done the damage, anyhow. But you hear me good. This has to happen soon. Very soon."

CHAPTER
_17

ABBY'S HOSPITAL ROOM

Mara McQueen now sat beside Abby's bed in a hospital chair whisked over after a glare and an imperious gesture at her assistants, demanding something in which to sit. Comfortable in her bed nearby, Abby stared ahead, fully immersed now in the account and oblivious to anything physical happening around her. Just a moment before, technicians had removed the distraction of the late afternoon sunlight by pulling shut the shades and curtains.

"I guess I should have known that actually seeing heaven would blow off their hinges every notion or fantasy I'd ever dreamed of. I mean, my friends accuse me of having an overactive imagination anyhow. But now, having seen it for myself, it's like my mind never even touched on it before. Like I'd never even pictured it at all, although I had so many times.

"But the real experience was so much more intense, more vivid, more joyful, more comforting, and more ecstatic than I ever allowed myself to imagine. And of course that in itself is unbelievable. I mean think about it: When's the last time something you'd fantasized and dreamed of since childhood turned out to be not only as great as you'd imagined, but a thousand times better? I'm not very old, but I'm already used to the familiar pattern of having everything I'd fawned over as a girl turn less shiny and glorious than I'd always pictured it. I'd kind of accepted that that's how life is. Making the most of unmet expectations.

"Heaven was the radical opposite of that. Now, when I think about it, I should have known. I mean God is infinitely creative and resourceful. A bit of a showman, I might add. He never misses a chance to knock our socks off with an outrageous display of beauty in His creation.

"But this was the ultimate. The greatest example of all.

"The first landmark was this huge gate. I don't know how large it was, because I didn't know how high I was flying above it. But if you think the *Arc de Triomphe* in Paris is a big arch, well, this one dwarfed it. And I have no idea what it was made of—it looked as solid as stone, but it shined so brightly that it almost seemed to glow from the inside. And it was probably the most intricately shaped structure I've ever seen, just crawling with carvings of angels and beautiful faces and these long, flowing shapes.

"As I passed above it, I saw three groups of people in pretty much identical formations. In each case, a single person walked alone toward the gate from the same direction I'd flown. And just beyond the arch stood this crowd of people, awaiting the one walker. I could hear calls of greeting and these kind of touching outbursts that seemed drenched in love, even if you're too far away to hear individual words. I heard snatches of delight and welcome. The sounds of people who've missed each other terribly and are being reunited at last.

"Then the gate was past and I was flying into the face of this energy I'll just call light, because that's the easiest way to describe it. Problem was, it was far more than just brightness or warmth or brilliance itself. I mean, for sheer intensity I'm sure it rivaled the sun, but it was far more. First of all, like a rainbow it seemed to hold every color in existence, in such a richness and intensity that I felt for a second like someone who'd worn dim, crusty old sunglasses her whole life and had just now gotten permission to tear them off. I wondered for a moment if someone had replaced my world with a shinier, brighter, younger version of itself. Everything around me was crisp and colorful beyond any standard of measurement. I even remember seeing colors I'd never seen before, which seems impossible now, because I know what the spectrum is and I've seen my share of rainbows. But still, there they were. I was just . . . stupefied.

"I laughed out loud, in part out of wonder at everything I was seeing, but also because it seemed that joy, even love, was just infused in the air around me. See, as awesome as the colors were, this light contained more than color. Its bandwidth, if you want to use tired-out Internet language for something like this, was much broader than that. It was also made up of emotions. Good ones, that is. Great ones.

"Mara, I just don't know if I'm conveying this in a way that sounds halfway coherent or makes any sense. The problem is, there are just no words for what I'm trying to describe. . . ."

NEARBY ROOFTOP, DYLAN'S OBSERVATION PERIMETER—
ONE MINUTE LATER

No reply had come back in the thirteen minutes since the Manhattan boss had asked for a pause. Dylan closed his eyes and innately realized that, despite Manhattan's indecision and his clear orders to wait, this was the kind of tunnel-visioned client who would irrationally turn around an hour from now and blame him for the consequences of delayed action.

He rose from kneeling and slapped a holstered handgun onto his belt. He pulled out his wallet and sifted through a small stack of business cards. Selecting one, he crammed the others into a front pocket.

"Listen, you watch all you want," he spoke into his radio mouthpiece. "I'm going in, and I have an idea. Please, no voice traffic. Listen in if you want, but I'll call you later to check in."

Without waiting for an acknowledgment, Dylan flipped the frequency dial on his belt radio, stood to his full height and began running straight for the shadowed hulk of the hospital wing.

ABBY'S HOSPITAL ROOM—THE NEXT SECOND

"And so I found myself responding without even thinking about it—laughing out loud for no reason. If I'd been on earth, you'd have thought I was bipolar or in need of some serious tranquilizer. But I was just fine. In fact, *just fine* in a truer way than ever before. I felt like I'd come home, to a home I never even knew I'd left.

"And that's not even the best part of moving forward into this light. Probably the most amazing thing I experienced just then was the music.

"*Song* was everywhere.

"I say *song* because just calling it music seems to oversimplify, even trivialize it somehow. It was so much more than just a sound or a melody. I even wonder if it can be called sound, it was so complete an experience. Part of it was breathy, like a million harmonized voices in total ecstasy. You might have mistaken it at first for some awesome melody being pumped in from someplace.

"First of all, this music was everywhere. I felt like I was inside it, rather than just a front-row hearer. My whole body was part of the instrument. I felt every part of me resonate like some tuning fork that's waited its whole life to give out just the perfect pitch. Inside me, even. Not only did it penetrate every inch of me, I *was* music.

"The only way I remembered that it came from other places was that every few seconds, just barely in hearing range, I'd hear a word, or part of one that I couldn't quite make out but I just knew was praise to God. It was an expression of adoration so perfect and exquisite that it took me a second to realize it was actually a nearly infinite number of layers of praise. Then I found that I could tell each song from the others. A few of the melodies came from classic hymns I remembered as a young girl. Some of the words were those of popular choruses from church days. Others were straight from the Bible—psalms and words of Jesus. Once or twice I heard *hallelujah* or *praise God*, although they were just a few words among millions.

"Still, this let me know that the music was coming from the mouths and lungs of real people, all around me. In fact, since the singers of these songs were somewhere just beyond my sight, it came to me that the reason I could even hear these songs was *because* they were praise. As though the adoration inside them was the force that powered them, made them strong enough to be heard, broadcasting them into the air.

"And you know how, sometimes in the best earthly songs, sometimes there's rhythms and melodies that barely belong together, and then at the song's peak they seem to bend toward each other and resolve in a harmony that's so poignant, it just snaps this little string in your heart? Well, these songs were like an ocean of those. As if all these people were singing their own individual, very different praise tunes, very serenely, very softly, except that instead of clashing with each other, a soft current was lifting each one up and mixing everything together into a blend that was so much more beautiful than the sum of its parts. Those kinds of exquisite resolutions kept weaving into each other, over and over again. And my heart kept aching at the sweetness of each one.

"I kept wondering if this music was being lifted toward me and my companion as we flew over. I was never sure exactly. But I was highly aware that the presence behind me was the object of all this adoration. Again, it's so hard to describe how, except I sensed almost physically that all this love was gathering, concentrating, on a point just behind my back. And what flowed out from Him in return—in some ways I couldn't even *look* at that emotion through any of my new ethereal senses. It was so powerful, so pure. But just let me say that it was joy—joy more intense than an industrial-strength spotlight, pouring into my face.

"Would you believe that wasn't even the coolest part?

"There was something else about this music that's maybe the hardest of all to describe. I suppose it would be best just to say it outright.

"I heard the sound of angels' wings. And it was the most beautiful thing I'd ever heard."

CHAPTER
_18

At this point, Abby leaned forward and her voice refused to convey any more words. Mara leaned forward too, her face shining with tears, and clasped Abby's hand. The handheld microphone held so tightly during the introduction was gone now, replaced by an intrusive handheld boom hovering like a bat just out of sight. With Abby's account halted, tiny sounds could be heard around her like the whirring of a tape recorder, the crew's breathing, and even an odd sniffle coming from Mara and some of those behind her.

Abby smiled and shook her head, taken aback by the point in the story where her self-control had chosen to run out.

"You all right, honey?"

Abby's lips moved, but the word *yes* remained mute upon them.

Determined to regain control, Abby righted her torso in the bed, sighed, and wiped her eyes vigorously.

"Okay, I'm ready. I'm almost through, anyway.

"I realize now how weird it sounds, and I have no idea why, after everything I've described, that it's the brushing of angels' wings that sets me off like nothing else. But the sound had a haunting, startling, and yet somehow peaceful quality I will never, ever forget. It was faint, and delicate, and it was totally clear in every second of the music.

Somehow it formed its own melody and moved in its own soft rhythm. And even though it didn't stop for a moment, it just went on with the richest variety of any piece of music I'd ever heard. For some reason I never felt compelled to look and see where exactly they were coming from. Maybe I wasn't convinced I'd ever find their source. You have to remember that just like with the songs and the music, there was such a gentle chaos swirling all around me that I'd given up trying to nail everything down. I decided to just let it all swim over me. Or maybe I didn't consider the sight of them near as important as hearing their presence confirmed for the very first time.

"Maybe the wings' motion was my own guardian angels' way of singing, of giving praise. Maybe it was their way of announcing me in a way, of ushering me into heaven. I'm not sure. Either way, that sound just stays with me. In fact, I just realized why."

Abby broke away from her eye contact with Mara and looked around her as if she'd just arrived in the room.

"I know. It's because I've started hearing them *here*. Now. In this world. Just barely out of hearing, but more and more often, and clearer since my first vision. I hear them around those times when I catch one of those eternity moments, you know, one of those rare flashes when from out of the blue you get this mysterious little dose of pure joy or insight or encouragement. One of those little lightning bolts from heaven, when your darkest moment gets obliterated by something you just know comes from outside of you. Just then my ear cocks the slightest bit, all on its own. It does that because I've heard the faintest rustle, and my entire soul, my whole body even, leans toward the sound—what's that word, *keening*?—for it's like a good hunting dog leaning toward the sound waves of a silent whistle.

"I do know that right after I became aware of the sound, I started to descend. I'd been flying pretty high above this whole scene, you know. We started to turn back toward the gate. And as we did, I became aware of the actual streets of this city. And I know you're gonna start to doubt me here, or think I'm being way too literal. But here's what I saw—"

"No, no, Abby," Mara interrupted, her eyes scanning a sheet of paper just handed to her by an assistant. The sheet, in fact, bore tracking information from real-time ratings and viewer response sources from all across the country. Mara's eyebrows rose.

She was impressed.

"Well, we kept moving downward," Abby continued. "And with every second, each of these things got more vivid and intense. The light, the beauty, the joy. Then I saw the city itself."

Abby turned straight into Mara's gaze, startling the diva from one more perusal of the ratings results. "Did you ever think the Bible meant it literally when it said that heaven would have streets of gold?"

Mara scrunched up her face like someone who hadn't given the subject much thought. "Uh, like most people I guess I always thought it was figurative language," she replied. "A metaphor for great value, something of high worth."

"Yeah, and although I'm not sure I ever thought about it directly," Abby said, "if you'd asked me, I would have probably answered something like that too. But it's not true."

"What do you mean?"

"I mean, they're actually made of gold. I saw them. Paving bricks of solid gold. Only the gold wasn't this clunky yellow like I saw once in an old Sunday school comic book. It was a rich gold like solid honey, so pure I could see into each stone, and like the arch they glowed so beautifully that I had a hard time figuring if they were lit from some inner source or just reflecting all the light around them.

"And on every side stood these rows of the most incredibly cool, diverse, inviting buildings. Every shape and size and layout you could ever dream up if you went to architecture school for a hundred years.

"On these streets I saw a middle-aged woman walking, and I remember she looked up at me. I'd like to say she gave me a smile, only there was already one on her face. Even all by herself, while walking down the street, she was grinning from ear to ear. Seeing me only made her smile widen a bit more, as if her world was so crammed full of things to be happy about that she only had to turn her head to see another.

"Just fifty feet away stood this family who had just walked through the gate. I knew this because I had seen them greet each other a moment before. They were still celebrating, surrounding the newcomer, a woman in her early forties, clapping and laughing and tossing up praises to God. The young woman was absolutely boo-hooing with joy—I know because I listened hard to see if this would be the first sound of sadness or pain I would encounter here, only to find the weeping was completely blissful and euphoric.

"Her arms were clasped tightly around this other woman, who I guessed must have been her mother or her sister, because the two of them didn't look like they would ever let each other go. They had obviously been apart for a long time, yet the happiness of this reunion had wiped out any regret.

"And then we came even lower, Jesus and I. Then, just as I didn't think my sense of joy and wonder could possibly grow anymore, Jesus leaned forward and whispered into my ear, 'This is just the beginning, my beloved. Just a preview of a foretaste of a beginning. I have so much blessing in store, Abby, that you could not even bear the knowledge of it, right now, if I showed it all to you.'

"Just as He said that, I realized that we'd stopped moving forward. We had turned, in fact, and were moving back toward the gate.

"And this question sort of drifted into my conscious mind.

"*So is this my time, or not? What am I doing here?*

"'I am with you because this is *not* your time,' He told me. 'I have shown you this to comfort you. To give you the peace of knowing your homecoming will be a time of rejoicing. To give you the assurance that you have nothing to fear.'

"'Are we not going all the way in?' I asked Him.

"I felt Him hold me tighter to himself, gently. 'No, my dear. Not today.'

"And, Mara," Abby said, "I can tell you that hearing Him say that was the single most heartbreaking loss I ever thought I would live through. At that moment, I would have chopped off a limb to keep going forward.

"But He just smiled and said, 'My dear, I showed this to you for another reason, more important still. I don't want you to fear. You still have much to do, back in your life.'

"'But I'm dying.'

"He pulled himself around to face me, and He smiled lovingly.

"'You leave that choice to me, Abigail. I will tell you when it is time to come home.'

"'You mean—?'

"'I only mean this. You have nothing to fear. To live is a rich adventure. To die, for you, will be a joy beyond imagination. Either way, you are in me, and I have nothing but good things in store for you.'

"'But please, don't send me back. Please?'

"He placed a great hand upon my shoulder, and His touch felt like an ocean moving through my body.

"'You have a mystery to solve, beloved one. And the solving of it will save many, many beyond yourself.'

"'Are *they* a part of this mystery?' I asked, pointing in front of me."

CHAPTER
_19

"See, we'd landed, if you can call it that, and just ahead, walking slowly out from under the gate's huge arch, was a group of about a dozen women. They were young and strong. Beautiful. I'd say *proud*, if you could picture a sort of pride that contains no trace of arrogance or haughtiness, but signaling a confidence in who you are and where you came from.

"As they walked, they stared at me with these odd, knowing smiles. I looked into their eyes and felt love settle in and just cradle me.

"'Yes, these are the beginning of your mystery,' Jesus said.

"The woman closest to me, slightly ahead of the others, stopped and broke into a wide, glowing grin.

"That's when I noticed. The skin of these women glowed unusually bright in this light. And then something in my understanding sort of . . . clicked into place.

"It was because their skin was black.

"So black that it shined.

"Every one. Black, or brown, if you want to say it that way. In fact, it seemed each woman's skin color grew a shade darker from the first row to the last.

"'Who are you?' I asked the first woman. That question may

sound defiant, if you weren't there, maybe even impolite, but I asked it with wonder in my voice, grateful that I'd even been able to make a sound.

"She stepped closer, and I saw that her features were African. Her skin's lean, tight sheen reflected light like a sheet of glass. Her lips were full and rich, her nose bold and broad. Her whole face, eyes especially, had given itself over to this dazzling smile that seemed to reach halfway around her head.

"She did not answer, but from the warmth of her smile it seemed that she knew me. It simply wasn't the kind of a smile you give a stranger. Even one you're incredibly glad to see. Each face in that group wore the same expression. I could feel each of their smiles warm their way into my insides.

"Instead of speaking, the woman in front reached out her arms. At first, I started to think it was some kind of ceremonial gesture. But then it felt like an actual hand was pushing me toward her. Suddenly I was so desperate to connect with her that I thought I would drop dead of longing the very next instant if anyone prevented me from stepping into her arms—although I obviously had no idea who she was.

"So I did. I took one long stride and walked into her embrace.

"I had no idea what her emotion was coming from, but as soon as I felt her arms close around me, something new and huge opened up within me. The sense of reunion surged and just overwhelmed me. If someone had figured out how to distill the sense of coming home into some kind of elixir, then I was now swimming in it. I felt home in every sense—emotional, spiritual, physical. I felt like I'd turned some huge corner. Like a homeless orphan who'd just been handed an identity and a home and a sense that I belonged.

"At the same time, I became acutely aware that this made no sense. This reunion was supposed to happen between family members. I'd heard stories of souls being greeted at heaven's gate by what everyone euphemistically calls 'loved ones'—one's family. Yet, in spite of all the emotions rushing through me, these were not my kin.

"Then Jesus spoke again, and obviously He'd been reading my thoughts. 'This homecoming is different,' He said. 'Your earthly mother will be here, although not for the reason you think. And the others you expected to see, you will not see.'

"'Why not?' I asked.

"'That is *your* mystery,' He answered in a voice so low that it almost sounded like a whisper.

"At that moment, the lead woman released her hold and stepped back. She reached out and cupped my cheek and looked deep into my eyes. Still locked onto my gaze, she smiled a smile that was part wistful, part sad, part love, and part joy. Then she touched the center of my chest with the tip of her index finger.

"She said a single word. It sounded something like *Iya Agba*.

"Her gestures reminded me of Jane in that famous scene of *Tarzan* and his woman introducing each other. Like *Iya Agba* was my name. So I made to correct her, as gently and politely as I could. I touched my chest and said, 'Abby.'

"She nodded and smiled, like the sound of my given name was no surprise. She seemed to know Abby after all. But she reached out and touched me again. Only this time she did not speak the strange word.

"*Iya Agba* rolled over me from just beyond her shoulder, this time loud and strong as a storm, deep and throbbing like the sound from a thousand mouths. Or maybe a million. I leaned and stared behind her. She had stood before a group of a dozen when I had first landed here.

"Now I saw a crowd reaching farther back than I could see. The sensation of so many eyes fixed on me, so many faces smiling right into mine, almost knocked me back a step.

"'Lord, who are they?' I asked.

"'Listen, my child,' He said.

"'I've heard their name for me,' I said, 'but who are they?'

"'Listen, and find them,' He said. 'Find them and you will solve the mystery. Heal the breach. It is all I can tell you. I will see you soon, my precious one.'

"And just that quickly I was back in my bed, sitting up and panting like a marathon runner. That was this morning."

"Wow," said Mara, moving her eyes sympathetically toward the camera. "What a story. What an unforgettable journey. Now, what is this great mystery He was talking about?"

Abby chuckled at the woman's relentless journalistic instincts. "I have no idea, Mara. I'm still processing all this as I speak to you."

"Do you think He was telling you that you weren't going to die?"

"That's a good question," Abby replied. "But I don't think He was telling me that either way. He was, for sure, telling me that I didn't need to be afraid of either outcome. That no matter what, I had only wonderful things to look forward to."

"What can you tell our viewers about the aftermath of visiting heaven? Has it changed you? Has it changed your outlook?"

Abby looked straight into the camera, her eyes bejeweled with tears. "Don't fear death. Not if you know God. If you know Him, you have the most awesome experience ahead of you. There is a heaven. It's completely real. A real place. A real destination. Before last night I had this hazy notion of what heaven would be like. It didn't seem real. But now all that's changed. I know it's real. I know it's incredible beyond words. My fear of death is just gone. The only fear I have left at all concerns this life. Here on earth."

"You mean physical suffering. It's a universal fear, you know. Fear of pain, isolation. The process of . . . death."

"No, although I wouldn't mind skipping that either," Abby answered. "I mean wasting this time. I'm afraid of dying with the knowledge that I wasted the last days of my earthly existence. These days have a purpose beyond my knowledge, yours and anyone's. And I'm feeling fairly good right now; the pain comes and goes. I have some good days left. Not a lot, at least not for certain. But just enough to make a difference. And whatever that difference is, I feel absolutely driven to make the most of it."

"So you're going to leave this hospital?"

"Absolutely. In fact, I might do it right after this interview is over. I want my last days on earth to be significant . . . to Him. To God. I'm not just going to lie here and wait for the end to come. I mean, once you know for certain that heaven is waiting for you, it puts everything else in a whole new light. My only fear is going into eternity with regrets. Grief for opportunities I had to make a difference, and squandered."

She turned back to Mara.

"That means I'm going to solve this mystery even if it takes every hour I have left on this earth."

CHAPTER

_20

"Well, honey," the talk host replied, her face aglow with the knowledge that the camera was back on her, "if there's anything I can do to help you, I will. If you need an introduction, transportation, a little boost in the pocketbook, you just name it. The whole world is watching to see what you'll do next—"

She never finished the sentence, for a fierce *boom!* barreled through the room. Walls and floors trembled, and the ceiling tossed a fine plaster mist into the air. The overhead lights flickered and went out, leaving only the beams of waving camera bulbs, sharp as spotlights in the swirling dust.

Somewhere, deeper inside the building, two gunshots rang out over the shouts of those trapped inside.

And so it begins, Abby heard a voice warn deep within her.

Fighting back the urge to cry out, she pulled up the sheets to shelter her face from the debris and her ears from screams assaulting them from every side. Something long and metallic fell from the mangled ceiling across the bed, striking her painfully on the calf. Mara was somewhere close, yelling out, "Extraction! I want an extraction!"

Danger hung in the air, lying in wait—in the sting of her leg, the smell of smoke and dust, the desperation of anxious cries. Yet something strange was happening to Abby. She didn't feel panic but remained totally calm and at peace. Fear seemed to approach her and then fall away, defeated. Could it be her brush with eternity had rendered her impervious to terror?

Abby rolled off the bed, clutched a pillow over her head, and muttered into the linen, "God, I accept this mission. I'm dying to find out what this is all about." Then she realized the words she'd used and let out a laugh. "Yes, Lord—no pun intended. But really, I can't stand not knowing. I will leave here now and go search for the answers. So will you please get me out of here?"

Just then, so soon after the prayer that Abby actually grinned at the timing, she felt a strong hand grip her by the upper arm and pull upward. *Hard.*

"Please come with me, Miss Sherman," a male voice spoke, close to her ear. "There's been an attack against the hospital and we believe it may be directed against you. We need to make an emergency evacuation. Will you let me carry you?"

"My father," she said, "he's here somewhere, looking for me."

"If he's not in here now, then he's being evacuated. No matter what. It's best you come with me and let us find him later."

Before she could utter another word, strong hands forced themselves under her knees, lifted her shoulders, and pulled her effortlessly into the air. Abby opened her eyes and looked into the face of a lean man in his early thirties. His features were twisted by the strain of carrying her and peering through the smoke for a path, but he looked harmless enough. More important, he radiated strength.

The familiar setting began to blur. Hospital room walls, which had been her home for two weeks now, morphed into a darkened, cramped hallway and then a nurses' station jammed with green-garbed nurses and street-clothed media types all jostling each other and crowding the elevator and stairway entrances in their desperation to escape. The air about her grew thick with the clamor of panicked voices. Abby could hear Mara's trademark drawl somewhere ahead of her, shouting for folks to stand clear, that Miss Sherman was coming through. Abby shook her head. *Miss Sherman.* She hadn't been called that in years, and then only by a bossy high-school gym instructor.

It struck Abby as strange and slightly wonderful that in a day's time she had gone from being anonymous patient to having the world's most famous woman acting as her *de facto* bodyguard.

And then a wondrous thing happened. Despite the chaos and desperate self-preservation engulfing the room, the volume dropped entirely. Faces turned her way, suddenly calmed.

With the shuffling of a hundred feet, a path opened up before them. A narrow one, perhaps, yet still a free space leading directly to a door marked with the brightest sign in the room, the one marked EXIT.

Abby felt her breath pull up short and her eyes mist in amazement. A wave of humility and sharp gratitude descended on her.

"Thank you," she muttered as she passed by. "Thank you all so much . . ." She leaned over and tried to make eye contact with *someone* as she passed. A woman's face floated into view—a nurse in her midforties, sandy blond hair pulled back tight, her face flushed, lips parted and panting. She stared at Abby with eyes wide and filled with wonder.

A chill flew down Abby's spine. *I'm becoming a curiosity,* she said to herself. She wondered if this was how accidental celebrities felt— you do something instinctive, some reflexive, inevitable deed, and as a result find yourself the object of a perplexing, if not frightening, adulation from everyone you meet from that day onward. And the thing just keeps on growing beyond control, all on its own power.

Abby moved her gaze to the next person and gasped.

It was Gladys, the African-American nurse who'd risked so much to come warn her about the Sight. The first one to give her a clue of what lay ahead. The brown face which had one day earlier brimmed with such resolve now seemed banded with strings of jewels. Abby blinked, looked again, and realized that they were everyday, beautiful tears.

"I'm gonna find out," Abby whispered fiercely. "I'm going."

Gladys said nothing, for she did not appear capable of words. She smiled lovingly, nodded and held out her hand. Abby reached out and managed to hook the tip of Gladys's fingers as she passed by.

"*Iya Agba*," Gladys said. "I know that word from somewhere. Dreams, echoes, somewhere . . ."

Their grasp pulled free, and just as quickly Gladys fell back into the crowd, her voice with her. Abby cried out her name, but her friend was instantly beyond reach.

They passed through the door and suddenly found themselves in a tight space, descending steps two at a time. *This man is strong.* Or maybe just desperate. She thought she heard another gunshot from somewhere above her, but the sound was too muffled and distant to be certain.

"Hang on," the man huffed. But it seemed clear to Abby that, despite his strength and skill, the man was under stress. Something had him scared. She decided he was her best bet and hung on tight for the ride.

She felt him lean back, then lift his leg and strike something hard. A metallic door groaned out into twilight. The penumbra of a turquoise sunset and a parking lot, punctuated by swirling police lights, swerving headlight beams, and the racing of engines from those frantic to leave the area. A breeze she hadn't felt in an eternity coolly greeted her cheeks and forehead.

Things grew so frenetic on every side that Abby felt the need to close her eyes; the sudden motions were making her nauseous. Suddenly Mara's shouting grew closer, and for the first time the man carrying her let out a shout.

"Here! Right here!"

She opened her eyes just in time to see a black Hummer dart beside them and shudder to a quick halt. Doors flew open and without hesitation she was carried inside. Deep leather and a luxurious hush greeted her at once. The doors slammed shut as a monstrous engine roared to life beneath her.

She leaned her head back onto a cushioned rest, closed her eyes and breathed a quick prayer of thanks. Then, feeling the same resolve pour into her veins once more, she opened her eyes and straightened herself.

CHAPTER
_21

"You've done a good thing, sir, but I have to ask. Who are you, and why are you in my Humvee?"

The voice belonged to Mara McQueen, turning and peering back from the vehicle's front passenger seat in an uncharacteristic state of dishevelment. The unfortunate recipient of her razor-sharp inquiry was the man who had just pulled Abby from the floor of her hospital room and carried her to safety, the man who now sat next to her in the backseat.

"I'm sorry there was no time for introductions," he replied. "My name is Lloyd. I'm a retired Navy Seal and a security consultant in L.A. And I'm very sorry to say that your bodyguard, Barry, was this afternoon's one fatality. He had just called me in for backup twenty minutes before the first shot rang out. I'm his local contingency man, so to speak. You probably knew that Barry had one of us in every city."

Her mouth hanging open in shock, Mara shook her head, incredulous.

"As the afternoon wore on and more and more folks started figuring out the origin of your broadcast and crowding into the hospital, your bodyguard grew nervous about securing the area. That's why he called me. I was pulling into the parking lot when the first shot occurred."

"Well, what exactly happened?" Mara demanded. "What kind of attack was this?"

"You have to understand that, since I got here, I've been running and then carrying Abby. So I haven't had much time for intel. But judging from the little I saw around me, it looks like a sniper was working in conjunction with someone inside the building. Either that or the sniper planted the bomb himself, way in advance. The fact that they shot your bodyguard tells me they'd been reconnoitering for some time, so had a good lay of the land and a specific plan of attack."

"And their target was Abby?" Mara said.

"Your man Barry had briefed me by phone before you all came. Seems the FBI has a very thick jacket on Abby and some pretty specific threats against her life."

At this, Mara turned toward the young woman and gave her a scowl, the one she notoriously turned on uncooperative guests and folks who managed to invoke her ire.

"You're just full of interesting stories, aren't you?" she said, her voice tinged with suspicious irritation.

"The night I got my infection," Abby responded warily, "someone broke into my house while I was sleeping and killed our housekeeper, who was more like a surrogate mother to me. Then he tried to kill me in my bed, but something scared him away. No one figured out what or who that was."

"And that's *it*?" Mara cried out. "I mean, I don't mean to be crass, but I've got a longer list of stalkers and enemies than the president does, and I didn't seem to rate here."

"There is something else," Lloyd interrupted.

"What now?" Mara said.

"When Barry gave me the advance word on today, I did a little prep work and called some of my friends at the L.A. field office."

"FBI?" Abby said.

"That's right."

"I thought L.A. County was investigating it."

"It was, until two weeks ago. And the reason they're not anymore is the something else I'm about to tell you. It seems there's a pretty solid cross-reference in the jacket to one of the oldest and most secret serial murder investigations in the bureau's history."

Mara turned completely around in her seat, so enthralled now that she didn't even bother to utter a word. But her message was clear. *Keep talking!*

"Doesn't make much sense to me," Lloyd continued. "You see, the victims are all older, vulnerable African-American women. All shapes and sizes, and from every part of the country. None of the common-alities that usually make for a single perpetrator. Except for one thing."

"What?" Mara snapped.

"Well, Mizz McQueen," he said, darting his eyes over at Abby, "it's fairly gruesome. And I was hoping to spare young Abby here—"

"I read Narbeli's autopsy report," Abby interrupted. "I imagine I can stomach whatever you can dish out."

"Then maybe you know exactly what I'm talking about," said Lloyd. "Because that's seemingly what ties your incident to all of these. It's the brutality of the killings, all of which is tied to the nature of the murder weapon. It's the handheld version of an old agricultural tool."

He looked down and lowered his voice.

"A scythe."

A long, dark pause fell over the Hummer's interior. For a moment the only noise was the huge engine speeding them along a crowded Los Angeles boulevard.

Abby did not glance out at the river of taillights streaming past her, not now. She kept her head down, her gaze aimed somewhere at her feet, and thought of her dear old friend, so cruelly dispatched by the whim of some homicidal aesthete, a bloodthirsty collector of antiques.

Didn't make sense.

"Hey," Mara broke in at last, "we need to get Abby somewhere safe, make contact with her father and find out which new hospital to drop her off at."

"Yeah," the driver agreed.

"No," said Abby. "Absolutely not. No more hospitals."

"What are you talking about?" Mara said.

"Please lend me your cell phone." Abby took the unit from Mara and dialed quickly. "Dad, it's me," she said. "I'm safe . . . There was no time. Mara's security people got me out of there and quick . . . I'm sorry, I called for you and looked for you on my way out, but everybody said it was better to just hook back up later . . . Now we're driving downtown."

She paused while her father talked for a while, her jaw muscles working feverishly.

"No, Dad, I'm not gonna do that," she finally responded. The occupants around her dropped their pretense of not listening and suddenly turned toward her with staring eyes. "Dad, you heard what I said in that interview. Well, I meant it. I'm not gonna spend another minute in a hospital bed. I was put on this mission by no less than Christ himself, and I'm *not* about to let Him down . . . Well, I'm feeling better. I'll pick up some of the medicines before I leave. Lord knows I've got their names memorized . . . I understand your concern and you know I love you, but I'm not going to change my mind on this. Besides, there's nothing more the doctors can do for me other than pump me full of drugs and wait for the end . . . Why can't you just wish me luck, Dad? Better yet, why don't you come with me? What? . . . Where am I going? . . . I don't know yet. Now that I think of it, I'm going somewhere where I can find a half million African women worshiping God at the same time. Someplace where the word *Iya Agba* makes sense."

Mara leaned in and whispered, "Nigeria."

"What?"

"You'll find a million brown-skinned women worshiping God just outside of Lagos, Nigeria," Mara said. "I did a report on last year's

Son of God Assembly. Did you see it?"

"Apparently no," Abby replied.

"I'm no expert, but while I was there I listened to many of the women speak in their native tongues. *Iya Agba*, if I'm not mistaken, sounds an awful lot like Yoruba."

Abby cocked her head and wondered for a moment whether she should tell her father what she had just heard. She shook her head slowly, whispered "I love you, Dad," and closed the cell phone.

_22

"Now, I didn't tell you that to give you crazy ideas," Mara said. "Do you have any clue what a dangerous and difficult place Nigeria is today? In twenty years of television I don't think we had a tougher time pulling off a production."

"Barry told me about it," Lloyd cut in. "He had to basically hire a freelance army regiment to travel with you."

"Forgive me, but I don't plan on going with a huge camera crew and an entourage," Abby said.

"That will make it infinitely more dangerous," Lloyd said. "The size of her contingent actually worked in Mara's favor. If you go as a single, sick, rich and famous Western woman, you won't reach the city gates of Lagos before getting kidnapped. Kidnapping and murdering Westerners is a cottage industry there."

"Do you know anything about this country?" Mara asked with a sudden fire in her eyes. "The State Department has a travel advisory strongly urging Americans not go there. Warning them specifically about lawlessness and kidnapping on the nation's highways."

Abby stared ahead and flexed her jaw stubbornly. "I appreciate the concern and advice, but you guys are *not* talking me out of going."

"I'm not trying to talk you out of going, dear," Mara countered.

"I'm trying to get you to accept my help. Do you remember what I said on the air? Well, I've never reneged on an on-air promise—and I have no intention of starting now, girl. So if you're so bound and determined to go somewhere—"

"To Nigeria," Abby interrupted.

"To Nigeria," Mara conceded with an affectionate roll of her eyes, "then you'll take my plane. And my help. The only thing I'll ask you to take along as a personal favor is one of my video crews. If your trip's a disaster, I swear to you now that we'll toss the footage. But I can't resist trying. I am a TV woman, after all."

"I've never known you to go anywhere without a camera in tow," Abby said, smiling.

"Oh no," Mara said, "*going* is the one thing I can't do. As much as I'd like to be there, I can never go back to Nigeria."

"But why?"

"I made some enemies. I spoke plainly about conditions there, and the official corruption. Nigeria has enough oil to be one of the wealthiest nations on earth. Instead, it's one of the poorest, while a tiny slice of the population live like emperors. I spoke about it. My army colonel warned me when the episode aired that I could never come back and expect to live."

"Well, so . . ." started Abby.

"Take my plane. Take Lloyd here, and all the security help I can hire. My producers will work the phones before you ever land, lining up for you a front-row seat at Nigeria's biggest church service. The Believers Gathering, largest in the world. And we'll find your *Iya Agba*."

God, this is crazy. I mean, here I am, very, very sick—"terminally ill" seems to be everybody's favorite word for it—and here I'm running off to the literal ends of the earth. Without my dad, my friends, or any of what I would have called, until today, my support system. Or at least what seems like it from here. From a human, commonsense point of view, my dad's point of view, this is nuts.

And, Lord, if I've somehow deluded myself into this escapade, please find a way to break through my stubborn skull and let me know. Would you? Because all I know now is, in spite of what common sense tells me, I had a real encounter with you the other night. And the promise of what you have in store is so real to me right now, it seems the only true craziness would be to throw away the opportunity you've put before me and just lie down and die quietly.

Maybe I am going crazy. Maybe some kind of brain-fry is part of my dying process. I mean, if you take all this one piece at a time, it makes me sound like a complete idiot. A word, Iya Agba. A strange occurrence in a waking dream. Wild stories over the Internet. Individually, they sound like nothing. Yet somehow they add up to my being here in this airplane, gambling the last days of my life on the ultimate wild goose chase. With the whole world speculating on whether I've lost my marbles.

The whole thing seems to require a heaping dose of faith, I suppose. After all, some days you haven't seemed like the surest bet in this world. Forgive me, but it's true—though on some days you are more real to me than my next breath, on other days, every once in a great while, when I've stuck my heart too deep in the things of this world, I look up and you seem so unlikely, so far-fetched. The whole thing—the Incarnation, the Atonement, the Cross, the return to heaven, the promise of eternity with you . . .

On days like that, I have to just take a deep breath and talk to you anyway. Act in faith.

And that's what I'm doing now, Lord. So please, don't let me do this alone. Don't go silent on me now, just as I'm taking the biggest plunge of my life based on things I believe you told me.

Please?

INSIDE A GULFSTREAM G550 PRIVATE JET, OVER TEXAS

They had barely reached cruising altitude before Mara McQueen, the jet's owner, held up a remote control and pushed a button, causing a mahogany cabinet door to slide open with a whir. Inside, three parallel monitors glowed with high-definition footage from each of the major cable news networks.

All three were running breathless, saturation coverage of the afternoon's events, beginning at Mara's dramatic interview with the world's newest-minted Internet celebrity, followed by chilling images of the camera shaking suddenly, the room going dark and the once-calm frame erupting into frenzied motion, anguished voices, and rounds of gunfire. Then the most dramatic of all: the unexplained disappearance of the episode's centerpiece, the seemingly ailing Abby Sherman. Not to mention her media champion, megastar Mara McQueen.

Speculation was rampant. Had the two women run off together? Had they both been abducted? No one could say for certain. Abby's father was on record as having fielded a cryptic cell phone transmission from his daughter, but its abrupt and ambiguous ending had left him with not much more knowledge of the truth than anyone else.

Someone whom security cameras had identified only as a tall, white male—who seemed to know exactly when to turn away from the lenses, but whom no one had correctly identified as one of Mara's personal staff—had gained admittance to the Sherman home, then mysteriously departed with Abby's passport and many of her clothes. Was the whole thing a hoax? Some tasteless publicity stunt?

In the absence of proof, any verdict would do.

"Honey, I think the time has come for you to set people's minds at ease," Mara suggested. She reached the media cabinet and pulled out an ultra-thin laptop computer. "Your native medium?"

ABBY SHERMAN, BEACHDREAMER@MYCORNER.COM

Dear Friends,

I must start with an apology. I can't imagine how much concern, fear, and grief today's events must have caused some of you. While I didn't cause the attack at my hospital or the chaos that followed it, I should have paid more attention, in the hours that followed, to the millions of people who have become my "virtual friends" of late.

Please know that I haven't meant to ignore or disregard your concern for my well-being. I value your faithful prayers on my behalf more than you'll ever know.

The answer to why no one has heard from me until now is complex. Even more difficult, circumstances dictate that I can only reveal some of that answer to you now.

Please remember, as you read this, that the events in question didn't happen with the neat, cut-and-dry simplicity that media reports always convey. While you may now have been able to re-create nearly every step of the attack, when it happened it was sudden, brutal, and incredibly disorienting. We didn't make calm and deliberate decisions with the full weight of consequences in mind. We reacted. And, under the circumstances, we made the best choices we could.

So what happened? Basically, when the room first went dark, the first explosion and gunshots were heard, Mara and I both escaped. Tragically, as you probably know, Mara's longtime body-guard was killed. Thankfully, a trusted backup was entering the scene just as it all fell apart. That person picked me up and hus-tled me to safety through the back of the hospital.

Once outside, I was taken away by a vehicle in Mara's convoy. At first, there was discussion of taking me to my family or to the nearest hospital. But the longer I thought about my conversation with Mara, the more I began to have second thoughts.

Eventually, I realized what the interview must have made clear: that I have a job to do. A mystery to solve. And that I had nothing better to do with my remaining days on earth than give them some meaning and purpose.

I can't tell you where I've gone. I'm so sorry—I've tried and tried to figure out a way I could safely do that. There simply isn't one. In order for my mission to succeed, and for any of this to have any meaning, I must go alone. Or at least try. Please—if you care about me and my fate, don't give encouragement to the papa-razzi or tabloid journalists who will try to track me down no mat-ter what the cost. Say a prayer for me, and if you want the verifia-ble truth, stick with this website.

Above everything else, remember I am doing this completely of my own free will. Believe me, I'm the only one who's truly excited about my taking on this quest. I have not been influenced, com-pelled, and definitely not forced to carry out any of the searches ahead of me. This is one hundred percent my attempt to solve the mystery raised by all those e-mails from so many of you to my MyCorner site, along with the amazing episodes from my visit to heaven.

Please pray that my health and courage will hold up. And ask

God for His favor on me, that I can figure out what in the world this *Iya Agba* Sisterhood, as I'm starting to think of it, is all about.

And for those of you who have the Sight, please let me know what you're seeing, would you? I need all the intel I can get. Just e-mail your sightings right here, and I'll be sure to get them.

Love to all,

Abby Sherman

CHAPTER
_23

NEW YORK, OVERLOOKING CENTRAL PARK

The two Scythian Elders, men who spoke three times a day but had only met in person four times over the last twenty years, stood clasping each other's forearms in the granite splendor of the palatial entry hall.

The oldest, the penthouse's owner, leaned in and stared suspiciously into the other's eyes.

"Have you come to give me bad news?" he asked.

"Please don't believe what you see on television, my Brother. We have the situation completely in hand."

"You know where she is?"

"Absolutely. She's on McQueen's plane and headed straight into the heart of the war."

"You mean—?"

"That's right, sir."

The brittle old voice creaked out a curse. "Didn't take the little vermin very long to sniff out the action, did it? There's no denying it—her awakening has been most dramatic and powerful. So if she's going there, tell me, why shouldn't I interpret that as the worst possible news?"

"Because our man is right with her."

"On the plane?"

"That's right. Under deep cover. She's completely at his mercy."

"Well then, why doesn't he just harvest her now and be done with it?"

"It seems that would be too complicated. He would also have to kill the pilots and then be forced to fly the plane himself back across the Atlantic. Our man is an accomplished operative, but he's not a pilot. Besides, I urge you to think of this as a massive opportunity rather than focusing on the risk. Think of the knowledge we can gain by letting her meet up with her side in Nigeria and having her die with them. That approach would produce massive intel on our enemies, and multiply the magnitude of the defeat already under way."

"I see. We make certain she's at the very same gathering when our forces attack, and that she dies along with the others."

"Exactly."

"Do we have real-time communication with our man?"

"No, we don't. On the plane it's only e-mail. But as soon as he's on the ground, I'll be in his ear and talking with him constantly."

"Good work, Shadow Leader. You know I had my doubts about using someone not fully embraced into the Brotherhood. But your unconventional choice seems to be paying dividends. As usual, your thoughtful preparations trump my impetuous nature. You've turned a possible disaster into potentially our most decisive victory of all time."

"Indeed. I am hoping for a death blow. Not only do we prevent the girl from igniting our opposition, but we wipe her out along with the heart of their strength. A masterstroke! Long live the Lord of the Air!"

"Long live! And speaking of strokes, let us celebrate. Come downstairs with me and pick out one of my best blades. I have a pair of fresh young victims waiting for us in my pantry."

Shadow Leader laughed. He had heard the old man's euphemism for a dungeon before, yet it never failed to tickle his funny bone. A dark soundproofed chamber used to warehouse stray human beings before their harvesting—to equate that with a room for storing dry goods struck him as the height of Scythian irony. Only a man drenched in the Brotherhood's culture enough to have his very own oak-lined library featuring rare antique scythes—expertly sharpened, oiled, and ready for use—could have thought of such a thing.

He laughed a rich, cultured laugh and followed his host past the recessed, nearly invisible door frame custom-built into the library's paneling.

He shivered with anticipation, for just then, standing very still and silencing his breaths, he had just barely made out the warbled crescendo of a scream.

THE MCQUEEN JET, MIDWAY ACROSS THE ATLANTIC

"I have good news and bad news," announced Paula, Mara's personal assistant, as she plucked headphones from around her head in the subdued light of the Gulfstream's cabin. Mara herself had deplaned hours before in Atlanta, her home base, where the plane had been refueled. Her place had been taken by a cameraman in his late forties, who sat silently filming everything with amazing unobtrusiveness.

Mara was confident of the trip's success, she'd reassured Abby, but her presence on the trip would have overshadowed and maybe even endangered this precarious mission. Besides, there was that *persona non grata* status to think about.

"Bad news first," said Abby.

"Mara was right. The State Department has just issued a strongly worded traveler's advisory, just short of an outright prohibition, against travel in Nigeria. Seems there's a rash of roving gangs, not to mention the usual bunch of Islamic commandos, who have been making incursions deep into the Christian parts of the country. Their stock in trade is kidnapping Westerners for ransom. Anyone who looks vulnerable and possibly rich. Two American and three British tourists have been abducted and slaughtered in the last three weeks. Basically, venturing anywhere outside of Lagos, Nigeria's largest city, is deemed borderline illegal and suicidal at best."

"Oh, great," Abby said in mock relief. "Glad it wasn't anything depressing."

"I've already arranged for the services of the colonel," Lloyd interjected. "A retired Nigerian officer who rents out his own private special forces squad. Just for Westerners rightfully concerned about their security on Nigerian back roads."

"But you haven't heard my *good* news," Paula said. "We just happen to be coming right in the middle of a Believers Gathering. Six hundred thousand Nigerian believers are, well, gathering, just east of Lagos. Seventy percent of them will be women. It started yesterday and won't end for another three days. They'll send an emissary to meet our plane and guide you personally to the site."

Abby's face broke into a wide smile. "That's exactly what I was hoping for. Six hundred *thousand* worshipers?"

"That's what I hear. Don't you know that the world's largest church, numbering over a million members in a single service, takes place in Nigeria?"

Abby began to nod intensely. "This is it, I can feel it," she said. "How long until we get there?"

Paula glanced down at her watch. "Only an hour and a half. Why don't you try and get some rest before we arrive?"

Abby nodded, for that sounded like a most wise idea. Buoyed by the good news, she reclined on a long leather couch, pulled a wool blanket over her body, and within three minutes was snoring loudly.

SEVENTY MINUTES LATER

Abby's in-flight nap ended with her shout and a fierce forward pitch of her torso, as violent as if her whole upper body had been propelled upward by a giant spring. Her eyes flew open and just as quickly met the alarmed stares of Paula and Lloyd. They had both whirled around in their captain's chairs, anticipating the worst. Even the cameraman lurched forward in a far corner, comical in his attempts to steady the lens even while his body was pitching sideways.

Paula lunged forward onto her knees and snatched up Abby's

hands into both of her own. "Are you all right?" she pleaded.

Instead of replying at once, Abby caught her breath and swept the cabin with probing glances. "I'm not sure," she answered at last. "Something's happening. Something just tore me from my sleep. It doesn't feel good." She cast a quick look at Lloyd. "I'm scared. I just don't know what I'm scared *about*."

Then she looked out one of the plane's oval windows beside her.

She screamed again. Then sprang backward so powerfully that if Lloyd had not thrown himself from his chair and caught her midair, the petite twenty-year-old would have struck the other side of the fuselage.

"What is it?" Lloyd asked, holding her now-quivering face in his hands.

"Look! Look!" she ranted, pointing to the window.

"All right." Lloyd released her and moved over to peer closely. He turned back. "Abby, I'm sorry, but I don't see anything but sky."

Abby looked at him as though preparing for a reply, but her stare turned into a scowl. She reached out her hands toward him and began to knead the air in front of him like a suspended pile of Play-Doh.

"Of course you wouldn't," she said in a low, almost whispering voice. "But what is that in front of you?" She squinted harder and leaned forward. "I can't quite . . . see . . ."

Bewildered and alarmed, Lloyd drew back, scowling himself now. He glanced at Paula to see if she was registering Abby's strange behavior. Paula was also scowling at the scene.

And then, in a fraction of a second, Abby's expression changed. The alarm fled her face and her muscles relaxed into a mixture of resignation and dread.

"Oh, I get it," she muttered to herself. "It's back. It's back . . ."

"*What's* back?" Paula asked loudly.

"The Sight," Abby replied. "I'm starting to see again. I hoped it had left me forever, but it's back."

"What is she talking about?" Lloyd asked Paula with an exasperated tone.

Paula breathed in and out at great length. "Spirits. Angels. She sees through the veil. Into the spiritual world—"

"Angels," interrupted Abby, still wide-eyed and speaking distract-edly, as if talking to herself. "Demons. And everything in between."

"Sounds like a real hoot," Lloyd said with a hint of a grimace.

"No, actually it's more like a curse," Abby said.

"What did you see out the window?" he asked.

Abby only shuddered and turned even farther away from the aper-ture. "Are we flying over land?" she asked, and it was unclear whether she was clumsily changing the subject or merely pursuing the subject further.

"We're overflying Cote d'Ivoire," he told her, stumbling a bit over the French-pronounced country name. "We're getting quite close to our destination."

Abby shuddered and grasped Lloyd's hand. "Even from this alti-tude, I can see carnage."

"What do you mean, carnage?"

"I mean warfare. Bloody, vicious spiritual warfare."

Lloyd grew still, and his eye movements suddenly became very controlled.

"You don't believe in that," Abby noted, staring at him.

"I am, for better or worse, a warrior," he said carefully, unable to conceal the incredulity in his voice. "A fists and weapons, stuff-you-can-see kinda guy. What you're talking about sounds like a lot of fairy dust."

"I wish it were," Abby said. "What's happening out there is hor-rific. The whole atmosphere is filled with it. Every altitude."

"Can you close your eyes and . . . spare yourself the sight of it?" he asked.

"Yes. It's almost the only thing I *can* do. The problem is, the only reaction inside me stronger than my revulsion is my curiosity."

"Why were you making those strange motions in front of my face?"

She did not answer right away, but just stared at him enigmati-cally. Then she shook her head in confusion. "I couldn't make you out," she said. "You were . . . fuzzy. There was something happening around you, but it was too fast. Too crazy. I couldn't see clearly what was happening."

"I guess that makes me a complex guy," he said with a touch of sarcasm. "I am, after all, an ex-soldier and cop."

Something about what she saw troubled her, except she couldn't determine exactly what it was. Then she had an idea, looked up at Lloyd, and asked, "Have you killed . . . another person?"

He stared at her, hesitating with his response. When he finally nodded yes, it was so faint that Abby didn't notice the motion at first. "I was in Desert Storm," he finally said. "And Iraqi Freedom. So, yeah."

She reached out to touch his arm. "It's all right," she murmured. "Most of us are in some kind of turmoil. I appreciate your service."

"Thank you."

"No, thank *you*, Lloyd," she insisted.

"Yeah," chimed in Paula. "Thank you for your service."

He nodded absently, looking genuinely disoriented by the conversation's odd turn.

"Howdy, folks," came the pilot's voice, jarring in its metallic loudness. "We're now about to descend over Eastern Ghana, which means we're only about fifteen minutes from Lagos Airport. Because of security concerns I'm going to make a pretty steep approach, so y'all may want to strap in tight. Thanks, and on behalf of my copilot and me, our best wishes on the mission at hand."

"We're flying straight into Lagos?" Abby said. "I would have thought we'd find some out-of-the-way place and avoid prying eyes."

"I checked into that," said Paula, "but it turns out we'll attract less attention coming straight into the private aviation sector of the national airport. Believe me, there're enough luxury jets in Lagos to match any strip in Aspen or Geneva. No one will even notice us."

"Better strap in," Lloyd warned Abby.

"Can I do that while I'm still lying down?" she asked in a frail voice. "All of a sudden I don't feel so great."

"Is it the pain?" Paula asked.

Abby nodded in the affirmative, holding her side and wincing.

"First the Sight, now this pain. Something about reaching Nigeria doesn't seem to agree with me."

The last word of her sentence went largely unheard, because at that instant the entire cabin jerked forward and downward at a precipitous angle. Instead of response, all Abby received for her words were her companions' respective groans.

CHAPTER
_24

LAGOS, NIGERIA, MURTULA MOHAMMED INTERNATIONAL AIRPORT

At most of the world's other commercial airports, the Gulfstream's final approach would have provoked immediate alarm and even specific countermeasures. At a contemporary American airport, for instance, its dramatic plunge from a blue sky would have sparked several moments of heated speculation over whether the craft had been commandeered by hostile parties and possibly a frenzied warning to Homeland Security. The pilots would have been sharply queried over radio as to the meaning of their actions. At the very least, it would have earned them a warning from the FAA and a likely reprimand from their employers.

At Lagos Tower, however, the maneuver was nearly routine. On any given day, there might be a dozen reasons why a wealthy Nigerian's airplane might attempt to evade potential hostile fire by shortening its final approach. They ranged from reprisals of a political, financial or even ethnic nature, to specific kidnapping or blackmail threats, to seething discontent among the earthbound class. Nowhere on the planet festered such a gigantic gap between the corrupt and wealthy—who collectively siphoned off enough oil from the world's fourth-largest petroleum producer to match the wealth of Bill Gates every single day—and a starving, teeming underbelly. That resulted in plenty of reasons for the incoming jet-set to be careful, and plenty of ready pretexts for attacking them.

Inside the jet registered to Mara McQueen, however, the maneuver had one overriding effect on its most important passenger. Strapped in tight to a leather divan, Abby was pitched forward into an optimal position from which to view the Lagos panorama at a most acute angle. Even as she gripped the nearest arm with white knuckles and strained audibly to keep herself upright, she found her eyes riveted on the sight reeling outside the portholes beyond her perch.

"If you're seeing more visions, please, just close your eyes!" offered Paula.

"No, it's not *that* at the moment," she answered. "The Sight seems to have dissipated for a second. I'm just looking at the city!"

Paula followed Abby's gaze out a nearby window. Through ribbons of smoke and haze, it seemed the dingy brown re-creation of a third-world slum had flooded the horizon. A sea of hazy brown rooftops, punctuated by whitish hills, stretched as far as she could see.

"Why are those hills that strange pale color?" Abby asked.

Paula made a face. "Those aren't hills. They're junk piles. Lagos has no—"

She did not finish the sentence, for just as abruptly the plane leveled its exaggerated descent with a groan of engines, flaring off its approach for landing. The sudden shift and the pressure of the positive *g*'s sent an army of needles through Abby's joints and midsection. Despite her continuing curiosity, she could only grit her teeth, close her eyes, and lean her head back against the couch.

There came a screech, and a jolt, and with a surge of cold reality came the sobering realization that *she was here*. Second thoughts, misgivings and all, she had irreversibly arrived on the next and scariest stage yet of her quest.

After the jet cycled through the familiar stages of reverse thrusting and hard braking, they began to taxi through a bewildering maze of aircraft—lumbering 747s, luxury business jets, and single-engine propeller planes scurrying haphazardly through the midst like a swarm of aeronautical gnats.

Despite her pain, Abby found herself fascinated by the crowd of planes, their sheer diversity of size and shapes, their exotic tail logos and country names, their deceptive appearance of taxiing without guidance. She peered intently through the portholes, her discomfort momentarily forgotten.

She gasped loudly, unbuckled her strap, and fell to her knees.

The two others rushed to her side and stared along with her. Out on the tarmac less than fifty yards away weaved three camouflage-green Hummers, their hulking outlines punctured by the barrels of upraised automatic weapons, circling around nose cones as they sped straight in their direction.

"Oh no!" Abby cried. "They're after us! They're following our plane!"

Lloyd's body tensed from head to foot and seemed to channel all its power to his eyes, which bore down on the pursuers with a calm intensity. The man seemed at home in this kind of situation. In fact, he looked more comfortable than he had appeared since Abby had met him.

"Abby, stay down," Paula warned. "Just lie on the floor and take cover."

"You too, Paula," barked Lloyd, his eyes still riveted on the soldiers outside.

Abby couldn't help but take one final peek. Soldiers—or she had to assume they were real soldiers as they wore no coherent uniform, just flapping clothes of a roughly similar green hue—were now waving their machine guns, signaling for the plane to stop.

Lloyd, now crouched down, pulled a large revolver from a previously unseen belt holster and began checking his ammo load. The cameraman swerved quickly between shots of each of them and the drama unfolding outside the plane.

The aircraft turned violently, tossing all three passengers to the left. The shadow of a towering 747 tail passed over them and left just as swiftly. An apparent near-miss. The wall of a huge hangar loomed on their left, and it seemed they had entered the airport version of a back alley.

Quite suddenly, they braked to a complete stop. The halt was so abrupt that the brakes screeched painfully and the entire plane slid forward on its wheels. It seemed to strain there, in a momentary shiver of inertia, before settling back again.

Lloyd stood up, his revolver now held against his chest, just as the main door whooshed open and filled the front of their cabin with harsh, menacing sunlight.

Abby heard the *click* of Lloyd's weapon being cocked. She searched his eyes for signs of fear, but saw only a resolute focus on what lay ahead.

Through the doorway came angry-sounding, high-pitched shouts. Orders in an unknown tongue. The pilot came walking out of the cockpit, a reassuring hand held out in front of him. "Please don't worry, folks," he said in a tone which, despite being professionally warm and personable, did nothing to reassure Abby. "This seems to be our welcoming party." His dark-blazered shape disappeared out that terrifying doorway.

Abby turned to Paula. "What does he mean?"

The younger woman roused herself into a state of uncertainty. "I'm not sure. Except that the staff back home was talking about—"

"Come on out!" came a clipped, imperious shout in thickly accented English. "Carefully!"

Lloyd tucked the gun behind the back of his belt and stepped forward into the light.

Cowering as far away from the opening as she could, Abby whispered a prayer. "God, surely this can't be it! Could I have misread you so badly that it all ends here, on the backside of a tarmac before we've even started? Please ... please don't let this be it, Lord. Rescue us. . . ."

Paula, now crouched in the exit, motioned for Abby to follow her. The bleakness in her eyes could easily have matched that of Anne

Boleyn on her way up the steps to be beheaded.

"You sure?" Abby asked tentatively.

Paula did not reply. Nevertheless, Abby turned and proceeded to follow her downward. She heard no gunfire. *Has to be a good sign*, she told herself.

Blinking in the glare, she glanced down and focused on keeping her footing on the metal steps poised midway between light and shadow. Feeling solid ground at last under her final step, she ventured a look upward.

The first thing she saw were the gleaming, intent eyes of a tall black man in impeccable green camouflage, staring at her. He stood above the windshield of an open-air Humvee, surrounded by four others crammed with nearly a dozen Nigerian soldiers. All of them staring straight at her.

Abby stepped forward. She felt her free hand, the one not being held by Lloyd for stability, creep upward in a gesture of submission.

She tried not to look at the gleaming gun barrels, the cold gazes behind them, or feel the menace they seemed to exude. She tried to force her mouth into a smile. Normal airport noise engulfed her: a taxiing jetliner somewhere behind her whined loudly on its way past. She breathed in deeply. The air was stifling, hot and humid. Her nostrils filled with the smell of jet fuel and a background bouquet of sea spray and rotting trash.

Can a person smell danger? she asked herself. So often she had heard of a dog smelling danger. Now she stood in a situation where she could almost discern its acrid scent, weaving faintly among all the others.

CHAPTER
_25

The tall soldier leaped from the Humvee and swaggered toward her. As he approached, she saw that he truly was an officer of consequence: a garish ribbon adorned his front pocket and his shoulder bore an epaulet gleaming with a golden eagle and two stars.

"You Abby Sherman?" he asked with accented voice.

She nodded. "Yes, sir," she said.

"And *this* man?" he asked derisively, looking at the cameraman. "This, we cannot have. I will not allow it."

"Sir, his presence was one of the chief conditions of your . . . retainer. Please verify that with your people, because our staff was quite explicit about that."

The officer stepped forward in front of the lens. The cameraman backed up, both out of necessity and, it seemed, self-preservation.

After brooding for a moment, the officer relaxed his posture and turned back around. "Welcome to Nigeria, Mizz Sherman. I am Colonel Anthony Shawkey," he said. She thought she discerned a softening in his voice. "Colonel Shawkey, for short. I am to be your protector during your sojourn in our country."

She cocked her head in surprise. *Protector?*

Paula stepped forward and whispered into her ear. "I was starting to tell you when we went into our final descent. It's a fairly common practice for high-profile visitors to employ, let's say, highly placed escorts to ensure safety. This seems to be our *ride*."

Struggling to process such an abrupt reversal in her expectations, Abby nodded numbly and shook the colonel's proffered hand.

"Pleased to meet you, Colonel," she said after regaining her senses. "I am most grateful that you and your men are on our side."

At that, the colonel threw his head back and launched an explosive laugh into the sky. He turned and walked back to his Humvee, paused beside it and held out his hand. A small brown arm reached out and grasped his.

The arm was attached, as the next moment revealed, to a diminutive African woman in her sixties who stepped gingerly from the vehicle and came forward. From this distance, the most remarkable thing about her was her dress. A resplendent wrap of emerald green silk crowned her head, but her exit revealed the garment's full glory. A flowing robe with the same iridescent sheen folded neatly over her small shoulders and encircled her tiny frame, ending with a flourish just above a pair of matching leather sandals.

Abby gaped unashamedly as the woman approached. Between the splendor of the old woman's clothing and the radiance of her countenance, the young American was unsure if she had ever seen someone so striking. Finally the two stood face-to-face. Close proximity only confirmed the older woman's beauty; her smile seemed to glow from a place deep inside her.

"Sister Abigail," the woman said as she lifted both of her arms for an embrace.

"Yes, and you are, ma'am?" Abby answered, utterly befuddled.

The smile only widened. "Sister Abedago, at your service. Your Nigerian brothers and sisters have all heard and been inspired by your story. And now, for you to choose coming here at this hour, with nearly the whole world concerned with your whereabouts—we are all overwhelmed. That's why I have been sent by the Believers Gathering to greet you in the name of our Lord and invite you to return, along with our brother the colonel here, to our assembly grounds."

The old woman's hands ventured closer, and Abby gave herself to a warm hug, careful not to rumple the lady's elaborate wrappings.

Suddenly, Abby remembered. She pulled back and asked the question she'd come here to answer. "Sister, have you ever heard the word *Iya Agba*?"

The older woman's expression underwent a fascinating series of reactions upon her hearing the word. First came abject surprise, manifested by a sudden relaxing of her facial muscles and a slight stare. Then bemusement, along with a faint smile. And finally, her guarded reply.

"Yes, I have, my dear," she said in a near whisper. "And I will tell you all I can when the time is right—"

From overhead came the thunderous interruption of chopping helicopter blades.

Without warning, the world began to swirl menacingly around Abby. Something in her knees gave out. The sight of the soldiers fell away from her. Mortified, she felt herself slump forward into Sister Abedago's bosom, precisely where she didn't want to end up. Then, gratefully, she felt arms behind her, pulling her up and away.

"Forgive me," she managed to tell her new acquaintance. "I do not feel very strong all of a sudden."

But Sister Abedago seemed quite agitated at Abby's collapse. Her regal glow instantly transformed into an expression of sharp concern. Looking around her with questioning eyes, she finally turned to Lloyd. "Should we still proceed?" she half shouted against the continuing blast of the offending chopper.

He only frowned and shook his head in response. "We've always known Abby was in precarious health. We're only here because of her sheer conviction that she's been sent by God himself. And if that's true, then I suppose she can drive out in any condition."

"Go, please," Abby said faintly. "I want to go *now*."

"Sister Abigail," her host said, leaning in to her, "you have come to a place of miracles, at a time of miracles. Let us take you and claim a healing for you. Will you let us do that for you?"

Abby nodded and allowed herself to be lifted into the lead Humvee.

Colonel Shawkey jumped up snarling, grabbed a machine gun from one of his nearest men, and unleashed a single blast into the air—a warning shot to the media bird still roaring overhead.

The aural onslaught sent Abby into a convulsive shudder of mixed fear and shock. "Who are they?" she asked, too weak to shout but strong enough to point upward.

"News media," said the colonel. "They already know you're here. There's been a leak!"

Abby returned to full awareness a moment after the Humvee clunked into gear and the wind of a headlong rush struck her in the face. As difficult as it was to keep her eyes open, she found it just as difficult to close them, for the sights flowing past on either side proved simply stunning.

The first reason was speed—the colonel's armed contingent concerned itself neither with speed limits nor the safety of other motorists. The four military vehicles roared down the tarmac like a sovereign's bodyguards in a royal motorcade.

The second reason was the incredible cityscape before her. Her first locale was the airport tarmac. As exhilarating as it had been to watch the Gulfstream weave its way through ground traffic after landing, she found it now doubly thrilling, although terrifying as well, to weave around the huge wheels of a departing jumbo jet, then race forward, narrowly escaping not one but three smaller propeller planes, execute a death-defying turn around a decrepit hangar, then rocket toward a side gate at the speed of an Indy Pace Car.

Soon afterward, however, it was the unrelenting squalor and humanity of outlying Lagos that kept her staring about in amazement. Granted, the daredevil driving had hardly ended; they were now on a regional highway the colonel's convoy treated as a personal racetrack. They flew on, oblivious to speed laws, blinking their headlights and honking their horns, and the few motorists who did not anticipate their passing, by pulling off the road, soon found themselves treated as highway cones in an improvised slalom derby.

But even through the vertigo and dizziness, Abby was transfixed by the row after row after row of unending shacks stretching out in slums so vast and desolate that she felt her soul shrivel at the mere sight of them. The lanes between them were jammed with people, and it was the sight of them which kept the young woman from growing totally demoralized.

They seemed, despite their surroundings, a remarkably energetic and lively people. Even as they skirted or jumped over trenches of raw sewage that transected every single lane, she saw folks laughing, saluting each other, children running barefoot with the same joy as kids back home. Men in sharp suits navigated precarious moat tops on rickety bicycles, and yet despite their tenuous balance, found the temerity to look over and wave at her out of sheer friendliness. It seemed the cameraman could not bring himself to stop filming.

"Lagos is rumored to be the second largest city in the world," Paula commented in her ear. "Official sources say tenth. But it has no sanitation whatsoever. No garbage pickup, no sewage system."

"I gathered that," Abby said.

"The people are amazing, though. They don't let any of their country's problems get them down. They have such spirit, such optimism. Mara fell in love with them when she was here."

The infernal drive did not relent for a second. But what kept Abby thankful for the Humvees' excessive speed was the stench, which, even with highway winds snapping about her, assaulted her nostrils with a strength and pungency that rivaled Manila. Beyond that came the assault of thick, heavy humidity.

For the second time, they approached a barrier of vehicles and vicious-looking, rifle-brandishing men who jumped aside at the last second for them to pass. "Who are they?" Abby whispered into the ear of Sister Abedago.

"A gang of local boys, asking for *dash*," she sighed. "An ordinary motorist cannot go more than five miles without being stopped at gunpoint and asked for dash. That's our name for a bribe, which is one of the most common daily facts of life here. The richer you look, the more pressing the request. The more serious the consequences for not paying. Another good reason to thank God for the colonel."

As they sped by, Abby glanced at the cold sneers directed at their camera and shivered. That smell of danger returned, more pungent than before.

"Are you seeing it again?" Lloyd asked in a concerned voice.

She nodded wearily.

"Tell me what you see," he said.

Sighing, Abby closed her eyes. "I don't really like to talk about it. But I will. The evil spirits are so ugly and terrifying that I'm not sure I have the language for it. I don't even know what's worse about them—their distorted, reptile-like appearance or the sense of hatred and hunger that seems to just reek from them in this awful stench. They're all different yet share the same qualities, or should I say distortions. Huge, leering eyes, mouths lined with limbs and fangs and dripping with some kind of caustic substance, everything backward and bloated and a grotesque mockery of the human body. The worst part is to see a human being walking around with one of these beings perched with its huge mouth halfway over its soul, its spiritual body. The person believes they're just walking through life and yet they're already half consumed."

Lloyd shivered. "But you see angels too, right?" he asked, as though considering such a prospect for the very first time.

"Oh yeah. And you've probably heard more about the true appearance of angels than of demons, just by being in our culture. What the stories and statues don't capture is how it feels to actually see one. Your body just comes alive with chills. I mean, to have one appear and know it's not a weird dream or a hallucination, and then realize all at once that your seeing this means everything about God and His Son and the Bible was true all along."

"I never thought of it that way," Lloyd said thoughtfully. "But I suppose you're right. You can't have angels without having confirmed the rest of the story too."

"Exactly. Everything just falls into place."

"And you're sure you've seen them," he said, more of a doubtful question than a statement.

"Yeah, I have," she answered with a good-natured chuckle. "Lloyd, it's kind of refreshing to talk with someone who hasn't read my story.

Everyone else I've met in the last two weeks knew more about my strange condition than I did."

"The price of celebrity, I suppose."

Lloyd—or his real name, the assassin Dylan Hatfield—turned away from the young woman and, for the first time in years, found himself in the unlikely battle of fighting to maintain his composure.

First of all, he had never spent this amount of time with a mark just prior to killing him. Or *her* in this case, which was one of the other sticking points. In fact, he had never spent any time with *any* mark. But her being a woman, and a woman this disarming, made things even worse.

But surely, he told himself, if he had ever done this before, it would never have come down like this. He had gone into this operation without the usual internal reassurances that he was truly neutralizing a righteous target. That, despite the fact that this particular one warranted more information than ever. He had lowered his standards for various reasons, which now struck him as trivial and beneath him—fatigue, intimidation, greed, resignation, blind faith.

But now, sitting here after hours in this young woman's presence, the questions throbbed so powerfully that they seemed poised to rip the breath from his lungs. How could, as Shadow Leader had so emphatically asserted, this beautiful girl and her ethereal Sight be such a threat to all humanity? The proposition seemed contrived and exaggerated at best.

Bottom line? *It didn't feel right.*

And it always had before.

Even if he'd been given a clear formula to how she threatened the world, killing her now would prove quite difficult. He'd grown to like the girl. She was down-to-earth, self-effacing, despite her beauty and sudden fame, curious and humble and funny at the same time. A real *girl*.

Had he met her in the course of his ordinary life—that is, the transitory and artificial cover identities he adopted between assignments—he surely would have been knocked out. But would he have had the insight to cast his eyes away from promiscuous models, and see what Abby had just now revealed to him?

He shook his head to dispel the thought.

This was madness. He would have to dispatch this girl with a bullet in the head within the next several hours.

The prospect brought her descriptions suddenly back to him. *Angel or demon.* Regardless of whether it was all true, he pondered a question in his mind that came whole and was utterly compelling.

Which one are you, Dylan? Which side do you serve?

He truly *felt* evil, insinuating himself into this girl's trust and loyalty under the falsest of pretenses. And yet his expressions of concern and interest had not felt like pretense. Because he wasn't pretending at all. He genuinely cared about the girl, and *that* not only made no sense but violated every operational philosophy he knew.

As the drive continued, he could sense their destination approach by the moment. The place where he would have to decide, once and for all, not only what kind of operative he was but what kind of human being. He tried not to think of it, but instead to return to the moment at hand. For the very notion made him want to vomit.

He shivered and looked aside, down into the squalor of the Nigerian suburbs.

Anything but to glance at Abby.

The lethal procession had rocketed away from the city's center for a solid half hour, with their straightaway speeds blurring in Abby's mind to some unthinkable velocity somewhere north of eighty miles per hour. All of this had produced the unforeseen benefit of reducing the beleaguered Lagos ghettoes to an eye-numbing stream of dried mud and refuse.

Abby had uttered her third prayer for safety when Lloyd whirled around in his seat next to her, holding up a pair of the colonel's binoculars. The cameraman swiftly followed suit. Curious to see the source of all the dismay, Abby forced herself to turn as well.

The horizon behind them resembled a scene from *Apocalypse Now* or *Black Hawk Down*. Its grayish smog was thick with the pursuing silhouettes of no less than a half-dozen helicopters, cameramen hanging dangerously from their sides.

Lloyd lowered the scope and shook his head angrily. "They're catching up! How in the world did they find out about us?"

Sister Abedago leaned forward in her seat and made a sad face. "I am afraid that even as we prepare for a healing of Sister Abby," she said loudly, "the word may have gone out a bit too far."

"It was inevitable," Paula added flatly. "We can take precautions, but even Mara always knew it would come out. That's why we have the colonel."

Then Abby saw Lloyd's arm stretch out straight, pointing to the highway's edge.

There bobbed a large, crudely lettered sign.

Welcome Sister Abby! Be Healed!

The placard was being held by two adorable little girls wearing plain flowered dresses, who waved and jumped wildly at their approach. A woman who appeared to be their mother stood to one side waving, aglow in a piercing blue smock.

Church clothes. Just for her.

Replaying in her mind the little girls' smiles, Abby found it hard to rue the obvious evidence of being known by everyone. Instead, she felt herself fighting back tears at their spontaneous and selfless display of love.

Just then, Abby's Sight returned with a vengeance. She realized she was grimacing and groaning in horror before the vision fully registered on her conscious mind—impressions of beings in all shapes, sizes, colors and shades of black or white, grappling with each other in a vast orgy of mortal combat.

Then the truth of it struck her. This was not a purely demonic display. Here were angels: large, bright, humanlike beings in similar numbers to the evil ones. That was why the fighting was so fierce and deadly, precisely because combatants from both sides contended for this city in near equal strengths.

As though reading her mind, Sister Abedago leaned to her and offered, "Sister Abby, did you know that the world's largest churches are here in Nigeria? The Lord is doing a wondrous work in our country. In spite all of its darkness and problems."

Of course, Abby realized even as she nodded her understanding. Without even trying to appear complimentary, Abby could see that the nation's Christian population had indeed brought to their land a spiritual potency unmatched anywhere in the so-called *First* World.

That was when all of Abby's careening emotions, her pain and the horror of her Sight seemed to gather themselves into a single, magnanimous cloud, which floated above the squalid and beautiful sights around her. And it struck her with an emphatic drumbeat that *yes, this is where I need to be.* Here was an adventure, regardless of its outcome, worthy of her last days on earth. A journey bold and desperate and far-flung enough to easily warrant the discomforts of leaving her deathbed to reach it. Suddenly the smell and the slums' hopelessness no longer oppressed her. She felt at one with the passing grandmother asleep on a woodpile and the man hawking peanuts from a two-legged street stand and the pair of boys throwing stones at an outraged rooster.

She felt, or thought she did, a faint glow in a fleeting instant. Jesus' satisfaction at seeing her here, obedient despite the cost.

Picturing this, Abby smiled peacefully for the first time in days.

_26

"Miss Abby? You awake?"

The piercing voice belonged to the colonel, who had turned around in the Humvee's front seat to face her.

"I'm sorry, Miss Abby, I know you don't feel well, but I must inform you of pressing matters."

Something in the soldier's tone jerked her back from her reverie and planted her, now wide awake, in the present. She nodded for him to proceed.

"You see, we haven't had any real trouble at a Christian gathering in a couple of months. In the past, these large services practically invited attacks by everybody from jihadist murder squads out of the north to garden-variety kidnappers and murderers working for all the folks who fear the influence of the body of Christ."

"Amen, my brother," interjected Sister Abedago, who sat listening intently.

"However," Shawkey continued, "the Gathering where we're headed has already been threatened. Because this is a strongly female assembly, and mainly led by women, it has attracted unusual criticism from local Imams. And the army's been tracking a large gang of trained insurgents who've assembled just two miles from the site. I'm afraid that was even before the news of your coming broke in the media. Regardless, the Army of Nigeria is going to do its level best to protect you, Miss Abby. But you have to know that your being here turns this gathering into a world media event, and Nigeria hasn't had such a thing before—broadcast live over every news network on the planet. You're making a lot of people nervous, from the prime minister on down to the lowest oil-stealing billionaire. What I'm saying is, you have a lot of enemies here today. You can thank God I'm not one of them."

Just then the Humvee took a sudden turn, which nearly pitched the colonel out of his seat. He turned angrily to the driver and glowered, then reconsidered.

"Now, when we arrive," he said after righting himself, "they're going to escort you straight to the front platform. For all intents and purposes, you'll be beyond my protection. But I'll be off to the side, and my men will be deployed all around the perimeter, talking to each other. And if something happens, anything alarming such as a loud noise from the crowd or a strange cry, you take off running to me as fast as you can. I know you're not in sprinting form, but I'll be on my way to you, so we'll meet in the middle. All right?"

Abby nodded, the tightness in her stomach betraying the sobering effect of his warning.

The colonel reached out and laid a thick hand on hers. "If the prayers of the saints hold sway, there'll be no need for this, my dear. But I'm a military man, and contingencies are my life. Your being led to me represents the most important mission I may ever undertake. I know you're braving death in coming here, and I want you to know that I and my men are freely doing the same today."

She glanced at the battle-hardened men surrounding her, their fingers tight around their trigger guards. She could hardly believe how dramatically her assessment of them had changed since that first, terrifying meeting outside the plane.

"Thank you, Colonel," she replied at last. "You have no idea how grateful I am for you and your men. Please find a way to tell them that before this is all over, would you, sir?"

He smiled and looked ahead. "Hopefully, you'll have occasion to do so yourself, miss. We're almost there. And may I say, from the looks of you, not a moment too soon."

The first and most obvious sign of their having arrived at the site of the Seventh Annual Believers Gathering was not massive crowds, as Abby had expected, but the hovering of more television choppers.

With a sinking sensation she remembered that arriving at the service would also mean giving up the convoy and its dizzying escape speeds. She would now be captive bait for the unrelenting media machine that had somehow tracked her all the way across the Atlantic.

The second sign was something only Abby saw. Looking ahead, she leaned forward and gripped the seat in front of her. Her eyes grew wide.

"What is it?" asked Sister Abedago. "What do you see?"

At first, Abby's only response was to recoil back into the seat and clasp the sister's hand. Then her voice returned and she spoke in a breathy, high-pitched tone. "I see angels. At least, I think I do. They must be angels, although I've never seen them anywhere this large before. They couldn't be the other, for they're shining and white and beautiful."

"How large are they?"

"They're—it's hard to compare using human measurements. But they must be taller than a house. Oh, they're so huge! And powerful!"

Sister Abedago's eyes gleamed with delight. She leaned in to Abby, still holding her hand. "You asked me about the word *Iya Agba*," she said emphatically. "Do you really not know what the word means?"

"No," she confessed. "I have no clue."

"*Iya Agba* is *you*, my dear. The word means a special gifting, endowed to certain women who can see into the spirit world. It is a name they take when the gift manifests itself."

"No. The word can't be all about me. I came here looking for its meaning!"

"Oh, but there are others," Sister Abedago assured her. "Many others. And dozens are here tonight. I will make sure you meet one of them."

They stopped talking as Colonel Shawkey, pressing an earpiece for an incoming radio command, held up his finger for silence. After several seconds, he nodded and grumbled, "Yes, sir. We will hold the line."

Looking up, the colonel tapped the earpiece again and addressed his charges in the backseat. "Things have grown quite serious," he said. "Our intelligence confirms the approach of a large force from the north, definitely headed our way. They are Islamic extremists, very dangerous and armed to the teeth. It is too late to evacuate the worship grounds, so we will have to keep everyone contained here and defend the perimeters. None of them know what is happening, and we must keep it that way as long as we can. It is the best we can do."

"I'd like to fight with you, sir," Lloyd offered in a grim voice. "I'm ex–Navy Seal, and I have several good weapons with me."

The colonel gave him his second appraising glance of the day, seemingly in search of a second opinion. His eyes passed over Lloyd's broad shoulders, fit frame, and level gaze. "All right. But you obey my orders. No freelancing, understand?"

"Yes, sir."

"What about me?" Abby complained to Lloyd. "Aren't you here to guard and protect me?"

"You're not going to be anywhere near that stage," Lloyd snapped. "I'm going to have you sequestered in a secure location."

"No, you're not. I didn't come here to cower in some lockup. I came here to meet these people."

"Did you come here to get killed?"

"I came here ready to die."

Lloyd rolled his eyes and laughed. "I'm sorry, Abby. I admit, I was testing you," he said. "I'd lock you away if I could, but I know how much good that would do."

"That's right. You just *try* to keep me from these people." Abby turned to Shawkey. "By the way, where are all of the worshipers?" she asked.

"We're coming in from the ministers' entrance!" Shawkey called back with a smirk on his face, as Abby had nearly strained her neck trying to spot the assembly grounds. "If we entered on the main route, we'd never arrive!"

Thinking of six hundred thousand attendees and all the vehicles they must have taken along, Abby realized that the man had a point.

But what Abby did not anticipate was the wall of photographers awaiting them. The trucks roared into a circular driveway adjoining a large tin-roofed building, braked hard and skidded to a stop. Like an ambush of waiting commandoes, the paparazzi unleashed a blinding volley of flashbulbs at Abby's Humvee. Almost by reflex, she grasped her jacket over her face. Then, reminding herself that she was no criminal and had nothing to hide, she remembered to trust the colonel's men and turned to face the exit ahead.

Shawkey's soldiers had lined up before her door and shoved away a narrow yet secure corridor between the vehicle and the building's front door. The reporters' shouts ignited into a roar. The flashes of lights aimed at her were so overwhelming, they seemed intent on searing her retinas.

Abby kept her seat and did not blink. For she was not looking at them. Her eyes were closed as she desperately begged God for the strength to make a mad dash. A few seconds passed. Finally, concluding that she would have to launch into the run to find out if God had answered her prayer, she opened her eyes. There hovered Sister Abedago's face, soft and filled with concern.

"Are you ready?" she asked Abby. "I hooked this Mr. Lloyd to prevent him from leaving without you."

Abby turned. The cameraman jumped out and instantly blended with the mob, just one more of the media horde. Lloyd sat perched half in and half out of the Hummer's seat, machine gun in hand, one eye on the surrounding chaos and another on Abby. He flashed her a smile and jerked his head to encourage her along.

"Let's go, shall we?" he said with forced good nature.

She leaned forward and felt the two friends' hands bear her up. Clumsily, they climbed out of the Humvee and started for the ministers' door. The clamor from the reporters tripled in volume. She heard callously shouted questions.

"Why are you here, Miss Sherman?"

"Do you believe in faith healing?"

"Why abandon your family now?"

"Are you in fact dying?"

Thankfully the two hands under her arms bore her down the gauntlet. From somewhere that felt far away, she heard Lloyd shout dire warnings to everyone near if she was hurt. She smiled, although it did seem like her protector had slipped into a surly mood of sorts. The bombardment of flashbulbs, shouts, and helicopter noise reached another crescendo, and for a second she felt more like a criminal than a free person on her way to a worship service.

Then, finally, she was through. A door opened and she entered a hushed, well-lit hallway, lined with wonderfully dressed Nigerians staring at her. Strangely they seemed to Abby as though they were spinning slightly. And then sliding sideways.

After a moment of shocked inertia, the observers converged on her and a dozen arms stopped her fall. In Abby's ears, the photographers' raucous shouts were now replaced with cries and shrieks of encouragement, along with rapid-fire bursts of prayer language from every side.

Luckily, Sister Abedago was beside her to restore order.

"You all stand back and just pray, you hear?" she shouted, more confident here than she had ever sounded in the Humvee. "We need a healing service for this young sister, and now! Is there a woman with the gift, an *Iya Agba*, anywhere on the platform? What about Sister Okoye? Is she here?"

Just hearing Sister Abedago speak those words shot a thrill of hope straight into Abby's veins. She felt herself recover and stood up at last.

"I . . ." she began haltingly, "I don't want to interrupt anything. I just want to speak with this Sister Okoye in private, and then perhaps watch some of the Gathering. That's all."

"But this is a blessing to all of us," cried a nearby woman, a young beauty with stunning ebony skin and a lilting, almost melodious voice. "Maybe you don't realize, but we've known of your arrival since five minutes after you landed. Ever since then, we have prayed for God not only to spare you and your group, but that He would lead you to us. You see, we had no idea where you'd be headed. And now to see you here! Will you not let this body of believers minister to you?"

The passion in the young woman's plea clearly melted Abby's resistance, for her eyes softened and she turned to the group with an amiably defeated look.

A cheer engulfed the hallway.

CHAPTER
_27

NEW YORK CITY, CENTRAL PARK

Only one participant in the tense conversation was even physically present. The Scythian Elder who inhabited the palatial Central Park penthouse now stood with his hands planted on his hips, facing a large plasma television in a vast room a real-estate prospectus had once christened *The Parlor*.

The other party to the exchange, glad that he was absent in the flesh, tried his best to diplomatically admonish his boss over a remote speaker.

"With all due respect, sir," said the disembodied voice, "you're mistaken. Not only are we *not* losing control, but everything is actually in place and moving rapidly toward our complete victory. I assure you, Brother. The pieces are exactly where we want them."

"Where is the girl?"

"She is inside for the moment, but she's about to be brought to the podium for some kind of healing nonsense. She won't live two minutes once she hits that stage. Our Islamic friends will strike the moment she walks out. And if they should happen to miss her, Dylan will finish the job. And then it will be a cakewalk. A massacre, to be candid."

"I'm in the mood for a massacre, to be honest with you. This operation has sorely tried my nerves. It has required far too much scrambling and improvisation for my taste. Far too much of what the French would call *débrouillage*—the art of untangling oneself from one's mistakes."

"I understand. But given the fluidity and chaotic nature of this whole situation, couldn't we view that as a compliment to our man in the field, rather than a failure?"

"We'll see, Shadow Leader. The coming hour will determine the fate of many, many souls, will it not, my friend?"

LAGOS-BENIN CITY HIGHWAY, NIGERIA

The massive crowd assembled for that day's session of the Believers Gathering was just ending a soaring chorus of "Lord Most High," a favorite praise song, all with the help of a two-hundred-person choir, a gifted song leader and rock band, when things began to truly rock.

Before the last note had even finished echoing across the vast human expanse, the Gathering's host, Reverend Evelyn Ebando, one of the most revered of Nigeria's female pastors, took the pulpit with a stunned look on her face. "My brothers and sisters," she began, then paused for the loudspeakers to carry her final syllables to the edge of the crowd, "we have prayed mightily. And I am here to inform you that she is here. Sister Abigail is in our midst. This Gathering, this assembly turned out to be her destination!"

A veritable tsunami of cheers and applause rose and rolled over the woman. She took one step back, then another. Although she seemed about to fall over backward, the ecstasy on her face confirmed that she was in fact fine. *Just fine.*

She turned and motioned for Abby to walk out. After some shuffling of bodies, the backstage crowd parted. Held up by Sister Abedago and a strapping young man in a broad-shouldered suit, Abby stepped forward with the halting gait of one using her last ounce of strength.

Amazingly, the ovation grew in volume. Doubled in intensity and power.

She reached the podium, gripping its sides, and her helpers stepped back. As the greeting crescendoed she stood motionless, blinking, staring at what sprawled before her.

Blinked. Stared.

Concentrated very hard on continuing to breathe.

And all the while, a massive roar of love and greeting rose from beyond the stage to wash over her in deafening waves.

Breathe . . .

You can do it, Abigail.

Problem was, her eyes simply could not process the scene before her, the sea of humanity, the sheer scale of it all. What lay beyond the stage seemed to violate some law of nature. You simply weren't designed to see humanity in this kind of abundance. The human faces, all crowded together into such a profusion. Individual bodies standing close to each other and swaying as if from some invisible breeze, forming a single, intricate quilt that stretched half a mile from horizon to horizon. The endless smiles, one after the other, and in infinite variety. The shimmering dresses of turquoise and cerulean and purple and white, crowned by head wraps of diverse shape and hue.

It all struck Abby as the most beautiful of sights. In another realm, another sense that her soul found truest, this vast array of souls gathered in one place seemed perfectly natural, a vestigial image ingrained deep inside of her, one which had never been coaxed into betraying its presence . . . until now.

The ovation finally subsided. It was time for her to speak. She had avoided thinking about this moment and therefore had not composed anything. She closed her eyes, breathed a quick prayer, and began to speak.

"My brothers and sisters, this is a great and fearful day for me. To say that God has led me here is without a doubt the greatest understatement I may ever speak."

She took another deep breath and during the pause realized with astonishment that the crowd had fallen silent.

"He's led me here without a doubt, and I'm not entirely sure why. Some of you believe He led me here to be healed. And while I don't presume to know His purposes, I can tell you that this wasn't in my own thoughts. And yet, as I've been told that amazing signs and wonders happen here in Nigeria, which would be considered unbelievable back in my so-called Christian country, I would never reject that possibility. Without being melodramatic, I must tell you that His reason may be for me to die here among you today. Like all of us are, I am dying. And this would be a wonderful day, and a wonderful place, to go and be with Him. Here, with all of you."

A tentative ripple of applause and cheers arose in response.

"And, although some of you may know this—and I have no idea whether or when Mara McQueen airs here in Nigeria—but the Lord recently erased all my misgivings about going to be with Him. You see, I believe with one hundred percent certainty that He showed me what awaits all of us who know Him. I can tell you . . ."

"Shadow Man, are you in position? Everything ready?"

The voice stuttered with bits of static and distortion, but considering that it was being bounced from three satellites all the way from New York City, Dylan thought it remarkably clear.

At that moment Dylan sat perched just below a light pole at the rooftop of a tin building backing up to the assembly stage. The spot afforded him an unbroken panoramic view of the surroundings: from the stage to the nearly 360-degree-wide audience to the outermost edges of the site. He could see also, merely because he had been given their positions, where Colonel Shawkey's men had stationed themselves at the rear of the crowd to buffer an initial onslaught.

"Yes, Shadow Leader. Everything is in place and proceeding perfectly. Our mark is just seconds away from her final position."

"And the defenses?"

"They have no idea what's coming. They're good soldiers, but they're few and outmatched. Over and out."

Dylan knew he had rushed an ending to the conversation, but he had intended to. Given all the thoughts tumbling over each other in his brain, Shadow Leader was the last person he wanted to talk to.

On every op until now, Dylan had always found it a worthwhile exercise to warm up by mentally picturing the hit, over and over again. In fact, the ritual had evolved over the years into an essential part of his preparations. But today, he simply could not force himself to even begin. Trying to picture Abby, of all people, in his scope's crosshairs, then watch his finger mercilessly squeeze the trigger to send a bullet hurtling through her brain—he just couldn't bring himself to conjure the mental image.

He could feel a moment of nearly suicidal choices rushing toward him, but felt powerless to either stop it or delay its coming. Neither choice would be simple, easy or painless; he knew that with a cold certainty.

And yet, as much as he dreaded its arrival, Dylan felt that if the moment didn't come soon, he would doubtless go insane.

CHAPTER
_28

Abby was still speaking, in a halting but heartfelt voice, when Reverend Ebando walked up behind her and gently placed a hand upon her shoulder. The reverend looked at Abby with kind, deep-set eyes and a warm smile, and said, "I'm sorry to interrupt, my dear sister, but I feel the Lord leading me to introduce you to Sister Okoye."

At the sound of that name Abby abruptly stopped speaking and turned to see the newcomer. The two locked eyes. Something passed between them that was both mysterious and quite visible to the audience. For her own part, Abby froze midway through offering her hand to be shaken. Again, she blinked and stared.

Then her face twisted, and she began to weep uncontrollably.

Abby cried not in a guarded way but in an abandoned, childlike flood of tears. Her knees began to waver, and Reverend Ebando had begun moving forward to offer support when suddenly Sister Okoye stepped in with a forbearing smile and wrapped Abby in her arms.

"What is it, my Sister?" she whispered into Abby's hair.

"I've seen you before," Abby managed to stutter between gasps. "I've met you."

"How is that, dear?" Okoye asked in a tone of voice remarkably clear of incredulity.

Abby pulled back to look at her again. "I saw you in heaven."

The woman stared at Abby, the breath seemingly torn from her lungs.

"It's true," Abby continued. "I saw you with a group of others. It's the mystery—the great question that drove me here. Who you, and all the others, were. Why He showed all of you to me. And now, here you are. Right here. Alive."

"My dear, does your spirit bear witness as mine does?"

"I can tell that we're bound, somehow. I feel like you're family, just as I did at the gates of heaven, where I first saw you."

"*Iya Agba.* It means Seer. Watcher. A gift you did not choose."

"Yes. That's why I'm here."

"But I am not only here to meet you. I am here to do much more. This is a great and terrible day, and I am here to pray for your healing."

Sister Okoye turned to the microphone. The crowd had never stopped its murmuring during the private whispers between the two women. Yet despite not knowing the precise nature of their conversation, the Nigerian believers were mature enough to know that something mighty was brewing.

"Brothers and sisters," Okoye began in the traditional way, "I am about to lay hands on our dear Abigail. And with the whole world watching, I beg you to pray with me as never before that the seed of death inside this dear girl will be destroyed in Jesus' name!"

At the farthest edge of the horizon—a hazy fringe where the carpet of humanity seemed to finally thin out and shimmer into forest—a faint row of gray dots rose silently into the sky and began to grow. They did not stay distant for long, for they were overflying the tree-tops at a full intercept speed of nearly two hundred miles an hour.

They were not, as some of the first worshipers to spot them casually assumed, more media helicopters. Their doors stood open, and from those gaping apertures bristled automatic weapons well known to veterans of a century's worth of Nigerian conflicts.

Islamic insurgents, hidden just beyond the perimeter, took that very first hum of rotor blades as their cue to launch a simultaneous volley of mortar rounds upon Colonel Shawkey's outlying positions.

The result was a single thunderous boom which seemed, to those who would describe it later, as a sonic complement to the great cheer that had just risen from the Gathering.

When a chattering of machine-gun fire broke out in reply, however, the worshipers farthest back immediately knew the truth.

Like a great football audience performing the wave, the human sea turned as one toward the back of the site. Already, five columns of smoke, punctuated by cores of flame, uncoiled into the sky.

And now, instead of joyful voices lifted in praise, there came the sound of screaming.

"Operation Intercept is under way," Dylan declared into his headpiece. "Ground attack has commenced."

"Shadow Man, do you hear me? I'm watching the networks. They're all carrying it, and they all note a disturbance at the rear of the audience, but they haven't moved their cameras! They're still fixated on the girl and this old woman!"

"Give it a second. Fatalities are already mounting."

"No! I will not wait! This old woman is doing something to her, and if the coverage goes on a moment longer, then they've won! They've won, you hear me?"

"*Who* has won, Shadow Leader? You never explained this."

"Forget it! Just follow orders. Obey now, before it's too late! Take the shot yourself!"

"I can't. The old woman's draped herself over her. Unless I take them both out . . . but I can't do this surgically."

"Doesn't matter. Take them both out, take out the whole Christian trash heap, I don't care. Just stop it!"

Christian trash heap—the odd excessiveness of the phrase gave Dylan a moment's pause. He was already on fire now with curiosity about just what Shadow Leader had failed to brief him on earlier— the supposedly ironclad rationale for "harvesting" this young girl in the first place. But now this strange, hateful term. It seemed to push the absurdity of this whole operation right over the top.

The moment is here, Dylan . . .

. . . make your choice.

Seething with unfocused anger at the dilemma now upon him, he returned his sniper rifle to the two women at the podium, searching for an opening, some random development that would take the conscious decision away from him.

"Hey! Lloyd! The fighting's begun! Who are you aiming at?"

Dylan pulled away and looked down, swiveling his rifle barrel with him. The voice belonged to Colonel Shawkey, who was rushing by with three of his men, their weapons at the ready.

"Come with me, Lloyd," Shawkey ordered. "We need you at the rear. No freelancing, remember?"

At that moment, Dylan's world groaned into a slow-motion, gray-tinged nightmare. A snail's world where the point of his index finger grazing the trigger loomed as large as a mountain. And where the sweet spot at the center of Shawkey's forehead, its every bead of sweat and buried capillary, seemed to throb in anticipation of a bullet.

"Lloyd? I'm serious!" warned Shawkey's stern voice from a place seemingly far away.

Dylan yanked himself into real time, jerked his weapon away and fired two rounds in Shawkey's direction. The colonel's men stiffened and shouldered their weapons to fire, but the sound of bodies falling just behind them stopped their motion.

They turned.

It was not Colonel Shawkey dropping to the ground like a rag doll, but a pair of jihadist gunmen who had been running up from behind, clearly intent on murdering them. The two now lay quivering in their death throes.

Colonel Shawkey and his men turned back around to face Lloyd. The colonel stared from the man's face to his still-smoking gun barrel.

"I need to stay here," Dylan said, his face a bit dazed. "I'm covering the podium."

Colonel Shawkey quickly cut his eyes over to Abby and Sister Okoye. He nodded and said, "You do that." And they strode away.

Dylan returned his aim to the two women, who, swaying together, had yet to leave the stage.

ST. LOUIS, MISSOURI—THAT VERY MOMENT

A guard walked up to the cell door just as the charge nurse settled back down from her tiptoe look through the observation window. The windows were all too high; it was the way the place had been built. Since the facility had been constructed sixty years before as a prison, not a mental hospital, this was far from the only indignity visited by its design upon the nursing staff.

"Patient 64," she half whispered to the guard, who was already pulling out his nightstick. "You know how docile she usually is—only reason she's in here is her delusional state, not her behavior. But I've never seen her this agitated."

The guard walked up to the tiny window and glanced in. Patient 64, a white woman in her early fifties, looked as disheveled and disoriented as he'd ever seen her. Eyes bugged open, she walked manically the length of her cell, turned around, repeated the short trip, all the while shouting, "God save her! God save her!"

The guard turned back. "Has she hurt herself? Hit the walls, even?"

"No. I just don't know if she's going to escalate."

"Well, it's God she's harassing," he said in a sarcastic tone. "I don't know how high she can escalate from there. . . ."

The nurse rolled her eyes and walked away.

JERUSALEM—ALSO THAT MOMENT

It was almost sunset when the monk found her cot empty, its former occupant facedown on the still-scalding surface of the roof, moaning softly. Convinced that her weakened state had taken a turn for the worse, he jumped down and began to ease her backward by the shoulders.

She turned to him with an exasperated look.

"Brother Brehan, I am fine. I assure you. I was in urgent prayer!"

Mortified, the monk released her and stepped back. "I am so very sorry, my sister. Please forgive me."

But she did not answer. She was already back down on her face, her arms and legs now extended outward as abject and prostrate as she could stretch them.

The monk took three more steps back, his gaze still fixed on her. In all the years she had been up here, he had never seen her adopt such a desperate posture. He stared closer. Was it delusion? Some kind of grandiose personality disorder?

He listened for the words of her supplication.

". . . dear God, my dear God, will you spare her, whoever she is? Wherever she may be? And heal the breach?"

BELIEVERS GATHERING, NIGERIA

Although Abby and Sister Okoye could hear and sense the growing commotion on every side, a sense of driving intention fell upon them. They both, without saying it to the other, became filled with a mutual adamancy to finish the prayer.

Abby could not tell whether Okoye was praying in an African dialect or a prayer language. What she did know was that the healing was proving a bizarre and harrowing experience. The woman, who at closer look appeared to be in her sixties, seemed intent on forcing the illness from Abby's body by pressing with increasing strength on her side. As Abby was already in great pain, the pressure quickly became excruciating.

Beyond that, her strange gifting had chosen this moment to shift into overdrive. A kaleidoscope of spiritual impressions reeled through her in a dazzling yet mind-numbing cavalcade. Images, rainbow spectra, strange colors, beautiful voices—all these and more flooded through her conscious mind and threatened to overpower her.

As if that wasn't enough, the torrent of strange words pouring from Sister Okoye's mouth grew in volume with every second the woman did not receive satisfaction. Abby winced and wondered how long this could continue without some sort of resolution.

Suddenly, Okoye stiffened and jerked backward with a loud, plaintive sigh. Her hand remained on Abby, but the grip relaxed and the cadence of Sister Okoye's prayers changed abruptly.

"Dear God, take it, take it . . ." she said in almost a lament.

The sense of anticipation became nearly unbearable.

JERUSALEM

"Sister? Sister? Are you sure you're all right?"

The woman was rolling around the burning roof dust like a veritable autistic, and that was something the monks had never counted on. Some sort of noise was issuing from her mouth, but the lone monk in charge here on the rooftop could not tell if it was speech or dying sentiments.

Brother Brehan bent down to hear, to try to wrest some closure from this impossible dilemma.

"What is it, my sister? Can we be of help?"

She did not look up but pulled back from the surface an inch or two. Caked onto her smooth cheeks was the dust of two days' prostration. She continued to pray without pausing to address these simpletons and their cardiac paranoias.

"Dear God, take it, please take this from her, whoever, wherever she is. . . ."

CHAPTER
_29

Sister Okoye's shift in position had finally afforded Dylan the shot he'd been waiting for. He steadied his grip, slowed his breathing, and began to tighten his finger on the trigger.

Apparently, he noted with a resigned sort of detachment, he was going to make his choice by letting the force of habit carry him straight through the moment. A lazy method, perhaps even a cop-out, but it seemed preordained somehow. The way it appeared destined to unfold.

He centered the crosshairs on the back of Abby's neck, but then lost his focus to the explosions and gunfire shattering the air on every side. He felt something foreign on his face, then realized that tears were running down his cheeks.

Get it together! he warned himself.

What was it? he asked himself as his finger hesitated on the rifle's trigger. *What had Shadow Leader said?*

". . . what this young woman threatens to unravel is incredibly dangerous. Dangerous to the whole world, in ways I could take days to explain to you. She cannot be allowed to continue. . . ."

A question emerged and refused to vanish, even as he tried to shake it off and finish his job. What observation from his forty-eight hours in this girl's company had confirmed even one iota of Shadow Leader's assertion?

And what had that assassin told him? The one Shadow Leader had sent to supposedly "train" him?

"... *these are men who wouldn't bat an eyelash at killing a child.*"

They'd been the man's final words, just before Shadow Leader had unceremoniously put a bullet in his head.

You can't turn back now, another voice told him. *You're a professional. Your client's seven-figure down payment is already in your Swiss account, drawing interest. You're in too far. You've never before aborted a job, you fool . . .*

He tightened his finger to what he estimated to be three pounds of trigger tension. One and a half more pounds to go and the choice would be made. And hopefully these yammering voices in his head would shut up.

He pulled a tiny bit harder . . .

. . . on the stage, Sister Okoye seemed to go limp. She reared back, her right hand still planted on Abby's side.

Then Abby began to jerk stiffly, like someone being electrocuted. Her mouth lay open, though it wasn't clear whether this was in sheer joy or mute suffering.

. . . Dylan blinked one last time, then focused his gaze.

No way. There is no way . . .

A large, luminous being had just appeared in front of the pair, blocking his aim. Not only did this . . . creature have its eyes focused squarely on him, but he was holding up his hand.

A clear gesture.

Stop.

You're going crazy! Dylan admonished himself. He gritted his teeth. *Get it together and do your job! Kill the girl. If your intel was wrong, that's not your fault. You were trained to do what you were told, by far more accountable sources.*

He lowered his cheek to the rifle again, resolved to just pull the stinking trigger and be done with it.

He blinked in disbelief. *Now there were four of the beings, forming a ring around the two women.*

Fine. He'd shoot these ghosts first . . .

He pulled, felt the trigger give way, heard the blast. Winced as recoil drove the rifle butt back into his shoulder.

But he knew, almost after the fact, that he'd pulled his shot off to the side. Missed on purpose.

He saw the muzzle blast drive through one of the being's shoulder. The driving projectile seemed to smudge the ethereal body as a tiny finger would a fresh sketching of pastel. If not the bullet itself, at least a strange coil of turbulence, a tiny smoke-like curl.

Did the being flinch at its passage? Did its face even budge? At first, Dylan thought so, and just as quickly could not remember. All he could see now was the slightest trace of something like disappointment coming over the being's face, even as it continued to stare straight at him.

It melted away. Then the other three too.

From the ring they had protected, a blinding starlike flash of light erupted where Sister Okoye's hand met Abby's side.

Dylan felt himself fall backward, propelled by the brilliance magnified in his rifle scope. Free air, then a shocking pain—the impact of stage flooring against his back. He contorted himself in agony.

Rolling on the floor, he looked over at the podium through partly blinded eyes. Through roving spots of black and brown he barely made out the two women, who now were kneeling, intact, holding each other. Obviously celebrating something.

He scrambled to a sitting position, panting furiously, his gaze wide and terrified. He threw down his rifle and stood impulsively, stupidly. Good way to get himself killed. But he didn't care just then. He'd made his choice.

No way would Dylan Hatfield take out an innocent girl, no matter what. And no way was he going to defy a being such as the one he'd just encountered. He knew this with the unshakable certainty of someone whose destiny had just walked up and introduced itself to him, like a stranger offering a handshake.

Not only did his employer's arguments not add up, but the assignment didn't add up to *him*. And he knew that whatever pretext had been fabricated to justify killing someone like Abby had to be a lie. He might never find out why, but he would also never come this close again. He would not tiptoe over that moral precipice.

He chose good. Right.

And maybe, immediate death.

Abby!

His voice hardly carried across the stage, given all the screaming and detonations shattering the air around them. He just had to tell her. Tell her, and then follow through on his words. Turn from her undercover assassin into her genuine protector. He had helped to set in motion this homicidal deception; helped locate, recruit, and plan the operation from the United States just before taking off for Lagos. The jihadist attack now upon them had been his clever way to get rid of the target without casting suspicion on anything other than Islamic terrorism. However, he had never intended for there to be this much loss of life. He'd designed the diversionary attack to consist of shots fired over the crowd's heads, scary flashes of light and harmless explosions intended to send everyone scattering and so disguise Abby's murder. Nothing more.

Nevertheless, he had set this thing in motion. And now that he'd defected to the other side, he wasn't sure how to turn it off.

He now turned his attention to the huge crowds and the carnage taking place among them. Another, lesser-trained operative would have found it impossible to do his job in this madness of blood-curdling screams, gunfire, and explosions. But Dylan had been specifically trained to take his shots regardless of any mayhem occurring around him. Now everything he had blocked out assaulted his conscience like a hammer blow.

He assessed the situation. Scowling, he glanced all around him. And then he saw it: a trail of strafer bullets, cutting a swath of death through the very center of the assembly. He mentally computed its path.

It would lead straight through the center of the podium!

He jumped up and, while shouting at the top of his lungs, began sprinting toward Abby. . . .

Something's happened to me. The message pulsated through Abby's entire body, while at the same moment she saw Lloyd fall out of the sky and then run madly toward her.

Something profound and incredible had just taken place in her body. The fog slowly began to clear and she looked around for Sister Okoye. The woman lay prone on the stage floor, her limbs slightly shaking. Abby threw herself on her friend's body and pulled her up.

"You are healed, my Sister," Okoye said to her with a smile.

"Is that what it is?" Abby cried.

Just then Lloyd struck them both with all the brutality of a linebacker. Her newly healed limbs once again screamed in pain as she slid across the stage, along with both Lloyd and Sister Okoye.

Bewildered, she glanced behind her, at the site of the collision.

There, punching upward a uniform row of pockmarks and sending up small showers of sawdust, came the approaching row of bullets. And there it continued, right through the spot where she had been lying just seconds before. She started to flail around for Lloyd, but he was too quick, his hands already pulling her up, and then doing the same for Sister Okoye.

"Let's go!" Abby called out to him.

Abby rushed to help Sister Okoye to her feet, and together the pair scurried with their protector off the bloodstained platform.

If Lloyd had been given more time to analyze the voice he had just heard, and the body from which it had just escaped, he would have realized that one Abby Sherman might have stepped slowly up to that podium, but another Abby Sherman had just stood and run from it. The ailing young woman he'd come to know had since undergone a complete transformation.

Meanwhile, Mara McQueen's expert cameraman had somehow remained functional and stationary during the entire massacre. And although he was here to cover the story of Abby Sherman's bizarre journey to Nigeria, the cameraman suddenly found himself recording history in the making—the brutal attack on the assembly as well as a jumpy glimpse of Abby's escape.

And then it was over, both the main assault and the brief resurfacing of Abby Sherman. For no matter how thoroughly they scoured the parking lots and roads surrounding the Believers Gathering site, the authorities would later find no more trace of either Abigail Sherman, the man known only as Lloyd, or Sister Okoye, whom Christians-in-the-know also called "Mummy Iya Agba."

BELIEVERS GATHERING, LAGOS-BENIN
CITY HIGHWAY, NIGERIA

That day's attack went down in history as the bloodiest and most galling example of religious fratricide to stain the African continent that whole year. By the time the remaining insurgents fell back and seemingly melted into the bush, over 300 Christian believers had died. As for the number of slain attackers, the numbers varied widely between the army's official estimate of 425, the media's number of 78, or local eyewitnesses' accounts of three or four dozen bodies lying in a dismal heap right in front of the stage.

Almost as dismaying to the Christians of southern Nigeria, however, was the fact that even though the world press had fixed its eagle eye on the Believers Gathering that day, the only story which survived into the following news cycle was not that of their people being massacred, but of the appearance and mysterious disappearance of Abby Sherman.

By the time press-pooled footage of Abby's cryptic speech, her bizarre contortions with Sister Okoye—who soon became a house-hold name in her own right—and her narrow brush with death was analyzed and talk-showed into oblivion, the attack itself seemed to have been reduced to a convenient catalyst, a mere backdrop for the main event.

Nigerians who had lost their loved ones on that horrific day had another perspective on the matter.

Yet, thankfully, many of them pointed to Abby's speech itself as their solace. The young American had described for them her visit to heaven and the incredible peace that had since come over her. For those forced by the day's later events to contemplate eternity in a fresh new light, her words proved life-changing.

Of all the facets of this story that kept it *page one* worldwide, how-ever, the one aspect most compelling in the hours and days to follow was the simple question, *Where in the world did Abby and her friends go?*

OUTSIDE THE BELIEVERS GATHERING—
LATER THAT AFTERNOON

The simple explanation for Abby, Lloyd (or *Dylan*) and Sister Okoye's unlikely, and nearly invisible, escape was that it had been aided by the giftings of not one but two Iya Agbas.

After the threesome had run from the stage, they had not stepped ten feet inside the ministers' shelter when Okoye had stopped, her eyes blinking rapidly, and warned them of evil approaching. They then made an abrupt turn and raced down a flight of stairs into a basement area when, just as Okoye had warned, a phalanx of radical Islamic guerrillas burst onto the floor above them and mowed down a dozen prominent Nigerian clergymen, all in a matter of seconds.

Fearing the gunmen would follow the stairs and find them hiding below, the three rushed to the far end of the dark basement where a bend in its corrugated tin wall had allowed a sliver of sunlight to intrude. From there they heard the appalling massacre as it was taking place above them.

Unwilling to exit into an unknown location, Lloyd had fished out a small mirror and positioned it on the other side of the wall to have a look. After quickly pulling back the mirror, he warned them with alarm in his eyes that escaping from here was out of the question. Three enemy pickups sat parked right outside the shelter wall with aft-mounted fifty-millimeter guns at the ready.

Sister Okoye laid a calming hand on Lloyd's shoulder and told him that, despite the threatening presence, it was safe for them to pass that way.

"You're crazy," he said. "I'm telling you, there're men out there with their fingers on triggers right this second, aimed this way. We wouldn't make it two yards."

Okoye smiled and glanced at Abby. "Sister Abigail, do you wish to tell him why we *can* pass this way?"

Indeed, Abby had snapped back to the present and told him with a smile, "Because there's a mighty warrior angel, Captain of the Ranks, standing right outside this wall, ready to blind their eyes."

Lloyd began to protest again, but then he remembered the reason why he was here and stopped himself. Had he not halted his killing because of supernatural sights—a flash of light which seemed to have healed Abby? Glowing beings guarding the pair?

"All right," he said. "I still wonder if this isn't suicide, but if you'll let me go first, I'm willing to give it a try." He pulled a handgun from a side pocket in his pants and quickly checked its load. Then, scrambling down gun first, he squeezed himself through the wall's small opening.

The two women stood and watched each other, waiting for Lloyd's "all clear." It came as a soft *thump* on the metal wall. Next, Sister Okoye clambered down and disappeared. Abby, now more at ease with the reliability of her Sight, followed eagerly. She rose up in a twilit strip of grass, crowded with pickup trucks, seething with men and their demonic controllers, and in her myopic surface vision she'd failed to look up and notice the angel her Sight had shown her just a moment before.

Lloyd was standing motionless before the pickup's grill, immobilized by either fear, wonder at his not being detected, or some combination of both. As Abby dusted herself off, Sister Okoye nudged

Lloyd's shoulder and roused him back to reality. "Come with us, warrior man," she teased him with a decided edge to her voice.

They took off running, away from the trucks and the shooting, and toward the trees. The men with the guns never looked their way. And the cameras, which remained fixed on the official entrance to the ministers' shelter, never caught them as they hid behind a helicopter and waited thirty seconds before sprinting into the nearby forest, just after a patrol of jihadist killers sauntered by.

CHAPTER
_31

Within minutes of their escape, Abby found herself jogging through knee-high grass behind Lloyd and Sister Okoye along a lush green wall marking the edge of Nigeria's rain forest. She did not yet realize that behind this very rampart of leaf and vine, equatorial jungle stretched across a broad swath of coastal Nigeria all the way east to the Cameroon border.

Mere hundreds of yards behind them, isolated rounds of gunfire still popped every few minutes. Screams from the wounded and dying drifted over on a late afternoon breeze. Abby shivered and quickened her step each time one of the sounds reached her ears, for she could hardly wait to travel beyond earshot of the horrors.

Suddenly a shot rang out more loudly than the others. A faint whistle and a hiss came from the grass just beyond her head. Harsh shouts echoed behind them.

They'd been spotted.

Sister Okoye, who swiftly took the lead despite her age, did not give an outward sign of having heard anything. Instead, she surged ahead with several lunging strides, then turned left without warning and disappeared into the trees. Too hurried to even register her surprise, Abby followed.

A curtain of bright green leaves and vines tried to block her progress, but she just gritted her teeth and plowed ahead. Abby was too determined to be stopped or even slowed by anything like undergrowth. She pushed through, feeling leafy cords drape across her face and neck. Blinking, she forced her feet to propel her forward.

Abby opened her eyes. She was shocked to find, instead of gloom and shadows, a vaulted, leafy cavern. It was like stepping into a whole new world. They were in that interlude between late afternoon and evening when the sun expends the last of its light in an eerily diffuse glow. As a result, the entire forest seemed alight with an unearthly, radiant green.

Her head craned upward, toward the distant canopy. The only sounds reaching them now came from nearby: the chattering of birds, the piercing shrieks of howler monkeys, echoes of untraceable cries against the cavernous jungle roof. Closer still could be heard the slapping of their shoes, the unavoidable thump of their breathing.

Sister Okoye continued to amaze Abby with her competence and fitness. Still arrayed in her silk dress, the aging woman hiked the fabric about her knees and moved just as gracefully and tirelessly as the younger two. In fact, she was now their leader; it was Okoye who had run unerringly to the fringe of rain forest a third of a mile from the Gathering compound.

For Abby, a jungle that at any other time might have felt gloomy and dangerous now felt like a haven. Every step away from the horror behind them seemed like a mile toward safety and calm. Not to mention the chance to sit down with Sister Okoye and ask a few pertinent questions on the real purpose for this journey.

Roughly a half mile into the forest, Okoye's remarkable endurance ran out and she asked them for a pause. They stopped under a break in the canopy, where stars already twinkled in anticipation of dusk.

"It'll be nighttime soon," Lloyd warned. "Are we heading somewhere specific?"

Okoye smiled and said, "Yes. We are."

"Well? Are you going to tell us about it?"

She shrugged. "It is a place where we will be safe. Or safer—"

A helicopter thundered overhead. A spotlight beam shot through the canopy and lit up the ground at their feet. Behind them, a rustling in the leaves betrayed the approach of a group along the trail.

His eyes as large as quarters, Lloyd yanked the two women back from the trail and flat onto the forest floor. Their only shelter from the eyes of those approaching was a low depression in the ground and the trunk of a huge ginkgo tree.

Resentful of Lloyd's rough tactics, Abby looked up to see battered Nike shoes strike dirt just five feet away. Then, as she stared at the machetes and AK-47s dangling from their belts, the Islamic symbols stenciled on white headbands, she vowed never to find fault with Lloyd's tactics again.

Abby cringed, for her sense of cozy safeness in the jungle had just been dashed to pieces. The killers were actually on their trail!

The unthinkable happened—a loud shout, and then she looked up into a row of gun barrels trained at them. Faces staring into hers, filled with hatred. The truth sank in with a bitter tug at her insides.

They'd been caught!

The shouts multiplied into a storm of angry voices. The barrels motioned upward. *Stand!* The three slowly rose to their feet.

The disk of light from the helicopter found them, blinding them and beating their heads with the downdraft from its rotor blades.

Abby felt *fear*. And once again that smell assaulted her nostrils— so strong now that she could taste it like a bitter, metallic tablet on her tongue.

Sister Okoye met Abby's eyes and grabbed her hand. Abby blinked and then peered closer at the row of guerrillas. She almost jumped back at the horrors that greeted her sight. Every one of these men was almost wholly consumed by a group of the most grotesque and revolting evil spirits she had yet seen.

The middle guerrilla moved forward and leveled his machine gun at his waist, preparing to fire on them.

"Stop!"

It was Lloyd. He had his hands held high as though the gesture might stop the bullets. The guerrilla smirked at the desperate stall tactic and tensed his muscles again.

"Brotherhood!" Lloyd shouted.

The man relaxed a bit, scowling at Lloyd. "What you say?"

"I am the Brotherhood's man. The inside source."

"Then what you doin' out here with *them*?" he said with a con-fused expression.

"Finding out the Iya Agba safe house," Lloyd replied. "The old woman's taking us there."

The guerrilla said nothing but stared at Lloyd through an angry sneer. "Who's your boss?" he asked.

"Shadow Leader."

The man rolled his eyes, apparently placated. But not enough. He then asked, "What's the sign?"

Lloyd stepped forward, closer to the lead man, and pointed to the sickle blade that hung loosely at his waist. It was the last thing Shadow Leader had taught him about the Brotherhood before his departure for Los Angeles. The name of the Brotherhood. Their symbol and the instrument of their harvests.

"This," said Lloyd, pointing. "This is the sign. The scythe."

The man's face relaxed, and he nodded to Lloyd. He then made a sudden arm motion to the hovering chopper overhead. The spotlight blinked out and the chopper flew away. Next, he gestured to Lloyd to leave the two women and join the other men behind him. Lloyd quickly complied.

"What does this mean?" Abby whispered to Sister Okoye.

"It means he is a traitor," Okoye answered in a flat voice. "Could you not sense it? Did you not feel the darkness around him?"

Abby turned to the older woman, shaking her head. "I felt nothing of the sort," she said. Inwardly she chastised herself for having allowed her latent attraction to blind her to Lloyd's true character.

"So, if you are Shadow Man," the lead gunman said, "your final test, then." He tossed Lloyd an AK-47 rifle. "You do the harvest."

Still holding the machine gun in his left hand, Dylan held up the scythe in the other. The men had made a mistake. For a true Brotherhood harvest, he only needed the scythe, not the gun. He gripped the scythe by its handle in the proper manner, turning and examining its blade with a pensive expression on his face.

Then his arm recoiled suddenly, sending the blade whistling through the shadow. It struck the lead gunman across the throat and sliced open his jugular vein.

Before the others could react, Dylan swung the AK-47 into both hands and opened fire.

Abby shut her eyes from the scene and turned away. Sister Okoye did not flinch at all but stood without blinking and gazed steadily at men who would have surely killed her as they now jerked wildly and crumpled to the ground.

The gunfire ended. No one spoke as the smoke swirled upward in the humid air. One of the bodies twitched; Dylan stepped over and watched the dying man carefully, his weapon aimed at the man's neck. But he expired soon after, sparing Dylan from having to shoot him again.

Satisfied that all the men were dead and that he could relax his guard for at least a moment, Dylan lowered his barrel and glanced around him. His look landed right in the hostile glare of Abby Sherman. He did not meet her gaze, but his face hardened again into a professional veneer.

"Come on, let's get going," he said, motioning toward the forest's interior and hoping neither woman would want to hash things out just then. "We've made a lot of noise and you can count on serious pursuit."

"I'm not going anywhere," said Abby. "I'm confused, and I'm not moving until I get an explanation."

"You deserve one, Abby," he responded. "But we don't have time for it now. We really have to go."

The thunder of not one but two helicopters rolled overhead, their speeding shapes banking low and hard over the treetops. Undeniably looking for them once again.

The three stepped back against thick tree trunks. The choppers climbed and flew away.

"We don't have to go anywhere with you," added Sister Okoye. "I'm the only one who knows where we're headed. I'm the only one who can help us avoid your colleagues' patrols."

"Look, if things really were like those guys said, then why would I have killed them? Why would I have signed my own death warrant?"

"I don't know," Abby replied flatly. "That's exactly why I want an explanation."

He squeezed his eyes in frustration and glanced wearily at the embers of dying sunlight streaming through the trees.

"Okay. Short version. Am I a trained killer? Yes. Have I performed some unusually harsh missions on behalf of my country? Or for the cause of freedom? You bet. But was I reconciled to carrying out this particular mission and killing a girl? No way. Not even before I met you. Afterward, it got even worse. I've been delaying the moment of decision ever since I met you in that hospital room. I've saved your life a half dozen times today, ranging from the tarmac at Lagos to a minute ago in this very place. And I've made my choice—I've rejected the assignment and in doing so I've turned my back on every oath or principle of my profession. I've chosen something else, something I don't even know, instead of the pinnacle of my whole career. In the process, I just plopped my own head on the chopping block. The people I work for will never settle until I'm dead."

"So what's your real name, *Lloyd*?" Abby asked.

"Dylan . . ." He hesitated, realizing it had been over a decade since he had simply, plainly, given a new acquaintance his real name. "Dylan Hatfield."

"So, Dylan Hatfield, having come here with the express intention of killing me, what exactly changed your mind?"

Emboldened by her question, as well as the answer he knew he harbored, Dylan explained, "It all started with you, Abby. The more time I spent with you, the less I could picture you as the mortal danger I'd been told to expect. But that was just the beginning. The real clincher was what I saw when Sister Okoye laid her hands on you." He turned to the older woman. "I saw it, the moment you healed her. I saw *them* first. The angels, I guess you'd call them. They were standing and staring right at me. And then this flash of light flowed from your hands to Abby's side. I saw proof, Abby, and I just don't know what to make of it. None of it squares with what I believe. I feel unhinged. Afraid too, I mean at the implications of it all. But I decided then and there I wasn't going to kill you but instead try to save you. All I know now, though, is that I'm lost and confused. I'm completely over my head . . ."

With the fading of that sentence, Dylan's cheek began to twitch, his breathing to race, and his chest to heave of its own accord.

It took Sister Okoye to break the awkward impasse. "I believe you, young Dylan," she said. "I've searched my heart and tried to sense the spiritual firestorm raging around you right now. I see your soul, and I believe you are truly broken. But also on your way home. You made a good choice just now, actually several good ones today. For that reason, Dylan Hatfield, I will allow you to venture farther in with us."

"Thank you . . ." he said.

Abby could see him struggling to shed the pain and weakness from his face, to force a little of the former pride and competence back to his features.

"And now let us go," said Sister Okoye. "I have no cause to belittle this moment, but you made enough noise for three counties, and as you said yourself, there will be pursuit. So please, follow me."

And with that she began walking down the trail at a fast clip. Late afternoon had now turned to night, and by the time Abby could even fall into line behind her, the Nigerian had disappeared in the brush. Dylan, for his part, had a flashlight, and he was currently using it to see as he stripped the dead gunmen of every useful weapon and tool they'd had on them.

"Are you coming, young man?" came Sister Okoye's voice from somewhere in the gloom. "You were so anxious to leave."

"Yes, Sister, I thought I was," he called out to her between breaths. "But then I remembered the weapons these men were carrying. We may end up needing these more than food."

"We have *no* need of those whatsoever," she said sharply. "If you really wish to learn about God's power, then please set those aside. Let us rely on Him to rescue us. There has been far enough shooting of guns for one day."

Reluctantly, he let the bigger guns fall to the ground, then slipped the small sickle around his belt and a revolver into the back of his pants. With the flashlight in hand, he ran to catch up with the two women.

Abby found that her former misgivings about the jungle had come to roost after all. At night, the jungle turned into a deafening echo chamber of animal calls, exotic birds and wild beasts. If she looked up at the distant canopy and squinted, she could make out the friendly disk of a full moon. But focusing on the trail ahead, precious little of that yellow dribbled down to where she stood.

On one hand, Abby reveled in the feeling of newfound vitality in her limbs, the chance to exert herself and be a fully physical being after so many weeks of stagnation. On the other, the darkness and unfamiliarity of her surroundings oppressed her so deeply that if it had not been for the proximity of her companions, she might well have sank into a fetal position and whimpered in a ball until dawn.

Yeah, great security that would have been, she admonished herself at the thought. *You'd have been leopard bait inside the hour.*

CHAPTER

_33

Abby had run distances before, so she knew to send her mind down a fruitful and engaging line of thought as a distraction to the pain. But even as she tried, the sound of gunfire echoing across that precious ocean of people kept reverberating in her memory. The sight of all those faces suddenly splitting apart like the Red Sea before Moses' staff, their retreating feet and legs revealing the shapes of abandoned bodies, prone and bloodied on the ground.

Her thoughts traveled back even further, to the death of Narbeli.

All of them, she could hardly bring herself to admit, had been her fault, one way or another. Because of *her*. On account of who Abby was, or what she'd done, or some sorry combination of the two.

What was it, she wondered, *about this primal flight into a dark jungle that's releasing such painful thoughts?*

She almost bumped into Sister Okoye, who had stopped running all of a sudden. But instead of leaning forward with her hands on her knees, the old woman was ready for her. With a forceful right palm she grasped Abby's forehead, and with the other, cupped her neck.

"Sister Abigail, I can feel you getting attacked back here," she said. "Making the hairs stand up on the back of my neck! I mean, you are feeling oppressed, aren't you? In your thoughts? Just now?"

Mystified at the immediacy of the woman's gift, Abby could only nod.

"Well, then . . ." Sister Okoye's hands tightened around Abby's forehead and neck, and she began to pray in a loud, singsong voice. "My Lord, through your almighty power, take these little familiar demons and cast them so far back into the void from whence they came that even their own master will never remember anymore, ever again. I ask you to free young Sister Abigail from the dangerous invitation of her dark thoughts, and return to us the woman she can be, and will be again. I ask this in the most holy and mighty name of Jesus Christ, amen."

She released Abby, then turned back toward the path. "Now back on the road, you children. We have much more escaping to do before the light returns."

Indeed, it still felt like escape to all of them. Most of all to Abby, who felt breathless and grateful for having avoided another day in the hospital ward. She did have to admit that in her current famished state, even the horrid hospital food sounded like paradise. Yet starvation was not a compelling enough reason to regret being here. Her most compelling reason to rejoice in these surroundings was the sense she still harbored of a vast, homicidal army pursuing them from the forest's edge, just a few missteps away. In fact, thinking about it made her want to run that much faster.

Eventually jogging turned to brisk walking as the three followed the ancient path from thinner outlying groves into a far denser portion of the rain forest. Every few minutes the vegetation struck Abby as having thickened discernibly, along with the oppressive humidity. Now, over two miles in, they found themselves in genuinely stuffy, mosquito-infested jungle. Thankfully, the path proved well-worn and quite passable through even the thickest and blackest tunnels of vegetation.

Some time later—how long was unclear, as the mad escape was beginning to blur into an eternity of running in darkness—they descended into a broad moonlit valley along the opposing ridgeline. At its heart ran a narrow but lively stream whose waters struck Abby as alive in the evening light, cascading in briefly glimpsed silver splashes.

After following the creek for a while, Sister Okoye paused, glanced around her, then turned and began walking uphill through a lessening of undergrowth. Abby and Dylan found her crouched next to a small natural basin of glistening water.

"A spring," she said through a mouthful that dribbled from her chin as she spoke. "It's the only safe water source for miles. Drink up."

As they were all dying of thirst, her words were the only permission they needed. Soon both were on their knees, scooping up bracingly cold handfuls with sighs of contentment.

Satiated at last, the three sat still, breathing deeply and enjoying the sensation of being safe. For Abby, the jungle was provoking a set of contradictory reactions—at once fear and intimidation, but now, increasingly as time wore on, feeling welcomed into an infinitely rich and reassuring hiding place. A refuge.

"So what I want to know, Sister, is what happened when we were captured?" Dylan said. "I thought you could see dangers like that ahead of time!"

The old woman turned to Abby with a quizzical look, then back to him with a dose of hilarity playing across her features. "I am a human being, Dylan. The Sight comes and goes. It especially goes at times when I am overly fatigued."

"Well, thanks for telling me. I thought you were fail-safe; I'd stopped looking."

"You did just wonderful. If not for you, I'm sure Abby and I would not have been so lucky."

"I don't understand," he said. "I mean, here you've led us without a scratch through a live battlefield. And now, just when it looks like we've escaped, you imply that you have no guarantees."

"That's right," she replied. "That's because there is no substitute for a walk with God. Without Him, none of these giftings mean anything. The Sight comes from Him, and so do extra warnings that reach me when my body is otherwise engaged or deeply worn. Remember too that He uses everything and everybody. You, Dylan, gave us a warning. Who am I to say that it did not originate with Him?"

"Because I don't believe in Him," he said sharply.

"Oh, that doesn't matter. God can use you anyway."

"I seriously doubt that. So far I've only been used by the kind of people who would kill you rather than acknowledge they even exist."

"Dylan," Okoye continued, "if you don't believe in God, then why have you placed your trust, your very survival, in the hands of someone who depends utterly on Him?"

"Because you've proven yourself, that's why. I've never seen an ordinary street magician get it right as many times in a row as you have."

Okoye fell silent for a moment as though listening to a voice from far away.

"What is it?" he interjected. "Another danger?"

"Yes, I believe so," she said. "Sister Abby, do you feel it? Do you see what I am seeing?"

"No, I don't," Abby conceded. "I see nothing."

"What's the danger?" Dylan broke in again. "Please tell me what it is."

Abby looked at him strangely and backed up a step. She knew precisely what Okoye was about to say. But the import of it was shocking, even catastrophic.

"It's you, Dylan," she said, clearly and without inflection. "It's *you*."

"But I thought I'd made the right choice. Taken the right path."

"You did, but that was merely the beginning. You still do not know God, or anything of His ways. You still have no idea what it is to be a warrior in the realms of the Spirit."

"Sister Okoye," he said with a tinge of exasperation in his voice, "when it comes to being a warrior, please don't presume to teach me."

The older woman fixed him with a challenging gleam of the eye. "Oh, but I *will* presume, young man. And do not forget who is leading you right now, lest I send you to find your way back by yourself."

Dylan nodded, for there was no denying the older woman's mastery of the rain forest.

Which was why, when Okoye stood and took off again, the others followed without saying a word.

CHAPTER
_34

He was only three-quarters of the way across the Atlantic, yet from his telecommunications-laden captain's chair, Shadow Leader was already well under way in organizing a tightening knot of pursuit around the escaped girl and her accomplices three thousand miles hence.

He had acted with such swiftness partly out of a lifelong habit of extreme efficiency. In this case, however, that had been last among his motivations. Rather, the situation itself had imposed upon him more urgency than usual. In fact, he had left New York hyper-aware that the scythe was poised to swing toward him.

He had failed, and he knew the price for failure. He had already been warned. He had harvested that price many times himself. As a result, he had not waited for his superiors' responses to the initial failure in Nigeria. And he certainly wasn't going to wait on the initiative of his African counterparts. Instead, he chartered a private jet and vowed to travel there and extract a victory in person, no matter how brutal he had to be.

He was on the phone to one Nigerian general, on hold with one member of the Nigerian cabinet and a source at the NRO, the American National Reconnaissance Office, on the subject of acquiring real-time satellite data of the fugitives' escape path.

Then the call came from on high. The one he always dreaded.

"Shadow Leader," growled the voice from hell. "I see you have deemed it wise to take the initiative."

"I have indeed, sir. And things are going so well, we may have the situation in hand before I even land."

"Pray tell me?"

"Well, to begin with, within the hour I will have twice-hourly thermal images from the NRO."

"Please explain, my dear boy. You know I come from another generation. . . ."

"The National Reconnaissance Agency maintains all of America's intelligence satellite fleet. If they feel the need, they can provide imaging of any spot on earth, except for the poles, I assume, down to a one-foot radius and tasked according to a dozen different variables. The thermal, or heat-sensitive filter, does the best job of spotting human bodies against a wilderness background."

"And what does this pie-in-the-sky picture do for you?"

"First let me tell you about our mop-up assets on the ground. I have a third of the original attack squad, augmented by a hundred more jungle-trained guerrillas just waiting for the go-ahead. They'll be supported by three Nigerian Army Hueys, a dozen mortars, and one American-made cluster bomb, armed and loaded."

"Is that all?"

"Plus we have all the national borders sewn up. The Lagos air traffic control is on a heavy lookout for any unauthorized traffic. She won't be leaving by any airport, that's for sure."

"And our Shadow Man, are we sure that he turned?"

"It appears that way, sir."

"You should have brought him all the way in to the Brotherhood."

"Yes. That appears to be my mistake."

"You know how much I care for you, my son."

"Thank you. I . . . feel likewise, sir."

"Of course our masters have expressed a certain affection for you as well."

"You know that I serve them utterly."

"I would hate for them to call you to their bosom now. I would miss you terribly."

"As I would prefer to serve them here in the flesh, my Elder."

"Good. Because one more failure and I'd wager you'll be assessed to be of better service, as they say . . . you know, in the other realm."

"That's why I'm here, sir. Getting the job done."

A click, and the merciful dial tone returned.

Shadow Leader sighed. Despite being a warrior, he found that he was not impervious to his Elder's perennial rudeness. He fought a geyser of resentment seething up inside him. *I'll do it, old man,* he found himself thinking. *And by the way, if mere affection from our masters determines when we're harvested ourselves, and you've been their favorite son for decades, why have you remained in this mortal coil for so stinking long?*

Yes, he'd do the job. He might be pushing fifty now, but at one time he'd been the baddest Ranger of his generation. Every bit the equal of Dylan Hatfield. If need be, he concluded, he'd strip down and plunge into the jungle himself.

NIGERIAN RAIN FOREST—LATER THAT NIGHT

Three hours later, their joints burning, their stomachs ravenous, their throats parched again, and, above all, their minds astonished at the endurance of their much older guide, Abby and Dylan watched Sister Okoye leave the trail once more. This time she strode confidently up a smaller path, up to the side of a low, overgrown hill. She leaned into a depression and pushed hard. The other two were amazed to see the mat of vines sway open—clearly a door. Abby reached out to the hill, pulled away some vines and discovered that, rather than a cave in the ground, this was actually a stone building that long ago had been covered by undergrowth.

Even before entering, it was possible to see inside a glowing of candlelight and the reflection of a large, open space.

Sister Okoye turned and barred the space. "Dylan, you are not yet allowed to enter," she said sternly.

He stared at her, glanced at Abby, then back to Okoye. "Sister . . . you know what we've all been through today. I admit, I have a long way to go, but is it necessary to punish me now, after all the miles we've traveled together?"

"I am not saying this to punish you, Dylan," she answered. "I am not allowing you entrance into the Iya Agba safe house because you are still a creature of darkness. You do not know God. And despite the choices you've made for the good, you are festering with not one but two familiar spirits of killing and revenge. One of them happens to be a strongman. There is no way you can enter into our midst until you make even more godly choices."

"You mean I haven't made enough of these choices for one day?" he asked, sounding all at once petulant.

Her fists found the sides of her hips, and her face took on a maternal bemusement. "Dylan, what two items did you plant about your person three hours ago, when we left the bodies of those you killed?"

His eyes fell. He had forgotten about his earlier weapons stash.

"Just a small sickle and a revolver."

"Dylan, I have several sisters just inside, fellow *Iya Agba* who have awaited our arrival for quite a while. Do you know how terrifying it would be to have a man with a scythe come walking through their door?"

"I don't understand."

"You already know a little about the Brotherhood of the Scythe; we heard that earlier. Perhaps you do not know much. Perhaps you do not know that the Scythians have been mortal enemies and sworn assassins of Iya Agba for centuries. They have never missed an opportunity to kill any one of us they could find, not to mention torturing and killing millions more with their blades through the years."

"I'm sorry. I will leave it out here."

"Yes, you will. Because you will be staying out here until all the Iya Agbas inside reach agreement about you. Please be patient, my son. This is all part of what you need to learn. Part of dealing with the truth of what you saw."

Okoye and Abby stepped inside, shut the door, and left Dylan feeling more lost and bereft than he had felt since learning of his father's death, fourteen years before.

CHAPTER
_35

AIR FRANCE, FLIGHT 292, OVER THE MEDITERRANEAN

Robert Sherman reminded himself for the thirtieth time to stop flexing his thigh muscles and rocking his left knee up and down. The tics, after all, would get him nowhere. The plane would arrive when it arrived, not a moment sooner. Air travel was the fastest means of transportation known to man. No matter how frantically impatient he was, that impatience wouldn't help him sprout wings and beat the 747 to Lagos.

He sighed and tried to keep his attention away from the onboard television monitor. Like every other instrument of worldwide media at the moment, it could not pass five minutes' time without some sort of update on his daughter. And while it had proven surreal to see her face on-screen a dozen times through a single airport terminal, it was far worse now to be a captive audience as some frowning Frenchman babbled in perfect Parisian an update he could hardly understand, while behind him flashed pictures of the appalling massacre where she was presumed to have died.

He groaned and tried to focus on his newly purchased map of

southern Nigeria. To have the leading global story be your own personal nightmare—it turned out *that* was the essence of surreal.

And an apt definition for sheer torment.

At the moment, no one knew if Abby was even alive. There were
rumors and inconclusive video snatches of someone resembling her,
running away from the scene. But if that was the case, why had she
not surfaced? Why had her protectors among the Nigerian military
not produced her, smiling gamely and none the worse for wear? Far
more likely, at least implied by most knowledgeable commentators,
was that Abby Sherman would be discovered among the piles of
corpses now lining the Assembly grounds.

Sherman shook his head, trying to banish these thoughts from his
mind. Foremost among his afflictions was the fact that he didn't know
with whom to be the angriest. Even Abby, despite the love and concern he felt for her, had enraged him by leaving the country with
nothing more to comfort him than a cell phone call. And a call, to
make matters worse, which hadn't even informed him of her destination.

Mara McQueen, who now found herself under a cloud of public
scrutiny over the affair, was also in Sherman's rogues' gallery. So was
this Colonel Shawkey, who after convincingly showing that he had
saved Abby's life, later conceded that he had virtually abandoned her
to an unknown security guard when the time of reckoning had
arrived.

He thought of all the bad television movies where heroes instinctively sensed if a lost loved one was truly alive or not. Then he decided
to try it. Removing his glasses, he squinted fiercely and tried to force
his mind outward, into the universe.

Is Abby alive or dead?

No matter what, he knew he would be expected to be there. For
her body to be found and her father still be in California conducting
business . . . no, that couldn't happen. It would be a public relations
disaster from which he'd never recover.

No, he had to be here, come what may. No matter what sort of
death Abby's silly god had in store for her, Robert would be the one

to do the hard things. To gather the body and take her home.

He replaced his glasses—the test hadn't worked. Deep in his most covert mind, he still hadn't the slightest notion whether or not his beautiful one had survived.

Or how long, once he did find her, she would still have left to live.

IYA AGBA SAFE HOUSE, NIGERIAN RAIN FOREST

Abby gazed at her surroundings: a large, clean hall dominated by a central table of rough-chopped wood and lit by the flames of a dozen large candles. Despite its exceeding plainness and humility, it radiated warmth and welcome.

Her perusal lasted only a few seconds, however. Almost immediately her eyes were drawn to the fiery gazes of three other women who had stood and now faced her as she entered. Their modern yet colorful athletic attire seemed to clash both with their mission and the room's almost medieval appearance, its stone walls and Spartan flooring.

Abby took another step forward, blinked and tried to refocus her vision. She found that she couldn't. No matter how hard she strained and groaned in frustration, she opened her eyes to the sight of swirling white robes, shining faces, and otherworldly silhouettes blocking the forms of her newfound friends.

She found herself ruing the power of the Sight, for now it was practically rendering her blind.

"Okay, God, I get it," she said, smiling in mock exasperation.

"Get what?" asked the first one.

"That you are surrounded by the presence of the Lord and His angels," Abby responded. "And if my instincts are still on track, that you are spiritual sisters of our mutual friend Sister Okoye."

"Our mutual sister, actually," said the second of the three.

"Yes, of course," conceded Abby. "In the broad family-of-God sense."

"Do you know nothing about *Iya Agba*?" asked the third.

"Sisters," reproached Sister Okoye, "that is exactly why Abby risked so much to come to Nigeria. To find us and ask us these questions. True, she knows very little about who we are. Or why she seems to be one of us. So let us tell her, in patience and grace. First, I must confess that I smell food cooking. Has anyone prepared something, or has this table lost its legendary hospitality?"

The first woman, who gave her name as Saronu, stood with a smile and walked to the back of the room where there sat an ancient hearth Abby would have labeled a *kiva* back in the States. Next to it was a peculiar construction: an outthrust piece of wall that held a small pool of water so clear that Abby had trouble identifying it.

Abby found a rough-hewn wooden chair, accepted a gift of water from a pewter pitcher and a plate of something the women called *moin-moin*—a half dozen cakes of a gelatinous bean mixture wrapped in what turned out to be plantain leaves—and a pair of hard-boiled eggs.

There had been a time in her life when she would have been embarrassed to eat and drink with the abandon of a rescued shipwreck victim under the gaze of a tableful of people. There was also a time when food this exotic would have taken her a lengthy period to work up the courage to dig into.

That time was not now.

Sister Okoye asked if a plate of food could also be brought to Dylan outside. After a few dubious looks, the other three relented and honored her request.

"There's no use torturing the young man," Okoye had said simply, to no one in particular.

Meanwhile, Abby had cleaned not one but two platefuls of the dish served her, feeling grateful for finally chasing away those hunger pangs.

It was now time to talk.

CHAPTER

_36

The second host was a woman named Motumbe, middle-aged, who bore a bright red scar along her left cheek and who turned out to be the group's designated historian.

After the food and drink were all gone and the table meticulously cleaned, Motumbe sat down before Abby like someone who had prepared something to say for a very long time. Sister Okoye had retired to a wicker rocking chair in the corner and sat with her eyes closed, her task for the day duly completed. Abby had no doubt that she was not simply dozing, however. Everyone in the room seemed to be listening as Motumbe began speaking.

"Iya Agba, you see, is an old Yoruba word that means *Respected Mother* or *Elder Woman Who Sees*. There are not so many of us as there once were. Our Sisterhood once numbered in the tens of thousands across all of Africa."

"Over the whole continent?" Abby asked in amazement.

"Yes. In fact, it is the oldest strain of Christianity in all Africa. Most of today's Nigerian believers are spiritually descended from the European missionaries who came here in the nineteenth century. But we Iya Agbas represent something far older and deeper. Exactly what, or where it came from, has become lost over time. But we know that an ancient heritage made its way across Africa over a thousand years ago."

"The first missionaries who came were actually intimidated by our presence," Sister Okoye added without opening her eyes. "They did not understand how a bunch of African women could know the truth. And so many of them feared us. They thought we might be some kind of soothsayers, some kind of occult knowledge. They urged us to forget about the Sisterhood and just blend into the emerging church."

"But there are others in other countries?"

"By different names, yes," Motumbe replied. "Clearly we all possess the same gift, but warfare and mistrust between nations have cut us off from each other."

"Do most of the other nations use a name meaning *Respected Mother*?"

"I believe some do. It is usually also a name referring to how we can see beyond the veil that separates the carnal realm, or that of the flesh, from that of the Spirit. Of course we see more than that as well. We not only see the state of spiritual matters all around us, but we seem to be connected with each other, somehow, in a way that none of us fully understand. We sense when another is sick or endangered. It wakes us up in the middle of the night or in the heat of the day, often when we least expect it. Or at least, it used to. We Iya Agbas have dwindled of late. Our bonds have weakened, and our influence has waned dramatically."

"And the Sisterhood is completely unorganized? No leadership, no hierarchy?"

"Some people call me the 'Mummy Iya Agba,'" said Sister Okoye, "because I seem to have a gift of leadership, and because I have studied at several universities. But that is a completely local title."

"I can't believe this . . ." muttered Abby admiringly.

"We have heard rumors that somewhere, in a place we do not know, there exists some sort of matriarch, a living heart of the Sisterhood. A leader, if you will. It is merely something we have sensed for a very long time, and many believe it quite strongly. And now our sense of her has declined quite dramatically as well. We fear that this person may be diminished in the same way that the Sisterhood has been. But it is not the only weakness. We have been weakened by division among believers. By the disbelief brought in Western modernism. By a lack of proper teaching among our young women. By old wounds that have never healed. And to be honest, we have been decimated by the Scythians' systematic murders."

"Did you know that there was an attempt on my life?" asked Abby suddenly. "That's the reason I was sick—at least until I was healed. I was supposed to have only a few weeks to live."

"Did the assassin come at your throat? With a scythe?"

"No, it was some bizarre, untraceable poison. However, my housekeeper was murdered that night, and they said her throat had been cut by a curved blade!"

Their eyes brightened, then darkened again as everyone realized the somber nature of their discovery.

"How awful to think that the Scythians might be at work in America too," Sister Okoye said from her chair.

"Do your gifts develop," Abby asked, "after a strange dream about the prophetess Anna at the Temple, meeting Jesus?"

"Yes! Yes!" Motumbe looked like she might jump onto the table from sheer delight at the disclosure. "Oh my. It is beyond doubt now that Iya Agba truly did cross the Atlantic."

"You see, Abby," said Sister Okoye, "one of the great unhealed wounds of Nigeria is that our harbors served as the launching point for the American slave trade. Many, many of our people enriched themselves and indulged their old tribal hatreds by selling each other into slavery, just a few miles from where we sit. We know from our prayers that a great wound was inflicted on our body when this happened. We know that territorial spirits have jealously guarded their holds over parts of our land and its people. We know that a number of Iya Agba women were sold and taken away. And we have never been able to sense their bond, or even know whether their gifting survived into the New World."

"'Heal the breach,'" Abby said in a strangely breathy voice.

"What?" said Motumbe.

"'Heal the breach.' It's the main command Jesus gave me to carry out."

"If there is a breach, a wound here, it concerns that subject. Our lost sisters in America, and the horrible sin that led to their being taken from us."

"Yes—except that I have no African blood in me whatsoever. That is the greatest question in my own mystery. The women who responded to me by the thousands were African-American. Women who had an awareness of something they called the Sight, but no idea where it originally came from."

"The Sight," sighed Sister Okoye, savoring the words. She now sat at the table, having completely abandoned her pretense of sleeping in the chair. Her eyes were filled with tears and her voice had grown husky. "So even the name survived somehow. Our sisters knew their name, but they did not know their heritage."

"It sounds like we are healthy in numbers," Abby said. "But it seems we are being destroyed by our isolation."

"Yes," agreed Motumbe. "It's as though the old sins and offenses continue to fester after all these years, keeping us separate and weak."

"That's my mission," Abby said with a new resolve in her voice. "To heal this breach. I see it now, clearer than ever."

"Oh, if you could," said the third woman, who up until now had been silent. "If you could only help revive us! Do you know how many good things these sisters have done through the years? We once functioned like what they called, in your American West, *scouts*. Literally scouting the spirit realm for attacks on our people, our children."

"Iya Agba leaders," added Sister Okoye, "often warned kings and generals of upcoming attacks, either from enemy nations or from within their own people. We saved thousands. We prevented wars, helped clear up misunderstandings between tribes. We were considered indispensable at the court of every sovereign in all Africa, whether they believed in Christ or not."

"Can you imagine how much good we could accomplish today across Africa?" Okoye said. "There is so much darkness to be dispelled. In Darfur, in Uganda. If only we could have had an influence in Rwanda, warned the poor Tutsis there of what was to come."

"They wouldn't have believed us," said Motumbe. "No one wants to believe in the purest forms of evil."

"If that's true," Abby interjected, "then why didn't anyone predict the attack on the Gathering today?"

The other women faced each other with blank expressions. Sister Okoye closed her eyes for a moment. She opened them again and said, "I think several reasons. First, I think the idea came from somewhere beyond our land, beyond our influence. It was hatched and conceived by the American side of the Brotherhood, whom we never even knew existed, and yet now it seems is far stronger than our own contingent. That means the spiritual currents around the plot were beyond our detection. Second, we were so completely wrapped up in your appearance and all the media madness that surrounded it, we were distracted. I myself was so intensely engaged in prayer for you that a bomb could have gone off and I would have hardly noticed."

"One practically did," pointed out Motumbe.

"Indeed. And last, I hate to say this, but again it shows how far we've fallen from our former days of usefulness and relevance. Our enemies have grown strong. We've become scattered. Our gifts have become diffused and weak."

"Tell me," asked Abby, "how do these gifts transmit themselves? What are their means of traveling from one believer to another?"

Motumbe shook her head. "That is one of the great remaining mysteries. Here, all we know is that only women receive the Sight, and that all harbor this ancient strain of the faith."

Abby fell silent for a moment, thinking intensely. Then her face brightened. "You know, there is so much talk about sisterhood among you all. And such a spirit of family. I haven't felt part of such a tight-knit family since before my mother . . . well, since before she left my family."

"What are you trying to say?" asked Sister Okoye.

"I was just thinking back to my trip to heaven. About being greeted at the gate by a group of Iya Agba instead of family. But maybe it wasn't *instead*. Maybe they were family."

"I'm not following," said Motumbe.

"Earlier, you said the other Nigerian believers were spiritually descended from European missionaries. What if the bond from that kind of ancestry was more tangible than we imagined? What if it goes deeper than just the vocabulary we use to describe each other? After all, each of us have what we could call a 'spiritual genealogy.' Isn't that true?"

"I suppose it's beyond debate," mused Sister Okoye.

"What if the ancient strain really did carry the Iya Agba gifting into Nigeria, and your common spiritual ancestry distributed it to each of you? From your spiritual mother? Your grandmother in Christ? Your great-grandmother?"

"Like some kind of spiritual DNA . . ." said Motumbe.

"Exactly. I mean, think about it. Why is it we're so interested in our biological family trees, but most of us, at least in my country, couldn't follow their spiritual family tree more than two generations back? I know my mother led me to Christ and taught me about Him. But I don't know who led her."

"Maybe that's an important part of the answers you seek."

Abby suddenly fell silent again. The very same thought had just occurred to her too.

CHAPTER
_37

Invisible in the midnight shadows, Dylan sat with his back to the small stone building and savored the first prolonged stillness he had allowed himself in a very long time. He closed his eyes and imagined that the chatter of nocturnal creatures and the dappled light of the moon were actually water, trickling cool and pure over his face. He then realized the sound of water was in fact emanating from somewhere around him. Sending out his awareness like a stealth probe around the building's edges, he finally located the source, peered forward and spotted it.

How odd. The building itself must have been intentionally built on top of the small spring whose leftover flow spurted out of a small aperture with the rhythm of a heartbeat, down through a bed of ruddy grasses and reeds.

Returned to the pain-ignoring mindset of his special ops background, he leaned back on his haunches and willed himself not to move or register pain from thighs or ankles. Despite the localized burn, he found it indeed refreshing to sit and simply let his muscles remain motionless, no matter what position they occupied.

He tried to shift his mind away from the emotional disarray of the last few hours by pondering instead the tactical realities of their situation. In a small-numbers guerrilla scenario, the building and its elevated location would prove more than adequate. He had decent concealment, good sight lines, a solid half dozen firing solutions, multiple means of escape, and only one feasible direction of hostile approach.

The problem was, their enemies weren't likely to come at them in a simple patrol. He had a good idea of the resources available to Shadow Leader, and it didn't take a genius to compute the massive resources necessary for that day's raid on the Believers Gathering. In an afterthought, he glanced back at the building's roof to see if there was a chimney and any smoke rising from it.

Good, he noted. They'd had the sense to keep things cold.

All he had at his disposal was a small blade and a revolver with four rounds remaining. In the coolness of retrospect, he inwardly kicked himself for having heeded the old woman's harangue and left so many weapons behind. Now it was clear how much he could have used a spare machine gun or two, stashed at strategic points around the perimeter. If only he'd had his old Delta Force mission pack, complete with claymore mines, grenades, booby-trap tripwires, and infrared gear. He could have made any intruder regret sneaking up on this place, that's for sure. . . .

Slowly it came back to him that all these thoughts ran completely against what Sister Okoye and the Iya Agba were all about. Now, given the indignity of being refused entrance and the old woman's high-handed description of his soul, he began to question his surrender to her fuzzy worldview. What were they supposed to do now, he wondered, sit around and pray while their killers came for them? If not for him and his allegedly excessive tactics, they'd already be cooling bodies in a clearing several miles back, victims of that first gang of thugs.

And yet—if he rejected Abby's world, where did that leave him? The killer of an innocent girl? Accessory to the indiscriminate slaughter of several hundred innocent worshipers? He groaned and kneaded his forehead with stiff fingers. On top of all that, there was the evidence of his very own eyes. He knew what he'd seen back on that stage, and he knew that it was not of this world. He'd witnessed a miracle. And even in his limited experience, people who ignored miracles generally did not go down as geniuses in the annals of history.

He tried to chase the maddening thoughts from his head. Problem was, his only true distraction was to once again address the physical defense of their position. He was a man, and men were wired to take action, to accomplish something.

He thought of the Australian sheepdogs whose urge to herd animals was so ingrained in their little brains that if deprived of the chance to harass sheep, they would instinctively start to wrangle small children or pets around a backyard.

Yep, that's me, he thought with a wry grin. *Give me a mission or tie me up.*

He calculated that they had traveled a total of three and a half miles from the initial trailhead. From the maps he'd seen, he was fairly confident that the forest extended on behind them for an indefinite distance. For a satellite or a chopper, that distance was essentially nothing. He remembered the power of contemporary satellites and regretted not having urged the women to trudge through the middle of the stream on their way here, to dispel their heat signatures. But then he thought of their overall condition at that point, and knew such frigid and slippery conditions would have been impossible to bear. Somebody would have broken a leg.

With an inner chill he realized that if this house was known in any way to their enemies, or if their approach had been detected, they would have a warning time of only a few seconds before an attack helicopter or hunter-killer team struck. He could rig up a few diversionary tricks like rock-falls or bunji pits, but he doubted the time spent would prove worth it. With today's firing distances and lethal rockets, close distance was no longer necessary. They would be toast against all but the most primitive attack.

So what do I do then? he asked nobody in particular as he leaned back. *Pray?* The poor victims of the day's shootout had done plenty of praying. It hadn't stopped hundreds of them from winding up dead in a pile too horrific to look upon. Come to think of it, it hadn't done much for all those victims in Rwanda, or Sudan, or Uganda, or a dozen-plus killing fields on this whole blood-soaked continent.

So what was it? Had he let himself fall victim to a bunch of pie-in-the-sky, fuzzy female illogic?

Somehow, in a place deep down within him, it didn't feel like that. In fact, everything about it had the strange, uneasy feel of unlikely truth.

But how *could* it?

He was about to stand and make his presence known to the ladies inside when he heard the door screech open. He turned and saw Sister Okoye leaning out with an intent look on her face.

"We're leaving, Dylan. We're taking a trip."

"Good," he answered, almost to himself. "Not a minute too soon."

"And oh," she said, turning around in an afterthought. "You can keep those weapons if you like. But just remember. They're not our first line of defense."

CHAPTER

_38

The first ruddy streaks of dawn had just begun to smudge the horizon when Sister Okoye and Abby emerged from the building and, without a pause, began running downslope toward the valley bottom. Feeling his dignity and male pride almost completely in tatters, Dylan nevertheless jumped up with a shout and started off behind them.

At an impenetrable thicket near the water's edge, Sister Okoye reached in and grabbed hold of a tree trunk. To the others' surprise, the trunk gave way and lifted in her hands. Dylan stepped in to help, only to find that he was holding a long, thin canoe of hollowed bark, uncommonly light and strong.

Carrying the craft over his head to the creek, Dylan couldn't help but glance around him anxiously. As glad as he was that they were leaving, and leaving on water no less, he remembered that right now they were operating smack-dab in the center of what he'd picked as the likeliest attack zone. He breathed in relief when Sister Okoye stepped in expertly, picked up a steering rod, and started instructing Abby on how to step in and sit properly without tipping the boat.

"It's going to be difficult, honey," she warned.

Abby gave her an understanding smile. "Don't worry, Sister. I'm a surfer. If you've never seen that before, it requires excellent balance."

Sure enough, she stepped in with perfect control and quickly sat down on her haunches, hardly lurching the boat at all.

Dylan had far less luck. He stepped in and nearly launched the whole canoe downstream with only a single foot planted inside. Catching himself, he used that lone foot to steer the front of the canoe closer to him, then gingerly placed the other one inside.

"Good," said Sister Okoye from the rear of the craft, and with one long plunge of her rod they were off.

It was a strange navigation for both Abby and Dylan, for the stream's channel was incredibly narrow, just barely deep enough to accommodate the canoe's shallow hull. At nearly every push, Sister Okoye's choices of navigation angle narrowed down to one thin slanted approach through thick undergrowth. Often, passage required a helpful push against a tree trunk or even a hand-paddle from Dylan in the front. It impressed the two how skillfully the older woman managed to steer their ungainly boat through the bottlenecks and sharp turns required to proceed downstream.

Soon a second lively creek joined theirs, then a third just minutes later, and before they knew it the stream's volume had doubled, making their path far easier. The three began to breathe more freely and glance around them. Three thick, mist-layered columns of sunlight had just pierced the jungle ahead of them, testimony to the coming dawn. A huge flock of birds chose the moment to launch into a vigorous chorus, filling the forest with a soaring crescendo.

Again, Abby thought about how Nigeria and its people continued to confound her expectations and surprise her at every turn.

"So where are we going?" Dylan asked at last, breaking the blissful silence.

"We're taking the next step in Abby's search," Sister Okoye said. "A place called Sungbo's Erebo. One of the most amazing spots in all Nigeria, and it's right at the end of a few miles' boat ride from here."

"Will we be exposed between here and there?" asked Dylan.

"No, although such concerns mean very little to us now. We're in God's hands, not that of G.I. Joe or anybody's armed guerrillas."

"I understand, Sister, but if this is God's route for our leaving, I'll just say that God has an excellent nose for tactical planning. He made a call I would have heartily approved of."

"I'm sure He'll be glad to hear that," Sister Okoye answered with a defiant grin.

Just then, as in counterpoint, a pair of choppers bellowed overhead, just a half mile or less in front of their position. Dylan ducked by reflex, but noted that where they were on the creek was well concealed by tree branches extending from the banks. Only northward, in the distance, did open sky even reveal the passing aircraft.

He shook his head in relief. Had they been delayed by just a few minutes more, or been a few hundred yards still upstream, they would have been caught and—unless Abby's and Sister Okoye's God performed a feat worthy of the Old Testament—would be dead by now.

Then he saw them—his blood froze in mid-heartbeat. Mere hundreds of yards behind them, but headed in the opposite direction, ran a dozen barely visible silhouettes. Armed *machete men*.

He pulled out the gun, his fingers straining for action. He turned, raised an index finger to his lips for silence, and gestured for Sister Okoye to slowly push them farther downstream.

She complied. Her motion produced the sounds of wood creaking and water lapping. He gritted his teeth in dread, then breathed once as the motion caused them to float forward nearly ten feet.

Dylan looked back at the human caravan. He gripped the stock and trigger guard, hard. But he could also see that the gunmen were not looking around. Although distant, they were clearly fixed only on what lay ahead. They were preparing for a raid, and their gazes were locked resolutely before them.

Dylan inwardly gave thanks for every yard of waterline that slipped by, taking them out of sight by the thinnest margin of safety.

He continued to shake his head, with the relief turning to amazement as he considered it. *Abby's God pulls through again, but He sure has a perverse affection for close calls. . . .*

He glanced ahead and almost laughed. Here came a large tributary from a steep channel on the right, so ample that it instantly doubled their channel's width. A minute passed like an hour. The threat was swallowed up in jungle and then faded away. Like a promise of easier days, the dawn started up in earnest, inflaming the sky to their left in a dozen shades of orange and turquoise.

"Will the three other women be around to get caught?" he asked Sister Okoye in a still-cautious whisper.

"No, they left in the opposite direction right after we did," she answered. "They're on foot, but they're local women and they will be hard to catch. Besides, they will try and create a diversion. God willing, our pursuers will never even think to look south along our route."

The next few hours would prove to be among the most beautiful and memorable Abby would ever spend. The stream broadened into a river whose path through the rain forest was a never-ending display of wonders and rare snapshots of natural life. By trip's end, she had spotted a python slung ponderously over a tree branch, a leopard and her pup drinking at a small pool of still water, a small crocodile weaving across the waterline, and more birds of every iridescent color and exotic shape than she even knew existed. An unlikely cool breeze, heralding the rainy season to come, even lifted itself across the path for their comfort.

The fact that she was encountering these sights as spontaneous and natural accidents, not from the pixels of a television screen or even the deck of a tourist boat, but here in the middle of a legitimate adventure, one that had nearly cost her life, made the apparitions that much more thrilling. After all, she told herself, the formaldehyde smell of the hospital had hardly faded from her, and here she was in a canoe, holding her breath against being discovered by assassins and jungle beasts alike.

You've come a long way, baby . . .

At some point, Sister Okoye asked Abby whether her Sight was showing her many disturbing apparitions.

"No," Abby said. "Actually, I just realized I've hardly seen any spirit life all day. Just fleeting shadows. Runners, I've gotten to calling them. But that's all. It's quite a relief."

"That is because nature is generally free of demonic concentrations or strongholds, unless you happen on a spot where something truly evil or provocative has happened. You may catch a glimpse, as you mentioned, of individual sprites on their way here and there. But those are usually in a weakened, famished state, anyway. Not much of a threat."

Her peace momentarily disrupted by the exchange, Abby was only glad to let the conversation lapse and the river's beauty return to settle back over them.

Some of that peace admittedly dissipated for good when, halfway through the trip, Sister Okoye, true to her word, started in on Dylan and his reeducation.

"So you are a great warrior, it seems," she began.

"I wouldn't presume to put a label on it, Sister. But I have done a great deal of fighting. Much of it solo work. By myself."

"I know what *solo* means, Dylan. You are proud of this work?"

"Much of it was in direct service to my country, to what I would consider the cause of freedom. So yes, I am proud of what I've done. It's not easy, and it's not for the faint of heart, as we like to say. Sometimes that makes me even prouder still."

"Have you killed many men, Dylan?"

"Yes, I have."

"How many?"

"To be honest, I try not to keep count. It's not exactly the part of my job I like to think about the most."

"But . . ."

"I don't know, maybe three dozen. Maybe as many as fifty."

Even though she was quite gratefully staying out of the conversation, Abby visibly stiffened at that response.

"What is your view of spiritual things, Dylan?"

"What do you mean? Whether I believe them or not? What kind of spiritual construct I subscribe to?"

"Let's start with whether you believe in a Creator God."

Instead of the rapid response, which so far had characterized the exchange, this time the question was greeted with deep silence. Finally he answered just as Sister Okoye was about to take a new tack in her questions.

"I would usually say no, and I always have," he answered in a suddenly mild voice. "Only today, I just now realized. Right this second, my answer is yes. I do believe in a Creator."

"Of course, what kind of fool would you be, here, in this place, to look around you and not believe."

"It seems that way, yes," he answered in a reflective tone.

"And yet, Dylan, believing in a Creator alone distinguishes you from almost no one. Even the animists out east of here believe in a Creator. So does Satanism. So does witchcraft. So does Islam."

"I suppose you're right. Yet so far I haven't signed up for any of those, have I?"

She paused while pushing the pole backward, something she needed to do less and less with the strengthening current. "But, Dylan, you should remember that in the last twenty-four hours you've been a witness to more signs and wonders of the Christian faith than just about anyone ever has without throwing himself to the ground and begging to be received into His kingdom. You've seen angels. You've seen a terminally ill woman be healed of her illness. You've seen the power of an actual miracle. Most people could hardly ask for more proof than that."

Another pause. If the other two had been sitting close enough to see his face, they would have seen his jaw muscles churning as Dylan brooded.

"Do you need to see more?" Okoye asked.

"Not really," he replied lamely. "I don't know."

"I don't mean to push, and you don't have to decide right this second, even though there are hundreds of men hunting for you in order to kill you, and this may be the last calm moment you have before meeting Him face-to-face. Other than that . . ."

She broke into a soft laughter, and so did Abby and even Dylan.

"But I do know this," she continued. "Even though all of this business pales in comparison with the importance of knowing Christ and finding your name written in His Book of Life, I can also tell you this: I can teach you nearly everything there is to know about becoming a true warrior. Not some caricature of manhood running around half drunk on rage and revenge, but a warrior far more valuable to his King than anything you've even heard or read about."

"And how do you know all this?"

"Because I am a proud warrior in His service. And while I don't have the power of a young man, or even of a young woman for that matter, I know about spiritual power. And I'll venture to say, Dylan, that it is exactly the opposite of everything you've been taught."

"Well, it sounds fascinating. I'd like to learn, if you'd care to teach me."

"Unfortunately," she snapped like the closing of a trap, "it is of no use to someone who does not know Christ and follow Him."

"All right. I've probably heard a hundred different twists on this through my life. So what, once and for all, does it mean?"

"Can I answer this?" Abby broke in.

Sister Okoye nodded with a smile.

"Dylan, it's simpler than you could ever imagine. And also harder, I suppose. God says that He just wants us to walk humbly with Him. To abide with Him, which basically means to hang out with Him—emotionally, spiritually. To spend time the way we would with a perfect father, if we could. Talk to Him, read His letters to us, tell Him how much we love Him through something called praise and worship."

"What about the big, all-important prayer at the finish line?"

"You mean the *altar*? Yeah, I think sometimes we make too big a deal of that. A lot of people respond to what's called an altar call and get the impression that if they just say this bunch of words their whole eternal destiny's taken care of. I think that's hogwash. Sure, it's a good beginning. It all starts with a prayer, but then it grows and ends with prayer as well."

"That's enough for now," said Sister Okoye. "I don't want Dylan to think he is being sold a cow. Son, when the time comes where in your heart you want to pray that prayer, just ask one of us to pray it with you and start your journey. That is all."

"You promise?" he asked, laughing.

"I always tell the truth," she said, then stopped speaking, for just at that moment a midmorning rain shower grayed over the sun and began pelting them with large, warm drops.

The rainy season had just arrived.

CHAPTER
_39

Drenched to their skin by the prodigious downpour, the fugitive threesome floated from the confines of the river, which had swept them thus far down into a broad grove of swamps and marshes. Even with a cool wind whipping against her soaked clothes and chilling her to the bone, Abby found the experience refreshing, even exhilarating. She lifted her head into the torrent, flung her hair back behind her, and abandoned herself to the sensation of gliding through an unending lukewarm shower.

Just a few feet ahead of her, Dylan glanced back and felt himself pierced by the beauty of a young woman in the grip of such freedom. Was that how it felt, he wondered, to just surrender yourself to the will of a sovereign, loving God?

He could hardly imagine how it would be, after having lived for so long according to the highly strung confines of his own abilities. Self-reliance had been his life, his credo, indeed his very survival. A tightly strung dependence on his own instincts, his own wisdom, his own gifts. Right now, however, none of it seemed as fulfilling as this young beauty's blissful abandon.

Without even making a conscious decision, he found himself leaning his head forward and speaking inwardly.

God, if you're really there, I guess I would like to start—

A sharp bump jolted him from the awkwardness of his prayer—the side of their canoe striking the hard bank of their apparent destination. Sister Okoye now stood and was prodding the nearby soil with the rod.

It struck Dylan at once that what he had started to pray was far more important than exiting the boat at that moment. So even when the boat lightened with the departures of Sister Okoye and Abby a few seconds later, he remained seated and lowered his head again.

"Dylan . . ." Abby called out impulsively. But Sister Okoye, who had sensed what he was doing, stopped Abby by placing a hand on her arm.

. . . God, I really don't know how to do this. But for some reason I find myself totally believing in you. In your existence, in your love for me, in your love for this messed-up world. I know this involves Jesus somehow, and what He did on the cross . . . that He died for me. I get that now. He died for me so that you and I could . . . what's the word, abide *in each other? Abide. I like that word. God, I'd very much like to abide in you, forever. Will you forgive me for being such a moron and take me in?*

He opened his eyes and turned to the sight of two women standing motionless in the middle of a driving rainstorm, yet weeping so hard that even with a wall of water falling across their faces, he could make out tears streaming from their eyes.

He stepped from the boat and felt the pair converge on him at once. Sister Okoye's arms were short but strong and threatened to squeeze the air from his lungs. She spoke as she wept, using words no English-speaking person—perhaps no one but the angels and God himself—would understand.

Abby, for her part, knew how to hug like a good American girl. He could feel her tears fall into the crook of his neck, warmer than the surrounding raindrops.

"Oh, Dylan," she cried, "you should see them! They're surrounding you!"

He knew precisely what she was speaking of, and the thought of it sent a shudder of wonder down his spine. He pulled his head back and glanced around him to see if he now had the ability to see them. Both women took his tiny release as a cue to withdraw, and suddenly he was standing alone in the downpour. And amazingly, the clouds over the sun thinned all of a sudden, casting a bright pale backlight onto the sheets of falling water. The effect was both dazzling and profoundly affecting. Dylan blinked again. Had he seen something, *someone*, in the wet radiance of the light burst?

Maybe so. But for now he was content not to look too closely, because the outward picture could hardly match what was happening inside of him. For the instant that he'd lifted up his prayer, he'd felt a proverbial weight lift from his shoulders—from his heart, and most of all his mind. The sensation had been so specific and vivid, he could still hardly believe it. It felt like someone had just sprung loose a ratchet that had been pulled tight for years, against every muscle in his body.

Then, at once, he knew what it was.

It was the tension of self-reliance, of feeling every second of every day that he had to be perfect, the by-the-numbers solo performer.

Although the old tightness was such a familiar old companion that he almost felt a twinge of sadness at feeling it melt away, the new reality of walking freely was so breathtaking that he could not bring himself to mourn the old.

He looked up. Sister Okoye was shoving their canoe off into the current. Even though he knew she was just wisely ridding them of a dead giveaway, it struck him in a rush of coincidence that her act was the perfect mirror image of what he was feeling. To cast off the old into the current and let it float off into oblivion. Amazing.

How thankful he felt, all at once, for the arrival of this monsoon! It was perfect, because just then he truly felt washed clean, immersed in something cool and pure. Feeling stupid and bold all at once, he felt his arms rise into the air and his fingers point up into the rain.

Thank you, God. Thank you for making yourself so clear to a confused and dense fool like me.

He felt someone else's soft fingers strain to wrap themselves around the digits of his right hand and pull them downward. Looking down, he saw Abby moving to tug him away from the swamp's edge. In the distance, Sister Okoye was already a wet smudge against a drenched backdrop of stone, beckoning for them to follow.

He did not feel the need to release her hand as they ran after their mentor, through a foot-soaking morass of mud and matted grass. When they caught up with her, she was hurrying down into an oddly formed passage between suddenly towering walls.

"This is our stronghold," she announced proudly, pointing up. "The Iya Agba heartland. Sungbo's Eredo."

"What is it?" asked Abby as she craned her neck in every direction.

"Is this man-made?" asked Dylan, trailing his hand across the wall's weathered surface.

"Exactly," said Sister Okoye with a smile of a schoolteacher receiving an unexpectedly correct reply. "This is the least known yet most important historical relic in all of Nigeria. It is a wall over one thousand years old, over one hundred miles long and seventy feet high. It is the outer rampart of a kingdom largely forgotten by history. But not the lore of the Iya Agba. Abby, this is why we came here. Here we will find the next stage of your search. Come, follow me and I will tell you more."

Energized by their arrival, not to mention the relief of not having to sit in a narrow canoe, she bolted forward and began to run along the rampart's edge. It proved tough going, for veils of rainwater ceaselessly poured from its flat expanse, directly over their path. Twice Abby slipped in the mud and fell hard against the wall, stopping herself just in time with an outstretched hand.

They turned a corner and saw that, indeed, the wall continued just as straight and as tall for a great distance. The depression at its foot deepened into an overgrown channel. "That's the moat!" Sister Okoye called back, playing the enthusiastic tour guide.

They continued on for over an hour, feeling their awe at the massive construction deepen by the minute. And just as they began to weary of its unceasing height, Okoye leaned sideways into its slope, stepped upward, and began somehow to scale its face. Abby and

Dylan peered, and finally saw that she was climbing with the aid of cunningly positioned natural protrusions in the earth.

"Iya Agba created these patterns in the wall long ago," she called down. "We memorize them, for they seem invisible to all others. And they are the only way to safely reach the top."

Glad to be moving somewhere different and decisive, Abby planted her foot into the first indentation and forged ahead. The way up proved surprisingly easy, although the constant rain was beginning to wear on her. She looked ahead and saw that Sister Okoye was almost three-quarters of the way to the rampart's top, scurrying like a Sherpa. Well, she'd just have to catch up . . .

. . . with a horrified rush of blood to her head, she felt her foot slip into free air, her body slide sideways. Her perch alongside a veritable mountainside sheared off into nothing.

She felt the scream of the doomed begin to gather air within her. Her will rebelled, her sense of destiny recoiled at the fate of such a capricious ending to her life. *After all those close scrapes, only to perish now in a fall off an archaeological relic? No, it couldn't end this way, it just couldn't!*

The reply came courtesy of a painful grip on her right hand. The hand forming this grip belonged to Dylan, who forcefully yanked her back up to the stepped path. Her legs flailing, her feet kicking the air in their desperate bid for purchase, she finally felt one foot nick a step's base and burrow in.

"Thank you!" she gushed while pressing her side against the comfort of solid flatness.

He smiled, not trusting himself to utter a word. Again, her hand sought his. He reasoned that given her near fall, there was every innocent reason for the clasp to take place. Yet as he stepped up the wall's side, hurrying to match her enthusiastic ascent, he couldn't help but thrill at the touch.

Soon they had reached the top, the very lip of the massive wall. Stepping up, they saw that it was much thicker than any wall they had ever known, nearly fifteen feet across.

Sister Okoye was nowhere to be seen.

"Sister! Sister!" shouted Abby into the unrelenting shower.

"Sister Okoye!" Dylan yelled now, with a man's force and command.

Then the older woman appeared, her face peering out and smiling through the rain. A stray hand beckoned them to her side, behind an outcropping that curled deceptively around what proved to be a sheltered hole.

Bending down through a low entrance, Abby and Dylan stepped into the shocking sensation of dry air, accompanied by the stale smell of a cave and the sudden flare of a torch bursting to life.

"Welcome to our place of refuge."

CHAPTER
_40

AMSTERDAM

"Is Shadow Leader in our custody?" the Elder asked, not bothering now to conceal his rage.

"The man knows his fate, my Brother," replied the voice on the television screen. "He avoided it first by hopping that plane to Africa. Now he has undertaken to find them all by himself. Hearken back to his younger days, I suppose. He seems to think he can emerge a hero and avoid any consequences whatsoever. Wouldn't we all—"

"I wouldn't," barked the Elder. "I would run a proper command post and coordinate the people working for him, like a proper leader of people. Instead of jumping in like some overage Rambo."

"Well, we have a very capable younger brother running the logistics during his absence. And by the time this operation is completed, he will probably be our newest Shadow Leader. But please remember. Our brothers in the area, while they have made a great harvest over the years, are not as organized and disciplined as we are. They are of very little use in a pitched conflict such as this one."

"Yes, well at least they have stayed loyal to their priorities. They've come far closer to sanitizing their surroundings than we have."

"I don't argue that. I merely mean that we can't count on them now."

"You fool, do you realize just how high the consequences have become? This blasted girl could reawaken the entire Sisterhood. Just when we stood on the brink of total victory."

"I do realize that, my Elder. That's why we're dedicating so many resources to resolving the problem."

"I'll tell you what you're going to do, my boy. You're going to issue the final mop-up order."

"Now?"

"Absolutely now. Every brother, American and African alike, is to kill as many Watchers as is humanly possible. Annihilation. I want it done."

"Gladly, sir. I cannot wait. Annihilation it is."

EREDO RAMPART, OGUN STATE, NIGERIA—
SEVERAL HOURS LATER

The rain had finally paused, allowing a lull in the changing of the seasons. Abby, Dylan, and Sister Okoye stood on the wall's summit like spectators in their own private skybox, looking out over an eternity of shining trees like sailors stranded in the Sargasso Sea.

"Look down," said Sister Okoye. "See how the moats were designed to catch and hold all the rainwater right here? In an odd way, we might be standing in the most secluded place in all of Nigeria. At least for the next day or so."

Dylan observed the pool below him. Indeed, the fortification had been cunningly built to allow rain in, while not allowing it to flow out.

"The moats have filled," she continued, "and the rest of the system filled right afterward. So now we have ten square miles of water between us and any hostile pursuers."

"Incredible," said Dylan. "I can see why you called it a 'stronghold.'" He paused, then said, "You know, the water could turn out to be a mixed blessing. It could also make it easier for an enemy to approach. It's true the moats keep the water contained right here, in the open and under our noses, but with the whole area flooded like this, anyone coming this way from the jungle will only have to float from tree to tree and will have excellent cover to do so."

"No, the water isn't that high," countered Okoye. "If you tried to swim it right now, you would be fighting your way through the tops of every kind of vegetation imaginable. Not to mention crocs."

"That's assuming they don't have watercraft."

"But isn't this still a safe place to be?" asked Abby.

"It is," Dylan conceded. "It's a very safe place. Plus, it offers some strategic advantages. Such as the great visibility from this height, the moats' exposed border, good shelter, for starters."

"And the disadvantages?" said Abby.

"Well, our enemies have the cover of the jungle, and presumably all the weapons in the world at their disposal. Besides the element of surprise—"

"Now wait," interrupted Okoye. "You forget that you're standing here with two Iya Agba with their hearts set on hearing from God. If He is willing, there won't be any sneak attacks."

"Good point," said Dylan. "I hadn't thought of that."

"I brought you here," explained Sister Okoye, "for many reasons. One of them was the attributes of this site. The second reason is probably the most immediate. We had to move, of course, from where we were. The northern safe house was never meant to repel real pursuit."

"That's for sure," said Dylan. "I don't think we missed being caught by more than a few minutes."

"The other reason I brought you here is that it could contain the answers you need to continue along your journey. You see, while a host of completely inaccurate stories have circulated about this place, the truth will help to tell us where you should go next."

"This is where we'll find more about the Iya Agba family line?" asked Abby.

"I hope so, my dear. Our own lore claims that this is the place our sisters came to when they first entered Nigeria, brought by the lady named Sungbo whom the locals believe is the woman who started this Ijebu kingdom. They think she was actually the queen of Sheba. They revere her so faithfully that her grave nearby is a guarded national monument."

"Is the belief accurate?" asked Abby.

"No, the Sheba story is not only untrue, but historically impossible. These fortifications may be formidable, yet they have only been here a thousand years. The queen of Sheba lived nearly three thousand years ago, during the time of Solomon, if you recall. And yet we do know that a wealthy, powerful woman did come from Nubia, or Ethiopia, built this place, and established the vast and influential Ijebu nation. I think, Sister Abby, that if we can find out the truth about her and where she came from, we will find the next step in your quest."

"I don't follow you," said Dylan.

"Well, while you waited outside the safe house," Sister Okoye said, "Abby had a fascinating idea that hadn't occurred to any of us before. A simple notion, really. She thought that perhaps the Iya Agba gifting travels through a spiritual family line, a genealogy of faith. Most of us have neglected the knowledge of our ancestry in Christ, but perhaps it is the very means by which our Sisterhood has grown and traveled. Through our spiritual mothers."

"A matrilineal genealogy of the Spirit," said Dylan, as though trying out the verbal mouthfuls for size. "And that's how a white girl could be related to thousands of African-American women? How would *that* have happened?"

"That's the problem. I have no idea how or if it ever did," Abby said.

"Why is that?"

"My mother led me to faith when I was young, but I haven't known her since then. She disappeared and I have no idea where she is."

"Would your father know?"

"My father loves me, but he knows nothing of this. When it comes to anything religious, he doesn't care. Sister Okoye, was the woman who led *you* into the faith an Iya Agba?"

"I believe so, although I think she resisted it. But now that I recall, she most definitely saw beyond the veil. People always thought she was a little crazy, so she largely kept it to herself. But I remember her saying some things. . . ."

"And *her* spiritual mother?"

"I'm as ignorant as you. I know no further than one spiritual generation back."

"It is an intriguing notion," said Abby. "And it truly is puzzling why no one pays attention to such a thing. Even sad, if you think about it. Imagine all these great family lines, all these heritages and sagas that must have woven their way through history. So many stories gone to seed. Yet we have no clue they're just sitting there, unknown, in all of our pasts. And maybe, like in this case, that genealogy could hide a major secret. Something really important."

"Why would it be only mothers to daughters?" Dylan asked.

"That's another mystery," replied Okoye. "Remember, we're just now pondering this whole idea. Maybe it's because African culture is so very matriarchal; here it's only the mothers who talk to the daughters about spiritual things."

"If that's the case, then I could be the first male in history. . . ?"

"Just remember that this is nowhere near as important as the parenthood of our true heavenly Father, and the kinship of our ultimate spiritual family, which is the whole body of Christ. This is just a fascinating side note in comparison to that."

They laughed heartily at the notion, then turned back as another wave of rain began to approach. But as they reentered the cave, a certain gleam never left Dylan's eye.

CHAPTER
_41

Stepping in, Abby noted that the cave was even more Spartan than the first safe house. It consisted of a long, clean, narrow space with little furnishings save for four thick hammocks, a folding metal table, and a small gas stove set on a stone. In a far corner sat stacks of dried food, bottled water, and assorted supplies.

And yet, for her, the hammocks made it luxurious and equipped beyond desire. After a day on the run, a rainy day seemed the perfect excuse to settle back and relax awhile, buoyed by the idea that a hundred miles of flooded swamps lay between them and any intruders. Within minutes she was snoring lightly, her face more serene than it had looked in days.

Sister Okoye took the occasion to have a talk with her young protégé.

"Did you know that you are the first man to enter this room in probably its whole six- or seven-hundred-year history?"

Dylan, who was relaxing in one of the hammocks, chuckled inwardly at the notion. "I am truly honored," he said. "Although something tells me I'm not through paying for the privilege."

"No sir, you are not. You have much learning to do. Or should I say, *un*learning."

"Oh, really? So my many years of studying warfare and tactics at various schools and war colleges, not to mention active duty carried out all over the world, now goes flying out the window?"

Sister Okoye struck an accommodating expression. "No, I would never tell you to forget it entirely. I don't presume to know what God will call you to do. But if you are to be an Iya Agba—a *male* Iya Agba, imagine that—or even just the champion Abby needs for you to be, then you must add a whole new world to your . . . your repertoire."

"*Arsenal.* I think the word is arsenal."

"Perhaps. You see, young Dylan, I think I've discerned what really drives you. What gives you such pleasure from your work. What keeps you trapped in your world of secrecy and isolation."

"Oh, and what is that?"

"You know what it is. Self-reliance."

His face seemed frozen in mid-breath. He was clearly at a loss, unprepared for such a bull's-eye.

"Tell me I am wrong," she said. "You thrive on being a one-man show, to use American lingo. On being a self-sufficient killing machine one needs only to set in motion and then sit back to await the inevitable success. The confirmed kill. No support needed, no backup, no emergency personnel. You succeed, or you die. You take all the risks, and you reap all the praise."

"Not really," he interjected. "In secret ops work, there's not much praise. It's too covert."

"Dylan, you know what I mean. Don't change the focus."

"So there's something wrong with all that?"

"Not in your world. But in the world of the spirit, it is the way to be destroyed, because almost every spiritual being you'll encounter is stronger than you. That's no reflection on you; remember, you're not on your native soil. You're out of your element. But the One you serve is the strongest in the entire spirit world, by an incalculable margin. You remember that. Even His angels are formidable allies. But in the world of the Iya Agba and of the spirit, independence is the antithesis of strength. Self-reliance is weakness."

"Really. So what is the preferred alternative?"

"Utter reliance on God, of course. The starting point is a complete assurance that the world of the spirit exists. You don't know how many so-called believers go through their lives only half believing in the spirit realm. Yes, they believe in God, and in angels too, though more in a sentimental way. But when it gets deeper, down to the evil side, Satan and his minions, the principalities and powers—most turn off their ears. They selectively believe. They even laugh at those who take it seriously, as though they are too impressionable, easily swayed, even childish."

"I understand what you're saying. But Sister Okoye, believe me when I tell you that if these last two days in Nigeria have taught me anything, anything at all, it's the reality of the spiritual dimension."

She laughed heartily at that statement—a bold, rich outburst that nearly woke Abby from her profound slumber. Soon he was laughing along with her.

"Fine. You can skip the preliminaries, Dylan."

"Thank you."

"Unfortunately, admitting its existence is truly just the beginning. Next comes the realization that this realm has its own set of laws and principles. Just as basic and important as our law of gravity. Harder still, most of them are paradoxically and diametrically opposite from those of our world."

"Sister Okoye," he said, "you never cease to amaze me. From a pious older lady to a tireless jungle runner and now a spiritual instructor. You've confounded every expectation I could throw at you."

"Well, thank you," she said. "As long as you're not implying that a woman, or worse yet an African, cannot throw around sophisticated ideas."

"Absolutely not," he replied. "And I will gladly listen to you. But I must warn you: If at any point my ears hear the words *dark side* or *listen to the force*, I will be obligated to either burst out laughing or start singing the movie theme song."

She looked at him blankly.

"Oh, it's a movie called *Star Wars*," he said, embarrassed now. "It's a huge classic; I was sure folks had seen it in Nigeria. . . ."

She glared at him. "I *have* seen it. But this is serious, Dylan. You don't know the whole story of the Brotherhood of the Scythe. A group that, never forget, has its clutches already deep into you. Oh yes, even to this day, even though you have begun to follow Christ, you should see all the clinging little familiar spirits pining to hook themselves into you at the slightest provocation. When my Sight engages, I can hardly walk for trying to stay out of their way. You're still paying a price for your associations, my Brother. And those old friends, my dear Dylan, happen to be the original prototype of the modern serial killer."

"Serial killer?"

"Actually, I understated that. Not only are they the originals, but they are the most prolific masters in their twisted field. I mean, none of the poster-boy murderers you have probably heard of on television ever killed with the relish and efficiency of the least junior Brother of the Scythe. These men kill because they are taught to enjoy the act of taking life with an almost sexual pleasure. While that is not unique to them, add the fact that their killing volume also causes them to climb the ladder of a very elaborate and ancient chain of command. So even as they become desensitized, requiring more and more victims, they acquire ever greater ability to gain access to them, then to escape detection and perfect their so-called skills."

"I had no idea . . ."

"Wait, Dylan—I'm not through. It is very important that I finish telling you this, and that you listen very closely. You see, the Scythians have one vastly preferred kind of victim. And that is a member of my Sisterhood. Iya Agbas. They track and slaughter us with a relish that rivals that of the SS and the Jews, if you forgive my imprudent analogy."

"I don't see the connection."

"You can't see it because the war between us is too ancient and distant for anyone to see. It is like the chicken or the egg.

"The Hatfields and McCoys," added Dylan pensively.

"What is that?"

"Oh, it's an ancient feud between two families that became quite famous from the American South. One of them, the Hatfields, were ancestors of mine. Their hatred became synonymous for the kind of feud that was so old and buried in myth that even its participants forgot how it started."

"Except, unlike that example," Okoye pointed out, "ours is not morally ambiguous. We know who started it. We know who the evil side is. But we do not know much more. All we know is that since the dawn of our known history, the Iya Agba have fought the evil of the Scythians, and the Scythians have murdered as many of our kind as they could catch. Now, there is one more dimension I have not touched on."

"You mean it gets worse?" he said.

"It does. You see, it's not only the volume of the Scythians' blood-thirstiness which makes them so evil. It is the underlying reason they kill. Or should I say the underlying function of their murders."

"Didn't you already say that? The almost sexual bloodlust?"

"Actually, that turns out to be merely a means toward the end. A pretext for the less initiated. We learned the horrible truth long ago, from watching demons converge on their dying victims like sharks in a rampage. Dylan, you must realize that we do not like to even speak of such things. I will try to say this quickly and be done with it."

He turned in his hammock to face her, amazed that any revelation could repel her so strongly. She breathed in calmly, seemingly gathering strength for the disclosure.

"They are actually *feeding* the evil ones. Do not ask me how or why. All I know is what we have seen with our very own . . . eyes, if you will. It as though the demons are feeding on the souls, or the residue, of the dying process. It seems the Scythians are their feeders, their gatherers of food."

"And this ancestral hatred of the Iya Agba," he said, almost explaining it to himself, "is why they feared Abby enough to coerce me into killing her?"

"Exactly. They are deathly afraid of her not only advancing in her gifts, but answering the questions you and I are solving right this very minute. Because with every piece of the puzzle we discover, the

Sisterhood regains a little of its former strength."

"No wonder they're so intent on stopping us."

"Indeed. They will not stop until they kill us, or until you and Abby finish her quest. And for that to succeed, she will need a godly warrior. Something you have yet to learn."

CHAPTER
_42

"My name is Saronu."

"Mine is Motumbe."

"And mine, Kofu."

"Yes, you have all three confessed to your names repeatedly. And for the record, we believe you. But what you've yet to tell us is—who else was with you in that forest?"

"God Almighty was with us," said Motumbe with a coy smile.

"Yes, He certainly was," rejoined Kofu. "He granted us perfect weather, right up until the end, and delightful fellowship."

"I'm speaking of human encounters, if you please."

"Well, we met you, right at the end of our journey," said Saronu. "And by the way, who might you be? You seem to be American, if my ear is correct. What is your authority to detain us, least of all interrogate us in this manner?"

"How spunky of you to ask. However, I will be asking the questions today."

"Couldn't you at least introduce yourself?" asked Motumbe. "After all, your proper name couldn't really be, as we overheard you called in the helicopter, *Shadow Leader?*"

Hearing himself addressed by his operational moniker caused the man to leap up, his eyes bulging with fury, and slap Motumbe across the face. A hard slap, which sent the woman and the chair to which she was handcuffed crashing into the wall behind them.

"We've committed no crime!" Kofu shouted at the man. "You cannot do this to us. We were hiking through the jungle. That is our right. It is not our responsibility to account for our lack of provisions or packing gear. We were walking briskly and expected to meet some sisters of ours that afternoon. If we were on a wrong trail, then surely that was our problem."

The man grudgingly walked behind the interrogation table and shoved Motumbe's chair back upright again.

"Nor must we surrender to anyone, especially as we are women alone in a wilderness area," said Saronu. "That applies even when the chase begins with a helicopter. Nor did it change when you people added squads on foot, and dogs too. If you want to chase innocent women through the wilderness, don't expect them to stop and offer themselves up. You should know the rule of jungle travel—you hide until someone is known to be friendly."

"Especially right after one of the worst massacres in our nation's history," Motumbe said sullenly.

"For the record, ladies, you are being held as suspects and material witnesses in the disappearances of Abigail Sherman, Solodra Okoye, and Lloyd Sanders. Two of whom are American citizens. Hence my jurisdictional authority, which, I assure you, is quite real, having been personally granted by the Minister of the Interior of the great nation of Nigeria."

"And we've told you," replied Saronu, "that we have neither abducted nor harmed any of the people you named, in any way."

Shadow Leader inhaled heavily, like a man laboring for breath. He reached down, pulled out a large chrome revolver, and laid it on the table with a heavy metallic clank.

"Last chance," he said wearily. "Where are they now?"

Ten, twenty, and finally thirty seconds passed without a single word from any of the three women. Wearing a disgusted smirk, Shadow Leader stood, picked up the revolver, and sighted it with a practiced swiftness—right at the center of Saronu's forehead.

His other hand then appeared, and the women gasped.

It was holding a scythe blade.

Just then a door opened loudly behind them. The scythe disappeared behind his back.

"Hold on, sir," called a bold African voice. The man swaggered into the room. He was large, muscular, and wore a perfectly tailored uniform of the Nigerian Army. "Why don't you let me do the honors."

"Why? I have authority."

"I know you do, but this is an official governmental facility. It would look far better if we simply allowed me to finish what you so ably started. With you completely out of sight. I won't need the blade, of course, but I can assure you I'll get the job done right."

Shadow Leader's eyes narrowed at the blade reference. The two men stared at each other. An almost palpable coldness seemed to chill the air between them.

Finally, Shadow Leader broke contact and walked away.

"Fine. You do the honors," he said before disappearing through the same back door.

The officer did not waste a moment before turning to regard the women through heavily lidded, hateful eyes.

And yet something about the man seemed to put the prisoners at ease. They glanced up and down and around his figure, and faint smiles began to appear on their faces. Even when the man picked up the gun, checked its chamber for bullets, then cocked it, they did not seem fearful in the least.

"Prisoners, I am with the Nigerian People's Army, and I assure you that I have the authority to act according to my own discretion," he said in a voice dripping with menace. "Your sentence has already been decided, and it is about to be carried out. Now stand and follow me."

He led the three out of the room and into a bleak prison court-yard. As soon as the door was shut, he leaned toward them and whispered, "I know you are brave women," he said, "but you had better be prepared to scream like you never have before. Now kneel."

All three women knelt in the dirt, with their faces low to the ground. No blindfolds were provided as he was an executioner's team of one. At last, he raised up his gun and then lowered it swiftly in Saronu's face.

"Where are they?" he asked in a suddenly kinder voice.

"At our Eredo safe house. Just downriver from the first house, where it meets the rampart."

He nodded. "Now scream for your lives."

A shot cracked in the humid air. Then another. And a third.

The officer inclined his head to the left, indicating with a fierce look a side door left ajar.

The women needed no additional urging. They stumbled to their feet, sprinted to the door, and disappeared through its crooked frame.

As soon as they were gone, the officer walked slowly back into the building where Shadow Leader awaited him in a conference room.

"They're gone," he said, quite accurately.

"Yes, and so am I," said Shadow Leader. "Taking off for a long canoe trip. Down the creek to the Eredo Rampart. Ever heard of the place?"

"I have. But why go there?"

"It's where our satellite picked up the escapees' boat, washed up."

Shadow Leader turned on his heels and began to walk out.

"Best be careful," the Nigerian called out after him. "It's quite the swamp down there. Better bring a lot of men."

"I'm going alone."

"You're joking. You'll never make it."

"Colonel—Colonel Shawkey, is it? I was belly-flopping through Laos when you and the Nigerian brothers were still stealing dash from your mamas at corner checkpoints," Shadow Leader snarled. "I'm through with your incompetent teams of teenaged machete wavers. I'm going in myself, and there *will* be a body count."

CHAPTER

_43

An idle observer would have had to stand within thirty yards of the insertion point, and even then with an unobstructed view in strong daylight, to make out what was taking place.

Silent inflating into the shape of a Kodiak boat, the large rubber sheath lay camouflaged in an interweaving pattern consisting of eight shades of green. Shadow Leader walked over to the creek's edge in a ghillie suit of the same design. Even his face and hand paint bore identical hues.

He was so well concealed that, running down to the boat, he appeared like little more than an undulation in the jungle backdrop. His intrusion resembled the blowing of a stiff breeze against the underbrush more than the passing silhouette of a warrior.

He patted his trunk and limbs as a last-minute weapons check. He would travel light. A fairly well stocked combat bag was strapped to the boat, but on his person he carried a relatively light load. A sniper rifle, three handguns of differing ranges and calibers, three grenades and an equal number of knives stashed in various pockets and Velcroed sleeves. No radio headpiece or any of that high-tech stuff other than a pair of infrared goggles, which was a point of pride. He had a last-ditch radio stowed away on the Kodiak. None of that battlefield GPS stuff either. Finally, he had a map and a compass and solid briefing about the terrain.

That was all he needed.

And of course a well-oiled, sharpened sickle blade—a *scythe* as he preferred to call it—dangled from his belt.

After all, this was in part an amped-up grudge mission. Not the best-advised strategy from a tactical perspective, but that wasn't the point. It was also a man's desperate bid to save his own life with a single grandstanding achievement.

He was well downstream from where they believed his prey had put in, so the Kodiak's girth was not an issue. Besides, a foot of rain had fallen since then, and every waterway within a hundred miles was now swollen to twice the previous day's volume. With this nimble craft and its silent but powerful trolling motor, the extra water was a definite advantage.

He jumped in, turned and waved off his men. At first, there was no need of the motor, even with its quiet propeller. He would need it later for steering more than for propulsion. His strong first push had sent him into a deliciously quiet glide, which the onshore men did not wait to watch. Their superior disappeared against the Kodiak's floor, lying prone for his first few, vulnerable moments as the support crew melted back into the jungle.

Time elapsed: four minutes, thirty-two seconds.

Three hundred miles above his waterborne path, a KH-12 keyhole satellite peered through the cloud cover with lenses using near invisible, thermal infrared plus radar enhancement to scan the targets' hiding place at a resolution four feet across.

The original source for this satellite-tasking request lay buried under layers of highly classified communications channels. It would have taken months for even an experienced navigator of America's covert landscape to discover the official with whom it had originated.

Then, even if the inquirer lived a week, which was not likely, he or she still possessed a miniscule chance of uncovering the person's link to the Brotherhood of the Scythe.

SUNGBO'S EREDO RAMPART

They spent the night warm and dry in the hammocks, swathed in light cotton throws and raised well above the cool floor.

The next morning Abby awoke to the sound of heavy rain pelting the rampart outside. She padded out to the entrance and, instead of light and an outdoor world, was greeted with a curtain of water nearly obscuring the entire outside view.

Dylan sat before the scene while he prepared himself to venture out to scout for enemies. But given the forbidding nature of the weather and the long list of things she wanted to teach Dylan, Sister Okoye had other plans. He protested weakly and only for a short time, for experience was teaching them that not only was the older woman persuasive, but her entreaties always wound up having ample merit.

So they spent the bulk of that day huddled in the cave, watching the rain and listening to Sister Okoye's lilting, patient voice.

What the Nigerian taught Dylan, in the course of those long hours, was essentially a reeducation into a whole new form of warfare. It began, however, with a primer on the most essential parts of his relationship with God.

"God is far less interested in what you can do for Him, or in all this spiritual warfare," she said, "no matter how important it may be, than He is first of all in knowing *you*. Abiding with *you*. That comes first. All the other wonders come second."

So she taught him the varied ways of being in Him—the vital role of daily time in His Word. The critical importance of remaining constantly in prayer instead of just speaking to Him at mealtimes or important occasions. Especially, she emphasized, during times of warfare. She stressed the enormous value of hearing His voice through the less reliable yet still crucial sources of creation and of other people. She told him about the gifts of the Spirit.

"I'm surprised, and fairly confused," Dylan confessed after several hours. "All this time and you haven't yet talked about do's and don'ts or getting clobbered for committing this or that sin."

"Well, don't get your hopes too high," she answered with a smile, "because following His commands for righteous living is definitely important. The problem is, most people get it backward. Living right is not the way you become saved by Him. It's the proof, the evidence, that you already *are* in Him. So it's not as high on the list as you might have imagined, that's all. First comes brokenness, then walking with Him. Obedience is a byproduct."

After a light lunch, she moved on to the rest of his warrior's training. Relentlessly, she verbally pounded on the notion of his self-reliance, of his turning his heart cold and hard during battle. Dylan argued that emotionally insulating himself was the only way he could do what had to be done. And Sister Okoye responded that it could be true in conventional earthly combat, but not in the spirit realm. In that realm, complete openness and receptivity to God's Spirit was a prerequisite. She insisted that he empty himself during battle and soften his heart to hear from a general who wasn't far away in some command bunker but right there inside him, trying very hard to speak to him right where he stood.

And if he had done the real work of what she had taught him that morning—the practice of abiding in Him every day—then his most crucial preparations for conflict were already in place. He would be already primed to hear God's voice clearly through His Spirit. He had already invoked the strongest angelic protection possible, already sharpened his spiritual senses by having cleaned away all the impurities clogging his soul.

Sometime around six hours later, at the crown of midafternoon, the expression in Dylan's eyes began to soften and relax. His gaze toward Sister Okoye began to ease and yet somehow grow more intent, more understanding.

Somewhere in his thinking, Dylan had just turned a corner. His comprehension of spiritual things had just reached critical mass. And yet his doubts over being able to follow through had just crested as well.

"I don't know if I can do this," he said. "It all goes so completely against the training I've imposed on myself for decades. I'll try, because I've seen what God can do through women like you. But I don't know . . ."

Both Abby and Sister Okoye smiled at him knowingly.

"What is it?" he asked, self-conscious.

"It's our Sight," Abby began. "We can already see a difference in your spirit."

"Yes, and by the way," said Sister Okoye, "the little nuisance spirits are gone. They've all fled, because you already have twice the angelic escort you once had."

"It's true," Abby said. "You already look different in the spirit than you did first thing this morning."

"Yes, but if you follow my advice," said Okoye, "you will soon be twice the strapping warrior in that realm than you are in the flesh. And more important still, your name will be written in the Lamb's Book of Life. You will be a follower of the Most High."

CHAPTER
_44

Soon afterward, a respite in the rainfall beckoned them out once again. The threesome exited the cave and stood peering out over mile after mile of thick emerald vegetation, punctuated only by clouds of fog which rose like white ships sailing a dark green sea.

"Let's not expose even the tops of our heads," Dylan warned. "Even now, someone could be in the jungle, reconnoitering."

"I'm seeing something," Abby said, her eyes closed as though experiencing some kind of torment. "I'm being shown an image. It just keeps blinking in and out, like something that's trying to stick in my mind's eye but keeps slipping away."

"Do you recognize anything?" asked Okoye, staring at her anxiously.

"Well, I think unless I'm fooling myself, it involves a thick mass of darkness moving down the river. That's all so far."

"A mass of darkness," Okoye repeated thoughtfully. Slowly, her hand crept up to Abby's head and settled there. Okoye closed her eyes and her lips began to move furiously.

Dylan instantly realized what was happening and felt his own hand moving forward, almost of its own will. He felt bashful for some stupid reason, as though it somehow corroded his manhood to join in earnest prayer.

Yet he also knew, more strongly than ever, how vital this all was. He had tilted his allegiances irrevocably, forever.

"It is a single warrior who brings with him a whole dozen demonic strongmen. And he is coming for you," Sister Okoye said in a somber voice.

"Coming for *me*?" said Dylan, scanning the treetops behind her.

"Yes. He is our enemy. *Your* enemy, if I read things correctly."

"I don't understand."

"The Lord just showed him to me. A soldier all alone, floating down the river toward us. Very experienced. Very capable. And filled with hate. Most of it for you."

The truth burst on Dylan with an almost visible reaction. "Shadow Leader," he said.

"Is that the leader of the Scythe?"

"One of them, I think. I don't know much about the Brotherhood, but I believe he is very near the top of its hierarchy."

"And do you have a relationship, a history with this man?"

Dylan shook his head in bewilderment. "I thought I did, but apparently the position is handed down from one operational manager to the other. The Shadow Leader of five years ago was a former army officer who was my superior for much of my military career. He was one of my best friends. Saved my life once, in Grenada. The one who recruited me into extra-governmental work. But he . . . well, I don't know what happened to him. I didn't even realize he'd been replaced until another of their operatives told me. His voice had been synthesized, I think, to sound like the man I knew. You see, after a certain point, we only spoke by phone."

"He is very angry with you," Okoye added. "In fact, he is coming down here as much out of a thirst for revenge as a desire to complete his mission."

"That's all right," said Dylan. "We can handle him."

"No, *we* can't, remember—?" Okoye insisted.

"You're not listening to me," interrupted Dylan with an indulgent grin. "By *we*, I didn't mean we three. At least not the three of us, alone." He took both her hands in his. "Don't worry, my Sister. I understand now."

Sister Okoye gave him a relieved smile. "Did I tell you what most authorities, even the archaeologists, believe was the primary purpose of the Eredo Rampart?"

"A military barrier, I'm sure," said Dylan.

Okoye shook her head. "It was almost certainly a spiritual boundary. They've discovered countless clues pointing toward it being like a barricade on a demonic highway: Do not go any farther. In fact, even today superstitious locals hike in here and make offerings on the rampart to protect themselves against evil ones."

"You mean this jungle used to be full of demons?" asked Abby.

"It seems that way. Or maybe a specific spirit war waged here. It's possible that's why the Iya Agba were brought here in the first place."

"So in a way," Dylan said darkly, looking out again, "this is just another skirmish in a war that's been fought here for a long, long time."

"You have no idea how long," said Okoye, closing her eyes in a way that suggested she was quietly gathering strength. "In fact," she continued, "neither do I."

They began their battle plan with a procedure that suited both the carnal and the spiritual warrior: a thorough circling of their surroundings. In this case, they were carrying out two utterly different objectives at once. First, cataloguing their position's most useful features and lines of approach, and at the same time laying down an intense prayer-journey around its periphery.

They walked as furtively as they could, mindful that their attacker could already be watching. Dylan had convinced the other two to proceed in a manner where, as two of them moved forward along the top of the wall, one would remain behind and closely watch for any sign of detection or telltale signs among the surrounding wildlife.

After several minutes of this, they regrouped at an odd hump-shaped rise on the ridgeline. Despite the fact that she crouched just two feet from a seventy-foot drop, Sister Okoye sat with her eyes shut, her lips constantly moving.

"What are you asking for?" Abby said in a soft, woman-to-woman tone of voice.

"For direction," Okoye replied without opening her eyes. "Simply direction from Him. For Him to move on our behalf. Lead us to His defenses, not ours."

Finally she opened her eyes and fixed her gaze on Dylan. "What are you thinking about?" she asked.

"I'm thinking our enemy will probably do his recon at nightfall, like most good special ops guys do," he muttered. "If we can trick him into misidentifying our position, maybe with some kind of an improvised heat signature, then maybe if we stay very quiet in an offset ambush spot, we can fool him into going after it."

"This is where this new warfare goes into action," said Okoye. "Be praying as you go that God will lead you to His place, and His solutions. No need to close your eyes or anything. Just say it inside as you go."

I feel weird, God, Dylan began silently, *asking the Creator of the universe with help on something as down-to-earth as a place to hide. Or a plan of attack. But if you're in the business of saving my sorry hide, then I guess I better ask you . . .*

They kept creeping along the wall's summit. Nothing happened, and Dylan felt the cold gray world returning hard, and for a moment despaired of his new faith.

"Look!" cried Abby, pointing.

At the base of a wall of rocks, covered by new moss, lay the remains of a shrine. A small clay plate, the rotted clumps of some kind of food offering, and scratched-up icons—a cross and a few symbols Dylan vaguely recognized. And a half-burned candle.

"There's your heat signature. Would that work, Dylan?"

He picked up the lumpy mass of old wax and turned it around in his hands. Nodding, he smiled at Abby. "Yeah, I think so."

"And look here." Sister Okoye was pointing just above the shrine, at a spot on the rock face.

Her discovery was a group of ancient-looking drawings, finely etched into the wall's surface. Most of the symbols were representational: a crocodile, a rain cloud, two beasts that reminded Abby of American pronghorn antelope. Then an eye. A strangely formed figure eight. A broad-hipped female form.

Sister Okoye could not tear her gaze away from the sight. She stopped moving. Her breathing seemed suspended.

"What is it?" asked Abby.

"Well, several things. First of all, that eye is the symbol of the Iya Agba. There's one in a corner of the cave we've been staying in. There's another one marking the beginning of the steps up the rampart; that's how I knew where to find it. I imagine they're all over this place. But I've never seen one grouped with other images. Or even heard of it before."

"Is that woman a fertility figure?"

"It appears so."

"Aren't those usually pagan?"

"Yes. The people around here mix everything together, often with tragic results. They don't know any better."

"What about that number eight? Isn't that weird? Isn't that shape a modern, or at least a Western number?"

Okoye frowned. "You're right, Abby. I wonder if it's supposed to be an eight at all."

"A coiled serpent?" offered the younger woman.

"I surely hope not."

"Yes, but look at how the bottom loop of the eight is sort of curled sideways. And there's a double shape inside. Another loop with a curled top. A baby serpent maybe?"

"Is it a kernel of some kind?" asked Dylan.

"Maybe," conceded Okoye. "There's definitely more to this shape than at first glance."

"Think of it according to the first principle," Dylan said. "Marcus Aurelius—'Of each particular thing, ask what is it in itself?'"

"Well, if I take the bottom of the eight by itself, it looks . . ."

"It looks like a flame." Sister Okoye had said it, staring ever harder at the image. "A flame whose uppermost tip curls into some kind of a ring around itself."

"Fire," said Dylan. "We have a flame, or a fire."

"A fire that's crowned by—"

"That's it!" he interrupted. "A fire with a crown."

"A royal fire. A fire of the kings."

"No," Sister Okoye said, "not a crown. Look how perfectly rounded it is. No points, no indents. That's no crown I've ever seen. But look how it's centered right over the top of the flame in a circle."

"It's a halo," said Abby.

"A holy fire," said Dylan.

Abby chuckled, thinking he was joking. Then, seeing his serious expression, she grew serious again.

"This is the next clue we've been searching for," said Okoye. "I can sense it. We're close. So close."

"A holy fire?"

"Yes, but look how close it is to the seeing-eye symbol. There are eyes all over this site, but all of them are alone. Nowhere near another carving. This is special. It's referring to one of our Sisterhood who is near a holy fire. She must be someone special. An ordained member."

"Maybe it's that matriarch you told me about," said Abby. "The one everyone thinks is ailing."

Sister Okoye looked up at Abby with a sharp, affirmative glance. "I think you're right. That could be it. God led us to the right clue."

"Really," Dylan said, sounding doubtful.

"Please don't let yourself fall into the skeptical Western mindset, Dylan," chided Okoye. "This is one of the biggest breaches between believers in the West and the rest of the world. And one of the Western church's biggest limitations. I told you that many Western Christians put the reality of the spiritual realm out of their minds. But here in Africa, we can hardly avoid it. It's always been right there on the surface, a part of everyday life. We've had witch doctors and shamanic occult and evil manifestations as long as we've had people. As a result, we've never been tempted to water down or explain away the powerful encounters between the armies of God and those of the devil."

"Maybe this is one of the reasons why, when our sisters were kidnapped to America," Abby interjected, "their impact never influenced American culture beyond the African-American community itself. Even to this day. Our Western mindset just wasn't ready to accept it."

"So where does all this leave us?" asked Dylan.

"Find a Holy Fire, and you'll find the source you seek," Okoye replied.

"You mean this woman you all think is the leader?"

"Yes, Dylan, and more. She will have the answers to all this mystery."

"So we're going to Ethiopia."

"*You're* going to Ethiopia. But yes, that is where the trail ends."

"We can't go there straightaway," added Dylan. "First we'll have to get to London where I have my European cache."

"Cache?" said Abby.

"All operatives like me have places around the globe where they can access money from a secret account and resources like new identity papers. I have one in L.A., one in Caracas, and one in London."

"Yes, but how do we get there? We don't even have papers to get out of Nigeria."

"I have no idea," he grunted. "One miracle at a time, princess."

"And He will give you one," said Okoye. "Do you see, Dylan, how just now He led us to both an answer to our mystery and a solution for your defenses?"

"I do," he said. "Pretty amazing."

"So you see, I wasn't trying to keep you from making earthly preparations. I just wanted for God to guide you into the ones He had for us. They tend to be far more powerful."

"Well, now that we've gotten that out of the way," said Dylan with an uncomfortable grin, "let's work on staying alive until we can get there. We're a long way from Ethiopia. And a long way from *safe*." He stood, holding the candle in his hand. "Besides, I have an idea. But we have to move fast."

CHAPTER
_45

Over the miles, the initial embers of Shadow Leader's resolve had stoked themselves into a virtual bonfire of revenge. Deprived of its true target, his hatred had fed, feasted actually, on his most primal companions—the solitude of the jungle, the thumping of his heart, the glide along a liquid highway, the silent flow of time.

Anything. Any stimulus at all.

When he finally arrived at the landing—which was no longer a shore but a mere left turn into deeper swamps—he felt himself rejuvenated into the deliciously unstoppable killing machine of his younger days. An unthinking force of nature.

Rejuvenated? he said to himself. *Forget that. I'm reborn.*

Nothing would stop him but nature itself—he could sense it within him. He hadn't felt this exhilarated in years.

He saw the rampart from the satellite photographs loom above a razor-thin layer of mist. Adrenaline seethed through every muscle in his body. He vowed to himself to line those three freaks' decapitated heads on top of that very ridge, then snap a photo of the sight and uplink it to the screen of every old fossil sitting in a rocking chair somewhere, deliberating his fate.

That would show 'em.

He pulled out his map, scrutinized its tracing of the rampart's path through the rain forest, and looked up at the real thing. There'd be a lot of ground to cover, and he wasn't going to wait for nightfall to start. He ripped an armful of reeds and vines from the jungle around him and spent twenty minutes fitting an intricate camouflage across the far lip of the Kodiak. *Perfect.* Now he was not only exquisitely disguised by color, but transformed into little more than a drifting clump of jungle flora. One of millions in the area, from the look of things.

Even his infrared goggles were painted camouflage, he noted as he strapped them on. He willed himself into invisibility. Resuming his stomach-down pose in the boat, he untied his tether and started the motor. He steered the disguised craft between his outstretched feet behind him and began to slide ever so slowly through the jungle's edge, just inside the canopy and the overfilled moats.

His nose crinkled under the assault of a foul smell. But just as quickly, recognizing its source, Shadow Leader broke into a savage grin. The flood had just offered him its first gift.

Swamp gas. *Methane.*

The sun fell, the moon rose, and an unlikely hush fell over the brooding heights of the Eredo Rampart. At the opening of their chamber, Dylan knelt, poised to set in place the last of his counter-measures. The half-guttered candle taken from the wall shrine now sat below him, ready to be lit and become their perfect lure: a self-perpetuating heat and light source. Just enough to seemingly betray a low level of human activity.

After fighting with a buried wick in the dim light, he managed to light the flame, then turned to the two women.

"I've put off saying this until the very end," he said, "but I think one of you will need to stay here with the candle. Not only to make sure it keeps burning, but to set the trap. He'll acquire a thermal sig-nature from a long ways off. But once he gets within any kind of sight line, he'll want to see an actual person or he may sniff a trap and bolt."

"I'll do it," said Sister Okoye. "I am not as mobile as you two. It is the perfect task for me."

"Yes, but it's the most dangerous," Abby protested.

"Exactly, my dear. After all, I am fairly old, even if you cannot guess exactly how old I am. I have led a full life."

Abby winced at the implications of Okoye's statement, but then let it go.

Dylan resumed his briefing. "If he's following special ops strategy, he'll strike fast and hard. The idea is to wrap everything up within thirty seconds. Granted, that's usually when you attack with a full squad. But I still expect things to happen quickly. Sister, just in case he considers sniping, stay just inside the entrance but no farther. Don't give him a target. If he climbs up, which I think he will, duck out of the way or you could get hit. I'll be just above you with the gun. If you see me wave, then slide away and get out of there fast, because it means I completely misread him and he decided to open up with explosives. But if he's on a personal vendetta to take me down, then he'll come up in person. Besides, he wants to kill Abby with his own hands."

Abby's face blanched.

"Sorry, Abby," he mumbled. "Now we should get into positions. If nothing happens by dawn, we just regroup here. Do so carefully in case it's a trap. But if your Sight was correct, he'll use the night. Oh, and one more thing."

"What's that?" asked Abby nervously, as if she could hardly bear one more of these nerve-racking disclosures.

"I suppose we should pray?"

They were holding hands above the rampart, each of them moving their lips in silence, when a loud but breathy *thump* filled their ears. Dylan's head shot up, his eyes sharp as knives, but out of deference to the others, he waited one second.

Two.

Three. He groaned inwardly. *Please, Sister, finish the prayer. . . .*

Finally out of patience, he dropped both hands and scrambled to the far edge.

The moat's waterline was on fire with an eerie blue flame. A foul smoke curled up toward them on a light breeze.

"Swamp gas," whispered Sister Okoye behind him. "He's using every advantage."

"He's good," agreed Dylan, nodding. "He'll use the smoke as his cover when he scales the wall. Let's get into position."

Shadow Leader had identified the distant heat signature over an hour before, then spent the bulk of that time approaching carefully for a better look. Surely, they wouldn't make it that simple, he warned himself. Then he remembered that the fools probably considered themselves undetected and had no notion of his coming.

Sure enough, as he approached in the twilight he'd seen the tops of one or two heads moving around, seemingly unconcerned. He had smiled, feeling a slight twinge of disappointment at the ease of it all. No matter, he had consoled himself, for he'd indulge himself in a full tactical approach anyhow.

Which was exactly what he was doing.

CHAPTER
_46

At the sight of the smoke—an unexpected tactic—Dylan felt the full weight of his old operational mindset come crashing back into his thoughts.

This is crazy, he heard the voice of his experience hiss at him. He'd finally cracked. Here he was, practically defenseless, facing a coordinated assault from a foe presumably armed to the teeth, defending a totally exposed shooting-ducks gallery overlooking a hundred miles of perfect cover. Worse yet came the hard-nosed voice from his past; he was heeding a couple of loony women so overdosed on religion that they wanted him to push aside the best military training in the world in favor of mumbled prayers and half-baked warm fuzzies.

Another voice broke in as correction, reminding him that Abby's and Sister Okoye's faith wasn't asking him to throw out his training but merely place it under the authority of someone other than himself, then add to it a whole new level of strategy he'd never known before.

Still, it felt—

Hatfield!—roared the voice of every drill instructor and field officer he'd ever worked with, barking at him in tandem—*Pull it together. . . !*

The smoke, now curling heavily about their position, embodied the rising urgency of his dilemma. He tried to analyze the situation with the same ease and calm he once had been famous for, but now the lateness of the hour made everything spin into a frantic, dizzy blur. A surge of panic rushed through him. His heart began to race like that of a rank amateur in his first simulation op. His lungs began to heave wildly in his chest.

And swirling around the core of this internal tempest was a maelstrom of old combat rules, warnings, war slogans and axioms, each one drilled into his subconscious many years before, each one now adrift and chaotic, crashing into the others and threatening to churn his brain into senselessness.

Should he stand his ground? Shock his enemy with a bold, random countermove? Abandon the position altogether? Wrack his brain for wily, out-of-the-box trickery?

After all, the latter had been his own choice, just today.

From somewhere in the mental carousel arose the calming, unlikely notion of praying. His soldier's mind told him *no*—that the time for praying was later, when all the action was over and the dust had settled.

Another consciousness, deeper and steadier, seemed to be whispering that *now* was exactly the right moment.

So Dylan started the prayer like an impatient teenager eager for his parents to leave. *God, seems clear that right now might be a good time to hear from you. It's just that you didn't wire me to stop and check out of reality right in the middle of a fight. So maybe, if you could make yourself really, really clear—and incredibly persuasive—and all in very short order, that would be great! Thank you. Amen.*

Another idea came to him from out of nowhere.

The lighting of the methane—it was too quick. Too easy. It was a diversion. Some kind of trap.

But what? What was he being diverted from?

The thought came hurtling through his brain like a stray bullet.

The other side of the rampart!

He'd focused on the jungle side of the wall because the rain forest at large represented the outside world, the direction of Lagos and civilization and the danger all those things embodied. But with a hundred-mile-long wall, how difficult would it have been to set off the swamp gas using some sort of fuse or delayed ignition, then double back and scale the rampart somewhere downrange, attacking from behind when the fire's commotion had sucked all his attention the other way?

And here he was—even now, straddling the top but clearly oriented toward, and looking down on, the moat side.

He pulled out the dead insurgent's revolver, the one with only four bullets left, and swiftly turned to the far side of the rampart's edge. This slope was dark, the night cloudy and moonless, the wall's plummeting depths only visible through the dimmest of shadows from the smoke rising above the opposite rim.

He'd sheltered Abby on a higher point of the wall's spine, ready and instructed on how to rain a half dozen boulders on Shadow Leader if he tried to climb the Sisterhood's ancient footholds. Hours before, he had agonized over the decision of what to do with Abby, mentally poring over contingencies of concealing her in the cave, taking her to a hiding place deep in the jungle or along the wall, even putting her in plain sight to draw out his enemy faster. Finally, the wisest course had seemed to give her a spot atop the wall, both within sight of him and reasonably protected from prying eyes below. It wasn't perfect, but given the circumstances it appeared the wisest choice.

Turning around, Dylan put two fingers to his eye sockets, the military symbol for *watch*, and pointed toward her appointed lookout area. *Keep looking*, he was saying, and she nodded knowingly.

While he scrambled along the edge and strained for any sign of attack, Dylan fought against yet another panic. This wave screamed at him that the situation was falling out of his control, that he was losing the initiative, hopelessly stuck in defense. He'd never been in this situation before. He'd always out-trained, out-thought, out-foxed, out-prepared, then flat-out outperformed any adversary he'd ever faced before. He'd never, ever been forced into playing catch-up.

That voice inside him wanted to curse those foolish women and their ridiculous notions for putting him here.

And they'd be the first ones to pay with their lives, the voice added darkly.

He gritted his teeth. Something else within him, from another place entirely, was warning Dylan that *no*, it was nothing like that—that, indeed, this very voice of anger and panic was his greatest danger, and listening to its bitter ravings would only lead to failure and death.

Shut up! he finally screamed, mentally, to his warring insides. *I'm sticking with God and His ways*, he said to no one but himself, reaffirming what he desperately wanted to do.

Lord, please show me . . . please guide me . . .

"Dylan!" came a masculine shout from behind him.

Before the bitter bile even had time to rise in his throat, he was already turned back around. And then he almost fainted in shock and disgust.

Abby faced him, her eyes wide with terror, a scythe snug across her throat. Behind her writhed a camouflaged jumble of limbs and ghillie-suit strips.

The realization sank into him like a poison. Shadow Leader hadn't come up from either side. He'd crawled right along the top of the spine like some lizard!

And now he had her. And him.

Dylan let go of the revolver, letting it drop to the ground.

"That was pathetic, my man," snarled Shadow Leader. "I mean, I'm a little long in the tooth, and I hardly broke a sweat cutting through your defenses. Sort of reminded me of your apartment, that cute little Chinese technology you had rigged up there. What's the matter, man? Did I just overestimate your abilities? Were you just overrated? Or have you been having too good a time out here with your little harem?"

"Look, if you're here to punish me, then fine. You can have me. Just let her go. She's of no use here."

"Ahhh, Dylan—are you still figuring me for a straight-up soldier? I know better than that, my man, and so do you. You may be *my* target, but I know more about the other side than you'd ever guess. And I know this one here's what this operation's about."

"What about Sister Okoye? She knows everything we do. She can do your sick cause a lot of damage."

"I'm killing her next, you fool!"

But Dylan wasn't listening. Hearing the word *next* was all he needed. With a quick, garbled *Please, God!* he launched himself desperately into the air. The impulse had thunderstruck him, with no plan or logic other than the knowledge that if he just stood there, he had seconds to live. Even with the sudden reaction, there came a gunshot and a bullet grazing the length of his side with a blaze of agony.

And he paid for the reaction's impulsiveness. His uninjured side slammed into the wall, shooting waves of pain straight through to his already seething flank. He rolled and felt gravity latch on to his limbs, warning him of a great fall just ahead.

Another gunshot, and a bullet whistled inches from his face.

Falling, he stretched out his hands in lunging, desperate clutches, trying to find a finger hold. Ridges, moss tufts, disintegrating clumps, all sheared cruelly from his grasp. He could feel his descent gain speed, gather momentum. The bottom wanted him. A cold fate had him in its teeth.

Then a single ring finger seemed to catch on something. Strong from years of rock climbing, he flexed the finger to hold fast. One, two, three more fingers joined it, clawing on to the outcropping. He swung his free arm around to strengthen his hold, then remembered this was the injured side and clenched his teeth in agony as he stretched.

Somewhere above him, Abby screamed. The sound of her voice in that state made him recoil so viciously that he almost lost his grip. He heard the body hit the wall above where he was dangling, then start rolling down toward him.

Please, God! he pleaded. *Save us. . . !*

CHAPTER

_47

But the falling body came for him anyway—a dark shadow bouncing grotesquely toward him. He prepared to swerve and try to avoid it. Then it passed, bouncing, striking.

Ghillie strips waved over his face. Camouflaged legs kicked the air viciously.

Dylan gaped, then turned downward to look.

Shadow Leader! Had she. . . ?

He saw a split second of hate-filled eyes and then . . . something he had never seen before. In the tiniest of fractions, a fleeting impression of fangs, of not two eyes but six, ten. A shiver of hatred so cold and intense that he felt as if he'd been plunged into dry ice.

Instinctively, he looked up.

Abby's hand filled his vision, outstretched from somewhere above him. His right hand shot up, grabbed hers and then pulled. At first he feared he might yank her over with his weight, but then he felt her impressive strength and so pulled hard. Seconds later he scrambled to safety, then to his feet.

Abby was beaming.

"How. . . ? Did you throw him over?" he said, hardly believing it possible.

She nodded through a wide grin.

"Judo. Grades ten through twelve." And she laughed. Actually laughed out loud.

Dylan felt the urge to laugh with her, until it occurred to him that Shadow Leader might not have been neutralized by the fall. With a body like that man's, an imperfect slope and a soft landing, you never knew. He reached for Abby and pulled her back, away from the far edge. He saw a shadow in her eyes and realized she'd misinterpreted his action.

"Let's be careful," he said, explaining a little too emphatically, "until we know for sure what happened to him. Stay down."

"How about I go to the back of the cave and get ready there."

"Good idea," he said, then watched her turn away.

As he approached the edge, he realized he was more engrossed in the new prayer he was thinking than the danger all about him. Perhaps this was growth, he wondered. Maybe this is what Sister Okoye had wanted for him so badly.

He peered down into the gloom. The bottom was smothered in total blackness, and yet he thought, with the briefest imprint of his peripheral vision, that he saw something. A silhouette? A writhing of animals? Something evil? Or just . . .

A grenade, its trajectory curving up around the wall!

The explosion rocked the wall to his left. Heat and a terrible force tossed him savagely aside.

He clenched his every muscle and rolled away, feeling his battered side absorb yet another white-hot impact.

Despite the pain, Dylan had to shake his head in admiration for his adversary's toughness. A seventy-foot rock tumble, right after a very hard landing on packed dirt—it was all pretty impressive for a man fifteen years his senior. And the man wasn't just sitting there thanking his lucky stars for surviving either. He was counterattacking, and with every resource available to him.

And if the grenades continued, and got any closer . . .

He pushed over one of the boulders Abby had lined up to knock down the other side. Rolling it to the far rim, he let it drop. He heard repeated impacts as it bounced down the side, followed by a flat *thump*.

Dylan vowed not to wait for the next grenade. He began running for the cave. That would be their final stand; he'd known it from the beginning.

He reached the entrance, saw Sister Okoye faithfully knelt before the candle, deep in prayer. "What's God telling you?" he panted, running up to her.

"He's here, along with His enemies," she whispered. "He wants you to trust Him. Listen for His voice."

"I have been," Dylan said as he took up a defensive position just outside the cove. "I'm just not sure I'll survive what He's telling me to do."

Another grenade exploded, forcing them all down on their stomachs. Facing the women, Dylan warned them through gritted teeth.

"He's coming back."

Abby could not tell whether it was a result of fatigue, stress or trauma, or even the surreal sight of smoke wisping about their once-pristine aerie. Regardless of the physical cause, she knew something was up.

She could smell the tiniest aroma of heaven.

Now came the faintest hint of that ethereal music. The exquisite brush of angels' wings. The inexpressible yet overwhelming joy, as singular as the taste of an exotic food, which had overwhelmed her before.

Yes, that was it—just a taste, an inexplicable crossing of spiritual wires.

Her vision began to blur again. But now it was smiles she glimpsed—white light instead of blackness, peace instead of turmoil.

Angels.

Now there unfurled a great unshaped purpose, welling up in her spirit. A wonderful *something* that was slowly gathering form.

Lord? What do you have in store for me? What do you want me to do? Please make it known to me. . . .

Then she stood, the idea fully formed and settled in her mind.

She picked up Dylan's sickle from where he'd thrown it an hour before, useless. Seemingly useless. Without even a pause to look about her for protection, she walked out of the cave and up the wall's spine to her former perch.

"Abby! Be careful!" shouted Dylan's voice behind her. "He's throwing grenades, remember?"

She turned and flashed him a defiantly blissed-out grin.

A few feet ahead, marked by a small hole in the rampart and a constellation of black and gray smudges, lay the spot where the enemy's first grenade had exploded. She reached it and held up her right arm.

In a single, emphatic motion, she raised the scythe with her other hand and sliced her wrist.

The sight of blood dribbling to the ground caused her to smile again, even more fiercely. *Am I indeed following a heavenly prompting?* she asked herself. *Or am I going mad?*

The world around her shifted into slow motion. Behind her, through a pale gauze of unreality, she could hear Dylan's and then Sister Okoye's voice rising in reaction. Dylan was shouting her name with palpable fear. Okoye called her name also but in a different tone.

Her legs were carrying her back toward the cave entrance. Sister Okoye now stood beside her, and she felt the older woman's hands bear her up, helping draw her back to the safety of the cave.

"Abby! What are you doing?" Dylan cried. "Sister Okoye, what is she—? Is she trying to kill herself?"

His face passed by, wracked by confusion, as the two women shuffled slowly deeper into the cave, with Abby's wrist still dripping blood as they walked.

Dylan looked down, and a sudden epiphany seemed to brighten his features. At the last second, Abby's hand trailed back and grasped his.

"Come with us, Dylan," she said in an otherworldly monotone. "Here is where we make our last stand. He will follow us now."

Dylan nodded, seeming to understand.

She looked up and saw Dylan glance back at the smoke from the latest explosion that drifted across the cave's mouth, faintly lit by the swamp's dying flames. The air of astonished calm on his face conveyed that he saw how perfect a plan it was. He turned back and locked eyes with Abby and nodded his acknowledgment.

Blearily she smiled back at him.

Abby allowed her knees to bend into a kneeling position, then held out her wrist for Sister Okoye to bandage. Neither one needed words to convey what needed to be done, for a kind of communion had gathered around the two of them. Okoye looked down with a soulful tenderness as she flipped a band of gauze around the wounded wrist.

Abby pulled back her arm and gave the other two a knowing nod. It was time. She crawled back a foot or two and lay down, curled into a fetal ball. Sister Okoye moved forward and blew out the candle. Near darkness settled over the cave. Dylan crept back, out of sight along the farthest wall, then sat down and clutched his injured side. Sister Okoye went and sat beside him, her eyes glued to the entrance.

Boom! Another grenade roared, so close now that it shook the entire wall and sent a rain of dirt down upon their heads.

They remained silent and still, and waited.

CHAPTER

_48

They did not have to wait long. A shadow stuttered across the penumbra, then stretched larger. A sense of pervading evil blew into the cave, its pungency almost suffocating to the three who lay prone inside.

"You fools," rumbled the half growl, half grunt from the wounded Shadow Leader's lips.

The man bent down toward Abby with the grimace of someone seriously hurt. A harsh light blinked on from the end of his machine gun and filled the room with a hazy glow. The barrel trained itself on Dylan, then Sister Okoye. It moved back to Dylan, lingered for a moment, then moved away when he didn't move a muscle. Blood-streaked eyes moved across the scene—from the girl mortally wounded, to Dylan almost dead against the back wall, to the Nigerian dazed and shaken up.

"Hatfield, you sure don't know how to protect your woman," the man chuckled. "Let alone yourself."

He returned his attention to Abby, prodding her motionless form. Spotting the scythe lying next to her, he bent down and picked it up. Confusion swept over his face. "What is this? You're offering yourself? You trying to deny me?"

He took the blade and pressed it against her neck. Seeing no wound there, he frowned. "Hey, where are you injured?"

He raised the machine-gun barrel to Abby's quivering forehead. Then he raised the scythe. . . .

"No!" Dylan bellowed, his voice thundering through the chamber.

He threw himself forward—the sacrificial plunge of a secret-service agent rather than a special ops man, and a reckless diversion intended to draw the bullet his way instead of harming the protected target. But it also had dim roots in the training of years past, when his Delta Force instructors had taught him that a bold, multisensory surprise would confuse the human brain for at least three seconds, rendering a coherent response unlikely during the interval. It wasn't much time, but enough for a skilled warrior to close the gap and engage the enemy hand to hand.

Only one caveat. This had always assumed that the enemy was marginally trained and unaccustomed to the savagery of tactical situations.

Shadow Leader screamed. Ripped a wild volley from his machine-gun hand. In a moment Dylan would later revisit in the agonizing, slow-motion replay of his mind, he twisted in midair and missed the bullets by so little, he felt their fiery path pierce the air along his left forearm and flank, then zip past him into the cave's far corner.

He struck the wall, winced in pain, and realized in a wrenching instant that he was a breath away from utter failure. His leap had missed contact with Shadow Leader, and Abby was no safer than before.

That was when, at the back of the chamber, Sister Okoye rolled sideways. Shadow Leader shot wildly in her direction, but she dropped down, throwing all of her weight onto a crude lever Dylan had fashioned there.

It was Dylan's great idea, the last bastion of his defense.

In the seconds that followed, the four hammocks, which had once hung lazily from the ceiling, now flung themselves from their restraints into an improvised catapult. At the center of this suspended web was the heavy cooking stone, hurtling through the air now at a stunning velocity.

Dylan shouted, Abby flattened herself on the ground, and the stone rocketed into Shadow Leader's midsection with a sickening crunch. His machine gun still scattering a spray of wild, random rounds, the enemy was hurled back out of the cave's entrance like a circus performer shot from a cannon. He landed stiffly along the rampart's rim, several yards beyond the start of Abby's blood trail.

"Stay here!" barked Dylan, and he bounded from the chamber to where the man lay.

Shadow Leader, aka Peter Sonnenberg of McLean, Virginia, now lay in a bloodied heap, disfigured, and in a state only vaguely resembling human consciousness.

In the physical realm, he was actively dying.

In the spiritual, he was being devoured.

The sight of his wounds, even dimly glimpsed through the alternating patterns of his uniform, was nearly impossible for even Dylan to look at. So was the sound of the man's voice, which came out pleading and frantic and drowned in a horrific gurgling sound. But even more unbearable was the presence of evil festering all about him. Dylan found himself barely able to stand it. The sensation oppressed and weighed upon him with an almost physical weight, and he felt something deep inside him recoil as though he were ingesting poison.

"There they are," Shadow Leader gurgled. "There they are. Liars, liars . . ."

"Who are the liars?" Dylan asked.

"They told me our masters were beautiful . . . sad and tormented, too beautiful for words."

"You're right. You served a liar," Dylan said.

"'Our masters are beautiful,' they said. They lied. . . . Oh, they're so ugly! You repulse me! Get away from me! Get back. . . !"

Animated by the strange, unexplainable strength of the dying, the man reached up and began to grapple his arms against some invisible foe. He opened his mouth, but only half a scream emerged.

"Get them away, Dylan!"

"There's only one way to do that. You have to cry out to God."

"No way!"

"Everything you were told was a lie. Didn't you just realize that? God loves you! He loves you more than you know."

"Not me! No way!" The man's eyes flew open now, wide and staring in terror at some unseen apparition. "You don't know all I did against Him!"

"It won't stop Him. He'll forgive you."

"All the people I harvested! All the killing! All the bloodshed!"

"He shed His own blood just so you could be forgiven of all that."

"No! It must be wrong! It's gotta be wrong! Get away from me! Oh, get away! Leave me alone—"

His eyes rolled to the back of his head. His arms fell to each side.

Dylan sighed heavily. For several long moments he sat staring at the fear-wracked death mask. Finally, he reached down to close the man's eyes and, despite having just fought him to the death, felt a thick knot of sadness take shape within him.

It struck him that there was no greater tragedy than the moment he had just witnessed. No matter how loathsome the man's existence had been, Shadow Leader had still been a fellow human, a deluded soul who had placed his trust in the wrong voices. Followed a horrific path and heeded its fellow travelers unthinkingly.

Saddest of all, here was a man so ingrained in his habits that even when he glimpsed the truth near the end, he had squandered his final chance rather than admit his mistake. He chose, however unknowingly, an eternity of torments over the humility of one moment's contrition.

Suddenly Dylan found himself fighting an overpowering surge of emotion—an equal mixture of sadness, relief, and awe. Maybe it was because, looking down on the destroyed man, he thought he could see himself. This was the path he could have embarked on, save but for the choice he made only two days before. He felt so eternally grateful for having been spared of his former direction that tears welled up in his eyes.

He looked back and saw Abby sitting at the entrance, shielding her eyes. He remembered. She could see for herself every revolting beast the dying man had been screaming at.

Only then, seeing the pain on her face, did he realize the truth. From the perspective of the Sisterhood, and of the Savior he now followed, this man's death had not been a victory at all. A narrow escape, maybe. But nothing to celebrate. Nobody had won, least of all Dylan.

His enemy's death was only a victory for the entity now in possession of the man's soul.

He stared back at Abby for a third time. She was gone, disappeared inside the chamber.

A howl of pain filled his ears.

Dylan would not remember running down the top of the rampart and throwing himself into the cave. He would only remember the pathetic image of Sister Okoye's body limply cradled in Abby's arms. And the incredibly poignant, full-throated grief of this young woman as she held the remains of yet another fallen mother figure and shouted out her rage to the four winds.

Then there was Sister Okoye's face. The life within it was fading rapidly, though her eyes seemed aglow with the dawn of a different world. Her pupils appeared focused on someplace else. Her mouth smiled at someone—someone clearly beloved, yet not in this chamber. Her lips moved faintly, slowly.

"I'm so sorry," Dylan mumbled, barely coherent. "I failed you. I didn't listen . . ."

Dylan bent closer, and her gaze seemed to settle back on him, delicately.

"You did not fail, my son. Please listen. You did not fail. This is gain for me, my son. My son in the spirit . . . remember."

A sudden tide of maternal love surged through him such as he had not felt since childhood.

"I will remember, I promise," he whispered into her ear.

Yes, without a doubt he knew it. This was his mother in the faith. The woman who had nurtured him and labored through his second birth. His spiritual family tree would forever begin with her.

Now, hard on the heels of realizing this, came the hammer blow of losing a mother once again—just as he had his earthly one only a few years ago.

Why—why did I let him get off those shots? he lamented.

"No grief, Dylan. Abby. This is my day of victory. Never forget." She reached up and, trembling, cradled his neck, then hers. "Walk with Him, and I will see you both. . . ."

The arm and her head fell limp.

For a long moment Dylan's world went gray.

Abby finally looked up from the sister's face, and her own features suddenly illuminated with the very same glow.

"What is it, Abby?"

She looked at him with blank incredulity. "You mean you don't see them?"

"No, Abby . . . forgive me," he replied. "I don't see them, whatever *them* is."

She scooted back as though allowing a new arrival the room to proceed forward. "Oh, I wish you could. They're right there, two of them."

She turned to him, eyes wide with wonder.

"They're taking her, Dylan. Two angels I've never seen before. I think they're escorts. They're being so kind, so gentle. They've both reached out a hand and eased her from her body. And oh—you should see Sister Okoye. She's free of that body, and she's so radiant . . ."

For Dylan, the moment was a bracing mixture of the wondrous and the unbearably bitter. Every inch of him could feel that something incredible was taking place all around him, although any outward evidence was confined to faint cues like the slightest warming of the light, in the temperature, on his own forehead. A faint but distinct quiver in the hairs along his forearms.

He looked down and told himself it could have been the guttering of the candle, which was finally beginning to burn out.

But no. He knew better, far better, by now.

At the same time, his heart still ached at his own failure, his self-directed guilt at Sister Okoye's fate. How could it not be abject defeat when he had not listened, not waited for God, but just thrown himself forward in some fearful reflex?

And the hardest irony of all—that if not for the heroism and sacrifice of the same woman he had imperiled, they would all be dead by now.

CHAPTER
_49

JERUSALEM

She reared up like someone who had been struck across the back—her eyes wide open, her mouth gasping for air.

A nearby nun hurried over, ready to administer aid, but the stricken sister did not require physical intervention. She looked like someone who had just awakened from a heartbreaking nightmare.

"Are you all right?" pleaded the nun. "Shall I get you some water? A spot of food, maybe?"

"No, thank you," she answered, as always. "But what happened? Was there a disturbance while I slept? A car bomb? Gunfire?"

"No, not anything, Sister. It has been a peaceful night."

"Not in the spirit. Somebody just went to be with our Lord. A sister of mine, somewhere. I have no idea who, just yet. But someone vital. A precious member of the Sisterhood."

"Was she close to here?"

"I feel it dimly, so I do not believe so. I believe she was from quite far away. If only I knew how far, perhaps some of my questions might find answers."

"So many who are known to you are praying without ceasing right now. I receive so many messages of support and concern."

"Please"—she tried to pull herself upright and in the process lost her breath—"tell them that God is showing me so many things. Good things. Promising things. I am very hopeful, my Sister, believe it or not. Ask them to share any unusual sightings with the rest of us. Will you do that?"

"I will, Sister. But please. Rest and be careful. Do not neglect your physical self, do you hear?"

The sister smiled again, indulgently, and closed her eyes once more.

The heat created by a hundred-acre swamp fire, burning against the contrasting backdrop of a thousand square miles of cooling nighttime jungle, did not go unnoticed for even fifteen minutes. The NSA satellite, operating in thermal mode, immediately registered the anomaly and began to burn images. Chromatically adjusted photographs were digitized and e-mailed along the army's private Intranet to the Scythian Brother sitting in Benin City, Nigeria, coordinating the vast search for Abby Sherman and her two companions.

The man called over a Nigerian Army official and arrayed the images before him.

"Look at these secondary signatures," he said, pointing them out to the man. "Are there combustible materials in the Eredo Rampart?"

The officer thought for a moment, then shook his head. "Those resemble weapon concussions. Grenades. RPGs."

"That's what I thought," echoed the Scythian.

"How many did your solo man go in with?"

"Three, I believe."

"One, two, three . . ." began the Nigerian, poking his finger at the photographs before him.

"Can we get some helos down there to check out the area? Right now, I mean?"

"I can authorize it. But you have to say please."

"Please." But the word did not include the inflection of a question, and the Scythian's eyes went cold as he said it.

Dylan and Abby fell asleep, both exhausted from grief and the stress of battle, near the spot they had occupied since their sister's passing. Her body lay not far from them, lovingly wrapped in wool blankets.

Drifting up from a troubled sleep, Dylan felt his eyes flutter open. His muscles, still wired to their former training, snapped taut for a split second. A presence hovered just before him. Someone less than a foot away. He saw light, faint and trembling, and nudged his mind into awareness. Was this the first spark of dawn?

The next second showed him it wasn't. Undulating in the tiny flickers was a face, male, perfect and totally at peace.

He heard words. It would not matter in the days ahead whether they had been audible or merely spoken into his spirit. In either case, he could no more deny their reality and power than that of his own speech.

Dylan, be free of regret and go forth in power. Your enemy is not yet vanquished. Bury your sister and leave this place at dawn to rejoin the battle. I will send you rescue.

Four Huey approaches had thundered overhead by the time Dylan and Abby—who stood huddled beside the fresh grave Dylan had prepared inside the chamber—saw a rainy dawn lighten pale and fresh against the earthen walls.

Ever thankful for the shelter of the hidden chamber, Dylan knew that their concealment was a godsend. At night, all the pilots would pick up was a cooling body on the ridge and maybe a couple of explosion signatures.

However, he also knew that come dawn there would be company. Lots of it, flown in and dropped from belay lines all around their current location. By midmorning they would be prisoners.

And yet, when he had told Abby of his ethereal visitor, she had readily agreed that they should wait for help. Dylan's residual instincts continued to resist this, eager to prod them into leaving their perch and putting as much distance as possible between them and the rampart before daybreak. But every time he remembered his otherworldly encounter, all resistance left him. He was too impressed with God's track record in their lives to risk fouling it up.

He has to fail us sometime, Dylan thought at last in the morning's wee hours, half deluded with pain and fatigue.

Abby had no idea how God intended to save them this time. She only knew that according to her "word from Him," they only had to wait and find out.

"Fine," he'd relented. "We'll see."

At first light came the sound of an approaching aircraft, and Dylan awakened at once, awash in disappointment that his darkest misgivings had actually prevailed. He glanced at the young woman, who leaned beside him fast asleep, her head resting on his shoulder. He would have liked nothing more than for this to continue, but being a man, he simply had to go and see for himself.

He carefully extricated himself from his companion, only partially waking her before tiptoeing warily toward the entrance. He began to frown even before reaching its aperture, for did modern armies still use propeller planes? He didn't think so. And yet the sound in his ears was now unmistakable. Not to mention baffling.

He stuck his head outside. The floatplane was a bright yellow, flying low just above the treetops and with astonishing skill. It was indeed a prop plane, which bore the bright red marking *His Wings Over Africa.*

"Abby!" he shouted. "Come here!"

The floatplane flew closer, then banked. Dylan saw an arm extend from an open window and wave. Then its wings dipped sharply, right then left. A greeting.

Friends!

Dylan looked at Abby and laughed. "You've got to be kidding!" he said.

After circling back, the floatplane began another approach toward them, this time even lower.

"No way!" Dylan said with a rush of astonishment, for he realized what the pilot was planning to do. "No way!"

Abby turned and gave him a smirk, whose meaning he translated right away. *So, are you through doubting yet?*

The moat, nestled up against the Eredo Rampart, might have been swollen from the recent rains, but it still was barely wide enough for even the most compact aircraft to use as a landing strip. And yet it was certainly the only place for a fixed-wing aircraft to land in many, many miles.

There simply was zero room for error.

This time, both of their mouths moved in the utterance of frantic prayers as the floatplane dropped and then lined up with a rapid series of nimble course corrections, gracefully flared its descent, and set its floats on the water dead center in the channel. To make things more difficult, the moat did not follow a perfectly straight line, forcing the pilot to continue adjusting even as he feathered the engines and steered furiously to bring the craft to a safe stop.

Sure enough, as the craft began to slow, its near wing clipped one of the rampart's edges, sending a dirty colored rockslide into the water. The plane then overcorrected a bit, shearing off a generous palm frond and sending it into the moat as well.

Regaining its rightful path, the plane pulled to a stop just opposite their perch, only sixty or so feet from their position.

"They're friendlies, of course," Abby said with a knowing glance at the resident skeptic.

"We're friends!" came a shout from down below. A white man was hanging from the window, waving a large bush hat their way. "Please, come with me! Hurry!"

The pair nearly skidded down the Eredo Rampart on the backs of their heels.

At the bottom, Dylan threw open the floatplane's side door, only to see its closest seat occupied.

"I thought my friends might need a ride this morning!" a strong, familiar voice said.

"Colonel Shawkey!" shouted Abby.

And if the man had not been restrained in a seat high above them, Abigail might have hugged her old protector to near asphyxiation.

SKIES ABOVE COASTAL NIGERIA

"Pleased to meetcha!" the pilot had loudly exclaimed over the clamor of his plane's engine, while extending a large hand into each of their astonished faces in turn. "Valdo Bittner!"

Then, in the ensuing minutes, Valdo Bittner proved again what a gifted pilot he was. Even as he continued to converse in a loud voice and swift, exaggerated gestures of both hands—hands that Abby would have preferred were gripped around the plane's controls—he retraced his flight's impossible landing in reverse, racing along the moat with no additional wingtip scrapes and putting to use his plane's incredibly short takeoff distance.

Their departure was unlike any flight its passengers had ever taken, for the steep ascent lasted only a split second. Their cruising altitude would remain fixed at somewhere around seventy-five feet, a height so perilously close to the jungle canopy that at times Dylan was sure the plane's floats were trimming leaves while they buzzed along.

"Where did you learn to fly like this?" Dylan asked.

"A school in Texas called LeTourneau," Valdo replied, grinning. "They have a whole program just for learning to land and take off in areas like this. It's called missionary aviation. These days, it's almost the last place left to have this much fun flying."

"I've never seen a landing like that one," Dylan said. "But if you hadn't nailed it, I think we'd be dead by now."

"Praise Gawd!" the pilot exclaimed again and again as he explained how persistently Colonel Shawkey had urged him to fly into a region not served by missionary aviation—all in the vain hope that they might rescue three people whom all of Nigeria could not locate.

Fortunately, the floatplane was accustomed to flying just above treetop level, so it avoided all radar detection as it took off and headed east and out of sight.

And not a moment too soon. No more than eight minutes after it disappeared over the horizon, a V-shaped formation of five Nigerian military helicopters came barreling down from the west.

The army choppers hovered so long over the point of the previous night's firefight that by the time they had delivered a half dozen paratroopers along drop lines to the ridge of the Eredo Rampart, their blades had blown away most of the evidence of what had taken place. All except for the body of the American "military consultant," a bizarre contraption beside a fresh grave, and a strangely bloodstained rock not far from his body.

Once again, the mystery of Abigail Sherman's disappearance had confounded local authorities.

By that evening, the President of the United States had graciously offered whatever assistance his nation's assets might offer the investigation.

Eager to remove the frustrating media magnet from over his country's life, the Nigerian Prime Minister wearily accepted the very next morning.

Thankfully, Pilot Valdo Bittner was also a man deeply in tune with God, so Colonel Shawkey had not felt forced into considering his last resort: veiled threats of bureaucratic reprisal. A small voice with whom

Bittner was quite familiar had impressed on him that no matter how unorthodox the mission, this was a flight he would regret passing up.

And so, even while the combined electronic surveillance capability of Africa's largest nation registered zero airborne activity in the sector over Abigail Sherman's escape zone, the plane continued a harrowing and visually engrossing journey across the surface of its coastal rain forest.

This aircraft used for missionary aviation was among the most remarkably nimble and expertly designed in the world. Indeed, few other planes could have carried off such an unlikely entry and exit. Colonel Shawkey had been fortunate to find Reverend Bittner along the Cameroon border, as missions like his usually serve in nations with large and remote indigenous populations. But a certain group of sisters, serving him in a covert advisory capacity, had been keenly aware of Bittner's existence.

Beyond that, their predictions of where to find the threesome had, despite their lack of external documentation, proven eerily accurate.

MALIBU, CALIFORNIA, THE COLONY

The Head Elder tensed and turned slowly toward the disembodied heads of the old men surrounding him. Oversized and glowing with the vividness of a million pixels, the flat screens bearing their images were so large and numerous that they nearly eclipsed the room's vast Pacific view.

"Thank you for waiting, gentlemen. St. Petersburg has now joined us. Welcome, my Brother. My fellow Elders, I have troubling news. Shadow Leader has failed in his Nigeria mission. In the process, he contributed his soul to the cause. I will soon name a new Shadow Leader, but before we can spare the time for such a transition, we must address the situation at hand. The first thing we're doing is gathering a longtime nuisance back under our control. You'll see it when it happens: just watch your screens. It will provide the young woman a powerful incentive to give herself up."

"And what if she doesn't?" growled New York.

"Our brother in Amsterdam and I," he said while nodding to

acknowledge the left-most screen, "issued an Annihilation order even before word reached me of his fate. Now the order will be enhanced. When we receive word of the girl's next destination, as we will quite soon, I'm certain, we make the order location-specific. Every one of our numbers, fully initiated or not, will be contacted immediately and ordered to converge as soon as possible on her location. Fifty warriors, on the scene with a maximum twelve-hour window. A fight to the death. As we've aptly named it—Annihilation."

"How do the higher ones look upon this crisis?" asked New York.

"I won't lie to you; they're concerned," the Head Elder replied. "I wouldn't take this extraordinary step if major stakes were not at play. But if we succeed here, we could still win a major victory against our enemies."

"What can we do to help, Brother?" asked St. Petersburg in his thick Russian accent.

"Well, actually, I'm going to ask you to do something I've never asked of you before. When that word comes, I want you to come as well. This is our fate on the line, and your presence could help turn the tide. We will need not only power and muscle, but wisdom and cunning. When the call comes, I will be expecting that from every one of you."

PORT HARCOURT, NIGERIA

It was almost midday when an unannounced and largely over-looked airplane executed a nonscheduled water landing on Bonny River just east of the busy harbor of Port Harcourt, Nigeria's fourth largest city.

In this industrial section of Port Harcourt, its polluted horizon dotted by the smoke of towering oil flares to the south, unscheduled aircraft landings usually signaled only one thing. Or perhaps two things—the arrival of another heroin shipment from South America on its way to Europe, or of heroin on its way to North America from the poppy fields of the Far East.

In fact, drug flights were a market second only to Nigeria's massive oil industry centered in Port Harcourt. Officially the world's fourth largest petroleum producer—and unofficially higher still if one chose to factor in the oil siphoned off by its staggering corruption—Nigeria exported all of its liquid gold from the oilfields of the nearby Niger Delta through the pipes of Port Harcourt.

The convergence of both bustling industries is why nearby dock-workers studiously looked away when the airplane pulled up alongside an empty quay and unloaded three passengers, a tall Nigerian man and two whites, and when the new arrivals just as quickly climbed into a large army van, which then sped off.

The van swiftly merged onto busy Aba Expressway and several miles later turned swiftly on Tombia Road, adjacent to the city's venerable Polo Club. Without even a touch of the brakes, the van swerved behind the white bulk of Le Meredien Hotel, admired by those in-the-know as the finest hotel in West Africa, and ducked into a basement-level entrance.

The doors were open before the van had stopped moving. No hotel personnel were in sight—the colonel and two Nigerian adjutants hopped out to help their slow-walking white passengers out of the vehicle and toward a nearly hidden service door.

For Abby, the sight of a polished marble hallway under elegantly recessed electric lights, after days of living in the jungle, proved overwhelming. She gasped and smiled, for she felt as if she had almost forgotten such places even existed. Her reaction was much the same when they reached a service elevator as its doors shut of their own accord and the motors whooshed them upward.

Colonel Shawkey had truly thought of everything. When the doors dinged and slid open, the two aides released her arm and quickly darted outside to make sure the hallway was unoccupied. Nodding the go-ahead, they resumed their places and escorted Abby to a door that opened into a luxury suite, which tore a sigh of relief from her bloodstained lips.

The rest of the day Abby spent in blissful recuperation. While Dylan conferred privately with the colonel in the sitting area, Abby stepped into the suite's spacious, white-tiled bathroom and bathed for nearly an hour. By the time she had dried off and retired to a king-sized bed nearby, a privately hired female doctor had arrived, carrying an IV saline kit in an oversized shopping bag.

Soon after that came food—so much gourmet room-service fare that it took two porters to wheel in the trays. Abby had been so pre-occupied with the preservation of life and limb that she'd forgotten how little and how infrequently she and her friends had eaten over the last several days. Wheeling in an IV-stand improvised from a coat hanger and a rolling lamp stand, she walked in and moaned at the mere sight of it all.

The doctor had helped her sit down and was preparing to make her exit when Dylan, who had yet to even change out of his tattered and spotted clothing, held up his hand.

"Doctor, I wonder if you could perhaps help me as well."

"Of course," said the doctor, eyeing his obviously injured side.

"Oh, it's not that," he said. "Well, at least for the moment. For right now, I wonder if you have a scalpel on you."

Looking him over curiously, the doctor reached into her shopping bag and produced the same. When Dylan stood and peeled the rem-nant of his shirt from the dried blood on his wounded side, she shook her head. "You do not need a scalpel for that, sir. I will gladly disinfect and perhaps suture, if it is needed."

"It's not the wound," Dylan said. "Please, come closer."

She approached him for a better look.

"Do you see the small teardrop tattooed there, just beside the wound?"

She nodded yes.

"I need you to make an incision right over it, exactly one half inch deep."

She stared at him as if he was crazy.

"Please. It's very important. I will pay a bonus, if you like."

"Could you tell me what we are doing?"

"Let's just say we're retrieving a buried artifact."

The Nigerian doctor shrugged, sat down beside Dylan, and took out some alcohol swabs. After cleaning the area thoroughly, she brought her scalpel blade against the skin.

"Sir, you do know this is going to hurt quite badly?"

"I was here when the thing was inserted," he replied. "Unfortunately, I remember it well."

"Would you like some rum?" asked Colonel Shawkey from a corner of the hotel suite. Dylan declined. And so the doctor slowly sank the blade into the area where most men his age would have located their "love handles." Dylan had none, although the blade did not penetrate muscle.

"Please, palpate the area," he asked in a pained whisper when the incision was complete. With a grimace the doctor reached in and closed her fingers around first one, then two round objects. Each one she dropped carefully onto the room-service tablecloth. Then she swabbed the area again, sutured the incision, and tightly wrapped a bandage over everything.

No one spoke as Dylan carefully picked up the two round objects, which seemed smeared with some kind of wax or oil. He rinsed them in hot water from the waiting tea service, finally holding them up to the room's light for all to get a better look. The objects glinted before their eyes, bright and dazzling. Abby gasped.

Diamonds! Big ones—easily twice the size of the huge rock her father had given Teresa.

"This is one of the oldest tricks in the game," Dylan explained. "A last-resort cash infusion—for emergencies exactly like this, when a secret operative finds himself hard pressed to get cash from the usual sources."

"Oh," sighed Abby in mock disappointment. "And here I thought you were about to give me a whale of a belated birthday present."

"Colonel Shawkey," Dylan said, ignoring her, his eyes still fixed on the jewels, "I have trusted you with my life. Therefore, as I have no other currency with which to leave this country, let alone reimburse you for this room, I trust you to fetch the highest price for these beauties on the local market. I know we're not in Sierra Leone, but I imagine there is still a good trade in stones of this value."

"Indeed there is," said the colonel, who seemed to avoid looking at the jewels himself.

"I know in New York or London, they would fetch around seventy-five thousand dollars apiece."

"They will not command that around here, sadly," said the colonel. "However, I can easily get you half as much in American dollars."

"That will be wonderful, my friend, thank you." Dylan seemed finally able to relax. He allowed a deep breath to escape him. "And now, Doctor, would you be so kind as to bandage up this other little scrape of mine?"

Dylan was fully clean, both his wounds and his body, when the colonel returned later—bearing not only a sizable brick of familiar green currency, but a Polaroid camera. One of the aides, who had hovered against a wall the whole time, photographed them both and disappeared with the documents.

"You are now as famous and sought after as Princess Diana once was," said the colonel. "Your name and likeness are on every television. Look . . ." He walked over and switched on a set. Without even changing it, he pointed with a smile, for right there loomed the faces of Abby, Sister Okoye, and a poorly drawn sketch of Dylan.

"Despite rumors of a recent close call near the Nigerian coast," droned a tired female voice, "the three remain at large and, much to the world's dismay, unaccounted for."

The next afternoon, two military vans pulled up alongside the terminal entrances to Virgin Airlines at the Port Harcourt Airport forty miles north of town. Soldiers emerging from both carried machine guns as they marched across the crowded sidewalk.

Twenty seconds later a gleaming white sedan pulled between the vans and stopped with a sudden chirp of brakes. The car disgorged three passengers: one tall African man in a military uniform, one slender and elegant man with hair whose gray color matched the pinstripes on his impeccable suit, and one woman in a full-length Muslim covering from head to toe.

The well-turned-out man and his cloaked companion turned and, quite surprisingly to the few bystanders who risked a look, embraced the Nigerian man with great fervor. The man, despite his air of panache, seemed to be teary-eyed when he released them. The woman, who impulsively tore down her veil in the process, embraced him far longer, and was clearly in tears when they finally separated.

The couple checked in their obviously light luggage at the curb, then shook hands with the Nigerian officer, also with great emotion, and strode resolutely into the terminal.

At the Virgin counter, Dr. Frederick Eggleston and his striking wife, Suleima, showed Nigerian passports, recently renewed, and Nigerian drivers' licenses indicating an address in a Port Harcourt executive compound. Their proffers aroused no suspicion, for sophisticated foreigners or employees of foreign companies, many escorting foreign-born wives, were the lifeblood of the Port Harcourt to London route.

They boarded the flight without incident.

One hour later, the jet landed at Lagos. Despite intense surveillance throughout the airport for the two Americans, Dr. and Mrs.

Eggleston were effortlessly shuttled to the Virgin Nigeria international lounge.

Granted, a closely observant Muslim might have noticed with some dismay that Dr. Eggleston's wife did not walk behind him, as a fundamentalist Islamic woman would. Had that person followed the pair to the privacy of their expansive first-class booth aboard the jet, he or she might have also been surprised to see her sit down and sip eagerly from the complimentary glass of champagne. Sighing in obvious relief, she seemed unashamed in the least to remove her headpiece, in the privacy of the bulkhead window seat, and reveal a closely shorn head of bright auburn hair. Her face bore not a trace of either Arabic or African ethnicity.

A very recent, and perhaps recalcitrant, convert to the faith.

CHAPTER
_52

LONDON, HEATHROW AIRPORT

Nine hours later, the Boeing 747 landed at Heathrow, marking the terminus of the pair's return to the West. The oddly matched couple silently parted in the terminal's main corridor and, carry-on satchels in hand, quickly made their way to the genders' respective rest rooms.

Fifteen minutes later, two sharply dressed and utterly transformed Europeans walked out. The husband, who greeted his exiting wife with a grin of barely concealed surprise, was now brown-haired and wearing the shorts and tennis shoes of an American tourist. The wife, her hair still auburn, was also attired American style, wearing a tight T-shirt, clingy skirt, sandals, and a pair of oversized, very dark sunglasses.

The husband leaned over and appeared to give his wife a lingering kiss on the earlobe as they walked. Instead, he was talking very fast.

"We've got to pull this off perfectly," he whispered. "London is the most heavily videoed city in the world. Cameras on every corner. They could follow us from this moment all the way to our hotel room. So don't let your guard down."

The pair jumped into a taxi to central London, where they quickly disembarked at Notting Hill Gate and hopped on to one of the city's famous red double-deckers. Grinning and craning their necks like a couple of ecstatic tourists, they rode on the bus's upper level for half an hour through the cold and crowded streets, finally getting off at Trafalgar Square. There in a spritz of fine rain they blended into the crush of milling tourists and allowed themselves to be swept, almost invisible amidst the masses, down into the stairway entrance of London's Underground. They boarded the Bakerloo line and abruptly exited at the next stop north, Piccadilly Circus. They crossed to the opposite direction, boarded again, then exited back at their original station and rode the Northern line up to Leicester Square.

Here the husband promptly located a branch of the Credit Suisse bank and, with the help of a retinal scan and nary a peep at his identification papers, withdrew the sum of one hundred thousand dollars. Next, he made a hurried visit to the safe-deposit vault, where he removed an American passport and Michigan driver's license, both in the name of Marcus Bryce, and finally a blank passport form—a document which, by merely possessing it, could mean a punishment of fifteen years in a federal prison.

The well-traveled couple then hopped another taxi into the heart of West Soho, one of London's more bohemian quarters. They disappeared through a side door adjoining one of the neighborhood's largest Internet cafés. Two hours later, and ten thousand dollars poorer, they emerged smiling more broadly than ever.

They found a bench and leisurely withdrew their purchase for inspection. An ordinary-looking cell phone, but which in fact was an untraceable, prepaid, and unlocked cellular device, with international phone rates already purchased through a coded phone card.

The husband made his first call, while the lovely woman beside him sat patiently and appeared to indulge in Soho's world-class people watching. The call was to his apartment. After spending fifteen minutes furiously thumbing the keypad, he hung up.

"Time to start taking the fight to them," the husband whispered to his spouse.

His next number was a classified number secretly assigned to a windowless room in Langley, Virginia.

FBI SERIAL CRIME UNIT, LANGLEY, VIRGINIA

"Task force, special agent in charge," answered the monotone voice of twenty-five-year bureau veteran Ken Grant.

"I have a breakthrough clue for you."

"Whoa. Let's start at the beginning. Who are you? What's your name?"

"Look. Don't handle me."

"*Handle* you? And who in the world are you to tell me that?"

"I'm a black-bag solo operator, veteran of Marines, Airbornes, Delta Force and beyond. Way beyond. So either let me tell you this, or so help me, you'll go down as the man who dropped the best clue this case ever had."

"Sure, buddy. Only one problem. You can tell me you're James Bond himself, but if you don't give me cause to classify you higher than the two thousand other whack-jobs who tell me junk like that, this call is over."

"How about, I know your withheld fact."

"Our what?" asked Grant.

"Come on. Don't mess with me. The fact you guys always withhold from the public in order to ferret out bogus leads and confessions."

"Oh, and what would that be, sir?"

"The scythe. Otherwise known as the sickle. They use it to slice their victims' throats. Sometimes they carve the symbol of it on their bodies. Am I right?"

"Okay. I'm listening. Where did you get this number? You called direct, right?"

"I got it from your SAC in Los Angeles. Under a cover identity."

"Yeah, and what's this clue?"

"I'm going to give you an address in Tribeca. Now, here's the rub. You're gonna find a week-old body in there with a bullet through the head. I didn't commit the crime, and I'll e-mail you video to prove it before the day's out. So to reach what's really important, you may have to shove around a little NYPD blue. I'm sure you feds won't mind doing that, though. Anyway, you'll have official permission, because the place is mine. I'm Dylan Hatfield. I've already e-mailed you the address."

"So what about this great evidence?"

"The man who committed the murder at my place is operational commander of the underground army that's been murdering African-American women all these years. You'll find his prints on my front door keypad and on a side table in the bedroom, the one with the clear glass vase on it."

"If all this is true, man," Grant said in a completely new, serious tone of voice, "you've gotta come in and talk to us. You must know a lot more than this."

"Believe it or not, I really don't, or I would tell you. But I am trying to bring these guys down myself, and as soon as I have anything more, I'll be in touch."

"Hey, bud. You want to freelance, be my guest. But remember that obstructing an ongoing federal criminal investigation is a felony."

"Do I sound like I'm obstructing to you?" Dylan was angry now. "Listen, you find that print. It's not to locate the man himself, by the way. He's dead. In Africa. And I just killed him. But trace his contacts, and you'll bring down the whole network."

"I've gotta have—"

"Go do it, and we'll talk soon."

Click.

LONDON, SOHO DISTRICT

The next call from the untraceable cell phone beamed out to Robert Sherman, resident of Pacific Palisades, California, but currently located in Lagos, Nigeria. The gap didn't matter, because Mr. Sherman's cellular account located him worldwide.

Abby spoke to her father for a little over three minutes. She apologized for not having called before, explaining that without a secure telephone, she would have given her position away to the authorities likely monitoring his calls. She revealed to him her safe condition, the fact that her quest was progressing well, and that she would be able to say more soon. Much more.

She closed with an urgent request. Would he refrain from telling anyone that he had heard from her? In fact, actively work to give the impression he was as frantic as everyone else? Her safety might well depend on it. After extracting a grudging agreement from him, she tearfully expressed her love and hung up.

She kept the phone in her lap and, for the next thirty minutes, labored to thumb its tiny letters.

Dear Friends,

Can't write much. But please believe that I am totally fine. Great, in fact. I am so sorry for all the worrying reports, but plz know they didn't come from me. Again, I am not kidnapped, prisoner, or anything. My quest continues. I have discovered much, and soon I will tell all. Please stay posted, and keep praying.

Love, Abby

CHAPTER
_53

After uploading the message to her MyCorner site, Abby stood and followed Dylan to hail another London cab, which they rode to Oxford Street, London's most famous shopping thoroughfare.

There, she and Dylan spent the next three hours on the from-scratch re-creation of a traveling American woman's wardrobe—everything from hats to tropical-weight dresses to underwear, toiletries, and cosmetics. And finally a fine, elegant, but not too elegant, suitcase.

They paused for a snack in the tearoom of Selfridges, the city's second most venerable department store, though much more affordable than Harrods. Their table was virtually encircled by bags; neither one had counted on just how much it would take to replace an entire traveler's wardrobe.

"So did you enjoy the shopping?" he asked with a quick glance around the loud, crowded room.

"Yes and no," she said with a sigh. "Yeah, after being hunted and deprived for so long, it was fun to shop like that. But another part of me feels completely lost. I take it I was supposed to buy lightweight things, suitable for Ethiopia."

"That's what I assumed," he said. "Isn't that what all of Sister Okoye's clues pointed toward?"

"Yes. I just feel so directionless. I mean, we have no clue other than the name of the country itself. What do we do? Waltz in and declare to the nation we're there to find out about some secret, a spiritual lineage we can't even name?"

"I don't know, Abby," he said pointedly. "You and the sister were always the ones who extolled the virtues of going on faith, stepping out and letting God lead your steps."

"I know," she conceded. "I know. But this is all a bit overwhelming. There's so very little to go on. Besides," she added with a small smile, "even the hyperspiritual have their down moments sometimes."

He smiled back, remembering at once why he liked this girl so much. "That's nice to know," he replied. "'Cause I am starting to have my doubts all of a sudden. Somehow it seemed easier, in that foreign jungle with only Sister Okoye to listen to. But now, here in the light of day, so to speak—"

"Let's pray," she interrupted.

"What?"

"It's time to pray." It was not a request. "Dear God, we need you to break through and keep ordaining our thoughts and steps. This is your journey, not ours. So we ask you boldly and expectantly. Please lead us now. In your holy name, amen."

She opened her eyes and looked around her with all the innocent anticipation of a child. Her eyes did not settle on anything.

"Maybe it's not supposed to work that way," Dylan offered. "Maybe we're supposed to get up and walk around or something."

"Or maybe we're supposed to wait just a second longer."

He smiled and barely suppressed a chuckle. For the first time ever, she was starting to sound her age.

"Look," she said. Her finger stabbed at a small advertisement in *The Times*, which lay folded neatly under his elbow. It was a tiny two-line box that read, *Ethiopian Cuisine—Soho. Most authentic in London.* And a pair of cross-street names.

"What?" he huffed. "A restaurant? You consider that an answer to prayer?"

"It's a direction. And at least it looks like an educational place to have dinner."

ETHIOPIA GOURMET, SOHO, LONDON

The couple rushed in within five minutes of closing time and without a reservation. Neither of those facts fazed the restaurant's owners, who dealt with culinary explorers, first-timers to Ethiopian cuisine, nearly eighty percent of the time.

The pair were promptly diverted to the innermost *mesab*, a small hourglass-shaped table made of woven fibers. When their hostess—a very old, hunchbacked African woman who took several moments to shuffle the ten feet to their table—motioned to the eight-inch-high stools along its edge, the young woman revealed her inexperience by shooting an anxious look at her companion.

"Forgive my friend," he said to the elderly woman. "We've been sitting on airplane seats all day and still feel a little stiff in the joints."

"Oh, you can sit at the bar," the woman offered.

"That won't be necessary," Abby cut in. "I need the practice. After all, we are traveling to your wonderful country in the next day or so."

"So soon back on the airplane?" the hostess said with a questioning grimace. "You two are travelers."

"Since we have no idea what to order," Dylan said, "would you kindly serve us your most common selection? At your discretion?"

The woman seemed pleased at this request, for she smiled broadly, nodded, and disappeared into the kitchen.

The couple sat on the stools and looked around for what came next. Their server, a tall, stunning woman with high cheekbones and creamy brown skin, emerged holding a long-spouted copper pitcher in her right hand, a copper basin in her left, and a towel. Bending over to them, she poured warm water over the fingers of their right hands and caught the runoff in the basin beneath. Then, setting it all aside, she did something else they didn't expect: she plucked the table right from before them and carried it off into the kitchen.

"Was it something I said?" Abby quipped.

"You wanted to come here," Dylan reminded her good-naturedly.

"And I'm glad I did," she said, suddenly serious. "I have a good feeling about this place. And about that lady who led us in here."

Abby glanced around her and realized that their cluelessness had made them the target of amused looks from the other diners. Soon the server returned holding their table. When she set it back down before them, however, it was covered by a large plastic dome. This the young woman pulled away, revealing what looked like a gray cloth covering the underlying tray.

"This is your *injera*," she offered, pointing at the object.

"Our tablecloth?" asked Abby.

The server graciously stifled a laugh. "No. Injera is your *bread*. Wait, and you will see."

Over the next few minutes she brought out four enamel bowls containing various thick stews and sauces, then poured them out on top of their "bread." Its entire surface was covered with concoctions named, as she announced each one, *Chicken Wat, Atakilt, Kitfo,* and *Yemisir.*

When the whole surface was covered, she knelt beside them. "Actually, injera is more than your bread. It is also your fork and spoon. See?" She tore off a piece two inches square, rolled it up around a lentil stew and, before Abby could react, popped it into her mouth with a deft little flick of the wrist. The mixture, once Abby had recovered from her surprise, proved pleasingly chewy, laden with a blend of exotic and delicious spices.

"I will come back with *Tej*," the server said, rising with a smile.

She returned bearing two longneck bottles of an amber liquid that turned out to be honey wine.

"I have to confess," said Abby after her first taste, "that I had no idea your cuisine was so unique."

"It is as old as our culture, which is as old as humanity itself," the server responded.

"I have to ask you," Abby began, earning a stern look of caution from Dylan, and just as quickly ignoring it, "does your culture make any special use of the eye? As a symbol, I mean, an icon?"

The young woman closed her eyes and grew very still; it occurred to Abby that all of a sudden even her breathing had ceased. At last she opened her eyes again. "I had better let you speak to my grandmother."

She left and brought back the elderly hostess, who now regarded them with a peering, intense look. She approached, sank to her knees, and knelt beside Abby.

"You wanted to know about the eye?" she asked in a near whisper.

CHAPTER
_54

"Yes," replied Abby. "I am very interested in whether the eye is a major symbol in your culture."

The woman looked confused for a moment. She pointed with a thumb back over her shoulder. "So, you are not speaking of our wall?"

"A wall? No. Which wall?"

"This one."

Abby felt a hand grasp hers and pull her gently upward. The woman led her through the other diners to the room's only smooth wall, shrouded from view by the restaurant's dim lighting scheme.

The woman stopped and pointed.

Abby stared at it, and then her hand flew to her mouth. She turned back to call Dylan, but he was already halfway to her. "Look," she told him softly.

The elderly woman was now looking into Abby's eyes with a strange, poignant expression. "You know about this?" she asked.

Abby nodded, unable to speak.

"This is more than just a symbol, isn't it?" asked Dylan. "It refers to a group, does it not?"

The woman nodded, wide-eyed. "You have been to my country, to ask me such a question."

"No, we have not."

"You are a follower of Christ, aren't you," said Abby in a voice that was more statement than question.

The woman nodded.

"I could feel it when I first walked in here," Abby continued. "My Sight has been dimmed by fatigue, all the travel, the stress, the distractions. But when I came in, I knew it was filled with . . . friends."

They returned to their table, too awed to make small talk. This time, the hostess sat down on one of the tiny stools like a dinner guest. In as few words as she could gather, Abby told the woman her story—of her dreams, the attempts on her life, her strange leading to Africa and the signs she had found there. She left out the part about her being an international fugitive.

As she spoke, her listener closed her eyes, and large, gleaming tears fell across her cheeks. When Abby finished, the old woman took a sharp breath, held Abby's hand, cradling it between her own, and began to speak.

"Now here is my story. I grew up in Addis Ababa in a large, fervently Orthodox Christian family. But it was my nanny, an old Coptic woman, who guided me into a walk with Christ. She led me in a prayer where I asked Him to come and forgive me and live inside of me. She taught me the things of faith, how to read Scripture and stay strong in Him."

"Then you dreamed of Anna," Abby interjected, smiling faintly.

"Yes, of Anna," she answered. "And do you know what happened to Anna after that event?"

"I have no idea," Abby admitted.

"History has no record of what befell her, but the legend I was told says that she traveled down to Abyssinia with one of the earliest Christian missions and helped start the church in my country. But that is rumor, and not the story I seek to tell you."

She took a long drink of the honey wine, glanced pleadingly at the ceiling, and continued.

"My father worked for the British consulate, and so during World War II we were called here to London. It was the safest thing, yet I was heartbroken, for not only did I love my country, but I knew my nanny was quite old and would not likely survive to greet me if I ever returned. The last thing she told me, the night before we boarded our ship, was that my coming here was a mission. She said God himself had told her I was to come here and start a gathering place, and decorate it with signs of the strange Sisterhood she belonged to. And someday I would be used in a mighty way to help heal a deep wound."

"A deep wound?"

"Those were her words. So I came here, and when the war ended and I married and my children entered school, I remembered my nanny's odd mission for me. I told my husband I wanted to open a restaurant celebrating our native land. In spite of many doubts, he supported me. The restaurant has thrived, and I have used it to help many of my people through the years, in the hope that each one embodied the one special calling I was waiting for. But I never felt like it had ever happened. So, still, I have waited."

"Do you have the Sight?"

The old woman looked away sadly and shook her head. "I did for a time, right after leaving Ethiopia. But living here, in the big city, with such a frantic life, I have neglected my walk with Him. I still believe, at least most of the time, but I grew busy and stopped attending church, stopped praying, reading the Scriptures. Now I feel things, faintly, like I did when you walked in tonight. But little more than that. The best I have done was stay true to this mission. Waiting. For you."

"For me." Abby said the words as if she was trying them out for the first time. "Tell me, what is your given name? Mine is Abby."

"Alemu."

"Dylan," he offered.

"Alemu, have you ever heard of a holy fire?"

The old woman's face twisted in disgust, as though a foul smell had just filled the air. "Yes, I know of the practice. It is a repugnance to me."

"What can you tell me about it?"

"You mean, you know nothing of it?"

Both Abby and Dylan shook their heads.

"Have either of you heard of the Church of the Holy Sepulchre?"

"You mean in Jerusalem?" Abby asked.

"Yes. Of course. The church built over the traditional site of Christ's crucifixion and burial. In the Old City. One of the most divided and fought-after pieces of real estate in the world. The Orthodox, Catholics, Coptics, Armenians, Ethiopians—they all fight over every square inch of the place so fiercely that legend has it a Muslim family has to keep the keys and open the place for worship every morning."

"How do you know so much about this?" Abby asked.

"Most Ethiopian Coptics know about the abomination of how their brothers and sisters have been treated there over the centuries. I do not have time to tell you the full list of outrages perpetrated by the Egyptian Coptics against the monks of my native faith. But enough to say that our monks have been attacked, lied about, stolen from, expelled from our rightful places, systematically harassed every hour of every day for decade after decade. Even when it cost the lives of our people. Today, the monks of the Ethiopian Coptic church reside in a tiny, stinking postage stamp they call a monastery, on the church's rooftop. With no running water, no electricity, no sanitation at all. Surrounded by snarling Egyptians who wait to strike them in the mouth for exceeding their territory by even an inch."

"And what does this have to do with us?" asked Dylan.

She looked at them again with thinly veiled impatience. "Because you asked me about the holy fire. That is an annual ceremony held by the Greek Orthodox clergy and thousands of their followers, down on the church's main floor. They claim that on Easter's eve every year, a pale blue flame comes to life above the sacred tomb and lights a candle in the hands of the Greek Patriarch. Then he turns around and lights candles being held by a crowd of worshipers packed into the church."

Abby fluttered her eyes for a moment, thinking back. "Dylan, do you remember what Sister Okoye said about a special person in the Sisterhood? A leader, maybe? And no one is quite sure where she is?"

"Yes. She's the one who's close to the holy fire. That's why we're asking about it."

"Right. I almost forgot."

"Yes," broke in Alemu. "That is what you are meant to do. The Spirit is telling me too. Go to Jerusalem. Find the church. Then find *her*."

CHAPTER

_55

As soon as they entered their hotel's two-bedroom suite on a clean but unpretentious Bloomsbury street, Dylan flew into action. Without warning he grabbed his new suitcase, brandished it high in the air, and shook all of his new clothes out onto the floor. Without a word of explanation he scooped up a large armful and carried it into his bathroom, tossing it unceremoniously into the large bathtub.

"What are you doing?" asked Abby. "Are you upset?"

"Abby, I couldn't say anything in the cab over here," he said without turning from his chosen task. "For one thing, I didn't want to rain on your parade. I know you're thrilled about finding this lead, and I believe it is the right one. But there is a problem. By the way, the second reason I couldn't talk about it until now is that it's too sensitive to speak of even within earshot of a cab driver."

"What is it now?" she said, suddenly burdened by the weight of all the *complications* she'd encountered since meeting this man.

He stood square to her and took her shoulders in each hand. "Abby, entering Israel under false pretenses is an incredibly difficult thing for anyone but the most highly trained liar. Israeli intelligence has taken a very unusual approach in identifying incoming travelers who have something to hide. Instead of trying to spot their weapons, they try to identify their lies. They'll take you aside and ask you a nonstop series of questions for three, four hours at a time. They'll intimidate you. Rattle you. Ask you seemingly random questions, then jump at you with a new one. They might even film you for facial parameters, which could be a disaster, because unless we rebuilt parts of your face with putty, you would be identified no matter how changed your hair color and cut was."

"What's with the clothes?"

"Oh, that's the other thing. They put everything you bring under a microscope—almost literally. If you have a cell phone, they'll call your most-dialed numbers. Yeah, they'll call them, then ask the person who picks up all about you. They'll read your journals. Hack into your PDA, right in front of you. And they'll certainly notice if you appear to have bought all your clothes brand-new less than two days ago in London. Addis Ababa wouldn't have noticed this, or cared. But Jerusalem would in a heartbeat."

"What if I said my domestic carrier lost my luggage?"

"Yeah. Then watch them call your domestic carrier to verify your story."

"Whoa. They're really that thorough?"

"More. I'm very worried about you getting through. And if they catch you, bam. It's all over. Deported back to the States, your cover blown, crowds of reporters, no chance you'd ever solve the mystery. High chance the Scythians would find us before any help would, whatever that might be."

"So what do we do?"

"We have no choice but to go. Jerusalem is clearly the next stop on the itinerary. But we'll just have to prepare very, very carefully. And as usual, I guess, pray our guts out when we get there."

"See, that's the problem. I can't picture myself asking God to help me be the best liar I can be."

"Then don't," Dylan answered. "Ask Him to make you invisible to the authorities. Or to keep you from being selected. Ask Him to keep you from having to lie at all."

"Yeah, but I'm still giving a false passport."

He sighed, then said, "Abby, try to see it in terms of the greater good—that, sure, we're breaking a rule, yet it's still the right thing to do. Didn't Christians during the Cold War used to smuggle Bibles into the Soviet Union? Well, they were breaking a law there and yet it was a good and brave thing they were doing, following a higher authority in that case. See what I mean?"

She pondered this. "You make a good point."

"I know I'm new at all this, but I'd imagine God looks at our hearts. Our motives. Why are we doing something? For the good of our neighbors? Out of love, or out of hate and malice?"

Abby nodded.

"And we have to focus on what you're trying to do here. In our case, we're not only acting out of love for others, but we're trying to carry out a mission God gave you. That mission is to prevent the slaughter of thousands, to conquer an enemy who has been killing your people for time immemorial. You're trying to prevent a victory for the forces of evil and death. Now which is more wrong? Which is more reprehensible? You presenting a false passport, or the forces of death winning this victory and spilling blood all over the world?"

"You're right," she said. "Besides, I just remembered something else. Jesus was arguing once with the Pharisees about doing stuff on the Sabbath. And He said something like the Sabbath was made for man, not man for the Sabbath. Our pastor called it the Sabbath Principle, and he preached on it—how God meant for the law to serve us, not rule us. Having pure motives was more important than following the letter of some rule scribbled on parchment somewhere."

Abby sat still, lost in thought, for several long moments. At last, she blew out a long breath and fixed Dylan with a relaxed, though still appraising, glance. "All right. I'll do it. Until, that is, I hear the first thing from God to the contrary. If I get the first inkling that He is displeased with this approach, I'll tell them everything. I won't hesitate to spill it all."

"It's a deal," he said.

For the next four hours, they meticulously prepared for the trip. After stomping on their new clothes in the bathtub for a half hour, they concluded that short of washing them with stones or pouring acid on them—then having them washed, dried, and ironed, which they had no time for—the new clothes had to be either thrown away or heavily supplemented.

They boarded a cab for the nearest late-night thrift shop and gleefully raided it for clothing, assorted toiletries, and worn-looking travel items.

When they arrived back at the suite an hour later, at nearly one o'clock in the morning, Dylan narrated their packing with his best improvised instructional lecture.

"I went through interrogation school at Fort Huachuca, Arizona, years ago," he began, pausing briefly to search his thoughts. "But the more I remember, the more I realize we're in a totally different situation. Military interrogation is trying to extract information whose general subject is already known, from someone already known to be, or highly suspected of being, a bad guy. Here, your interrogator doesn't know if you're a bad guy or not. He or she is only trying to determine if you're lying, and after that, *why*."

"Well, I better warn you. I've always been told I don't lie well. I'm not bragging or anything—I'm just naturally kind of transparent."

"Great," he said sarcastically. "Well, here's the basics of successful deceit. First of all, it's all about not breaking your pattern. Don't alter your manner no matter what. If you've been looking all around the room, using a certain tone of voice, a certain pitch, certain rhythm, anything consistent, don't change it. A change in pattern is the most obvious sign of lying. Don't even change your eye movements while answering a question. That especially includes bringing your hand to your face. Touching your nose or your mouth is another classic sign."

"Do I keep eye contact with them?"

"Only when you're hearing or processing a question. A lot of people think it's convincing to keep relentless eye contact with your questioner, but that's not necessarily true. No eye contact isn't good, but too much can also be a sign you're trying too hard. And again, it's your pattern that matters most. Don't start making eye contact at the moment you start covering up, or you've given yourself away. Besides, most people look up when they're recalling information, especially about their past. Although looking down is not a good idea. A downward look is a sign you're checking your feelings, which is a sign of guilt."

"So what's our story? Should we stay a day longer while we work on it?"

"No. The longer we stay in London, the more we risk exposure. We need to move on. The best kind of cover story we can make up is the kind with the most truth in it. Minimize your need to lie. Remember that the core you're trying to conceal is your identity. Everything else is open to being sprinkled throughout your story, or even used wholesale. Study your new identity. You're Isabelle Rawlins of Ann Arbor, Michigan. A college student on sabbatical. No previous stamps. You've gone to Mexico on spring break, hence your one re-entry stamp is all. But feel free to say where we're actually going, and what you're interested in. Just change a little about *why*."

"What do I tell them about us?"

The question seemed to catch Dylan completely flat-footed. He stopped in his tracks, without even turning around. "Again, as much truth as possible. While you find me devastatingly handsome and charming, the truth is that you know it's not safe for a young woman to travel alone anywhere, let alone the Middle East. So I'm just a friend. A male friend come to look after you during your research trip."

She smiled, then asked, "Am I going to be sitting in a chair with a lamp aimed in my face?"

"Nothing that campy. If you're selected for further interview, you'll be in a small room, though. Sparsely furnished. You could even be interviewed by a man-woman team. Just remember that they're going to question you along a story line. They'll get your rhythm going along a certain subject. Then they'll suddenly interrupt you with the odd, irrelevant question. Just to throw you off your game. See, it's only human to want to be heard when you speak. And it's confusing to be interrupted with an unrelated question. So if they get you going too fast on a given subject, watch out. They'll try to make you stumble and contradict yourself. It's okay to slow down, and to pause. . . ."

CHAPTER

_56

Both Abby and Dylan slept in until nine, then got ready and grabbed a cab back to the Internet café in Soho, where Dylan purchased a pair of tickets to Israel on an American carrier. They exited, then disappeared to the same upper floor they had visited the day before.

Forty-five minutes later they emerged, smiling, yet considerably poorer. In a carefully concealed waistband wallet, Abby now owned a freshly minted, although cunningly distressed, U.S. passport. Thanks to post–9/11 improvements in passport security, the required holographic and embedded detail work, not to mention the use of a verifiable American identity, had skyrocketed the cost of acquiring such a document by nearly twentyfold. And the exacting glue and laminate work had required an overnight waiting time for drying purposes.

But neither client was complaining.

Marcus Bryce—his original identity of Dylan Hatfield now almost lost for all time—had engaged the most skilled, discreet, and expensive forger of such things in all of Western Europe. And that kind of care took time.

The piece, along with its accompanying driver's license and Visa debit card, were foolproof.

They hopped another cab for the return leg to Heathrow. From her seat inside the speeding black Fairway, Abby looked up at the sky. It was a gray day, made overcast by the soiled underbelly of high, thick clouds—a typical London day. She looked out at the crowded street, listened to the honking and beeping of vehicles, smelled the urbane aroma of exhaust fumes and ozone. She glanced at her companion.

"You know something, Dylan?" she said, barely above a whisper. "You're going to think I'm crazy."

"No, I won't. What is it?"

"I miss Nigeria. I'd give anything to be back in that forest right now. I miss Sister Okoye. I miss those people . . . weren't they wonderful? The smiles, the children, the incredible women with their dresses and their voices and their wild, exuberant worship. I miss all of it."

She paused while he smiled dreamily back in the same places with her.

"Do you know that after all that time," she continued, "I never learned whether Okoye was her first or her last name?"

"Neither did I."

The silence descended back on them. The taxi picked up speed.

The young woman looked back out the window, trying to identify a difference in hue between the monotonous grays of concrete highway, soot-stained walls, and leaden sky.

She began to cry, softly, to herself.

JERUSALEM, CHURCH OF THE HOLY SEPULCHRE

The monk approached her usual sitting spot and froze in place. He stared.

She was sitting up like a normal, healthy person, the kind strong enough for everything from speech to movement of limbs to engaging in ordinary human conversation. He smiled and gave a prayer of thanks. How long had it been now?

And she so young. Or *seemingly* so young.

"You can come closer, you know," she said in a voice he noted was free of weakness, breathiness, and impediments of any sort. It actually had a ring, a timbre to it. *Praise God.*

He approached, trying to mask his relief.

"I feel better this morning," she said. "Do you know why?"

"No, I do not, Sister," he answered.

"I am having visitors tomorrow. Very important visitors."

"Oh. Well, I am glad for the warning. Perhaps I can tidy up the area—"

"Tidy up nothing, my brother. They are not people to try and impress. They will be people for whom I wish the warmest hospitality. A hearing, receptive audience for what they have to say. That is all, and no more."

"Perhaps we can show our hospitality by helping them up here in the first place. Helping them see our views."

"Helping them reach me would be more than sufficient. I realize, they will have no way to name me or identify me. They are coming for very mysterious and godly reasons. So please allow your most gifted colleagues out on the terrace tomorrow. Would you?"

"What are they?"

"What do you mean, 'what are they?' They are followers of Christ, that I know. They are adventurous, that I have heard. They are loving, that I can only hope. They are a man and a woman. And I have been told, on good authority, that they will be here tomorrow. That is all."

LAGOS, NIGERIA

"What do you mean, 'go *home?*' I'm not going home. *You* go home!"

"Mr. Sherman, I understand your frustration and . . . dilemma. And pain. But our government no longer believes she is in the country."

"Why?"

"I'm trying very hard to have that information released to me."

"Well, would you leave your daughter in some third-world country on the basis of *that*? Of the blubberings of some third-rate consular bureaucrat?"

"Now wait a minute, sir. There's no need to get personal—"

"You idiot, there's nothing more personal than the well-being of one's daughter. Are you married, by any chance? Got any kids?"

"I don't see why that has any bearing—"

"Yeah. Didn't think so."

"I can tell you, sir, and this is entirely off the record, that we have engaged an unusual level of . . . let's just say data-gathering capabilities, if you get my drift, to assist the Nigerian government in this search. Given the high level of media attention on this case, we felt it was only helpful. And those extensive capabilities have now given us ample reason to believe that she is no longer within these borders."

"Then where do you believe she's been taken to?"

"Sir, we do not believe she has been taken anywhere against her will. Given the amount of distance she has covered, as well as numerous other factors, we believe she is moving about of her own free will."

"Look. You tell your bosses that I'm going to hire my own merry band of Nigerian mercenaries to comb the savannah for my daughter. I hear you can buy them by the pound out here. I may or may not stay myself in this godforsaken place. But if I leave, you can be extra sure I'll leave behind a team so large and well financed that you'll wish you'd called in the marines to find Abby. Do you hear me?"

"Loud and clear, sir. Although I feel an obligation to warn you that the engagement of private militias for anything other than safe travel to and from various approved points within Nigeria proper is strongly discouraged by—"

A door slammed and Robert Sherman was gone. The consular official, clearly rattled by the encounter, allowed his sentence to trail off into the oblivion even he knew it deserved.

Beyond the door, Sherman walked away smiling. He knew his Abby was safe and sound, of course. But the leak-proof search teams would never know it until the end—not if he could help it.

Five minutes later, he was on the sidewalk, looking around impatiently for his hired security team.

They were nowhere to be seen.

Twenty seconds after that, a single black SUV raced up the street, swerved over to a stop, and produced three machine-gun barrels from its thrown-open doors.

Abigail's father did not even get the chance to protest. A bystander rushed up from behind him and brutally shoved him toward the gunmen. His falling body was swiftly swallowed into the vehicle, which just as quickly screeched back up to speed and into the careening Lagos traffic.

CHAPTER

_57

Abby had fallen into a near trance of composing and rehearsing her cover story during the quiet four-and-a-half-hour flight. As a result, the only distraction strong enough to break her concentration turned out to be the bump of their actual landing. Startled back into an awareness of her surroundings, she looked outside and gasped. A deep blue sky and palm trees whizzed past her window.

She reached out for Dylan and clutched his arm, smiling.

While she climbed down metal stairs to the tarmac, Abby felt herself torn between vastly opposing emotions.

First, she was thrilled to be visiting, for the first time, the "home turf" of her faith. It struck her as a powerful validation of her quest that it had now taken her to the very core of the Christian heritage. Even if her first sight of it was a large patch of concrete, the smell of jet fuel and a skyline of very Western, low-slung buildings. All around her, immigrants and Jewish seniors were kneeling and kissing the ground with loud, touching laments.

Second, however, she found her apprehension about the upcoming entry process climbing by the second. While she and Dylan waited on the tarmac for a cluster of security personnel to approach them, they both worked to mask their tension as simple travel weariness. But these were only cosmetic attempts. By the time Abby dared to look, only four people remained ahead of her.

A sheet of ice-cold fear descended upon her. She felt her heart break into a gallop. Her thoughts suddenly became sluggish and incoherent. She closed her eyes and tried to will herself into normalness. Perhaps, she struggled to tell herself, she could simply keep channeling these symptoms into the universal signs of a sleep-deprived flyer. A few yawns, eyes that refused to stay open, a twitchy agitation of the limbs . . .

The space ahead of her yawned clear.

Your turn.

"Madam?"

"Oh. Sorry." She shuffled forward, almost grateful for the veil of awkward self-deprecation her slow approach afforded her. She caught up and offered her passport to a man in his forties. Short hair. Cool, gruff expression. He'd been here awhile.

"Miss Rawlins, what is the reason for your visit today to the State of Israel?"

"Uh, re-research."

Great, Abigail, she chided herself. Stumble on the very first word.

His eyes rested on her face; she strained to appear tired and unfocused. Anything but dishonest.

"What kind of research?"

"Sociohistorical, I guess. A doctoral thesis."

"Please board the bus, ma'am. Thank you."

She met Dylan's gaze as they were heading to the bus, which had just lumbered to a stop beside them. "Is that it?" she mouthed.

He smiled with regret and shook his head no.

The fear returned full force. They rode the bus several minutes to the other side of the terminal, then disembarked. Dylan and Abby were both motioned into a door with the other passengers, then to the left side of a large, open room.

Abby blanched—it was full of interrogation kiosks.

Dylan reached out and gave her hand a friendly squeeze. "Just part of the Israeli welcome party," he said to her as though they had never discussed the subject. She knew what he was doing. A little banter to cut the tension.

They were quickly separated and led to separate cubicles. Now a woman in her twenties awaited her, already scrutinizing her as she approached. Abby handed up her papers and stood, wearing a neutral expression and wondering if the skin over her heart revealed any sign of the wild pounding beneath it.

"Miss Rawlins, why are you coming to Israel today?"

"Educational research."

"What are you researching?"

"Uh . . . the interplay of social, historical, and religious relationships between competing factions at the Church of the Holy Sepulchre, to put it succinctly."

"What factions?"

"Well, all of them in general. But specifically, the Egyptian Coptic and Ethiopian Coptic monks."

Great, Abby exulted inwardly. *I'm getting to tell the truth.*

The young woman opened Abby's suitcase and began tossing its contents on the table between them. All at once, Abby began to see gaps in her preparation—an unopened toothpaste tube here, an unremoved clothing label there.

"Did you come alone to do this research?"

"No, I came with a friend. He's over there in the other—"

"What is your relationship?"

"Friends. Just good friends. He's here to look out for me."

"Did he buy you your ticket?"

"I guess, technically."

"What do you mean, 'technically'? Either he did, or he didn't."

"Well, he purchased it on his credit card, although I'm reimbursing him."

"Miss Rawlins, I don't see any sign of information-gathering devices here. No computer, no camera, not even a pen and paper. You say you're here to conduct research?"

Inwardly, Abby groaned. What an oversight. She chuckled out-
wardly, trying to maintain an amiable facade. "I was told to pack light
and cheap. They said a laptop wouldn't be safe on such a long trip.
And that a camera would attract too much attention. I planned to buy
pen and legal pads here in Jerusalem, along with one of those cheap
disposable cameras. I love those things; they're so handy. Don't you?"

The woman didn't answer. Her eyes were fixed on the mess she
was making of the suitcase. Abby just stood there, silently exulting at
her deft handling of the crisis, and awaited the next one.

Just as quickly, Abby's eyes darted up and caught sight of a camera,
trained on her from just behind her questioner's head.

She began to pray.

Across one of fifteen monitors lining the wall of a nearby command center, a series of thin, blinking red lines swarmed over a still
image of Abby's face like warring laser beams. Red dots blinked and
tiny sounds emitted where vertical and horizontal lines intersected.
Within seconds a biometric mapping of her facial features announced
its completion with a low beep.

A panel glowed violently, angrily red. An alarm sounded.

A watching member of Ben Gurion Airport Security Service
walked over and shook his head as the captured still-shot faded,
whisked away to Interpol's alert system. The shot was replaced by
real-time footage of Abby's face. Blinking readouts of her skin temperature, pulse, and pupil dilation.

"Biometrics are a little elevated," the man said to a companion in
the corner, "but it's the actual features it really doesn't like. They've
triggered some Interpol watch list, but which one, it didn't say."

"Did it upload?"

"Yes. Just did."

"Fine. Then just wait. This girl doesn't trigger any serious profiles.
I think she's just tired. Unless Nadeena spots something, let's just wait
on Interpol."

CHAPTER
_58

ISRAEL, DAVID BEN GURION AIRPORT

"Please, Lord," Abby whispered, "let my fear and my guilt stay invisible to these people and their cameras. . . ."

Inwardly she repeated the plea over and over as she stood, her knees grown as rubbery as her brain cells. She could see Dylan standing at the far edge of the room. He was through. She could see that he was also sweating it out.

More than anything, she hoped he was praying.

"And what use will you make of this research?" the young woman continued.

Abby sighed. *The truth, if possible . . .*

"First and foremost, I've developed a practical goal. I want to help the Ethiopians win their fight. There's an important war going on, one that's far more important than a few square feet of church rooftop."

There. It was vague and imprecise, but it was the truth.

"What made you choose this subject?"

That tack surprised Abby. She strained a moment for words.

"Well, it's quite a story, with roots stretching back over centuries. All sorts of implications and subtopics reaching into nearly every level of religious and social history through the ages. Dramatic episodes too. Even in our own decade, there've been violent—"

"What is your true relationship to the man you came here with?"

Ah, there it was. The tossed-in disruptor question.

She paused. An honest responder would have paused before answering that one.

What is the truth? Abby asked herself. *What is an honest reply I can give to satisfy this woman?*

She wanted to answer that it wasn't any of her business. It was no concern of the State of Israel how she felt about Dylan. And she would have been right. But she would have also been inviting her own doom.

She sighed, the breath laden with reluctance.

She would speak the truth.

"I suppose it's because . . ." she said finally, then pausing again, "because I have romantic feelings toward my friend. Feelings I have never disclosed to him. And I was hoping that on this trip, those feelings might emerge and turn into an actual . . . relationship."

"Why would you hide such a thing from a public questioner?"

Abby almost guffawed out loud. "You're joking, right?" she heard herself saying, despite her own better judgment and inner protestations. "Would *you* offer up such a thing to a public official, in this kind of setting?"

The young woman looked at her closely. She seemed to be searching, Abby imagined, for signs of a motive behind the outburst. *Petulance? Impatience? Arrogance? A plea for sympathy?*

Out of sight, the young woman's right index finger trembled, poised over what they all called the "giveaway button"—the alarm that told every security person in Ben Gurion that a falsehood had been identified. A bad guy of some sort had been found.

The finger lowered. Its skin actually grazed the button's top surface.

Something passed between them. The tiniest spark of understanding. Of course, Abby was right. It was ridiculous to fault somebody for not informing an interrogator of a private crush.

And yet, she had to say something.

"I suppose it's because of my high regard for Israel and the religious heritage she represents. I'm very aware that I'm traveling alone with this young man. And of the . . . appearance of impropriety that might present."

Perfect. Her voice had dripped with an altogether sincere reluctance and embarrassment.

Her confession had been truer than she'd ever intended.

Abby met the young woman's gaze and tried to picture whether she too, somewhere in her past, may have harbored unspoken, possibly unrequited, feelings for a man she'd spent time with.

Please, Lord, deliver me from this nightmare. . . .

Abby leaned back and caught sight of Dylan, straining anxiously for a sight of her.

The young woman noticed the contact. Ever so slowly, her head turned until she got a glimpse of the man Abby had spoken of.

He was in mid-wave, smiling hopefully, when the young woman had seen him. He lowered his hand sheepishly.

Abby thought he had never looked more boyishly handsome.

The index finger withdrew. The young woman's face softened and became human again.

"You're free to go."

Unable to process the words, Abby stared at the passport and ID being handed back to her. The documents shook imperiously, a gesture of impatience on the young woman's part. *Take them and go!*

"Enjoy your stay in Israel, Miss Rawlins. And good luck."

Because Abigail Sherman's facial measurement did not reside in the fields reserved for criminal suspicion but rather for *persons of interest*, a rather hazy and more innocuous designation in Interpol's menus, the alert was not automatically forwarded to the customs booth as it otherwise would have. As a result, it was delayed for twenty seconds while the command center staff decided whether to forward it to the booth for action or ignore it altogether.

Several moments later, a red alarm began to blink silently in the bottom left corner of the young Airport Security operator's computer screen.

By then Abby was on the other side of the terminal, staring motionless at a suspended television as Dylan walked up briskly.

"Come on," he urged her in a low voice.

"Dylan! Look!"

Compelled by the panic in her voice, he glanced upward.

The red-backed text crawling along the screen's bottom read, *Breaking news: Robert Sherman, New Media chairman and father of Abby Sherman, abducted in Nigeria.*

Dylan shook his head in a brief concession to shock. "I'm so sorry, Abby. We can talk about this later, try to figure out what to do, but right now we have to move. Now. The cops are coming. . . ."

Security personnel spotted the pair just as Abby and Dylan disappeared onto the outside sidewalk, their bags in hand. Pursuers sprinting out to the sidewalk saw only a retreating taxicab, its license plate numbers and ID tags, only they were too distant for reading.

But Abby Sherman had not escaped. Not by a long shot.

Interpol knew, which meant that within an hour the entire world of secret organizations had learned she'd been spotted in Israel.

A half hour after that, an enhanced Annihilation was issued to every Brother of the Scythe around the globe. With blood stirring and adrenaline surging through their veins, every one of them stopped from fifty different ordinary activities. Twelve were in the act of harvesting victims, and even those ecstatic rituals went unfinished.

Fifty killers turned their homicidal gazes on Jerusalem and hurried there, as though their own lives depended on it.

CHAPTER

_59

They found her that morning standing, as motionless as a statue, facing out across the rooftops of the Old City. The monk came up behind her and she spoke without turning, without giving any sign of how she'd detected his approach.

"Brother Brehan," she said, still staring ahead, "I hope you've brought me some reinforcement."

"Indeed I have, my Sister."

"It is I, Sarha," called the female voice beside him.

"There is a great battle afoot," she said.

"I know. I sense it too. It is why I came. I sent out my best summons to all the sisters I know. They are all on their way."

"Good. I have never seen so many comings and goings over the skies of this city before. And never felt such foreboding. The battle ahead will be unlike anything we have known. But do you know why it is happening?"

"I have no idea, Sister."

"She is here. The sister we have prayed for all these weeks. I have felt her approaching."

THE OLD CITY—THE NEXT MORNING

Walking through the ancient stone walls of the Jaffa Gate beside Dylan, Abby gazed up at the deep blue, almost purple Judean sky, felt the Mediterranean sun warm her cheeks, smiled for a moment, then just as quickly willed the expression from her face. Frowning, she looked down while they walked.

"I just can't believe I asked him to lie to protect me," Abby lamented, "yet never thought of asking him to protect himself."

"That may be true," said Dylan, "but you didn't ask your father to go traipsing around the globe, making enemies."

"He didn't know what he was in for, you know that. He doesn't even believe in spiritual things."

"I predict he will soon," Dylan said.

"What are you saying?" she asked, fuming.

"Only that I think he's got quite a learning curve ahead of him."

"Well, regardless, we need to pray for my dad's safety, that God will protect him wherever he is right now. His life's in serious danger. . . ."

"I'm sorry, Abby. I didn't mean to sound so cold. And I agree completely that we need to pray for him. By the way, are you going to tell me what you said to that security woman back at the airport?"

She gave Dylan a long, appraising glance, and the faintest return of a smile. "Not on your life," she said.

"I didn't think you would. But you realize this only gives my imagination more fodder to imagine anything it wants."

"Imagine away, Dylan. It will never beat the truth."

Smiling at each other, they passed under the gate's arch and gaped in wonder. The sheer crush of humanity that greeted their senses nearly caused them to stop where they stood—except that in a crowd this thick and bustling, stopping was the one sure impossibility.

Beyond the strip of shadow sprawled David's Square, a marketplace crammed with street vendors, food stalls, souvenir stands, and more people than Abby had ever seen in such a small space. Abby glanced at a trinket stand beside her, piled high with copper pots of every size and shape. Just beyond it, a Palestinian boy barely in his teens hoisted wooden nativity scenes in both hands, screaming an incomprehensible sales pitch to all passersby. She craned her neck. Her gaze brought her exotic shades of blue and orange from a silk stall; her nostrils filled with hot steam and the aroma of fresh-baked pita bread, deep-fried falafel, and some kind of grilled kebab. As she walked by, she ducked to avoid the wild gestures of two men, one of them a Hasid wearing black clothes and a waist-length beard, haggling loudly over a large urn. Overwhelmed, Abby hopped aside to avoid being struck by a strange little cart, pushed along by a stone-faced teenaged boy.

"That's what passes for mules around here," Dylan explained. "You see that strip of rubber dragging along behind? That's the brakes. When they go downhill, the guy just steps on it hard and hangs on."

She laughed out loud at the thought. "Wow, you know so much! Do you know what it does for me, being back here?"

"Back here? I thought this was your first trip to Israel."

"Well, Dylan, that's the thing. All of this takes me back to the very first dream, or experience, that launched me on this whole journey. Remember, it was my experience of inhabiting the body of the prophetess Anna, on the morning her lifelong dream was fulfilled and she got to hold the baby Jesus, and tell the world that the Messiah had come. It all happened right here, and I can feel it, and taste it, and smell it."

"That's great, Abby."

"Dylan, are you all right? You don't seem all that excited to be here."

He turned to her, his features clouded over. "I've been here before, Abby."

"Oh. Well, is that such a bad thing?"

"No. I mean"—and now he adopted a low, menacing tone—"I've *been here* before."

She shook her head, a blank expression on her face. "I'm sorry. I'm not catching your drift."

"Do you even remember what I told you, back in Africa, about my career?"

"I know at first you were hired to kill me. But I guess I never put it all in a broader picture. Maybe I just didn't want to see the whole meaning."

He stopped walking, turned to block her way, then leaned in close as the crowd flowed around them, bumping their shoulders and assaulting their senses with an unending variety of foreign clothes, snatches of exotic languages, and questioning looks from faces of every description. David Street had now turned into a narrow bazaar—a claustrophobic, deafening kaleidoscope of people, shops, and foods.

"I've been an assassin, Abby," he whispered. "A professional hired by our government and . . . sympathetic parties. No fake movie stuff. No James Bond. The real thing."

"People like that really exist?"

"A few of us, yes. I was here in '01, right after 9/11. A small team and I helped Israeli Mossad find and sanction a whole PLO team that was here preparing to do some very bad things."

"Sanction?"

His face darkened. "You know what I mean."

"Oh . . ."

Abby nodded thoughtfully, and they continued walking, the moment's tension dissipated. She looked down at her feet and, for the first time, tried to absorb this deeper knowledge.

"I never would have taken you for that kind of person. Not that I'm judging your actions, but I always imagined that those who did stuff like that would be—" she paused and searched for the right word—"hardened. And you, you're not like that at all."

"Thank you, Abby. But you need to know: I only killed people that most folks would admit needed to be killed."

"Does that make it right?"

"When we're at war, it does. Whether our government declares it or not, we're constantly at war on about a dozen covert fronts all the time, on any given day. The world is crisscrossed with wars, covert and public, and most of them are being fought over human beings who seem to have no conscience. No heart or compassion or regard for human life whatsoever. Besides, hasn't God sanctioned war many times, you know, in the Scriptures?"

"That reminds me of what Sister Okoye was trying to get across to us. Only in another context. Just as I didn't have the perspective to see the wars you've just mentioned all around the world, so you once lacked the vision to see the spiritual wars being fought everywhere, probably even before your own nose. Right this very minute . . ."

"Hey, knock it off!" Dylan mock protested, pretending to swat away demonic combatants from the air in front of him.

"I mean it," she insisted.

"I know you do. And I believe it too. It's just a lot to absorb. Add it all up, and it's a lot of warfare for one sorry little world."

They turned onto Christian Quarter Road, which proved every inch as crowded and overpowering as David Street.

"Yeah. Speaking of which. . . !" she said, pulling up short.

"What do you see?" he asked.

She stared, letting the crowd jostle past her.

"You don't want to know," she replied, her gaze still locked ahead. "Dylan, you really don't want to know." She turned her head and kept walking. Then, just as suddenly, she stopped and shivered as though a cold front had just swept over her.

"Abby, what's happening?"

The levity she had worn like a good-natured mask that whole morning had abruptly vanished. Her eyes began to stare left and right, up and down. She edged closer to Dylan and shivered.

"I love this place, I really do," she said tentatively, "but it's also an intense place. A scary place."

Dylan became very still and his eyes began to flutter. After a few seconds, her wandering gaze caught sight of him.

"Dylan, what are you . . . are you praying? For me?"

Without looking at her, he nodded. "How did you know?"

"It's the strangest thing. I can *see* it. It's so vivid, like these beams of spiritual energy are just bouncing off you. And I can feel the love in them, somehow."

Now his eyes shot open. "Don't flatter yourself," he said with a smile.

There was an awkward, lengthy pause as they continued their walking.

"Anyway," he finally began, "can you tell what I was praying for?"

"You mean, *specifically*?"

"Yeah. Specifically."

"Well, let me phrase it this way. You're seeing so many disturbing things. But are you seeing anything good? Anything godly? You know, any players for the home team? Oh—" She stopped cold and peered ahead like someone facing a bank of fog. She breathed in sharply, and then her hand reached out and grabbed his. "Oh, my Lord . . ."

"What?"

"Why didn't I see this before?"

"See what?"

Instead of answering him, she turned to face him. He saw at once that her lips, her cheek muscles, even her eyelids were quivering.

"Thank you for praying what you did," she said. "I have this . . . this habit of looking so much more closely at the darker things. I don't know why I do that."

"I think we all do that."

"But you're right. They're everywhere." She pointed up at the old walls, then over at the window sills of an ancient church. "They're sitting, standing, flying around, some of them fighting in pitched battle right in full view of all the others. Oh, they're so beautiful—it takes me back."

"Back to heaven? Not literally, I hope."

"No. But thinking back . . . it's so encouraging. It reminds me of many wonderful things. Like the fact that I'll see Sister Okoye again. Do you remember how freaked out I was when I first met her at the Gathering?"

"How could I forget?"

"I lost it, precisely because I had seen her face before. I had met her, in a vision of my heavenly future. So I know for sure. I'm guaranteed to be reunited with her."

As they turned left under a thick arch and a road marked *Souk el-Dabbagha*, Dylan took a long, tremulous breath.

"What's the matter?" Abby asked.

"I can't believe I let her die. I should have listened to her more. She practically begged me to handle things her way. If only I hadn't been so focused on my own so-called strength."

She stopped him, placed both her hands on his shoulders, and faced him square in the eye. "Dylan, you listen to me. If you could hunt down Sister Okoye right this second and give her a second chance to come back to tired old earth, her tired old body, instead of where she's at now, what do you think she'd say?"

"I don't know. You tell me."

"Having seen it myself, with my own two eyes, I will tell you. She'd groan and say, 'Do I have to? Please, Lord, let me stay.' See, Dylan, you did nothing wrong, and her passing wasn't a tragedy. For her, at least. For her, it was the ultimate victory, just like death is for any believer. Okay? So drop the *pity me, I messed up* party."

He started to chuckle despite himself. "You're something else, you know that?"

"I take it that's good."

"It's something else, that's all I'll cop to."

They reached the bottom of a long staircase, turned left and looked up.

"And look here," he said flatly. "It seems we've arrived."

CHAPTER

_60

JERUSALEM, CHURCH OF THE HOLY SEPULCHRE

Abby looked up at a plain, open plaza flanked by a high wall featuring two arches, one of them bricked over and the other framing an open door.

"This is it?" she asked, her voice rising in disbelief. "It seems so . . ."

Dylan did not wait to hear Abby finish, but began walking forward as though pulled by some invisible force. She caught up with him by the time he crossed the threshold and into the church itself.

Surrounded by cool air and shade, for a moment they only stood and stared. The first item that captured their attention was a large, rectangular stone on the floor before them.

"Look at this," Abby said in a hushed voice, moving her eyes between a sign and the stone itself. "This is the rock where they say Christ's body was laid after the crucifixion, as they were waiting to bury Him."

They turned and climbed a set of stairs, only to be confronted at the top with nothing less than Golgotha itself—on the surface nothing more than a wall of white panels bedecked with sculptures and inlaid finery, but if the sign was correct, the actual hill itself, with the site of the cross indicated by a spot under a stone table.

Struck into awed silence, they continued to shuffle through an ever-unfolding maze of grand hallways, garish artwork, and random appearances of history itself. At one hand would loom a wall of intricately carved silver; another room would greet them with the pendulous shapes of a hundred suspended candleholders. They found the rotunda where the edicule—the structure built around the tomb of Christ—rose under an impressive marble dome. They found three of the actual Stations of the Cross, and chapel after tiny chapel dedicated to minute aspects of Christ's last moments on earth.

Finally, they both looked at each other with looks of weary overstimulation.

"This is incredible, but we can't play tourist anymore," he urged. "We've got to get serious about finding your mystery friend."

"Yes, we do," she agreed.

A tall, full-bearded Orthodox priest was walking past them. Abby reached out and touched the man's arm. He turned toward her with a scowl on his face.

"Uh . . . hello, we were wondering," she began in a wimpy-sounding voice, "where we might find the Ethiopian monastery."

The priest shot her an angry look and stormed off.

"Thanks for your Christian charity," she said under her breath.

"Come on, let's find somebody else," Dylan said. They walked for another ten minutes before spotting a Catholic priest and catching his attention.

"Excuse me, Father," said Dylan. "Could you direct us to the Ethiopian clerics?"

"I'm sorry, there aren't any Ethiopian clerics here," the priest said as if making a distinction.

"Really? There's no Ethiopian Coptic presence anywhere?"

"Why would you want to take up with those people, anyway?" he spat. "They're squatters. Beggars. Not real men of God."

"Forgive me," Abby broke in, "but if they are all those things, where are they?"

"Who?"

"These beggars you spoke of."

"Why, on the rooftop, of course." With that, the man promptly walked away.

Abby and Dylan exchanged amused glances. "They're not very nice people," he said, chuckling, "these men of God!"

She snickered and said, "Maybe they got a dispensation from the Golden Rule." Another ten steps later, she slowed her pace and looked up at Dylan. "If you saw what I could see," she whispered, "you'd realize all that's here is not as it seems. Some of these men had better learn the meaning of a 'broken and contrite heart,' or they just may find themselves in an eternity they never dreamed possible."

It took the pair another fifteen minutes to learn precisely how to find the ill-reputed Africans' rooftop abode. In that time, they walked approximately a mile, during which they also learned that the Church of the Holy Sepulchre actually contained thirty-six different sub-churches of every size and function, and that five different subtypes of Christian clerics shared jurisdiction so jealously that combat had broken out no less than four years prior, requiring the intervention and arbitration of the Israeli government. Finally, their Ethiopian hostess had been right—these men of God were so perennially fractious that her keys had been given to a faithful Muslim family for safekeeping. Every morning, the Arab Muslim rose at sunrise to faithfully unlock this bastion of Christianity.

It took a long theological harangue with an Orthodox prelate and a hefty "donation" to the man's unimpressive renovation project to obtain the directions.

By the time Abby and Dylan exited the church, walked around to its rear, and started climbing up a rickety metal stairwell, they had begun to realize the full extent of this divisiveness. Whereas they had walked on marble and gold a moment before, now they feared for their lives.

At the stairs' end, in a fleeting gesture of chivalry, Dylan allowed her to open the door and enter the rooftop area first.

He almost bumped into her, for Abby had paused at the first step and not taken another. He edged closer, feeling a nugget of impatience travel through him.

She turned to him. It could have been an accident of lighting or position, but he would forever describe Abby's look during that turn as a classic vision of a beautiful girl twisted into an enigmatic profile, alongside Vermeer's *Girl With a Pearl Earring* or Meryl Streep's *The French Lieutenant's Woman*.

He was mystified in an instant and followed her inside.

They both stood utterly motionless and silent for what must have been a truly long time, for some of the rooftop's occupants had begun to stare at them by the time they moved again.

CHAPTER
_61

What appeared before Abby and Dylan was a small and distress-
ingly humble African village, perfectly re-created on the very rooftop
of the Holy Sepulchre. Encircling a small dome that crowned one of
the chapels below, a dozen low mud huts sat amid the clatter of cooking pots and the stench of a broken sewage line. Two African men,
not attired in any sort of clerical garb but resembling instead the kind
of malnourished and shabbily dressed men one sees in Western relief
appeals, sat nursing a small fire into existence.

"Welcome to Deir es-Sultan," called one of them with a rehearsed
intonation.

"Hi. How are you?" said Dylan.

"I am blessed, thank you," he replied.

"Is this the Ethiopian Coptic area?" Abby asked tentatively.

"This is not an area, as in a sector of the church," answered the
man, who possessed only an eerie stare, blue-black skin, and a pale
gold robe wrapped neatly around a very thin, bald body. "It is the
rooftop, which is the home of Deir es-Sultan. And we are the Coptic
monks of the Abyssinian Community of Jerusalem. Spiritual and
physical offspring of the apostle Philip."

"But this is where you stay, all the time?"

"My dear, if our people were to quit this rooftop for even a second, even over the span of several centuries, we would forfeit even our contested right to be here. We would return to find any trace of our presence here erased forever."

"But isn't it cold in winter? And hot in the daytimes? And uncomfortable always?"

"It is all of those things. But we still consider it an honor when compared to the blessing of being saved by the sacrifice of our Savior."

"It's an honor for us to be here with you," said Abby. "Did you know that while the spaces downstairs are thick with demons and their combat with angels, that you up here have a spiritually clear space, defended by four of the tallest and most impressive warrior angels I have ever seen?"

"Thank you, my Sister," he said. "And yes, I have been made aware of this state of affairs. It is most gratifying."

"I must ask you something else," began Abby in a completely altered tone, "does the image of a female eye mean anything to you?"

The man cocked his head and smirked slightly. "You must look more closely before asking such things. Yes. It is our most common image, carved into our candles and necklaces, painted on our venerations and icon panels. It is, as you say, our motif."

"And is there anyone up here, a woman most probably, who seems to embody the meaning behind your motif more than the others?"

He cocked his head sideways. "So you truly are *her*. Come with me."

They followed him across the rooftop village, feeling like Western missionaries in some old tale of woe. Beyond the other side of the huts, against the vantage point where the church's most exposed side opened into a sprawling cityscape of Jerusalem, lay a cot.

Beside that cot, a woman was struggling to stand.

They said nothing but watched the woman rise to her feet with an inexorable slowness. Finally, now having stood on her own, she looked their way and flashed them an excited, even familiar look.

"For weeks now she has been waiting for a great breakthrough to arrive. A 'healing of the breach,' she calls it. Every day she grows weaker, and every day her prayer is not answered."

"Today is the day," said Abby boldly.

Helped by another of the nuns, the feeble woman had now approached quite closely.

"Would you excuse us?" Abby asked the monk. With a nod, he left her.

She stepped forward, and not knowing how to express herself, bowed awkwardly.

The woman extended her arms as Sister Okoye had, and her sisters at the jungle safe house, what seemed like an eternity ago. Abby saw with amazement that, while the woman dressed and moved like a mature woman, she had the eerily serene face and piercing eyes of a young girl.

"Welcome, my Sister," the woman said in a slow and breathy voice. "I have waited for you so long!"

Abby did not have the patience to answer but immediately moved into her embrace. The woman stepped forward and pulled Abby into her arms. They swayed and held each other for a long time. Sobs could be heard, muffled through fabric and skin. As they stood and held each other, it felt to Abby like she had never before felt such a nurturing and loving grasp in her life.

They eventually pulled apart, and Abby said, "I have searched for you all over the world! I can't believe I've found you at last."

"And I have prayed for you and longed for your coming," the woman replied. "What is your name, my dear?"

"It is Abigail. Abby, for short."

"I am Rulaz."

"I'm Dylan," he said, from what sounded like a mile behind them.

Rulaz nodded to him. "You are a very unusual man," she said. "Do you have the *gift*?"

"He may well develop it," Abby said. "In any case, he is a warrior. Both spiritual and otherwise."

"Yes," Rulaz said thoughtfully. "My guardians here," she said, smiling and pointing at the giants no one could see but them, "told me you would come."

"Your guardians," Abby added, "confirm to me that you are the matriarch of the Watchers. The one with the answers."

The old woman smiled the most mysterious and enigmatic smile. "I have managed to keep that role secret for many, many years, despite being out here on this open rooftop. One of the reasons is that my sisters and I never speak of it out loud."

"Oh, I'm sorry . . ."

"Please, do not apologize," Rulaz continued. "Today is not the day for such mincing of words. This is a rare day, with open warfare. Can you not feel it?"

Abby looked out over the nearby Alexander Hospice and a sea of roofs that stretched all the way to the sheer blue Dome of the Rock.

"Yes. Yes, I can."

"Around here, I am known as the Sentinel of Jerusalem. I spend most of my days looking out over Jerusalem, tracking the comings and goings of spiritual beings across the city. Watching. That is our oldest and truest name, you know, the women gifted like us. The Watchers."

"And now? What do you do?"

"I wait."

"The Lord himself told me to find you," Abby said through tears, "and heal the breach."

"Praise Him! He is so faithful."

"He is." The two women locked eyes, taking each other's measure.

"Dylan," Rulaz said, "I have seen a clouded account of your coming as well. And yet I see that your heart is pure, and that you follow our Lord. You are therefore welcome among us. I would gladly offer you chairs, but sadly even such items of basic comfort are denied us by our tormentors. I speak of our earthly ones, of course."

"I have so many questions to ask you!" Abby blurted.

Rulaz let out a delicate laugh. "And I have so very many answers to give you, my dear Sister. Some of them will require that you ask me their questions. Others will not. But we have little time. We will have to speak during the heart of a pitched battle. You two have brought great danger and conflict with you into this city today. Even now, the skies above us are stormy with the writhings of demons of greater size and influence than I have ever seen here at one time."

"Have we given you away?"

"I do not believe so. You have attracted a massive conflict to Jerusalem, but I think as yet my own identity is still protected. I think our enemies are searching for you, and that is why we must move quickly. Several of my sisters have come, and more are on their way. Brother Dylan, if you are truly a warrior of the highest order, then your leadership will be most precious today."

"Did you say we have both physical *and* spiritual enemies entering the Old City right now?" he asked.

"Yes. How coordinated they are I cannot tell. But they have definitely drawn each other to this place, all in search of you. They are bound to the death to stop Abigail and me from solving the mysteries between us."

"Does Abby need to be physically concealed from view?"

"Our guardian angels have the power to conceal, but I do think it would make things easier for everyone if she were disguised."

"Right," Dylan said. "Are there any monk's robes or similar garments we can give to Abby to wear while you talk?"

One of the sisters lurking in the background nodded, disappeared, and then quickly returned with a gray woolen robe that they draped over Abby's upper body.

"Why don't you crouch down against the wall and make your whole body invisible," he suggested.

Abby complied, only opening the fold enough to say, "I can tell I'm going to have an exciting role to play today," with more than a touch of sarcasm.

"Your role is to have a conversation," Dylan reminded her. "The whole reason we're here, taking the risks we're going to face, is so you and Rulaz can speak at last. Don't you forget that."

"Yes *sir*," she answered playfully, teasing him for his sudden turn toward the brusque leader.

"Rulaz, what can you tell me about the physical attack coming this way?"

"The Lord only showed me a symbolic cloud in a vision," she replied, "but from many years of interpreting such things I would say it was a group of four or five dozen men. All of them intensely evil, well trained and motivated in the extreme."

"They are Scythians?"

"I believe so."

"There is something else," Abby broke in. "They have taken my father. There's been no ransom demand or any contact, but I'm sure it's them, and they mean to take me out of the fight today."

"Does your father walk with Christ?" asked Rulaz.

"No. That's part of my concern."

Rulaz frowned and moaned softly. "He is in great, great danger. We will have to spend many resources praying for him as well."

"Rulaz, can you spare someone with the gift to go with me into the city?" Dylan asked.

"Sister Sarha," called Rulaz. "Would you go on a prayer-walk with this brother?"

From her vantage point against the wall, Sarha stepped forward and nodded vigorously.

"Sarha, I'm Dylan," he said, offering his hand.

She shook it and said, "Mr. Dylan, I would be most pleased to accompany you, and to pray as the Lord leads."

"Thank you, Sister. Well, we've no time to waste. Let's go."

And the pair disappeared into the rooftop complex.

"Brother Brehan?" Rulaz cried out. A man's lean face appeared from between two of the low-slung huts. "Today is the day of reckoning I have told you about. Could you gather your other brothers and spend the next few hours along the rooftop perimeter, praying without ceasing for our spiritual and angelic protection?"

"We think you are a heretic, Sister, you know that."

Rulaz froze and aimed a glacial stare at the monk, awaiting the end of his statement.

"Which is why we will be glad to pray for you in this way," he finished, smiling.

Rulaz chuckled. "Thank you, my brother."

CHAPTER

_62

With their defenses in place, Rulaz finally lay down on her cot, pulled a thin shift over her body, and turned to where Abby sat crumpled against the wall, well concealed.

"The evil spirits familiar to these skies are accustomed to the sight of me upon this bed, fighting for strength. They will think nothing of it and will not hear us whispering to each other."

"First of all," Abby asked softly, "are you the mother, the heart of the Sisterhood of whom they speak? The leader of *those who see?*"

"I am first of all the Sentinel of Jerusalem, as you have been told. That means that I and my predecessors use our gift in the service of Jerusalem, to watch, like a harbormaster if you will, over the departures and arrivals of spiritual beings at the city's holy places from all across our world. Then I dispatch this knowledge to the sisters I know, scattered though they are."

"But surely there is more," Abby prodded.

"Yes, there is. I am the earthly granddaughter one hundred twelve times removed, and spiritually descended just as many generations deep, from Anna, the prophetess who held baby Jesus in the Temple and proclaimed Him Messiah. "

"Whom I saw, or even inhabited, in my dream which began all this."

"Yes, as we all have. It is the surest sign of being one of us: having the dream of Anna."

"So the reason we all have this dream is because we are all her spiritual descendants, in an unbroken line?"

The woman nodded intensely. "Many, many of your spiritual relatives have not learned this. They simply look at the gift as a random occurrence, because almost no one has developed the practice of tracing back one's family legacy in Christ."

"How did this legacy build?" asked Abby.

"Well, the Word does not record it, but after meeting Jesus, Anna left the Temple and followed His ministry from afar. After His death and resurrection, she became one of the early church's most enthusiastic witnesses. Her spiritual family at the time of her death was rumored to be in the thousands. As decreed in this birthright, I am the matriarch of a spiritual family name of which the words *Iya Agba* are only the Nigerian variation. It is a very old and far-flung spiritual family, but its primary name around the world is *The Watchers*."

A NEARBY ROOFTOP

The photographer knelt only seventy yards from the rooftop enclave of the Ethiopians. In everyday circumstances, the leather-jacketed paparazzo would have felt more at home at a movie premiere in London or Cannes, jostling among the usual mob for a celebrity snapshot. And while Jerusalem was hardly considered a haven for the jet-set, the subject he was about to shoot represented the biggest name, the biggest media story in the world at the moment. Definitely worthy bait.

Still, he wasn't sure. The sleaziest of anonymous tipsters had called with a tip for the ages, according to him. Passed on to him from one of his coolest and most mysterious sources. Condition was, the tip went to just one person. Someone who was good. Someone who could get the shot sent out to the major syndicators in minutes.

He'd been flattered at the thought of it, if not the source.

He focused his longest telephoto lens, a contraption so large he sometimes found it hard to hold steady. There—right in the open on the church roof. Man, old woman, younger . . . had she died her hair? Made sense if she had. He bore down with his focus, trying to make out the face for certain.

Snap. He took a preliminary photo. His warm-up shot, he called it.

He flipped on the review button and studied the shot. Sure looked like her . . .

He decided to go with it. Aiming the lens again, this time set on rapid-fire, or one shot per second. The photographic equivalent of a Gatling gun.

Where were they? A sharp glare filled his viewfinder, dazzling him. The light forced him to put the camera down and regain his bearings. *Chill out,* he told himself. Strange, because the sun was nowhere near his shot. What was it, then? What obnoxious strip of reflective metal had he failed to identify? And why was it catching sunlight only when he looked through the camera?

He tried again. Same result. A pillar of blinding light assaulted his eyes, enough to sear his retinas.

ABYSSINIAN ENCLAVE, ROOFTOP OF CHURCH
OF THE HOLY SEPULCHRE

"I received nearly thirty thousand responses to my question within a day of posting it to my website," Abby said, midway through her description of the Sighted sisters in America.

Rulaz was staring at her in amazement when suddenly she almost jumped from her cot—the most dynamic motion she had made since their arrival.

Before Abby knew it, the woman was on her feet and pointing dramatically at the rooftop's edge.

"Abigail, do you see? What is he doing? What is that gesture?"

Abby squinted and tried her best, but the Sight was not upon her just then. It had not been the most ideal of days. Fatigue, preoccupation, not spending enough time in prayer. She had seen darkness in the church downstairs, but that had been all.

But this seemed urgent. She had to do something.

Lord, I don't deserve it, but please restore to me the gift you so gener-ously bestowed on me. Please allow me to see along with my sister. . . .

She opened her eyes again. Nothing. She knew what it was: she couldn't just treat God like that. He could grant her prayer in a sec-ond, but more than that, He wanted her to walk with Him.

Even though she knew it was for mixed motives, she began to praise Him. She started to hum her favorite worship tune under her breath, and despite being less than totally sincere, she felt her spirits begin to rise.

Then it came. She blinked against the brilliance pouring out of the two towering figures, standing at the rooftop's edge.

She peered closer. They were holding up their hands against something. A cascade of even more radiant light was pouring from those hands. Whatever or whoever the supernatural measure was being used against had better take cover. . . .

"Forget this!" the photographer barked in frustration. He already had the warm-up shot. It wasn't well focused, but good enough to identify the subject, which was all that mattered. It might have been a lucrative picture, might have even made his year. But for a profes-sional photographer, nothing was worth burning out a retina.

Even if its source could not be explained . . .

He trudged down to the corner Internet café, e-mailed the shot, then waited for his cell phone to ring.

Within ten minutes of its transmission, the photograph had aroused interest and even frantic activity among no less than thirty-four people in Nigeria, Europe, and the United States. At Fort Meade, Maryland, home of the National Security Agency, the half-focused pixels were resolved and Abigail Sherman was positively iden-tified with 94 percent certainty, including a margin of error of less than 3 percent.

By the time the photographer had returned to his rooftop post to make sure his prey had not escaped, his cell phone's voice-mail box had already logged in thirteen messages.

No matter, though, to the people involved. Although its ringer was turned off, its signal allowed a tracking to within fifteen feet of his location. The proximity to the Church of the Holy Sepulchre was noted within seconds—the nature of the building not lost for a moment on the Scythians receiving word on their way into the Old City.

CHAPTER
_63

OLD CITY JERUSALEM, CHRISTIAN QUARTER

Dylan and Sarha plunged into the thick afternoon crowd like tourists trying to win a footrace. Forty yards away from the Sepulchre walls, Dylan spotted a phone booth and nearly threw himself on it.

Accepting a phone card from Sarha, he covered the keypad with his body and dialed frantically.

"Hey, Reuven. Please don't hang up. This is Dylan Hatfield calling. I know this isn't a secure line, so I won't say Mossad and you won't say Delta Force, but you do remember me, from Tel Aviv? Early nineties...?"

Dylan laughed heartily. It appeared his contact had remembered him.

"Listen, I've got a lot to lay on you in a very short time. And I hope you remember enough to know that you can trust me no matter what. I'm in the Old City right now. You need to know that a group of thirty to fifty serial killers . . . yes, you heard me right, *serial killers* . . . right, they just entered Jerusalem . . . No, I don't know how they all got through airport security together, but maybe disguised as some kind of group? Maybe religious. So look for a large, all-male tour group, like a group of priests or monks. Anyway, it'd be a big help if you could come to the city and work with me on this . . . whatever that might entail, you know. Oh, and I'm completely free-lance now. I'm not on a formal op or mission for anyone else. I'll fill you in more later . . . No, I have no weapons on me—no comm., no cell phone, nothing . . . I'm just outside the Church of the Holy Sepulchre. . . . Fifteen minutes? That's great! One more thing—bring a metal detector wand. I'll explain later. See you soon."

Then he hung up the phone and exited the booth.

NEW GATE, OLD CITY JERUSALEM—AT THAT MOMENT

Dylan's off-the-cuff guesswork had actually described the enemy's tactics to the letter. For the very moment he left the phone booth and began making his way toward the rendezvous point to meet up with his old Mossad contact, four groups of twelve men dressed in the garb of Nazarite monks, each one led by a scowling man of advanced age, approached a different gate of the Old City.

Two of the groups were composed of dark-skinned men, though all the leaders were white. All had passed customs that morning on a chartered flight from New York, traveling as an international delegation of Nazarite Brothers in Intercessory Prayer for the Peace of Jerusalem. Religious groups, especially traveling en masse, tended to receive gentler treatment from Israeli security, since their common purpose of the journey was easier to determine. The authorities had failed to realize that Nazarites wear white Essene robes, not the black colors worn by this group.

On the outskirts of modern Jerusalem, their bus had stopped in an industrial area and taken on a large box from a van marked as a carrier of agricultural implements.

The box contained fifty-five razor-sharp sickle blades. Those deadly weapons now lay concealed from the walking public of the Old City by the thinnest of monastic garb: a simple fold of robe.

As for those leading each pack, each of the elderly men grasped a crooked staff for support, but the use was merely cosmetic and to evoke sympathy from passersby. Each of the senior leaders was actually one of the Elders of the Scythian Brotherhood. And the reason why none spoke to the men behind them was not a matter of protocol or religious decorum. It was because the Elders were in the throes of exercising the one ability that had elevated them to their exalted rank among their murderous brethren.

They were conversing with demons, as freely and fluently as language students on an immersion trip.

And they were headed, finally, to a certain destination. The Church of the Holy Sepulchre.

DEIR ES-SULTAN MONASTERY, ROOFTOP OF THE HOLY SEPULCHRE

"This is all incredibly fascinating," Abby said to the Sentinel Rulaz. "But there appears to be some great mystery surrounding me and all that's happened up to now. And somehow I have been promised that the solving of this mystery will heal a breach of some sort."

"Maybe we should say breaches, in the plural," added Rulaz. "Let me explain. This is a closely guarded history, one that few Watchers know, at least in full. After meeting the baby Christ, Anna the prophetess lived to see Him crucified and the fledgling Church grow and flourish. When persecution intensified, she fled with a large group to Ethiopia, where she became a formidable witness and evangelist. But something extraordinary began to happen. A large number of the women Anna had led to Jesus started to manifest visionary gifts remarkably like her own. It was as if her spiritual endowments passed on to her offspring in the faith much like parental traits in one's children. The women whom *they* prayed with to accept Christ witnessed them too, and so on. As the numbers and layers of these visionary women grew, they began to notice additional wonders. It seemed a spiritual thread of interconnectedness linked them all, alerting them to each other's dangers, victories, and fluctuations in the Spirit.

"That's why the Iya Agba in Nigeria are aware of you and were concerned for your condition, even though they have no idea who you are or where you live.

"Now, after Anna's death at an age approaching 130, an old age prolonged by the dry, healthful desert air of our country and the faithful care of her multiplied family, the lineage spread with the word of Christ across Africa. Amazingly, Africa's matriarchal tradition, with mothers not only leading the family but counseling the young girls in matters of faith, caused this heritage to remain confined to mothers and their spiritual daughters."

"Somewhere along in there," Abby interjected, "a wealthy royal from Ethiopia traveled to Nigeria and established the Ijebu kingdom. Did you know about that?"

Rulaz closed her eyes and fell silent for a few seconds. "Yes. I remember hearing something in my youth about our Sisterhood having seeded a kingdom far west of us. Something about helping its queen, who was a native of our land, battle a powerful evil."

"Yes. The Iya Agba of Nigeria are apparently descended from those sisters who came over."

"I am aware of the Iya Agba in the Spirit, although I did not know their name until just now. You see, this is one of the most painful breaches I have referred to."

"Please explain this to me."

"It all came about through the next chapter in our continued history. Through the centuries, the Watchers evolved into far more than a spiritual family. Our gifts made us a vital but highly secret asset in the battles between good and evil all across the globe. Watchers have acted as sentinels beyond Africa: in Europe and Asia as well. We have warned countless homelands of impending invasions, kings of imminent assassination attempts, popes and clerics of every stripe of demonic attacks against all segments of society. And in the midst of all that headiness lay the seeds of our alienation."

The State of Israel was home to twenty-one women descended from the spiritual lineage of Anna the prophetess who possessed the gift of the Watchers. These women formed an unusually tight-knit group as a result of living in a predominantly Jewish state and so close to the matriarch of the Sisterhood. They lived in virtually every corner of the nation: from the Golan Heights to the Sea of Galilee to the resort city of Eilat at the corner of the far-south Negev Desert.

At that moment, all of twelve who did not already live in the greater Jerusalem area were in their cars and within ten miles of the city, summoned by a powerful spiritual call.

Three had left children with their fathers. Five had left jobs mid-workday, having given their employers no warning or asked for time off. One would be investigated for desertion from her army post upon her return.

All but one of them had violated at least three traffic laws during their hurried trip into Jerusalem.

CHAPTER

_64

ROOFTOP OF CHURCH OF THE HOLY SEPULCHRE

Rulaz gazed back out over the Old City and blanched.

"Sister Abigail, whatever you do, do not look out there. First of all, you would be detected almost immediately. The air is thick with combatants. Secondly, the sight of it would make you ill. I have never once regretted having the gift of my Sight. Until this moment."

"Are we losing?"

"I cannot say who is losing or winning. The battle is fierce right now. But I'm speaking of the sheer blackness and repulsiveness of our enemies. Perhaps we in Jerusalem have been overly sheltered by our many angelic guardians all these years. But I have never seen such a grotesquerie before. It is as if the pit of hell itself flew wide open and disgorged itself into our skies."

"I am so sorry," Abby said. "I feel like I am the cause of all this."

"Do not say such a thing. If your coming caused this, it's because you are the greatest blessing to come our way in many lifetimes."

"Well, at least let's finish this and see if I can leave you in peace."

"Ah . . . now, where was I? Oh yes. The breaches arose from a myriad of sources. The Iya Agbas of Nigeria fell under a shadow when their countrymen started selling their brothers and sisters from all over Africa to the slave trade. Whether true or not, a rumor began that implicated a few of the Sisterhood in the heinous practice. But that was far from all. My own foremothers in the Ethiopian Coptic church became hopelessly embroiled in the eternally tumultuous politics of our country. As a result, we gradually drifted from fraternal contact with our neighbors. Some of our more zealous ancestors accused other sisters in Northern Africa of mixing their beliefs with the newly emerging Islam. Deepest of all was the heartbreak of our sisters over in America, whose fate we lost any ability to discern. And so it went. So after all these years, the Sisterhood's relevance, effectiveness, and anointing seem on the wane. A shadow of heartbreak and estrangement has corroded the invisible bonds between us all."

"Isn't it strange to you that, after all these centuries, the Sisterhood is still a black, African phenomenon?"

"I will say that it saddens me. It is a remarkable testament to how socially separate so many races remain, especially in the most intimate areas of their lives. But think about it: the Watchers are but one family line in a vast human kinship called the body of Christ. And consider how many amputated limbs litter that tree, how many breaches and schisms have caused whole parts of our strength to atrophy and wither away from isolation or under use. I mean, look at the awful way supposed Christians treat each other here at the Church of the Sepulchre, the very place on which we sit. We have struck each other with fists and quarreled amongst ourselves in a manner that shames the cause of Christ, all on account of grievances that date back centuries ago. My life is being afflicted and shortened because of the hateful pettiness of the Egyptians, who have a laundry list against us of their very own."

"Is this weakening of the Sisterhood the cause of your own physical difficulties?"

"Oh, I would like to think that because we all share this tenuous thread between us, our general decline has caused my own. And it is possible. It is also possible, though, as my brother and some of the monks here would argue, that I have simply neglected my health in my insistence on staying up here in prayer. In either case, I am certain that a healing of these breaches would be the best form of help I could receive."

"So the mystery remains," Abby said adamantly. "Why am I, a white girl brought to Christ by my white mother, apparently a member of this African Sisterhood? And why are the Sisterhood's enemies trying so desperately not only to keep me from growing but destroy me outright?"

"Because you represent two things they fear greatly: first, a healing in some of our deepest wounds, and second, a dramatic opportunity to grow the Watchers family in some whole new places. You are the greatest hope we have encountered in many, many years, Abby."

"But it still doesn't make sense. How, if the Sisterhood has remained confined along tight ethnic lines for so long, did I suddenly become the first breakout?"

Rulaz shook her head with a look of bewilderment. "That is why I am, unfortunately, not the end of your quest. You still have much digging to do."

Dylan walked up to a wedge of shadow alongside the intersection of David Street and Christian Quarter Road, raised his arms and threw them around the form of a lanky man of thirty, which suddenly materialized from the gloom.

"Reuven, I am so glad you came. I wasn't sure you would."

"You have a pretty incredible story, Dylan. If I didn't know what kind of man you were, I would have called out Shin Bet on *you*."

"I understand. And you haven't heard half the story yet. I've been through quite an adventure in the last couple weeks. Tell me though, are you armed? Do you have weapons? Do you have some backup?"

Reuven pulled aside a strap from his shoulder, revealing a machine gun. "This is all I could manage. Of course I can call in reinforcements the moment they're needed. But first, Dylan, you're going to have to tell me more."

Dylan stepped aside and allowed Sarha to step up. "Sarha, this is my friend Reuven, who is an officer with the government. He's going to help us. Reuven, you did bring the metal detector like I asked?"

He nodded.

"Good. Sarha is actually going to point these guys out for us." Dylan then took the wand and walked on ahead.

Reuven gave Dylan another incredulous look. Why in the world, if Dylan was so confident of his claim, would he have to rely on this young African nun to find these evildoers? He had known Dylan as a tightly wound yet professional and levelheaded special ops soldier. What had happened? Had the city claimed another victim of its famed Jerusalem Syndrome—that state of religious mania that gripped otherwise sane individuals in delusions of religious apparitions and apocalypse?

In either case, he would certainly stick around and find out.

Dylan and the young woman had already melted back into the crowd that packed Christian Quarter Road. Reuven decided it was worth finding out, and followed them.

But the rejoining did not come easily. For some reason, the pair had not chosen to simply merge back into the sluggish flow of people along the bazaar street, but to weave furiously through the bodies at top speed. Reuven was out of breath and thoroughly frustrated by the time he caught up with them again.

When he caught sight of their faces, he forgot his emotions altogether.

Both of them now stood stock-still in the street. Their eyes were wide open and fixed straight ahead. Reuven followed their gaze . . .

. . . to a group of about a dozen monks, turning onto Douk el Sharabba.

He watched warily as Dylan passed them quickly on the right, averting his eyes. The men seemed to be headed toward the front doors of the Holy Sepulchre, but as they entered the small plaza before it, Dylan had preceded them and was quickly shutting the church's two large doors.

"Gentlemen!" Dylan called out to the group in a loud, echoing voice. "Due to security concerns, we must reluctantly subject you to a metal-detector search today. No weaponlike objects will be allowed inside the church. He then waved the metal-detector wand above his head for emphasis.

The men said nothing, but just turned to their leader, an old man wearing a brutally dark scowl who began to visibly tense and look about them as though anticipating some kind of fight.

Reuven glanced over at the young nun. She had now shut her eyes and seemed to be praying fervently, one arm extended toward the group. Amazingly enough, it appeared that one, two, then half a dozen other women were joining her, only one in a nun's habit, yet all of them adopting the same expression and gestures.

A silent, coiled tension descended upon the plaza.

CHAPTER
_65

From the rooftop overhead, Rulaz had detected it too. She stopped speaking with Abby, hurried over to the edge and pointed down.

"It looks as if Dylan has confronted the first group, along with some more Watchers. They're praying to expel and banish the demons possessing most of these men. Let's join them . . ."

And they too held out their hands and began praying fervently.

Dylan wasted no time approaching the eldest monk with his metal detector, and the device wasted no time producing a loud, obnoxious squawk. Without a word, his eyes piercing Dylan with invisible daggers, the old man slowly reached into his cowl and retrieved something that, although expected, nevertheless provoked a loud gasp from the women watching.

The scythe was new, untried, and its half circle glinted cruelly in the sun.

The monk neither offered the weapon to Dylan nor did he drop it. Instead, he held the scythe high, and as he did the other men followed suit, filling the plaza with shards of sharply reflected light.

Reuven, without knowing why, found himself turning around his machine gun and seeking out the trigger with his right index finger.

The women's prayers suddenly became audible, and pleading.

Two of the monks nearest the row of women turned and lunged toward the women.

The plaza erupted into chaos.

The two out-of-control monks, as soon as they touched the women, were thrown to the ground in a fury of growling, screaming, and wild gesticulations.

Dylan swiftly broke the old one's arm with a dual twist and karate chop, kicked the man off his feet, and took up the scythe. In a split second he became a one-man killing machine, a whirl of spinning limbs, fists, and kicks against which the Scythians were no match. These men may have been hardened killers skilled with their scythes, but none were martial arts experts.

For his part, Reuven did not make a conscious choice to enter the conflict. Two monks had leaped on him, intent on gaining control of the machine gun. A deadly roar rang out across the square and the men fell dead, followed by three more who were attacking Watchers beside him.

But even as he concentrated fiercely on controlling his fire and not accidentally shooting any bystanders, Reuven's peripheral vision revealed to him something else which made no sense.

The remaining monks had thrown themselves on the ground and were rolling around, growling like animals and foaming at the mouth. It was almost as if some invisible sound frequency had assaulted something inside their heads and ripped their sanity from their skulls.

He stopped firing and stared at what was taking place. The monks were rolling away from a single direction—that of the women, their loud prayers and their outstretched hands. One of the men even faced the group and held out a hand like someone begging for mercy.

Reuven looked around. The entire group was either dead or incapacitated by this bizarre madness.

"Dylan!" he called out. "What in the world is going on here?"

Up on the rooftop, Rulaz did not dwell on the victory unfolding below, but immediately turned back to Abby.

"Where were we?" she asked the young American.

"Please tell me about these enemies of ours. I've found them to be vicious and resourceful. And they seem incredibly intent on killing me."

Her host stared at her with a sudden, cold fire. "Abigail, do you truly wish for me to tell of such evil? I will tell you: it is not something I discuss, ever. I do not wish to invite darkness of that kind into my mind."

Abby thought about it for a while. "No, I believe that if I am to solve this mystery, I need to know."

"Fine. But first let us pray for protection, even as I merely speak of these things. We are exposed out here, and we need as much cover as our Lord will grant us if such words are to leave our lips."

They both prayed briefly, individually.

A few minutes later, Rulaz asked, "Have you ever heard of the book of Enoch?"

Abby shook her head slowly, searching her memory. "I might have heard of the person, but not a book."

"That is most people's response. Enoch was a well-known figure. But the book that bears his name happens to be one which my church, the Ethiopian Orthodox Church, includes as Scripture. Even many conservative Protestants regard Enoch as a most unique member of the noncanonical writings, or books not voted to be part of Holy Scripture by the Council of Laodicea. By the way, that council voted it out of the canon because Enoch had been rejected by the Jews. However, the Jewish scholars had rejected it only because it contained prophetic references to Jesus Christ. Anyway—many of the early Church Fathers quoted from the book of Enoch, from Tertullian to Clement of Alexandria. Enoch is even quoted in the so-called canonical Scripture, the book of Jude."

"I never heard any of this before," admitted Abby.

"But the reason I bring it up is because the first part of the book of Enoch is titled *The Book of Watchers*. It describes how, early in history, God had ordained a special group of angels to watch over the affairs of mankind and teach us many of the most glorious artistic and technical innovations. These were the original Watchers. However, at one point, the Watchers became enamored with the beauty of earthly women and conspired to take them as their wives and lovers. This they did, in violation of every command of God, and you might cast a blanket over the consequences by saying simply, and without fear of being vulgar, that all hell broke loose. God cast the Watchers down and condemned them to wander the earth forever, without the ability to possess or interact with human beings as before."

Rulaz paused and leaned forward, and as she did it seemed her face visibly darkened.

"That is what Enoch's book says. Now hear what we believe happened after that. It is well known that demons have a desire to inhabit human form, which makes any human lust or hunger seem microscopic by comparison. And that was denied to them forever. So it turned out the only way these wandering demons could slake their great hunger, and their lust for human contact, was by gorging themselves on human suffering itself. Think of it as a refined form of spiritual nectar, a concentrated byproduct. Yet the only suffering powerful enough to satiate them was that of the dying process. So these condemned demons made contact with a small group of renegade soldiers, and then deceived these men by inducing them to kill others in exchange for some of the great secrets and lore of the ages. That is how the Brotherhood of the Scythe was born. And that is their primary purpose: to procure the evil nourishment these foul beings crave."

"If these wandering Watchers can't possess humans, then what just happened down there? Why were so many cast from those men?"

"Those were other, opportunistic, even ordinary demons, if you will. Think about it. You cannot devote yourself to sadistic murder without opening yourself up to, and being driven by, profound evil."

"How does this relate to our group called Watchers?"

"I believe the earthly Watchers, by which I mean *us*, were ordained by a new angelic host of Holy Watchers, as the faithful of their heavenly ranks were called, in order to assist the unfallen angels in resisting and destroying this horde wherever possible. We have always opposed them. We have always sought them out—even in the Sisterhood's most far-flung and isolated clusters. Over time, we have become mortal enemies to each other. And so it seems fated to always be."

Abby reared back in her sitting perch against the wall. "I can't believe all this," she said. "It's almost too much to digest, let alone how it all relates to my mystery."

"Tell me about your mother," Rulaz asked gently.

Abby's face fell and a pall of sadness came over her features. "I never really knew my mother."

She went on to explain how her mother had disappeared during her childhood, how her father had later divorced her mom *in absentia* and remarried, and that he'd long urged his daughter to let go as it concerned her mom, and to move on with her life.

Rulaz fixed Abby with a fierce gaze. "That is where our healing lies, my Sister. For you, and for us all. Heal the rift. Go to her."

"I can't," Abby replied. "I don't know where she is."

"Please," Rulaz insisted. "Try to find her. I can't tell you why, but I feel God telling me that it will lead to the breach you seek to heal. Everything depends on it . . ." She looked at the sky and winced. "What a fouling of this beautiful city."

Abby finally gave in to her curiosity and looked out above her, feeling her Sight almost beckoning her.

She almost fell backward. What assaulted her spiritual senses reminded her of a word she'd learned that year in an art appreciation class—*chiaroscuro*, or a sharp contrast between light and shadow. Blinding white light shot and waved all over the sky as intoxicatingly beautiful angels waged battle, punctuated by horribly distorted pockets of sheer blackness which, if she cared to focus, would resolve into the forms of ghastly and nightmarish beasts, grappling and struggling furiously.

She turned away. Even a moment's look seemed to have sucked all the strength and initiative from her body.

"Look over there," said Rulaz, pointing to the side, down toward el-Takiya Street.

The second group of so-called monks had now entered the horrific scene. Their elderly leader's arm was pointing upward, straight at them. The men ran over to the metal staircase and began sprinting up its steps.

Then a shout rang out. It was Brother Brehan, bounding toward the rooftop gate, shouting deprecations as he ran. "Nooo!" He launched himself over the wall and onto the metal staircase's top landing. The first Scythian stood only five feet below, his blade waving before him.

Brehan turned toward the wall and with two mighty yanks pulled a pair of ancient, rusting bolts out of crumbling limestone.

Rulaz threw her hands over her mouth and closed her eyes.

The staircase bent cruelly at the top, made a loud metallic creak, and collapsed. Brehan and the leading edge of Scythians were tossed mercilessly to the ground.

In the square, the remaining number turned about and glanced at their leader. Behind them advanced a row of emboldened Watchers, all of them holding out their hands and praying loudly.

Suddenly the elderly leader let out a guttural sound. He stiffened, and his followers mimicked him exactly.

He raised his sickle across his own throat, resting the blade tip just below his far earlobe. Eight more did the same.

He drew the scythe down in a fast, hard, swiping motion.

The men behind him performed the same motion in a single, precise rhythm.

It was Abby's turn to gasp at the horror below as nine bodies fell as one. Blood began spreading out across the plaza.

Rulaz turned to her, touched her forehead, and muttered a parting blessing. "It is time for you to go now," she said in an urgent whisper. "Find Dylan. Return to America."

"I thought it would end here," Abby lamented.

"It has not. And these men are defeated today, but not for good. They will keep coming after you. But it will end soon. Now go, while the fog of battle is still upon the Old City. There is another stairway that leads down from this place, right over there. Godspeed, my Sister."

CHAPTER
_66

OLD CITY JERUSALEM

Abby crossed the rooftop and fled the Abyssinian compound as swiftly as she could. Once she reached street level, she found Dylan, pulled him aside and told him what Rulaz had said.

After saying good-bye to Reuven, Dylan and Abby began sprinting down what they figured to be the least demon-infested street. Just minutes later they encountered a thick crowd along the narrowing lane where they felt it was safe to slow down.

The pair had vacated the Holy Sepulchre plaza with only seconds to spare. Only a moment after they had run from the site, two Israeli Shin Bet soldiers had ascended to the Deir es-Sultan rooftop.

There they found the nun known as Rulaz reclining as always, appearing only hours away from death. And yet, in a bizarre paradox, the barely living one struck the killers as the most vibrant person in the whole place.

They had intended to detain Rulaz and wait for orders over their cell phones. But a strange compulsion fell upon them. An unexplainable discomfort took hold of their extremities, and they began to shake so violently that they almost did not make it back down the steps and out into the street, where the symptoms immediately subsided.

From the apparent stupor of her weakened-again state, Rulaz smiled mildly and whispered a loving prayer of thanks.

KING DAVID HOTEL

Back in their East Jerusalem hotel room, Abby lay on the bed, trying to combine recuperation with brainstorming on their next step, which both of them knew had to take shape soon.

Very soon.

"Do you know what's strange?" she asked Dylan. "I never did tell Rulaz the highest likelihood is that my mom's dead. I don't know if that's denial, or some kind of deeper instinct, or what. It feels strange."

Dylan stiffened, the evidence of a new idea blossoming on his face.

"Look. I have an old friend at the FBI. Looks like for all its failings, my old life is turning out to have its advantages. Let's just see if he can run her name through their databases and come up with something definitive."

"All right," she said, her voice filled with dread. "Here's the phone."

She handed him the set and he swiftly dialed a number from memory. He waited almost a minute, then broke into a wide grin.

"Robert! Hey, it's Dylan Hatfield. Did I wake you up? I'm sorry, man, and you know better than to ask me where I'm calling from, but suffice it to say it's across the pond a ways. As if you couldn't find out . . ." He laughed awkwardly. "Actually, Robert, that's kind of why I called."

Dylan paused and listened for a moment.

"Well yeah, you heard right, or at least on the surface it's right. I mean, yes, I have gone off the rez, my man. Left the old company store, as it were. But you know me, Robert. You and I go . . . how far back? Twenty years now? Anyway, you know that I have more conscience than half of those guys put together. Right?"

He laughed.

"I thought you and I would agree. So here's the deal: I'm willing to pay good coin for a little of your telecom expertise. I need a domestic name run through the databases. Could you do that? This is very important, a life-or-death honest-to-goodness big deal. Freedom, the flag, all that good stuff. All right, the name is . . ."

He held out the phone to Abby.

"Susanne Louise Sherman."

Dylan broke out into a huge smile. "Did you hear that? Great. Thank you, buddy. I appreciate it."

He hung up, pumped his fists in the air, and cheered.

Within an hour a name appeared in Dylan's e-mail account, sent from an unknowable and untraceable web address.

St. Stephen's Home for Mental Health and Recovery, St. Louis, Missouri.

ST. STEPHEN'S HOME FOR MENTAL HEALTH AND RECOVERY—THREE DAYS LATER

Reverend and Mrs. Paul Skinner of Matewan, West Virginia, had arrived without appointment, with no records and, most of all, without the troubled and ailing teenaged son for whom they were "checking out" the St. Stephen's facilities.

However frowned upon by government regulations, such drop-ins were not a problem to the St. Stephen's staff. Turned out most parents did pretty much the same thing when first sniffing around, prior to the pain of involuntary committal. No one wanted to appear too serious before it was necessary. One understood such things in the mental health business.

So when Reverend and Mrs. Skinner arrived, the missus clearly distraught over the mere consideration of such an act as committing her boy to an "asylum," as she insisted on calling it, their impeccable dress and laudable concern warmed them to the facility staff.

The Reverend and Mrs. Skinner quickly discerned during their tour that Booneville was, despite occupying only a middle-tier status among private institutions, a most respected and well-managed private mental hospital. Its grounds featured one of the finest and largest specimens of Kentucky bluegrass of any place not already a horse farm, and its amenities were clean, non-odorous, and clearly above the norm. If the staff was somewhat less than stellar, and the success rate actually far below the national average . . . well, that only made for warm, long-standing relationships.

After they described their son as unusually strong-willed, physically strong, and resourceful, it seemed perfectly acceptable that the pair paid close attention to the home's security systems. The reverend, as most men of the cloth often did, protested a complete deficiency in technical matters and seemed lost when the home's director described to him the intricacies of the intensive ward lighting and locking grid.

But like most, he seemed mighty glad that the system was in place, whether understood or not.

The only disappointment to the director was that, as they left, they pointedly ignored three requests to leave their name and address in the brand-new contact-management system. They seemed sincere when they pledged to come back, but the hapless director now found himself, after the investment of an hour-long tour, completely unable to follow up with the decent couple.

He also wanted to express his goodwill to the poor wife, who seemed to be seeing ghosts, or some kind of frightening apparition, at nearly every turn of the hallway. He had never seen such a skittish woman. In fact, if he had been a suspicious man, he might have believed that it was she, and not some alleged son, who was the real object of their visit.

CHAPTER
_67

The perimeter lighting, which for most of the evening had kept the entire forty-acre grounds awash in an electric glow, blinked off at eleven o'clock, as promised. As a result, the cloudy winter night sank its unrelieved darkness down upon the campus like a thick black pillow.

The result? Conditions were almost too optimal for the man and woman, dressed in form-hugging black, as they scaled the high-brick wall and leaped inside. The two were so well disguised, they almost couldn't see each other.

Straining to spot his companion in the dark, Dylan almost wished he had skipped the black attire. If not for the ambient lighting from exit signs and night-lights inside the nearby building, there would have been no illumination at all.

That is, until the motion detectors set off a lawn spotlight. It was a windy night, so Dylan knew it would alert no one. As for the security guard who was parked in a truck on the other side of the campus, if he was awake at all he would attribute the spotlight to trees waving.

Finally he spotted Abby. She was standing still against the wall.

"Are you okay?" he asked, approaching her slowly to avoid causing a fright.

"I don't know if I can do this," she said, breathless.

"You mean, breaking in somewhere?"

She shook her head violently. It wasn't that. "It's the spiritual activity here. You wouldn't believe it. Things weren't this thick earlier today."

"Do you want to pray? We're not exactly on a time crunch, you know."

He couldn't believe he was hearing himself volunteer this, at last. Part of him, the perverse and heedless male, chided himself for capitulating to such a female-dominated perspective. *Religion's for chicks, and the guys they've whipped into submission*—something like that.

Amazing how quickly, once back in the United States, parts of him could begin to forget everything he had seen and learned overseas.

But another part of Dylan had forgotten nothing. Oddly enough, that inner guide was the same part of him that embraced discipline. That remembered to observe the tactical rules when on an op. That observed total operational control in following a plan, handling a firearm, heeding orders. The part of him that cared about the truth and took pride in doing what was right.

It was the part of him that never forgot what he had experienced, no matter how much time had elapsed or how many miles had flown by. . . .

Healings, angels, blinding flashes of light, prayers answered miraculously . . .

So yeah—it felt a little strange to kneel down on a mission, with a girl beside him, on-site, in full operational gear, and talk to someone who wasn't visibly around.

But Dylan was a different kind of warrior now.

The prayer over, they hugged the wall over to a low hedge, which they then followed, hunched forward. They reached the outer door with its simple numeric keypad, and Dylan almost laughed, remembering how easy it had been to glance at the director's proud punching in of numbers during their comprehensive tour.

The service entrance, he noted, was the only one without an attendant video camera, so Dylan merely pushed 4–3–2–1—the default factory setting, he was certain—and they were in.

Their earlier grilling of the director on security measures had, not accidentally, extended to the subject of nighttime staffing. Proudly extolling his facility's nocturnal vigilance, the man had told them exactly where the night-shift nurse sat for each of the home's major sections. The only one that did not rate a full-time desk inside was the high-security area, which, because of its narrow halls and highly medicated patients, could manage by sharing a nurse with the youth ward.

They wove silently through the hallways, easily evading the night desks by ducking into side halls and flowing along the length of the complex toward the high-security wing. But the ease of their access was not matched by ease of movement on the part of Abby. In fact, the farther she progressed into the building proper, the more her halting and jerky motions made her resemble one of the patients rather than a skilled intruder.

"Why now?" Dylan whispered to her during a break in one of the safer hallways. "Of all the places we've been, what's so bad about this place?"

"It's the patients. Think about it, Dylan. Most of the people in places like this are good, ordinary folks just having some problems. But if we know that demon possession makes people lose their minds, then how many of those folks also make their way to mental institutions? These hallways are full of . . . oh, there's, I can't even tell you . . ."

HIGH-SECURITY WING—THAT MOMENT

Unfold top half, open sideways.
Loving gaze. Pray.
Fold back. Trace the crease.
Unfold top half, open sideways.
Loving gaze. Pray.
Fold back . . .

That very day, Patient 64 had finally lost count of how many times she had performed the motion. It had taken years for the number to climb so high. Of the years—she had lost count of those as well. Decades' worth, to be sure.

She had kept a careful count for all those minutes, all those days, all those years. Somewhere in the thirty-five-thousand range. That was all she could remember now.

Today, something was different. A different-ness that had creeped all the way into her little world and chased the number from her mind. She would have collapsed entirely at the loss of it had the different-ness not felt so promising, so hopeful somehow.

She could feel her breathing slow and fall into rhythm. Her spine straighten. Her tear-caked eyes, her brittle mouth start to soften into those of a human being again. Her mind clear itself at last.

She felt her will return to itself and give her back her control.

Had someone forgotten to give her the medicine? Had one of the nameless authorities that ruled her life failed in its mission of keeping her perpetually fuzzy and confused? Or had something truly changed? Would she tomorrow find herself clearheaded enough to leave the ward and step outside for the first time in years? And once there, would she be able to walk like one of the higher-functioning ones, without screaming and running away at the sight of a monster?

Or was this something else entirely?

She held the paper again, her cherished treasure.

One more time?

She would unfold the top half and open it sideways. Then gaze at the photograph one more time. She caressed it gently.

She smiled at the little girl pictured there. A long-limbed, blond-haired girl on a beach, beaming the grin of a child who has nothing whatsoever to worry about. Whose world is intact. Whose family stands together on either side and above her. Who love each other. Who will not implode in three weeks' time.

She prayed, asked God to protect that girl, wherever she was. That He would make himself real to her. Teach her His ways. Lead her to the narrow path.

That He would bring her women to replace what had been taken from her.

She kissed the picture, although she knew the one in that image was not a little girl anymore.

And then she heard something, and her blood froze within her.

It was late. Very late. There weren't supposed to be sounds.

Yet she heard the familiar four tones of the code being entered on the outer keypad. The drone of the lock releasing, then its click as it drew back, open.

She turned, expecting anything. A demon. An attendant. Her guardian angel. Her executioner.

The door opened farther and she looked, unblinking.

She breathed in and out, in and out.

Stared.

She raised her hand and looked again at the picture in her fingers. Then back up at the young woman who stood in the doorway with tears streaming down her beautiful face.

The young woman took three long steps forward, into the cell.

Her voice was high, breathy and plaintive.

"Susanne?"

The pause continued, unbroken.

"Mommy?"

The word seemed to echo and quaver between them, for a long time.

The woman could not move. That was all right, though, because the younger woman could move just fine, and did so. Her long, lean arm left her side and reached up into the air. Abby's fingers extended and grazed the other's cheek. Traced the outline of her face with a fingernail. Descended the length of her nose. Caressed her hair.

"Mom. . . ?"

Only a sob came in response. The woman cocked her head sideways and moaned audibly. At last one of her hands trembled forward, inviting a touch.

"Mommy, I didn't know you were here," Abby said in the voice of a little girl. "Or I would have come. I would have been here, Mommy. You know that. Do you know that?"

Her mother did not answer, but a single tear had fallen from her eye.

"Please don't torment me," she finally said.

"What?"

"This is . . . a dream, right? Only are you a good dream, or a nightmare? Please, just don't hurt me. Don't torture me like this."

"Mom!" she said in a fierce whisper. "It's me! I'm really here!"

The woman's face recoiled at that, as though the words confirmed that indeed this would be a painful dream.

Abby gently picked up her mother's hand and brought it now to her face, released it. The hand almost fell back again, but then stopped its fall and returned to Abby's cheek. The hand began to trace, just as Abby's had traced her mother's features. As it did, her mother's eyes began to focus, to widen in gradually rising amazement.

"Thirty-six thousand, four hundred and thirty-eight!" She said the number proudly, like a youngster who has just labored through some thorny arithmetic. "I had forgotten last night, after keeping count faithfully, every single day I've been in here."

"What were you counting, Mommy?"

She held up the photo, its folds almost frayed into nothing. "The number of times I did this." She began to unfold it. Her fingers moved surely, smoothly, in discrete motions too well rehearsed for thought.

First, the lifting of the top flap. Then of the horizontal fold, opened sideways.

Now Susanne was holding the photo up for her to see. Abby stared, then turned back to her.

"Mom, I can't see what's on the picture. It's blank—too worn for me to see what's there."

Her mother looked at it again as though there was no issue, then faced her. "It shows my Abby when she was three years old. And her mother. Me. On the beach."

Abby leaned forward to gather her mother in her arms.

Her mother pulled away.

"But I'm not finished. It's not put away."

She turned the photo in her direction and gently kissed the figure of the little girl. Then she shut her eyes. "God, please protect my Abigail, wherever she is. Watch over her. Teach her your ways. Love her for me, in the ways I can't. Most of all, let her know you. Please?"

Then she folded it back up, just as efficiently and carefully.

She now faced Abby with a childlike look of anticipation.

"I'd like to hold you now."

There was no lag of anticipation. Immediately the woman was in Abby's arms.

Even though she had already examined Abby's face, it was the embrace that finally caused the truth to sink in. Holding her daughter's heaving torso and squeezing tightly into her shoulders, she finally gave herself over to an expression of wonder and utter shock.

"It's you, Abby. It's really you. God answered all thirty-six thousand, four hundred and thirty-eight!"

"He did, Mom. He really did. I can't wait to tell you how well He answered your prayers."

"I promised Him I wouldn't be angry, you know."

"Angry about what? About being in here?"

"No. About your never coming to see me."

"But please understand—I never knew. Dad always told me you had abandoned us. You had gotten tired of being a mother and just left."

Her mother now appeared crushed and deflated. "No, no . . . that's not true," she said. "He's the one who put me here. He's the one who kept me here, all these years."

Abby looked down and fought to absorb what she had long suspected about her father.

"Of course, it's what I needed," she added.

"What? No, you didn't. You didn't need this."

"Honey, I need to be protected."

"Protected from who, or from what, Mom?"

"From all the things I see that aren't really there. All the horrible creatures I see fighting and eating people right outside that door. I don't want to say too much. Tell too much about what I see. Gets me in trouble. But they do frighten me, sweetheart, in ways you couldn't imagine. Even though the doctors tell me it's just a hallu . . . hallucin—"

"Hallucination."

"And that's why I'm too sick to leave. Until they go away . . ."

"Mom, they're *not* hallucinations. Which is why they haven't gone away, despite all the medicine and everything they've tried."

"They're . . . they're real? No. They're too terrifying to be real."

"Yeah, but what about him?"

Abby motioned to the corner by the room's door. There, in a flood of light, stood her guardian angel, broad and quivering with power.

"You see it too?"

"Yes, I do, and it's not a sickness. It's a gift of spiritual sight."

Her mother shook her head. "No, it's no gift, that's for sure. If it's true, it's a curse."

"Not if you look at him. Not if you know the whole story."

"I do look at him. He's the reason I can even stay in here."

"That's great. But he's also the reason you can walk *out* of here."

"You mean, he will come with me?"

Abby sighed at the simplicity of the answer. "Yes, Mommy. He will. And so will I, and Dylan. And we'll hold you. And pray with you. Every inch of the way."

Dylan now stepped forward, a look of caution on his face. "I'm Abby's friend, Dylan. I think you two need to do a lot of talking and catching up. But unfortunately, this is not a good place to do it. We need to leave here right away, because it's going to start getting light soon, and when the morning shift nurses arrive, we'll be discovered for sure. So, Mrs. Sherman, we've come to take you out of here. For good."

She shook her head. "I don't think I can do it. I'm not strong enough."

Dylan turned to her. "You're right, Mrs. Sherman. You're not strong enough. I've just learned the limits of my strength lately too. But you don't have to be strong enough. God gave you this gift, and it is a gift, and He is more than strong enough."

"Well, He's going to have to come here and tell me himself. Because I'm scared."

"Ma'am, instead of coming in the flesh, He sent us here to help you. He uses His people like that sometimes."

"Mom, you remember the verse you once taught me, when I was too scared to jump off the diving board at the YMCA? 'I can do all things through Christ who strengthens me.' I remembered that verse, and I believed you when you told me. So all these years, when lots of things have scared me, I asked Him for the strength, and He always gave it to me. Always. Never failed."

Her mother nodded and shut her eyes. Her lips moved quietly. And moved some more. Then, it was over. She opened them and smiled.

It was the smile of a rational, if incredibly frightened, human being. "Let's go."

It was perhaps the oddest-looking patient discharge in the history of St. Stephen's Home. And not because of its covert and furtive nature either. The three people who hobbled through the hallways as a single clumped unit looked more like unshielded simpletons moving through a nuclear blast. Eyes half closed, their lips moving constantly, they each held up a hand against the darkness all around them.

This darkness had nothing to do with the lack of lighting in the hallways. This ethereal darkness, thankfully, had one redeeming feature. It fled swiftly before the onslaught of another outstretched hand accompanying them: that of the guardian angel, who indeed proved to be far from stationary.

It would be fair to say that Abby's mother prayed her way off the campus, each medicated shuffle step seemingly powered by at least three prayers each. It was wrenchingly slow, causing Dylan great uneasiness at the increased risk due to their snail's pace.

But even Dylan had to admit that God was working for them. This was November, and the same winter that had brought the rainy season to Nigeria brought a cold fog to the grounds of St. Stephen's. Even though cars were entering the distant driveway on the other side of the campus, the strange-looking trio slipped out the opposite side completely unseen.

Abby's mother was weak, and it took a great deal of awkward pushing and hoisting to get her over the wall. But once she fell into Dylan's grasp on the other side, and her slippered feet met concrete sidewalk, a sigh of relief tore through her body.

"I'm out, aren't I? I'm really free. . . ."

Abby wiped her eyes. "You really are, Mom. Now let's hop into the van and really get out of here. Because we have far more than just the home's staff after us."

CHAPTER
_69

Ten minutes later, three minutes before the disappearance of Susanne Sherman was even discovered, a plain blue minivan pulled onto Interstate 70 and into the lifeblood of rush-hour St. Louis.

It was the second vehicle used in the getaway. The first had been an old conversion van Dylan had parked under a highway overpass just down the road from the home. They had driven it four miles to an enclosed parking garage, then exchanged it for the newer, more dependable minivan.

One of their first tasks was to have Susanne Sherman change from the tattered old robe and shift she'd been wearing to the new silk tracksuit they had brought with them. The minivan's windows were not tinted, so Abby moved with extreme delicacy to help her mother change in the backseat without attracting the attention of other motorists.

"Oh, this feels marvelous!" her mother exulted in a voice that sounded decades older than it should have. "I wore the same thing for so very long."

Twelve miles later, the minivan exited and swerved rather abruptly into the drive-thru lane of a nearby McDonald's restaurant. Susanne, who could hardly remember the name McDonald's, let alone the last time she'd sampled their breakfast fare, gleefully ordered herself a sausage biscuit with egg, along with two orders of hash browns and an extra-large Dr. Pepper.

She reached down into the bag and withdrew the sandwich in a grip that shook so violently Abby had felt compelled to lend her mother a hand. Susanne's face slackened bitterly at the clear display of her deterioration. She bit down into the sandwich, chewed three times, and allowed the tears to run from her eyes once more.

Once her ravenous hunger had been satisfied, she glanced outside the van.

"Is it almost dawn?"

Dylan peered out the window. "Looks like it."

"I would like to see the dawn; I haven't seen the sun come up in all these years."

Then Abby remembered from her childhood the early morning walks on the beach she'd once enjoyed with her mother. She fought back tears at the thought.

"You're in luck," Dylan said. "We're less than two miles from the Arch, a perfect spot to catch the sunrise."

Soon they pulled off the Interstate on their way toward the Arch. Dylan parked facing the Mississippi, then he and Abby helped Susanne from the van just as the tip of the sun's orb crested the skyline of East St. Louis, across the waters of the mighty river.

Susanne said nothing as waves of golden light seemed to pour into the air around them, glinting fiercely off the sharp edge of the Gateway Arch. She continued to gaze at the sunrise in silence for a long while until finally she turned to Abby and said, "God really does answer prayer, doesn't He?"

Abby nodded.

Susanne Sherman's disappearance had just surfaced along the electronic fringes of the vast surveillance web stretched over the world, all for the purpose of locating and apprehending Abigail and her elusive companion.

Early morning fog might have concealed their escape, and Dylan's cunning had erased almost all odds of their being caught, but it did not prevent a tiny, invisible dot inside the lamination of Susanne's faded photograph from sending out a signal so weak yet so persistent that it could be traced in real time by highly trained operatives of the United States government.

Or, as in this case, the battered yet surviving organization with whom the operatives supplemented their appalling government salaries.

INTERSTATE 55, ST. LOUIS, MISSOURI—
JUST MINUTES LATER

While driving, Dylan glanced back at Abby's mother with a disarming grin. "Ma'am, I believe you're looking just a bit clearer and stronger with every mile we put between us and that place."

"I am feeling clearer," she said. "That's for certain. Thank you. Thank you for coming for me."

"Mom, do you understand now that your seeing all these things all this time was actually a spiritual gift shared by thousands of other women?"

In fits and starts, while omitting whole chunks of her tale to avoid spinning off into hours of digression, Abby told her mother about the Watchers and what she had learned of their plight. The account ended for Abby with a single, crucial question.

"Who led *you* to Christ? Can you tell us about that person?"

Regret and sadness washed over Susanne's face. "I grew up in the last tatters of the old South, you know. A big ramshackle house over in Webster Groves. A swing, huge lawn, fried chicken, and pot roast for Sunday lunch. But part of that world was . . . I wasn't raised by my mom and dad. I was raised by Marcelle."

"Marcelle? Was she African-American?"

"You mean *black*? I never heard of that other word."

"Yes, that's what I mean."

"Marcelle was definitely brown, or Afri . . . whatever you said. She was the great-granddaughter of slaves, who were literally sold down the river and separated, only they found each other and reunited after the war."

"World War I?" Dylan asked, frowning.

Susanne gave him a look as if she questioned his intelligence.

"The War Between the States."

"Oh."

"Dylan's a Yankee through and through," Abby explained with a smirk.

"What I'm trying to say is that Marcelle led me to Christ and taught me everything about the Lord and His ways."

"Did you go to Sunday school?"

"Not for a long time. Marcelle was my Sunday school."

Abby nodded, smiling to herself.

"In fact," said Susanne, "Marcelle is also the one who blessed me. Out of the blue one day, as we were reading the Word and talking about 'gawdly thangs,' as she used to pronounce it, she just up and laid her hand on my forehead and started praying something fierce. And something happened to me. I can't explain it."

"You don't have to, Mom."

"Now that I think of it, it's a funny thing. Because it's right after that blessing that strange things started to happen. A few months later I had the strangest dream, so odd I can even remember it now. I dreamed that I was the prophetess Anna. Meeting Christ in the Temple."

"It's the sign that you have the gift," said Abby. "It came to you through your spiritual family. Mom, as best I can tell, you might be the first white Watcher who ever lived."

"Does that make you the second?"

"I suppose so."

"Well, it hasn't been such a great thing for me so far. Right after I had that dream, I started seeing things. Spirits. Ugly creatures. I was only ten, so in Southern Gothic style, it was just written off as having a good, active imagination. I remember my father joking that as long as Susanne's ghosts were Yankee soldiers, he was all right with that. But then it got bigger. I started running away from seemingly empty chairs. I started talking to people, angels I guess, nobody else could see. I'd even give hugs to thin air. My parents got worried and thought that, without some kind of 'modern intervention,' I'd become one of those mad Southern ladies. So the first thing they did was fire Marcelle and banish her forever. She was forbidden to talk to me. I don't think they had restraining orders back then, or I think they would have gotten one. Then they sent me to a hospital for disturbed children."

"What was that like?" Abby asked.

She took a deep breath and continued. "Well, they started with lots of pills. Tranquilizers. Ten, twelve pills a day. Then the electroshock, which at the time was the worst thing I'd ever lived through. In between, we got slaps in the face, swats on the behind, some good shoves when we didn't cooperate. But you know what was the absolute worst part for me? Being separated from Marcelle. Not having her around to comfort and guide me, not to mention teaching me in 'the ways of the Lord,' as she called it. Now *that* was torture."

"How long did you stay there?"

"Eight months, if I recall. When I got out, I was one troubled teenager with a big chip on my shoulder. Then I went into a depression and started turning away from all that Marcelle had taught me. I stopped walking with God or reading the Word. I met a boy named Bobby in the neighborhood, and two months later I found out I was pregnant. He was from a good family and going off to an Ivy League school, so my folks arranged this quickie marriage. But as soon as you were born, he took you away with him to California. Next thing I knew, his daddy's lawyer had filed commitment papers with the state, and that got them full custody of you. And that's where I've been . . ."

Her voice had turned shaky, then trailed off.

After a pause, Susanne continued. "About eight years later the involuntary commitment expired and I got to come home. My daddy spent most of his savings getting a lawyer to bring you home and let me see you. Do you remember that?"

"I do," said Abby. "I've replayed those days in my mind a million times."

"I don't remember much of it, because it was a very difficult time. But the one thing I remember perfectly is the night you and I prayed together for you to receive Christ into your heart and start walking with Him."

"I remember. You put your hand on my head and prayed by yourself for a while."

"Yes. Just the way Marcelle had shown me to do it. And do you recall what happened then?"

"Something. Something weird. I remember feeling this strange jolt, kind of like when I stuck my finger in that old light socket in the garage."

"A bright light passed between us. Something incredible. But then your father stormed in to tell me that my time with you was up. He was very angry. He told me he was through putting up with this Negro witchcraft."

"He said that?" Abby said.

Her mother nodded.

"Dylan," she said, turning to him with a stricken look. "We have to find Marcelle. If this breach is going to get healed, we have to find Marcelle and close the circle."

Susanne took her daughter's hand and held it over her heart. "That would be even more than I've ever prayed for. That would be a dream come true."

Abby leaned her head against her mother's shoulder. They quietly savored each other's company, the flow of new time and the passing miles.

CHAPTER
_70

Turning south, they soon found themselves in a sprawling suburb. Dylan stopped at an electronics store, where he purchased a "screaming" laptop computer and a high-definition camcorder. Then the three retired to the nearest coffee and Internet haven.

"Do they really want three dollars for a cup of coffee?" Abby's mother asked, incredulous.

"For a good one, yes," Abby answered, chuckling.

"Maybe the coffee's expensive, but all the information in the world is free," Dylan said. "Look. I just enter the word *Marcelle* in a search engine and the World Wide Web goes out and searches databases all around the globe. Oh no . . ."

"What's the problem?" Abby asked.

"Three and a half million hits is the problem. This won't be much help."

"What does *hits* mean? When I was a girl, a hit was either the opposite of a strike, or a pull on a joint."

"Mom! I didn't know you knew that."

"Well, sweetheart, you didn't think I slept through my adolescence, did you?"

"A hit," explained Dylan, "is a reference to the word you're browsing. So I found three and a half million references to Marcelle out there, which is far too many to investigate myself. Where did Marcelle live most of her life?"

"I'm sure it was Webster Groves."

Dylan typed a bit. "Now we're down to one hundred hits. Problem is, they're mostly new and commercial sites. I'll scroll through, but it doesn't look like anything about an individual. Do we even know if this lady is still alive?"

"She would be well into her eighties by now," Susanne said, after some reflection.

"Are there any childhood friends you could ask for a last name? Any old tax records?"

"Dead and buried. But you know what?" Susanne added. "Marcelle is alive. I know it's a cliché to say this, but if she had died, I believe I would have sensed it somehow."

"Absolutely, you would have." Abby struck the table with a loud slap. "That's it! You may think this is crazy, but I'm gonna do something bold. Maybe even redemptive."

Dylan's eyebrows shot up. "What are you cooking up?"

"I know who knows this stuff. I'm gonna call my granddad."

The three of them left the Internet café and found a private place outside where they huddled around the phone. The dialing tone and beeps sounded over its speakerphone, then finally ringing. A static-like noise, followed by a male voice, gruff and somber.

"Heath Laidlaw."

"Granddaddy?"

"Abigail? Abby, what's become of you? We've been so worried. You're all over the TV."

"I'm fine, Granddaddy. And I'm starting to put a lot of very important pieces together. Try to guess who I'm with right now."

"Don't play with me, Abby. I'm an old man."

"I'm with my mother. Who I was told I would never find, but who's spent the last many years in a mental institution due to repeated commitments and interventions from her family."

"Are you calling to bawl me out, Abigail? Because I'm a little too old to put up with that kind of guff."

"No, Granddaddy. I'm not calling to condemn you or anything like that. But I did think you might want to speak to your daughter."

A faint crackling of static played over the speaker for a moment. When his voice returned, it sounded like that of a different man.

"Susanne?"

"Daddy?" her mother said, sounding suddenly a half century younger.

"Sweetheart, I'm sorry. So sorry . . ." His voice sounded as if he might break into a sob. "Oh, I wish your mother had lived to see this day, Susanne. Are you there? Can you hear me?"

"I'm here, Daddy" came her reply.

"I was wrong, Susanne. I know that now, and I've longed every minute of every day, for the last twenty years, for the strength to tell you that. But you know sometime even your worst mistakes just kind of get cast into cement and become stone, and you feel there's nothing you can do to make it right. After your mother died, I sort of gave up, telling myself it was too late. I believed the worst, that you were doing so poorly, my telling you wouldn't matter. My taking you out wouldn't matter. And of course that wasn't true . . ."

Susanne leaned back in the sunshine and shook her head, clearly overwhelmed by all that was happening to her that morning. She blinked a few times as though absorbing what she had just heard took extra brain-processing time. She leaned forward, smiled faintly.

"I forgive you, Daddy. You sound sincere, and in Jesus' name I forgive you. You know that I still have a great deal to work through. But with His help I know I'll be able to forgive you. I just need a little time to do it fully, to adjust to everything. Okay?"

"Thank—"

The final word of his appreciation was swallowed in some kind of vocal garble.

"Thank you." And now it was clear, despite the bad connection, that the man was weeping openly.

"Granddaddy," Abby said, "I've been learning a lot about healing old wounds and breaches. And we're doing more, having a greater impact right now, than you may ever know. Confessing and forgiving each other is kind of like repairing broken veins and arteries that have gotten clogged over time and now threaten the life of the whole body. It's big stuff, Granddaddy. Even God takes heed of it."

"How's that?"

"You wanna know?"

"Sure. Tell me."

"It's simple. God says that a broken and contrite heart He won't despise. He won't turn away. Ever. Those are the two conditions. Broken. And contrite. From our side, He also says that whoever doesn't forgive his brother won't be forgiven of his own sins. But that's for another day. Have you ever heard the word *atonement*?"

"Of course. It's a religious term, if I remember rightly."

"Yeah. Well, it basically means taking action to make things right. Something like that. And today is atonement day for you, Granddaddy."

He chuckled affectionately at his granddaughter's candor.

"We want you to give us Marcelle."

"Who?"

"Marcelle, Mom's old nanny. You've got to know something about where she went. We want to know. And we need you to remember."

CHAPTER

_71

Marcelle Reynolds, age eighty-two, lay in a bed of the Bonneville Care Center's nursing ward, listening to the gradual slowing of her heartbeat on the bedside monitor, and a syncopated, sanitized version of an old Otis Redding song she remembered from her younger days, drifting from the ceiling speaker.

Her body was failing her, failing fast, but thank the Lord her ears hadn't gone yet.

Now they brought her the sound of footsteps. Many of them—and they weren't the flat claps of the doctors' loafers or the soft padding of the nurses' shoes either.

She focused her bleary old eyes and confirmed it.

Visitors.

Then her Sight slid into place, and she grinned.

"Is that an old friend from Webster Groves, by any chance? Girl named Susanne?"

Susanne nearly collapsed from sheer surprise. "How did you know it was me?"

"I've been expecting you," she said, still smiling. "Some friends of mine told me you'd be coming soon."

"And you want to see me?"

The old woman exploded into a vocal barrage that was part coughing, part explanation, and part warm laughter. "Are you joking with me? My longing to see you is one of the biggest hurts in life I got left!"

Susanne then did something that startled and even frightened everyone but Marcelle. She broke into tears and collapsed, almost threw herself against the old woman's bed. The motion was so sudden and so forceful that Abby, thinking her mother was having some sort of episode, fell to her knees in an attempt to save her.

A nurse passing by, hearing the commotion, entered the room and was stopped by Dylan, who stood rigging up his video and laptop in a corner. "What's going on here?" the nurse barked.

"Oh, it's just some old friends stopping by," Marcelle called over, "mending some old *stuff* from the look of things! Don't you worry. I'm great."

The nurse glanced from face to face as though braving a band of criminals. "All right, then. But you all remember that Mrs. Reynolds is very ill. She needs her rest and quiet to recuperate."

"Miss Marcelle," Dylan said, "I'm rigging up a video camera and I'm going to try and show this conversation to some other folks around the country. Do you all mind that?"

"I suppose not. Is it okay with you, Susanne?"

They all replied except for Susanne herself, who was still weeping uncontrollably by Marcelle's side.

"Sister, what are you crying for?" Marcelle finally asked.

"Will you forgive me?" she asked between sobs.

"Gladly, but whatever in the world for?"

"I'm the reason you were sent away, Marcelle. Didn't you know that? I'm the one who ratted on you, who told Mommy and Daddy about how you'd prayed with me, and how it had been the start of all my . . . my seeing things. It's because of me you were banished."

"Oh my dear!" Marcelle exclaimed. "I never thought to blame you or have any unkind thoughts about you ever! You were just a child then. All you were doing is being honest with your folks."

Susanne looked up, astonished.

But Marcelle was equally amazed.

"Honey, I can't believe you'd spend so much time torturing yourself over things that weren't your fault, when I'm the one who ruined your life!"

"What? How did you ruin my life?"

"Susanne, I had no business layin' hands on you like that, a white girl in a culture that had no clue about giftings the way mine did. I made a terrible mistake, passing on the Sight like that, when you were neither ready nor of the right branch of the family. See, in my world folks had heard of the gifting for years, even if it was just through the grapevine or old legends dating all the way back to slavery days. But the separation of the races had kept it out of y'all's world. White believers are more cool and collected, and more into teaching and thinking everything through. Y'all aren't at home with signs of the Spirit, least ones that powerful. Besides, on Sundays the two races don't rub elbows all that much. It's two different faiths almost. So it was my fault. I was foolish and reckless. I just loved you so much, and I saw how you loved the Lord. . . ."

Susanne held up the withered brown hand and kissed it twice.

"You led me to Christ, and for that I'm eternally grateful."

"So you forgive me?"

"Of course I do. And I'm so glad that you forgive me too."

"Nothing to forgive."

"Ladies," said Dylan from the back of the room. "I'm sorry to interrupt, but I just wanted you to know that I'm filming this conversation. And I just got off the phone with someone in Atlanta, who was quite eager to receive the transmission of this video. Someone named Mara McQueen."

"You mean she's watching us right now?" asked Marcelle.

"Yes, along with probably a third of the world's population," he answered, laughing at the outrageousness of it all.

Abby turned back to Marcelle. "Miss Marcelle, I don't know if you've been told about me. But I was just in Africa where I fellow-shiped with the missing part of your ... I should say *our* spiritual family. To begin with, did you know that you are my grandmother in the faith?"

"Oh, darling, you come here," Marcelle said, reaching for her in vain.

As Abby walked over to Marcelle and took her place at the death-bed of her spiritual relative, Dylan glanced outside and saw something that caused him to stiffen and quickly leave the room.

CHAPTER
_72

BONNEVILLE CARE CENTER, MAIN CORRIDOR

Four, now five men, their long overcoats hiding automatic weapons . . . Dylan's old, internal tactical voice counted down in his ear.

They're here for a bloodbath. And there was no way, no way at all, that Dylan was going to allow that to happen. What was taking place in that nursing-home room was too precious and important not to defend with his life.

Instinctively now, without hesitation, he began to pray. He asked for guidance, for protection, for divine help, but most of all for wisdom—so he would know the right thing to do and when to do it as he faced the battle ahead. He finished by asking, *God, do I take action? Should I use violence against these men?*

This time the answer came back so clearly, it was almost audible.

Then, striding through the lobby, he heard screaming coming from the nurses nearby. He met up with two of the men as they were marching through the front entrance. In a single motion he launched himself upon them. A couple of kicks swept them both from their feet. Before they could recover, Dylan had thrown his whole weight on both of their chests and was wrenching the weapons out of their hands. One, then two blows with the gunstock to their heads immediately knocked them out.

He jumped up, dodged a woman in a wheelchair, punched through the door into open daylight and glanced around frantically for the best direction to run.

Away. As far away from this place as he could get. Yes, he had to lead them away from the women.

Gunfire shattered the air just beside him. The others had found him! He turned and took off running.

A line of trees to his right seemed to betray some kind of creek bed. At least that offered some cover, so he headed that way. A bullet zipped by his right shoulder. He veered wildly away again. The red dot of a laser sight now danced about his neck and shoulders. Seeing this, he lurched into a headlong zigzag pattern. Then the dust ahead convulsed beneath the sprays of a dozen sharp concussions. *Machine-gun fire!*

Doubt chose this moment to assail him. *Still think God is going to get you out of this one? How badly are you willing to be a chump?*

In the midst of his panting, he called out to God and kept running. The machine guns he carried in both hands were now, he realized, a hindrance. He tossed them down into the creek.

There were times for weapons of the Spirit, and he'd suddenly realized that time had come.

He felt his feet move into a renewed frenzy of speed.

God, he pleaded, *all this time I've waited for a sure sign from you. Waited while Abby and every woman we met heard your voice, saw your angels, received clear direction from your Spirit. It's my time now, Lord. Please. The time has come for me to receive something real and miraculous. . . .*

A cross street loomed in his vision. He abruptly turned the corner and disappeared.

God, please! The time is now. Not three seconds from now . . .

He looked up. There was a flash of bright light—a hand, a

shoulder, a burst of unspeakable power. Although he would have done so willingly, he fell to his face automatically, almost by reflex.

Three seconds later, his four pursuers rounded the turn as well.

Taking in the new street before them, they almost fell on their own faces in their joint effort to stop the forward momentum and halt their progress.

The man they were pursuing now knelt on the road's center stripe, one knee raised, an elbow resting on it.

The guy looked like he was praying, almost.

The lead gunman regained his balance and raised a Glock handgun. A professional's mark: one to the head, two in the chest.

The kneeling man began to shake. And so did the killer's gun hand.

"What are you waiting for?" asked the second gunman.

"Well, look at him! He wants us to do it. Something's not right. Gotta be some kind of trick. Either he's wired, or he's gonna set something off the second we do him, or maybe signal a sniper nearby."

"You got a point," said the other gunman, now too scared to even nudge Dylan with the toe of his boot.

The two men began to back away, guns at the ready.

The weapons fell to the street. The men backed up, desperate to get away but unwilling to turn their backs on the sight before them. Finally, twenty yards back, their terror peaked and they turned around to flee, disappearing into the neighborhood.

Dylan stood and remained still, looking up and down the full length of the mighty warrior angel standing guard just behind where he'd knelt.

"Thank you!" he said out loud. *"Thank you."*

MALIBU, CALIFORNIA

A gleaming stretch limousine pulled up in front of the bone white beach home. A patrician, elegant figure in an expensive European tracksuit ran his hand through well-coiffed gray hair, looked up at the sea gulls massing overhead, and jogged inside.

Lying against the far wall of an empty living room was a man with his arms tied behind his back.

The Head Elder of the Scythian Brotherhood walked over to him and kicked the soles of his feet to wake him up.

"So, it's our old secret friend. The man who, in a way, made all this possible. Hello, Bob Sherman."

"Yes, and here's the man who lied and went back on every promise he ever made to me," snarled Abby's father.

The man bent down and shouted in Sherman's face. "What are you talking about? Has your memory failed you, you idiot? Do you remember what you were, this loser at a state college, when we found you? When we offered to make all your dreams come true in exchange for some help with your whacked-out wife? Did we not deliver on that? Did we not make you a millionaire thirty times over?"

"You told me Susanne would get treatment and help for her delusions. Not force me to lock her away for three decades. Not tear my family apart!"

"Well, your daughter has taken revenge for all of you. Our Brotherhood is in tatters. Our leadership is dead, our rank and file decimated. And for me, the only joy I'm going to have before my masters come to claim my soul is that of making your last moments on earth as excruciating as possible."

He extracted a scythe from its hanging place on a side wall.

"And if I get the least impression that you're trying to talk with that putrid god of your daughter's during this time, I swear I'll make this more painful than anything this world has ever witnessed."

"You mean, since the death of Christ," Sherman said through gritted teeth.

"Whatever."

"Well, don't worry on that account. As it happens, what you're describing has already taken place. I read my daughter's account of heaven before you pigs found me. And I know she's telling the truth. Not only that, but what she described was so much more appealing than anything you and your men could offer, it was no contest. So if your homicidal existence is so pathetic that you can't stop yourself from inflicting pain in your very last moments of safety, then go ahead. Because I'm a follower of Christ now, and I know where I'm going. And whatever suffering you inflict on me will be so richly rewarded in heaven, I might be tempted to come back and ask you to inflict some more."

"Die, you pathetic kneeler," he growled, coming closer, his grip tightening on the scythe's handle.

Sherman began to speak in a loud, commanding voice. "In the name of Jesus Christ, I command you, foul spirits, to leave my presence. Leave this place. Leave this man!"

The Head Elder took one step back, for the foul beings all around him had responded hatefully to Sherman's words.

That one step, the impact of Gucci leather on Carrara marble, obscured the faintest sound of movement from outside . . .

Crash! The living room's picture window shattered profusely, deafeningly. Glass cascaded all over the space.

A black-clad male form flew into the center of the room, screaming "FBI! FBI!" at the top of his lungs.

The Head Elder called out for help, but none of the beings this leader of the Scythian Brotherhood had served would save him now. Bullets flying around him, he turned away from a row of white, translucent beings and dashed across his marble floor in terror. He reached the edge of his second-story veranda, framing that magnificent seascape, and leaped . . .

He struck the terrace below with unearthly force, turning his limp body into the mockery he had so often made of others.

CHAPTER
_73

MARCELLE'S ROOM—THE NEXT MOMENT

"Yes, I can remember in my childhood," Marcelle was saying, "hearing stories of these unbowed women coming over from Africa and singing praises to God even while they still lay chained in the horrible holds of those transport ships. I remember."

"It's amazing," remarked Abby, "that as hard as their lives have been here, with all the days of slavery, the hard years after Emancipation, or many decades later in the fight for equal rights—none of it's squeezed the gifting out of those godly women."

"Yeah, but still, we've all been hamstrung," Marcelle said, her voice starting to weaken. "It's a scandal, we've had so little to do with each other's faith that it took this long for the gift to cross racial boundaries."

"Maybe now it's time," Susanne said.

"Maybe it's time for all these old breaches and grudges to get washed out of our system," Abby agreed. "Can you imagine what the church could do, with our prayers alone, in this messed-up world? Without these divisions and grudges to sap our strength?"

Marcelle held out her thin arms, inviting Susanne, herself just a stick figure, to climb up onto the bed. Tentative at first, she crawled forward and lowered herself into the old woman's arms. Slowly, tenderly, they formed a mother-child embrace.

"O Lord," Marcelle called out as she tenderly caressed Susanne's forehead, "you know I have missed this. I remember, Susanne. And I know you remember."

Abby knelt before them, letting herself melt into their healing embrace.

Then Abby furrowed her brow and gazed up into the face of her grandma in the Spirit. "We've forgotten how sick you are."

"Oh, I'm all right. Fact is, this is the happiest day of my life!"

"And mine," said Abby.

"And definitely mine," added Susanne.

Abby leaned forward, took her mother's hand, and placed both on Marcelle's head. It was a posture she had seen only once before, when standing before Sister Okoye at the Believers Gathering as she herself was nearing death.

Both of the younger women began to pray silently, moving their lips.

It was at this point that television viewers all over the world, regardless of their set's quality or the reliability of the video feed, began to experience the old standby. Technical Difficulties. Some saw what were once labeled ghost images, or shallow transparent forms moving across the screen. The whole viewing audience noticed a brightening of the ambient light in the room; some even assumed that an electrical malfunction had overtaken the nursing home.

Only a select number of them realized what was actually taking place.

Suddenly a bright flash of light shot from the center of the room, and of viewers' screens. Thousands would report that their tubes had exploded, and scores would have to be reminded by manufacturers' help desks that their televisions no longer even possessed such things.

In the room, the bright flash and remaining glow revealed what video could not fully capture—the translucent figures of radiant beings standing about them.

Abby and Susanne scrambled from the bed as Marcelle shooed them off like an impatient parent, hopped off the mattress, and took them both arm in arm for a walk down the hallway.

Dylan met them there, a glow of intense satisfaction playing across his features. His eyes met Abby's, and they narrowed in a blissful smile. He came aside of them, draped his arm over Abby's shoulders and squeezed hard. Then he leaned over and buried his mouth in her unkempt hair. No one else around would know what was exchanged just then. A word of triumph, a bid of congratulations, or perhaps something more.

In either case, they had completed the quest. Finished the race. And there was one thing no one could take away from either one.

They were both warriors in the highest sense.

ATLANTA, MCQUEEN STUDIOS

America's favorite talk show host turned away from a giant video screen, which still bore the image of a smiling Marcelle. The host's face was slack with awe, wonder, and amazement. All she could do was shake her head, her arms crossed and her eyes lined with tears.

"I can't help but feel like we just set off a shock wave of the Spirit that's rocking across our country tonight," she said, accompanied by a roar of delighted applause. Her voice began to rise, drifting into the preacherlike cadence of Mara McQueen at her most inspired.

"I don't know if you felt it like I did, but all I can say is, *let the healing begin!*"

WESTWOOD MERCY HOSPITAL, LOS ANGELES

Nurse Gladys was walking down one of the hospital's gleaming hallways, carrying two cups of medication, when suddenly her muscles began quivering and her eyelids fluttering. Her fingers twitched, and the cups went flying as though flicked out of her hands by an invisible gremlin. The pills they contained scattered all about the floor.

Gladys lowered neither her gaze nor her hands in response to the mishap. Instead, her eyes searched out the nearest window through the open door of an adjacent patient's room. She stared out into the sky with a look of fierce curiosity.

Another few seconds passed. With a look of disapproval, a nurse behind Gladys dropped to her knees to pick up the tablets. Everyone on the floor knew Gladys hadn't been acting herself since an inappropriate conversation had surfaced several weeks before between her and Abby Sherman, the hospital's now-famous patient who had disappeared.

Still Gladys did not look down. In fact, she began to smile—a wide, beaming grin that transformed her winsome face.

She closed her eyes and two enormous tears flowed down her brown cheeks. Her lips started moving. A nearby colleague trained in lip-reading would later report that the nurse's only words were *Thank you, Jesus, thank you* . . . Over and over again.

IJEBU ODE, NIGERIA

Kneeling before the grave of Sister Okoye, Sister Motumbe quickly looked up from the clump of small flowers she had just transplanted.

A few hundred yards away, lying in a hammock restored to the ceiling of the Eredo Rampart, Saronu opened her eyes abruptly, jarred awake from a deep sleep. At first somewhat alarmed, she peered into the distance, then started to smile slowly. She nodded her head as though an inner question was being answered somehow, from somewhere.

Both women closed their eyes, serene.

JERUSALEM, ROOFTOP OF CHURCH OF THE HOLY SEPULCHRE

Facing the setting sun from her perch over the city, Rulaz closed her eyes and smiled blissfully. She held out her arms and extended her hands. It almost seemed like a faint, imperceptible breeze was washing over her.

She tilted her head back, heavenward, and began to laugh a rich, unforgettable laugh, which her brothers and sisters had never, ever heard her unleash before.

Pure laughter and praises to Jehovah began to drift downward across the crowded rooftops and alleyways of the Eternal City.

AUTHOR'S NOTE

Most of the Nigerian geography I depicted in *The Watchers* is authentic. The location of highways, rain forests, and most of the Sungbo's Eredo is all real. Everything mentioned about Sungbo's Eredo is historical, from its appearance and location to most of its history—except that it was not a fixture in Watchers lore, as these Watchers were my invention. Yet it was indeed reputed to have been built by an ancient, wealthy queen from Ethiopia. The rampart's remarkable water-gathering qualities were taken from archaeological literature. My depiction of Port Harcourt was all too close to the mark, as throughout the writing I'd continued to read media stories of abducted and murdered Westerners in the Niger Delta region.

My descriptions of London were culled, sadly, from the Internet and I trust, accurate.

As for Jerusalem, everything about the Abyssinian monks on the rooftop of the Holy Sepulchre church is true—except for the fact that no Sentinel of Jerusalem or Watchers matriarch lives among its beleaguered Coptic population. However, the entire account of age-old tensions, abuses, and even outright fistfights between the two Coptic contingents is sadly true.

Finally, I'd like to address the issue of "Spiritual Genealogy," which arises in this book. I encourage everyone to try to trace their spiritual genealogy as far as possible, as a fascinating and inspiring pastime. However, I have no desire to confuse, dilute or otherwise complicate the far truer and more edifying Scriptural nomenclature of the Family of God. God is our true heavenly Father, and our spiritual one as well. Those matter supremely. I only maintain that tracing the path of the one or ones who led us to Christ can often reveal fascinating and revealing truths of our spiritual heritage.

ACKNOWLEDGMENTS

A globe-trotting thriller like this requires one of two things: either unlimited airline miles, or some well-traveled friends. In my case, I was blessed with the latter.

My thanks go out to Rev. Joseph Thompson of the Nigeria Harvest Experience and The Church at the Well, as well as to his wife Sola, for their assistance with Yoruba vocabulary. Thanks to my longtime writing buddy, Stephen Bransford, for his help on Nigeria as well.

My friend Claudia Cross was essential in forming the concept for this story, and I'm grateful to her. My cherished agent Lee Hough was as always a source of profound encouragement and guidance both during and after the first draft.

A huge dose of thanks and *well-dones* belongs with this book's two primary shepherds at Bethany House, Carol Johnson and Luke Hinrichs. Both of you poured your hearts into helping me craft and hone *The Watchers* tremendously. Thanks for your wisdom, your talent, and most of all, your patience with me. It's been a great experience.

I must thank my wife, Connie, and my children, Ben, Abby, and Emma-Le, for their incredible patience and resiliency during the latter stages of drafting this book. Only you and I will ever know how grueling that period was for all of us.

Thank you all from the bottom of my heart.

ABOUT THE AUTHOR

MARK ANDREW OLSEN, whose novel *The Assignment* was a Christy Award finalist, also collaborated on bestsellers *Hadassah* (now the major motion picture: *One Night With the King*), *The Hadassah Covenant,* and *Rescued.* Mark grew up in France, the son of missionaries, and is a Professional Writing graduate of Baylor University. He and his wife, Connie, live in Colorado Springs with their three children.

Looking for More Good Books to Read?

You can find out what is new and exciting with previews, descriptions, and reviews by signing up for Bethany House newsletters at

www.bethanynewsletters.com

We will send you updates for as many authors or categories as you desire so you get only the information you really want.

Sign up today!